Green Fields #11

RETRIBUTION

Adrienne Lecter

Retribution

Green Fields #11

ISBN: 9781089669371

Editing by Marti Lynch
Interior design & cover by Adrienne Lecter

www.adriennelecter.com

Give feedback on the book at:
adrienne@adriennelecter.com

Twitter: @AdrienneLecter

First Edition August 2019
Second Print Edition November 2021
Produced and published by Barbara Klein, Vienna, Austria

To M

Even if he doesn't know why (that's what he said). He knows.

Chapter 1

"Let's get this party started."

It didn't feel like much of a party, I had to admit. Both the location and people present weren't looking very festive, or in the mood for festivities. All of us had good reasons for that, I figured; coming together to beat the crap out of some human shit stain wasn't necessarily a cause for celebration—and being on the receiving end of said intentions couldn't be that much more fun. I also wasn't sure if direct, physical aggression was the best thing for my two companions; neither Nate nor Bucky Hamilton looked very enthusiastic at the prospect, but that could have been due to months of trauma, lack of acceptable food sources, drug withdrawal, and sleep deprivation. I was rocking the tail end of what likely amounted to a tenth of what they'd been through, and curling up in a corner while listening to the storm rage outside sounded like a mighty fine plan. Compared to how I was feeling, Cindy—that would be Master Sergeant Cindy Cooper, formerly US Army and more recently pimp, drug lord, and one of my least favorite people around—looked downright peppy. The black eye she was sporting and light bruising along her jaw—both acquired yesterday when we'd hit the camp hard and had kicked the previous administration out—didn't seem to bother her. That she knew who we were was a given. She had previously been under Bucky's command from what I'd gathered, and besides, both he and Nate had racked up quite the notoriety status around here. I'd—not so gently—reminded her that we'd met two months ago when she'd shot me up with drugs that had almost incapacitated me but thankfully hadn't prevented me from killing my way out from under the threat of rape and murder. Her relaxed attitude toward the men lurking behind me must have been an act, but I had the distinct suspicion that she wasn't quite taking me seriously.

Nothing like dissuading people of that notion.

I was sure that she expected me to go right for a punch—and I was absolutely itching to oblige her—but if I'd learned something from how the previous leadership had handled things around here, it was that good ol' violence was by far not the worst that someone could do to you. She was currently sitting on a high-backed chair that was bolted to the floor, ankles bound to the chair legs and wrists cuffed behind her back to keep her where she was—ideal for me to straddle her thighs and plunk myself down on her lap, my arms casually slung over her shoulders, like you'd do with a lover. Her eyes widened in surprise, and while she locked her muscles in place, I could feel her try to recoil physically—which was, of course, impossible, with the chair setup and all that. We hadn't bothered with restraining her head or neck—mostly so she wouldn't break quite that easily when punched—so technically, she could have tried to head-butt me or spit, but instead she just stared straight into my eyes. From up close, it was impossible not to see that her eyes were wide with fear and apprehension, however blasé she tried to act. Three years ago, knowing that I was the cause for that would have made revulsion well up inside of me. As it was, I felt a certain satisfaction roll up my spine. I might not have been the most dangerous person in this room, but I was far from easily ignored.

"We can do this the hard way, or the really fucking awful way," I drawled, ending with a chipper smile that I absolutely didn't feel. "You know that we know what you did, and you can't expect any of us to go easy on you. So why don't you spare yourself the worst of it and spill your guts right here and now, and I can promise you that you won't go through everything that you've subjected countless women to yourself."

A muscle jumped in her cheek as she gritted her teeth, further steeling herself. Her tone was wry as she responded, not a hint of fear in it. Part of me envied her that level of composure.

"Gee, thanks. And here I thought you'd try to intimidate me." Her gaze briefly flickered to who was lurking behind me, but rather than snub me further and address the guys, she looked back to me as she went on. "It shows so fucking plainly that you have no fucking idea what you're doing. I'm not afraid of you, or anything you can think of threatening me with. I know that those are all empty threats. You don't have the guts to follow through with anything." Another pause, and her gaze dropped from my face for a moment. "And you are lacking the equipment to do so."

Involuntarily, my fingers flexed in the well-worn leather gloves, but I kept my arms right where they rested on her shoulders. I'd considered taking off the gloves—bodily fluids were a bitch to clean off—but more so than usual, being surrounded by lots of people who could all so very obviously physically best me made me self-conscious about the missing bits and pieces all over again. Yet since I couldn't very well 'fess up to that—least of all to this scum—I forced a bright smile on my face, deliberately ignoring her insinuation—and turning it around on her again. Sorry, missy—you won't get a chance to try to get into my head.

"Not having a dick just means I can go right on to shoving my shotgun up your ass," I told her conversationally, making sure my grin remained strong—and hopefully a little anticipatory. "I've always been curious what happens when you take point-blank range to the next level. And watching you bleed out on the floor from having all your internal organs perforated would be worth not getting all the answers." In turn, I ground my hips forward, as if the very thought did some interesting things to me.

Her face remained impassive, but I didn't miss her convulsive swallow. So she did take me seriously, at least to a point. Interesting. Also borderline useless until she started spilling her guts, hopefully before I had to pick up one of the knives set aside in plain view and help along with the physical analog of that. Yet rather than fold, she said, "Like that's very motivating." Her attention again skipped behind me, to the right, where I knew Hamilton was lurking. "Why do you indulge this damn imbecile? She's just wasting your time, and very ineffectively."

I wasn't stupid enough to look over my shoulder—and leave my nose, ears, and possibly eyes and neck exposed to her—but part of me was burning to check the look on Hamilton's face. Normally, I would have expected his favorite expression around me—a perfect sneer—but I doubted he would give Cindy that satisfaction. He didn't speak up, so I guessed he was holding her gaze evenly. He'd gotten really good at that silent "I'm still better than you" gloat—I'd been subjected to it all morning while we'd gotten some more caffeine into our systems and had pretended to do more than unenthusiastically push oatmeal around chipped bowls while Andrej and Pia had shot suggestions to and fro about how to best get started with the interrogations while the three of us had mostly just listened. Why it was us rather than them in here was easily explained—the Ice Queen had other shit to take care of, like getting the day-to-day of the new management sorted out, and someone needed to take care of getting more cars up and running. That left the three of us idle. I couldn't pass up the chance to haunt one of my new least-favorite people in the world, and as it stood, both Nate and Hamilton were amazing for scaring anyone shitless with their sheer presence. It didn't matter that there was a thick, dark bruise around Bucky's neck where he'd almost gotten strangled yesterday, or that he'd lost most of his physical bulk over the months of imprisonment in the camp; it just made him look even more the lean, mean survivor that he was. In turn, Nate's comparative bulk came with its own implications—and that was a can of worms I fully intended to keep the lid on as long as humanly possible. I hadn't been the only one who'd noticed that he'd barely eaten more than a single spoonful of oatmeal this morning. Granted, I was the wrong one to ask if it had been edible or not, but the fact that everyone at the table had been watching in silence spoke volumes.

Another fight for another day. Today, all that was on my agenda was to get some answers out of this fine specimen before me.

Absentmindedly playing with the hair at the nape of her neck—which made her already tense body go rigid—I went on chattering. "If I were you, I wouldn't count on either of them losing it and ending your miserable existence quickly. I could be wrong, but Hamilton must have a huge beef with every single one of his former soldiers who turned on him, and Miller... where do I start? With the fact that you murdered the one woman who showed him a thread of kindness, or that you prepped his wife to get raped to death? No worries—we won't go the eye-for-an-eye route, but when you bite it, we will have to bury you in pieces." Her eyes narrowed as she got ready to deflect that, but paused when I gave her a dazzling grin.

"You saw my hands, right? You really think I couldn't replicate how they worked me over?"

Confusion crossed Cindy's face, quickly followed by dread. This time when her gaze flickered in Hamilton's direction, it wasn't in challenge but seeking confirmation—that she must have gotten, seeing how she paled. "You're lying," she accused, her tone flat.

I allowed myself a snicker, hoping that my acting skills were a little more on point than usual. Being around Hamilton was a kind of torture, so I wasn't lying exactly, just not telling the truth.

"How did you think they got Miller to cooperate with them in the first place?" I asked, pitching my voice as if that was a rhetorical question. "I can tell you that pretty much every version I've heard of how we betrayed the scavengers is absolute bullshit, but you wouldn't know, right? Because you betrayed your people and slunk away when things went sideways at the base in Colorado." Cole had told me that she'd been part of the defense when we'd hit the base, and had been presumed dead when she hadn't been around after we'd forged our rickety truce—that had changed nothing, least of all for the better.

"They wouldn't," she insisted, sounding like she needed to believe that more than she actually did. "They must have known that you're useless without half your fingers. You're a damn scientist. What use are you if you can't do science?"

I was itching to correct her several misconceptions, but since that would likely have undermined my act, all I could do was shrug. "Guess all they cared about was my husband's cooperation." I paused, taking a moment to shift on her lap again. "But none of that is relevant now, except to stress just how low my bar for things I will not do has become. So why don't you do us all a favor and spill your guts, and we can be done before lunch break."

I already knew what was coming when she visibly set her jaw. "You're not getting anything from me, cunt."

I considered before I got up, finally getting a chance to glance at the men behind me. Nate looked grim, Hamilton eager. "Too bad," I muttered, then looked at the table with the extensive amount of scalpels and other things, and back to Hamilton. "Wanna lend a hand?"

"With pleasure," he drawled in what must have been the first agreement the two of us had reached without fighting beforehand. Oh, how torture and dismemberment brings people together! I cast a last glance Nate's way but still didn't get anything from him back, least of all a warning. I didn't know exactly how it made me feel that he was happy to lean back and relax while watching me torture a woman who, without a doubt, deserved to be punished—but maybe not quite like this.

"Then let's do this," I offered as I mentally squared my shoulders and picked up a scalpel.

Hamilton stepped up to our captive's back and grabbed her right hand, forcing her fingers apart. She tried to fight but to no avail. "How do you want to do this?" he asked, still jovial going on friendly, which weirded me out on so many levels—but was a welcome distraction from what I was about to do.

"Joint by joint," I shot back. "Let's take this slow."

And slow I took it—even if I was screaming inside every fucking second.

As it turned out, both Cindy and I had been wrong—it took us a lot longer than lunchtime to get her talking, but talk she did. And scream. So much screaming that I was loathe to continue simply because it grated on my very soul. But as it turned out, Bucky and I were a surprisingly good team—once we started, neither of us could stop or even ease up, a silent contest of gritted teeth and narrowed eyes going on that was so much easier to concentrate on than what we were doing... or the bucket full of discarded bits that rested on the floor right in front of Cindy so that she could easily keep track of our progress.

That she hadn't succumbed to systemic shock hours ago was a marvel—and plain testament to what the damn serum did to people. I'd know. I also tried very hard not to remember, which was impossible, considering the task at hand—ha!—and how much my fingers hurt, phantom pain included.

As we stepped back from the chair and its restrained prisoner—the wrist cuffs long having given way to rope around her elbows for practical reasons, also serving as a light tourniquet—screams were replaced by quiet, defeated sobs, which was ten times worse. I refused to even glance at Hamilton, instead focusing on Nate where he still leaned against the opposite wall, arms crossed over his chest, his body seemingly at ease, his eyes never leaving Cindy.

"Tell me about Nyah," he said, deceptively calm. It was everything but, of course, seeing how Cindy tensed—and then went slack in her bonds. Her head lolled to the side as she sniffled into her shoulder, taking a few labored breaths before she turned back to Nate.

"What about her?" Judging from her tone, she was stalling. I was tempted to give her an incentive to keep talking right there—I didn't know the name, but I could take a good guess at who it had belonged to, and that made me want to go all kinds of violent all over again. As it was, refraining from wiping the sweat off my brow and consequently smearing blood all over my face—again—was what I left it at.

Nate's stare turned harder—if that was even possible—the line of his jaw standing out. "Why did you fucking kill her right after dragging her out of my cell?"

The mental image his words conjured up wasn't pretty. I could downright taste his desperation and frustration as the guards held him down, forcing him to watch as that bitch executed the only person who had shown him any kindness—who had, maybe, even become a friend—right in front of his eyes. So much for feeling pity for her.

Cindy snorted—something I hadn't expected. The smirk crossing her face was way too satisfied for anyone's good, and it seeped right into her tone as she responded. "Why, isn't that what you do to a used-up, old nag? You put it out of its misery?" For a second, I thought Nate would finally break his stoic stance—that he must have been vibrating with the need for violence was clear, at least to me. The measure of self-restraint it must have taken him not to give in was impressive, and just a little scary. It sure belied the amount of poison that I knew must still be coursing through his veins. But, if anything, stubbornness and spite kept him rooted in his spot, not giving her the satisfaction of taking her bait. When Cindy realized that, she let out a small laugh. "Don't you get it? Any of the girls sent up from the kennels to the arena had long since lost any use for anything else. They only ever got served up to scum like you when they were too used and broken and diseased even for the lowlifes that made the barn their extended living room."

The implications of that made me want to punch her all over again. This was exactly what they'd had planned for me if I hadn't managed to break the hold the drugs she'd given me had on my mind and killed myself out of a glorious future of getting raped to death. It was impossible for me to shake off the horror of seeing Nate this way one last time; not for me, but for him. When we'd sprung him two days ago, he'd seemed composed enough—and except for tearing that asshole's head off yesterday, he hadn't lost control for a single moment—but I could tell from the way the tension in his body changed that he must have come to the same conclusion, and didn't like it one iota better than I did. There was no need to staunch jealousy; just because he'd cared about that woman didn't negate what we had. I felt like we were way beyond worries like that.

Good thing that I wasn't in control, because Cindy might have managed to goad me into action this way. Nate remained calm as he went on questioning her. "If you had no other use for her, why not leave her with me?"

"And reward you for what, exactly?" Cindy taunted. "Be glad I killed her. That way I absolved you of the decision whether you'd eat her or not. Or should I say, I made it for you?"

Surprisingly, it was Bucky who gave a jerk at that, if where our captive couldn't see him. Nate barely glanced at him—not enough to call it a warning—and I realized that the reason it was the three of us in here wasn't just because of the phenomenal chemistry we had going on, but maybe also because of the information we extracted might not be great for the public at large to hear, unprepared.

Nate's silence seemed to have been some kind of signal I missed, as Bucky took a step forward so he could aim another jab to Cindy's left temple that got her head snapping sickeningly to the side, blood that had previously stopped spurting coming afresh from her nostrils. Maybe I should have felt worry at the fact that it seemed more like retribution than encouragement, but I was beyond that. Cindy muttered a curse under her breath, briefly trying to crane her neck to glare at Bucky, but Nate's next question stole her attention.

"Care to tell us now why you chose to work with these assholes? From what I heard, you were a passingly competent NCO in your time." She didn't react to the barb, but Nate didn't look fazed by that. He quickly glanced to me before going on. "Spare me the sob story of how you had to so you'd escape worse. We've had plenty of time talking to the girls you oversaw. You weren't the one who showed them what little kindness they received."

I had been surprised to hear that, while not exactly being sorry that the madam who'd run the brothel died, most of them had seen her as the lesser evil. They had been very forthcoming with pointing out that dear Cindy here had quite lived up to the task of being their enforcer.

It was impossible to miss how Cindy tried to look at Hamilton once more, but he kept his distance now. When she realized how futile her attempt was, she looked back to Nate. "Wouldn't you like to know?"

"Only passingly," he responded. "But I'm sure someone will help you remember, if you need the incentive?"

She visibly jerked with apprehension, what little fight she'd showed leaving her with a labored exhale. If I had to guess—and there wasn't much actual guessing involved—she was in too much pain to want to add to that.

"Honestly? Bad luck, just like everyone else," she muttered. "You think your little ragtag band of misfits had it bad? Being in the army wasn't much better. I lost more friends and comrades the second summer than when the shit hit the fan. My tour should have ended that first winter but they didn't even give us a weekend of leave, if only to curl up and hide from the world for a sec. The toll got too high. So when someone suggested a way to drop off the radar, I took it. Just my luck that the alternative proved to be even more of a shit show than what I'd run from."

I was a little surprised to see an expression on Bucky's face that he usually reserved for me only. Great that in his view I was right up there with deserters. "I think that's called karma," I told her succinctly. "And reportedly, she's a bitch."

I shouldn't have felt that thread of satisfaction at seeing her flinch at the sound of my voice, but didn't find it in me to regret it. Cindy didn't bother with glaring at me; instead, she switched gears—and I hated how honest and raw she sounded as she started to plead with Nate.

"I beg you, please end this. Yes, I get it—you hate me. And maybe I deserve it—"

"You absolutely do," I happily supplied.

Another shaky exhale, and she continued. "Yes, I deserve it. I could have done what others did and acquiesced; only did what I was forced to do. But it's not like they didn't spare me, just because I got a promotion. I got caught in the same web that you did. Cortez made me an offer, and I was stupid enough not to read the fine print and expect the ramifications it came with. So maybe, a few times, my fear and frustration found ways to escape that made others suffer more. And maybe, sometimes, that made me feel a little better for a moment, like I had power. Control. Don't tell me you don't know exactly what I'm talking about! I watched you fight in the arena.

I watched you change. There was a time when you only fought to survive. What you did yesterday? And the day before? Nobody made you go all out and not just kill, but execute your opponents. I may be guilty, but so are you."

If she thought she could get under his skin with that, she was sorely mistaken… or was she? It hurt my very soul to listen to her accusations and see Nate not even try to protest. I wanted to jump into that breach for him—insist that, of course, things had been different. For one, he hadn't done a thing to play along—but his silence made me cut down on the impulse. Whether he believed her or not was anyone's guess, but he must have had a reason not to laugh in her face.

Surprisingly, Hamilton spoke up when neither of us did. "Yeah, because starvation for weeks at a time is no motivator at all." I didn't miss the glance he sent Nate's way before he stepped into Cindy's field of vision, taking over. That was concern, and not the kind that I was used to—sarcasm twined with disdain, usually centered around Nate's choice to stick it out with me. Rather than let her explain or respond, Hamilton hit her again, hard enough that something crunched—and I doubted that had been his fingers. Cindy seemed dazed rather than just hurt as her head lolled to the side, blood dripping onto her stained dress. Hamilton used the opportunity to push a jaw spreader into her mouth. I hadn't seen him pick it up. He sounded almost pleasant when he turned to me. "Get the pliers."

I didn't hesitate but felt like another layer of sanity fled from my mind. No idea why the prospect of tearing out her teeth next skeeved me out more than what we'd already done to her; maybe because I'd gotten so used to my own shortcomings that I no longer saw them as the most horrible thing in the world. I told myself that at least I wouldn't be the one using the pliers, since I lacked the manual strength for that. See, everything is good for something.

Cindy took that moment to shake off the daze, only to realize that because of the jaw spreaders, answering wasn't something she could easily accomplish anymore. Judging from the sequence of grunts and moans, she was regretting not having talked more when that had been an option. A small part of me waited for either Nate or Hamilton himself to stop and give her a chance to rectify that, but the expression on Nate's face was truly unforgiving. I wondered if that was the consequence of Cindy's barb hitting home—that if he wouldn't allow himself redemption, he certainly wouldn't grant it to her.

I realized I was okay with that. Maybe that made me a horrible person—but at least I was in good company.

Eventually, Hamilton eased up on her and let Cindy talk, and talk some more she did—if even more slurred than before, hampered by agony and swelling—but she might as well have kept her trap shut. The problem was, what she had told us was valuable information—and confirmed some of my guesses—but at the same time was utterly useless. Almost everyone she could implicate was dead, or wishing they were. Everything led back to the same: Cortez had been one manipulative fucker who had gotten off on reveling in the worst that humanity had to bring to the table—but there had been no other rhyme or reason to it, no method to the madness. And while horrifying in itself, "because he could" didn't help us at all, neither to make sense of this nor to plan ahead.

Maybe Scott and his team had been more successful today with some of our other guests, but as it was, I couldn't shake off the feeling that I'd just sold my soul for nothing.

Three of the marines came to drag Cindy back to her cell—or what was left of her. The serum would keep her wounds from becoming septic, but we'd banged her up enough that, just maybe, she'd die because of that. Or not. I couldn't quite find it in me to care about her. With no reason to remain in this fucking room for another moment, I wordlessly turned on my heel and walked out into the dark tunnel beyond.

"Good job," Hamilton called after me, the usual goading tone back. And all was right with the world again. "You'd make a half decent interrogator if you did a better job imitating me."

I forced myself not to turn back and instead keep walking—for three more steps, before I hunched over and hurled up what remained of my breakfast, the heaving so strong that I needed to brace myself with both hands against the roughly hewn wall. Bile followed, and I still wasn't done, the heaving painful as it ran dry. My entire body was shaking by the time I managed to straighten, only to find that I had garnered a small audience. Hamilton of course couldn't leave me be, and Nate hovering behind him wasn't much of a reprieve. But I could have done without Pia and Andrej joining them, with Andrej at least giving me a pained, sympathetic smile. The Ice Queen did her best to ignore my antics, instead conferring with Nate in hushed tones—and handing me a bottle of something green and vile looking as soon as I was done.

"Here, drink this," she needlessly stated, her tone leaving no question to the order.

I closed my eyes for a moment, swallowing hard to check if my saliva would stay down, and then downed the whole thing in a few sips. The consistency was thick, not quite like a smoothie, and from what little I could smell I was quite happy not to be able to taste it. As I finished the bottle, I saw that both Nate and Bucky held similar vessels, both still half full, and Hamilton watched with horrified fascination as I licked up the last drops. "You really can't taste that shit, eh? And here I thought Richards was jerking me around when he told me that."

I refrained from pointing out how little I gave a shit about who had told him what about me, and instead turned to Pia. "Any news?"

She shook her head, not even hesitating for a second to consider if some tidbit or other might have been worth sharing. "We have rooted out another ten of Cortez's guards and middle men who hadn't tucked in their tails yet and left in the night. Two still refuse to talk, but the others seem to have given up hope so they decided it was easier for them to stay."

"Hope for what?" Maybe it looked to them like our victory had been quick and easy, but the truth was far from it. And who would come to rescue them, anyway?

Pia shook her head, disbanding my unspoken theories. "Hope, in general. We have yet to round up anyone who puts up more than token resistance. Whoever has been running operations is either dead or left before we could accost them."

"Sounds like Harris will have an easy time running this shit show," I surmised.

Pia looked less than impressed with my assessment. Andrej grinned, but it wasn't a nice expression. "He just might," he pointed out. "If there's anything left to run. Most of the scavengers don't sound too keen on settling down and getting involved with the grueling day-to-day of running a settlement now that you've shut down their prime entertainment."

Too bad. Even worse, I couldn't find it in me to care.

"So, who needs dismemberment next?" And my, didn't I sound chipper?

The Ice Queen's pinched expression let me know that I was fooling no one, as much as I tried to pretend like this wasn't killing me. "Scott and his men aren't done yet," she explained. "We will meet in the central room by the kitchen in thirty."

"Outstanding!" Hamilton enthused, going as far as clapping his hands together once. Without waiting for our reactions, he turned around and strode down the corridor. Pia kept eyeing Nate and me critically, but at Andrej's nod she joined him in following Hamilton. Nate meanwhile finished his bottle with barely held-in disdain, leaving the empty container by the door of the interrogation room. I did the same, attempting to follow him—and made it exactly eleven feet into the corridor, to where Nate grabbed my hand and pulled me into a different room, shutting the door with emphasis.

Yeah, not socializing for a while sounded like a great idea.

Chapter 2

My mind was sluggish switching from revulsion to anything else, and my stomach definitely wasn't very agreeable with what it had been fed, but I did my best to push all that aside in favor of getting ready for some…

…of Nate leaning against the dusty table shoved into the glorified maintenance room, his head hung low but turned to the side so he could study me, arms crossed over his chest. It was awfully close to relief that I felt as I sagged against the closed door, meeting his gaze levelly. Dread clawed up my throat—and, right now, I preferred that to what else could be resurfacing—but did my best to shove that away to where I could continue to ignore it. I must have done a shit job considering how Nate's jaw tightened, making me raise a hand.

"Give me five more minutes and I won't barf in your face when you fuck me on that table."

A wry grin appeared on his face for a moment. "Don't you think I'd be more considerate? I would have turned you the other way round."

That dragged a chuckle out of me, but it was hard to hold on to the light, warm glow appearing in my chest. "Very considerate, indeed."

We kept staring at each other for several seconds straight, and I so could have done without the vibe of defiance that seemed to be coming off Nate in waves. Things had always been so easy between us—sure, emotionally mired in layers upon layers of complicated shit, but deep down, underneath all that where the base animal brain lurked, we'd always crashed together and fallen into step with each other seamlessly. That had been my mental fallback for way longer than I cared to remember, an unshakable union, more death-do-us-part than any spoken oaths could ever be. And now all that space was filling up with things unsaid—or said too much—and that rattled me more than the self-loathing still riding my conscience… although that didn't help.

"Talk to me," Nate more offered than snapped, making me even more annoyed. At my frown, he grimaced. "It won't undo the damage, but it will help take the sting out of it."

I was confused about what he was referring to for a moment, but annoyance turned to real vexation when I realized the truth.

"What, you think I'm all twitchy because I just absolutely needlessly soiled my soul for that piece of shit?" Silence met me so I went right on. "And can you tell me why exactly we needed to waste a day on that? She had absolutely nothing to tell. Nothing."

Straightening, Nate cracked his spine before he answered. "That's something. And it's something that we needed to know."

I didn't agree—not one bit. "She gave us no names. No connections. She couldn't even tell us who had established this camp here, and for what purpose."

"We already know that," Nate pointed out, interrupting me.

"We do?" I didn't have to feign anger.

The stare he gave me wasn't exactly condescending, but I could tell that he was getting annoyed with my tirade. Too bad! Yet he didn't stoop so low as to answer my question, instead jumping to the next point—and I didn't care for how his tone turned careful, as if he was talking to a shy, startled animal.

"Bree, relax."

I was sorely tempted to stomp my foot on the ground and insist that I would do no such thing, but refrained from giving him that much ammunition against me. I was already feeling raw like seldom before—and there I'd thought the early morning hours of yesterday had been bad when it had just been the two of us, talking.

"I am relaxed," I ground out between gritted teeth, not even trying to pretend like that wasn't a lie. "And why wouldn't I be relaxed? It's not like I have any reason to be wound tight and worked up, with no way of relief in sight—"

Probably the worst moment to cut myself short, and I didn't miss how a muscle jumped in his temple. We stared at each other for several seconds straight, both of us daring the other to say something—until I realized that we were having two very different conversations at the same time, both oblivious to what the other was actually saying.

Nonverbal shit will do that to you sometimes.

My confusion—and resulting realization—were likely plain on my face, but I still made a point of pulling my anger and frustration inward, hoping that my stare would turn level rather than challenging. Why, oh why, did this have to be so complicated? And why did we have to have that damn elephant in the room when, because of what I'd just done, I felt like I needed Nate to be my immovable rock, at exactly the one time in our shared lives when he needed me to be the very same for him? The incredible level of stupidity of that realization made me crack up, earning me a glare I absolutely deserved.

"Do you really wanna get it on?" I asked, shifting my position into something actually going on relaxed. "Because, truth be told, I feel like crap, and getting off is almost the last thing on my mind. I mean, if you feel the need to, I'm happy to just bend over that table and let you have a go, particularly if you do the main part of the job, but my heart may not be fully in it." What I didn't say—and what I had the sinking feeling he already knew in the first place—was that my hangover wasn't that bad, but I was happy to give him that excuse if he wanted it.

Turned out, he did, his brief smile turning from self-deprecating to pained for a second before it evened out into the slightly vexed glare my jokes usually earned.

"If you are that enthusiastic about it, let me spare you the ordeal this once."

Olive branch or not, that deserved a fitting retort. "You don't exactly look ready to perform, either." Part of me wanted to hit myself for the phrasing, but I'd never been good at pussy-footing around anything—and, deep down, I figured he'd appreciate that. I would have, had our roles been reversed.

Nate snorted, the look he gave me stating plainly that yes, it was a foot-in-mouth moment, but no, he didn't mind that much. A moment later, he sagged a little more into himself, and it was only then that I realized just how pale he looked. Not just having-been-locked-up kind of pale compared to my slightly sunburned, tanned complexion, but the plethora of unhealthy coloring that usually came with sleep deprivation and the wrong side of a hangover.

"Just how bad do you really feel?" I asked, making sure to disband the last thread of humor from my voice.

He considered for a second, raising one shoulder in a shrug. "On a scale of one to ten? Like death warmed over. It was worse during the interrogation, but I'm afraid that if we'd actually got down and dirty, you might not be the first to hurl up whatever was in that bottle."

So much for that. I winced, casting around for a witty response—but was absolved of one when a loud banging on the door cut the moment short. As if that wasn't bad enough, the grate of Hamilton's voice served as a good substitute for being doused with a bucket of ice water. "If you're done rutting around like animals, we have a briefing in five. Scott's getting impatient."

I was already pushing myself off my perch against the door when I paused, realizing that Nate hadn't moved a muscle. I couldn't help but grin when I caught him glaring at the closed door, pure annoyance on his expression. If thoughts could have killed, my master plan to ensure that Hamilton got to live an agonizingly long life with the knowledge of what had happened to him tormenting him forever would have come to an end right there. Of course Nate didn't miss my gloating, earning me a softer, more belligerent version of that glare, which I rewarded with a grin.

"Come on," I said, holding out a hand to him that I knew he wouldn't take. He didn't, pushing off the table in one smooth motion on his own volition. "We shouldn't keep the marsupials waiting."

The joke was obviously losing its power—if it had ever held any for anyone but me, which was debatable to begin with—but the smile remained on my face at Nate's vexed grunt. Not waiting for him to be done, I wrenched the door open, ending up right in Bucky's face, his hand raised to deliver another knock, I was sure. Absolutely deliberately I invaded his personal space as he didn't immediately step to the side, the two of us glaring into each other's face from up close. Instinct told me to recoil—we did have history aplenty for that, and while he hadn't gone as all out as Nate and embraced the easy road to survival, he had remained the reigning champion in Cortez's arena for almost a year. If anything, that kept me from backing down, turning our staring match into a stalemate. Only when Nate was close enough behind me that I could feel the heat of his body did Hamilton step aside, but he still managed to make it appear like a gesture of pure necessity rather than chivalry. I was tempted to keep my body turned so that I was always keeping him in front of me, but then deliberately forced myself to turn my back on him as I strode down the corridor. Feeling his gaze like a dagger between my shoulder blades sure helped clear the last dregs of sluggishness from my mind.

"It's such an absolute joy to be working with you both," I heard Nate mutter behind me—mostly to himself, but the fact that he said it aloud meant it was a warning to me; Hamilton probably as well, but I doubted he cared much about playing nice. I hated having to be the adult in this constellation; it absolutely crimped my style.

I made it two doors down before the guys had caught up with me, and while I didn't think it beyond Hamilton's pettiness to try to increase his pace to where I had to jog to keep up, we managed to settle into a leisurely stroll that quickly brought us to the common area that used to be the prep rooms and kitchens. While we were gone, someone had cleared away most of the sleeping bags and dragged a long table in devoid of chairs so that people could gather around it for a proper briefing. Pia and Andrej were waiting for us next to Scott and Danvers, his second-in-command. Of the other marines faction, only Sgt. Buehler was in evidence, standing at least as straight as Scott while stealthily nursing her injuries. She looked relieved to see us enter. Richards, meanwhile, did a great job of keeping his expression neutral, but I didn't miss the way his shoulders hunched slightly at our entrance. I still didn't know whether Hamilton intended to relieve him of his command but so far, the army soldiers continued to report to Richards. Last in the illustrious group were Harris and the ever-scowling Eden, although she did flash me a quick grin as her eyes fell on me—or maybe Nate, I wasn't quite sure. I was more than happy to let him handle that with his usual mix of arrogant ignorance and outright belligerent hostility. No, jealousy was the least of my concerns today.

I was about to demand a status update when Scott glanced up from a report that he had been perusing, the paper already crumpled and several times folded as it appeared. "So good of you to finally join us," he drawled not quite jovially. I would have drawn up short if I hadn't been certain Hamilton would have barreled right into me; this way, I had a second or two to think about my response until I came to a halt at the table opposite of Scott. I was certain that we hadn't used up the time Pia had given us.

"What can I say, I'm a busy woman," I said instead of telling him where to shove his misgivings.

The marine commander pointedly glanced at Nate, who held his gaze evenly and with downright infuriating neutrality. I'd had years getting used to his behavior—and it wasn't like I ever left out an opportunity to fend for my right to jump my husband's bones—so it didn't surprise or bother me, but anyone's need to make this an issue annoyed me. I was tempted to ask Scott whether he wanted a status report of what had happened in the meantime since I presumed Hamilton must have filled him in on the measly findings of our interrogation.

Just my luck that my body decided this was the perfect moment to remember that it had gotten pumped full of chemicals it really didn't appreciate, the need to hurl imminent once more—which I managed to suppress—and this time coming with some violent shakes—that I did not. Making a face, I clawed my fingers into the edge of the table until the worst had subsided, leaving me feeling lightheaded and weak. Nate ignored me but it was impossible to miss Hamilton's smirk, even though he looked decidedly pale and sweaty himself. He caught my gaze, snorting briefly. "You'd think you'd be relaxed and mellow afterward. Not that anyone could remove the stick that you have up your ass."

A plethora of retorts shot to the forefront of my mind, and for a moment, I was tempted to say screw it and dive right into the worst of them, never mind that a lot of the shit I'd fling at Hamilton would also land on Nate's head. The disdainful twist that came to the Ice Queen's lips wasn't enough to make me hold back, either. Andrej's chuckle egged me on more than anything. But I knew that Scott's acceptance of my authority was rocky at best—and now that I had Nate lurking beside me, Scott likely expected me to relinquish it— and the last thing I needed was for me to be the one to further undermine myself. Besides, what really annoyed me was the— likely unintentional—insinuation that Nate hadn't done a good enough job mellowing me out, and I wasn't going to set anyone straight now.

I sure felt like a responsible, capable adult as I turned my full attention to Scott, and thus hopefully annoyed the fuck out of Hamilton for not getting a rise out of me. "You have something? As Hamilton without a doubt has already told you, we got nothing that we didn't already know—but, as they say, sometimes you need confirmation that there is nothing to be found." If Nate got annoyed with me for hijacking his statement, that was his problem, not mine.

Scott looked disappointed that he didn't get to sneer at me again but was quick to answer. "Our interrogations went just as badly, but one of my contacts managed to ferret out one of the Chemist's assistants as he was trying to sneak out of the camp yesterday. We have now confirmed his identity."

I couldn't help but frown—and not just because he still wouldn't give up who his connections were. "Sneak out in this weather?" I hadn't been outside since the early hours of the morning, but the worst of the storm was blowing over the camp right now, audible even here, below-ground. From what little I'd caught was going on with the camp, several of the more rickety buildings had already caved in, making people flock into basements and the sturdy structures of the citadel—the converted upper levels of what used to be a coal mine, also housing the arena.

Scott allowed himself a small smile. "Might be a case of intelligence not necessarily translating into street smarts."

Before I could respond, Hamilton had to offer his two cents. "Sounds familiar, huh?" he drawled from way too close, not just the lack of distance making it too damn intimate.

And because I'd about used up my mature-behavior moves for the week, I had to turn my head so that we were almost nose-to-nose, and stared blankly into his grinning visage. "You wouldn't know."

We kept staring at each other, my skin crawling but my ego unwilling to move even a muscle.

Nate was the first to grow tired of our antics, speaking up for the first time. "I presume the reason you're not yet busy beating the shit out of him means that you want us to do it? Tell us where your people are keeping him and consider it done."

Scott's attention had jumped from our staring match to Nate but briefly flickered back once more. "Are you sure that you don't want them to hash things out first?"

Nate cast us both a look that was scathing enough to make me draw up short, but his tone remained jovial as he replied. "If I had an iota of hope that would change anything for the better, I would have herded them out into the arena and let them beat the crap out of each other. But since I don't, we'll have to do it the mature way and pretend to be working well together until something catastrophic enough happens that we actually do."

Hamilton gave a silent sneer—still more in my direction than Nate's—and I left it at a consternated glare. Scott found this surprisingly amusing, likely because it was a message received and neither of us was able to protest that fact. He certainly looked more at ease than the Ice Queen, who appeared more than sick of the holdup. The rest of the people were watching in silence, which made me feel actually chagrined. I didn't mind being the prime entertainment around but could have done without it happening at my expense.

"My men have stashed him in the Chemist's workroom," Scott explained. "You might want to take a look around as well."

Nate accepted the news with a nod, and after a glance at Pia—who gave him a similar gesture to show she had everything else covered—turned toward a different exit than through which we'd entered. I still found it eerie that he knew his way around this place so well although he must have spent virtually all of his time in his cell, but that was my husband for you. I would have gotten turned around in this rabbit warren all the time if I didn't have someone to guide me along. Bucky was right there next to me, of course, as apparently we'd already maxed out the alone time we'd get that day. I would have minded less if his smirk didn't let me know that he was quite amused at my obvious vexation.

I really needed to learn how to stop carrying my emotions on my sleeve, even if it was mostly the need for bloody murder, and usually centered on just one person.

I was surprised when Nate not only led us to the upper level of the tunnels, but on into an above-ground extension accessible from below that must have been some kind of admin building for the mines. Everywhere we turned, people stepped out of our way, most of them giving us as wide a berth as possible. I didn't mind at first—traveling with company again had accustomed me to not being on my own somewhat but the crowds here still made me uncomfortable—and it made getting to where we were headed easier. But it only took a few minutes for me to catch on that they not just responded to someone, armed and armored, being in a hurry, but they actually recognized Nate and Bucky. Hamilton, if anything, seemed to love watching them inch away from him, practically gloating at the mix of fear and awe that met him. Nate, already tense, seemed to get more so with every second that passed, his gaze unwavering in front of him as he pushed forward. Knowing him as well as I did, I could see his unease in every line of his body, making me want to punch all those gawking assholes in the face.

The door we were looking for wasn't hard to find, with Hill and Cole leaning next to it, pretending like they were on guard duty but mostly interested in watching the people pass by. To say they drew up short when they saw us round the corner was an exaggeration, but they seemed somewhat conflicted about whether they should salute or not. The marines were definitely having a bad influence on them. When they realized that Hamilton wasn't about to get in their faces, they relaxed, and Hill pulled the door open after rapping on it twice.

"Have fun," he told me, way too chipper.

I still managed a smile even though my heart was already sinking considering what I'd likely be doing five minutes from now. "You know I will," I quipped, increasing my speed just a little to be the first through the door.

Inside, Scott's other three marines were loitering around, if a little more present than the soldiers had been. I could immediately see why they weren't on high alert; the man they were guarding looked like the least threatening person I'd seen all day. That probably said more about the scavengers milling around than him, but he couldn't have been much taller or heavier than me. The marines had tied his limbs to the chair he was sitting on, but because it was made of wood, I figured I should maybe not punch him too hard or else the rickety piece of furniture might disintegrate. Maybe it was simple bias because of my personal beef with Cindy, but judging from the way his eyes went wide as he saw us come in, I didn't think I'd need much violence to get this one talking.

"You can leave now. We got this," I told no one in particular. When nothing came from either of my silent, hulking companions, one of the marines nodded and signaled the other two to beat it. The guy in the chair looked after them with something akin to longing before his attention snapped back to us—and he went a few shades paler. I was tempted to do some posing shit like crack my knuckles— not that they would do that, and even less so in the gloves—but left it at crossing my arms over my chest, remaining in an easy stance in front of him. "I hear you have something you want to tell us?" Which was a lie, but he did look ready to spill his guts.

"Yes!" he pretty much shouted, his attention still split between the three of us. "Please, there's no need to hurt me! I'll tell you whatever you want to know! I'll tell you everything!"

That was a nice change of pace—not that I necessarily trusted it, but after repeating the same questions over and over for hours and never getting anything to work with, far was it from me to protest.

"Fine with me," I told him, mostly so his eyes would finally stop alternately snapping to one of the guys and quickly skimming away once more, a new wave of horror making the prisoner shake like a leaf in the wind. "Let's start with who you are and what you've been doing here, and maybe what you think is the most useful information for us."

It didn't exactly work, but he did include me in his mad looking-around for a moment. Bucky let out a grunt, which made my annoyance spike. Glancing to the side, I realized that he was now leaning against the closed door at my back, staring with bright-bordering-on-crazy eyes at the guy in the chair, which made me guess he'd seen him before. "Yeah, I do remember you," Hamilton growled, which made the guy actually whimper. I checked with Nate next but he remained standing, his expression hard but neutral—and by itself no less threatening than Hamilton's grimace. Great—looked like I was going to have to pretend like I was the mature one. Again.

"Talk," I told our prisoner. "You have about ten seconds before either of them decides that—"

I didn't get any further than that as the guy started stammering immediately, his tone high-pitched in real panic. "My name's Mike. I got here around two years ago, in summer, just when they were getting started. I used to be the Chemist's assistant but I don't know his name or where he went, and..." He had to stop there to catch his breath—or take one, for starters—and I used that to silence him with a quick, raised hand.

"Okay, Mike," I offered, trying to be jovial but really, it came out more like a taunt. It was hard to step out of the confrontational mindset I'd been in most of the day, and Hamilton's presence didn't exactly help with that. "Let's start from the beginning. How did you become the Chemist's assistant? What did you do for him? And is there anyone else around that we could ask as well?"

He shook his head at first—likely in answer to the last of my questions—but quickly stopped when Hamilton leaned a little closer. "I didn't have a choice, you know?" he stuttered, his words still coming out pressed and too fast. "They signed me up for guard duty first but I knew I wouldn't survive that. You have no idea how horrible it was!?"

"I can't imagine," Nate more growled than drawled, apparently deciding not to sit this one out after all.

Mike's eyes went wider still, a visible shudder running through him as he realized what he'd just implied. I hadn't thought I'd ever meet someone who was scared out of their wits, but he seemed pretty close to the definition of that idiom.

"It was either that or the arena," he explained, slowing down a little when his stammering got too bad to get the words out. "None of the guards do it because they want to. Well, most don't. Cortez has a few who do. But the rest of us, we don't. They caught me stealing—food, because I was so fucking hungry, and back before the scavengers came to trade and we had the fields producing, there barely was food for anyone. Of course I chose guard duty, but they accused me of slacking off when I got beat up good by a few of the prisoners as we subdued them." His gaze again flitted between Nate and Bucky, but this time he managed to focus on me before anyone could threaten him further. "My supervisor was warning me off just as the Chemist came with a new round of drugs to test, cursing under his breath that he never had enough hours in the day to get the work done. I used to teach basic chemistry in school so I offered to help. It sure beat getting killed."

I was tempted to give him a "cry me a river" response but let the guys do that with their mere presence. "Exactly what was it that you did for him?" I hadn't had time to check if there was any documentation to be found, but judging from the empty spaces on the desk and few shelves that weren't full of tubes and flasks, I didn't hold my breath.

Showing a first hint of possessing a spine, Mike blinked in irritation. "I mixed up whatever he told me to. Some solutions were straight-up basic organic chemistry. We also did a lot of plant extractions and distillation. More often than not, I didn't have a clue what I was doing—he just had me follow the instructions he gave me. Sometimes he tested the results on me, too—you know, so I wouldn't deliberately screw with the outcomes. You'll likely not understand half of it if I tried to explain it to you."

I could practically feel Hamilton's silent laughter beside me, vexation sneaking into the relative relaxation that had settled over my mind. "Try me," I shot back, doing my best not to sound—and look—as offended as I felt.

Mike's beginning ire increased but he obliged me. "Some of the compounds I could guess at because of how he had me mix them—esters for the most part, some salts. The plant extractions were almost all psychedelics. Once the first batches produced stable results, that's what he had me use as a base for large-scale production. Most ended up crystalized. What the scavengers love to get high on comes from that." And whatever Cortez had shot me and Richards up with that gave me the hangover of a lifetime right now, if my guess wasn't completely wrong. That much made sense—the few glances I'd gotten at the shelves were enough that I could cook up a batch of acid if I found a basic recipe somewhere… not unlike the shit we had gotten up to in college sometimes, after hours, with the help of a TA who had dutifully signed out the respective chemicals from the general list that had existed to prevent that very use of them. I'd always had the suspicion that had come with decades of tradition.

My absentminded nod seemed to annoy Mike further—as did my next question. "That all you did?"

"I helped with injections, too," he professed, sounding a lot smaller now.

"And?"

He blinked—and that's when I started to suspect that at least some of the shuddering and stuttering was an act. "Producing drugs large-scale takes up a lot of time."

"Actually, it doesn't," I pointed out. "Only if you don't schedule the batches right. But yeah, it takes a day or two if you laze around on your ass, pretending you're doing something other than twiddling your thumbs." He didn't react, which in itself was confirmation enough—although not for anything I felt like further blaming him for. So he'd been a slacker. Considering the consequences— particularly for those who seemed to have been the guinea pigs for the test batches—that might have saved lives. "What else did you do for him? And before you keep on digging that hole you're in, we know that wasn't everything."

He drew up short but tried to hide it in another wide-eyed shake. "I swear, I—"

Nate let out another growl—this one nonverbal, and of the kind that made the hair all over my body stand up—and Mike thought better of it. "Yes, he had me synthesize other shit, too, but I bet all of that is way above your pay grade. And it wasn't like he was sharing his plans with me. I just got to do the lab monkey work."

"Like what?"

He sighed, exasperated—and I didn't miss how his focus dropped from my face to the side of my neck, where thanks to my tank top being my only clothing on top, the very ends of the X-shaped marks were visible. Ah—now things were about to get interesting. "You do know about the serum project?" A stupid question, as I was about to point out, but he went on before I got a chance to. "He was working on some improvements, from what little he told me. I won't bore you with the details."

Now that was where he was wrong. "Please do."

He actually went so far as to grunt before he caught himself—and it was that last bit of annoyance that made me realize where this came from. He did a good job hiding the arrogance in his gaze, but not good enough, now that I knew what to look for. "Why waste my breath—" he started, but cut off when I gave him a bright, albeit cold smile.

"You have no fucking clue who I am," I observed.

It was almost comical to watch him pause. Again his attention snapped to my marks, and he looked nervous for real as he licked his lips. "One of the scavengers, obviously," came his hesitant response.

Leaning back, I allowed myself a self-satisfied huff, then let my smile turn bright and toothy and possibly quite hostile. "The Lucky Thirteen sound familiar? I'm Bree Lewis, and this here is my husband." Mike's eyes went wide—no further explanation needed. Cocking my head to the side, I held on to that smile, but I could tell there was only sadistic glee in it now. Ah, how good it felt to, for once, get the recognition I deserved. "So when I tell you that I do, in fact, know a thing or two about the serum project—and basic chemistry—you know that I'm not lying. And if you don't spill the beans this fucking second, I will start to take you apart limb from limb and feed you to my husband, and make you watch how he will eat every strip of flesh, muscle, and tendon that I cut from your body." I chanced a look at Hamilton—less to gauge his reaction and more to indicate him—and found that, for once, he was playing along nicely, a look of gleeful if violent anticipation on his face. "He can do whatever he wants. He obviously has his own beef with you, but I don't expect that to go down any less painful or gruesome for you. We have been working quite well together all morning when we were cutting up that traitorous bitch." I considered if that was enough, but since he hadn't gone completely white in the face yet, I added, "And if their reputation around here isn't enough for you yet, let me explain that back before the zombie apocalypse, the entire serum project had somewhat of a reputation because of the people they recruited for black ops shit—and these two were, without a doubt, among the worst of what the army had no official knowledge of. Well deserved from what I heard, which is but a fraction of the shit they actually got up to."

Maybe I shouldn't have gotten so much satisfaction out of scaring Mike—and some of the glee I felt was definitely due to the last dregs of the drugs in my system making all kinds of things funny to me—but the sharp scent of urine tickling my nose was definitely rewarding. I didn't look down at his crotch to confirm; that wasn't exactly necessary. Before, he had been uneasy but putting on a show. Now, his panic was real.

"I didn't lie, I promise!" he cried, finally dropping the stuttering act. "I really don't know what that asshole was up to! I just did what I was told!"

I gave him a one-shouldered shrug to let him know I really didn't give a shit. "Then speculate. Please."

He swallowed convulsively, his attention only straying from me for a second. "I'm not sure how the two are connected, but from what I can guess, he was trying to find substances that cut through the protection the serum conveys, and to develop different stable versions going forward. We didn't work with the live virus here, obviously, but in the notes he gave me, a few version numbers were mentioned, in ascending order."

"What for?" I felt that question was more important than possible details.

Mike looked a little perplexed, as if he'd never asked himself that question. "Why what?"

"Why mess with the serum that's already working?" I asked, not hiding my vexation with having to spell it out. "I presume that's why you kept testing that shit out on the prisoners? To see if it had any effect?" That explained why they had a plethora of shit that worked on us. Nate hadn't gone into details when he'd talked about the drugs they'd shot him up with, but judging from the track marks on his body, it hadn't been just an occasional thing.

And it also fit with what Hamilton had said—that he'd dropped off the weaponized serum we'd brought from France with the Chemist.

Mike hesitated, his unease becoming apparent when he finally did speak up. "They would have had a much harder time subduing the surviving fighters otherwise," he pointed out, his voice cracking. "That it helped with the workers was mere coincidence."

That last bit grabbed my attention. "Say what?"

"The workers," he explained. "You do get that they are mindless, almost brain-dead worker bees?"

"Enough so to want to beat the shit out of anyone connected with forcing that state on them, yes," I let him know.

More convulsive swallowing followed. "It's not what you think."

I gave him my best naive expression. "So they aren't the soldiers who got inoculated with the wrong version of the serum that was meant to turn them into mindless drones?"

"Not all of them," Mike insisted—as if that didn't make everything worse. "Those were the first workers. But there weren't enough of them to work large-enough fields to sustain a larger settlement."

"So you, what? Accidentally shot up people with more of the same shit?"

He shook his head vehemently at the sharp tone of my voice. "Of course not!"

I couldn't help a derisive snort. "No. A bunch of assholes who hold arena death matches would never do that."

The guys got another round of fearful attention. "It wasn't that same serum variant," Mike said, trying to correct himself. "It's the side effect of one of the working ones, I swear! We discovered the downsides after the damage was done, and it wasn't like we could warn people after that, or they would have killed us."

"Wait, is that shit the reason why most of the scavengers are raving lunatics now?" This really got better and better.

"Some," Mike muttered under his breath, but was quick to speak up at my frown. "Most of it is the drugs—that we've had to test, extensively, beforehand. One in ten to thirty gets like that, but most not at first, or even for the first few months. Shit, how deranged do you think we are to condemn thousands of people to brain-dead slavery?"

"Exactly that much," I pointed out. But I had to admit, his agitation raised some doubt in me.

"Well, you're wrong," he protested. "They shot all of us up with that shit, too! And their command crew as well. Shit, I get why you don't trust me, but why would they have risked it themselves?"

He had a point—if I ignored my experience with Taggard and his boys. It stood to reason someone had learned from that—or not. "And the scavengers just let you do this."

"Let us?" Mike's voice took on a shrill note that I belatedly recognized as amusement. "They demanded that we do it. Almost rioted twice when there weren't enough doses for everyone right when they found out we had a working serum." He looked conflicted for a moment, as if trying to remember some detail or other, but finally gave up. "You know how dangerous it is out there. Weren't you damn glad you were immune to the zombie bites and scratches?"

I was the wrong one to petition for agreement with that. "I didn't get the serum until well over a year past the shit hit the fan," I succinctly told him, hard-pressed to pass up the opportunity to sneer at Hamilton, as he deserved. "It's convenient, but it's not the be-all, end-all, and it does come with some massive downsides."

Mike looked satisfied for a moment—making me guess that the status of my immunity had been what he'd been trying to remember just now; being what counted as a celebrity these days came with weirdness like that, I figured—but it quickly passed, leaving him wary and scared once more. "Well, most people thought differently. So we gave them what they demanded. There are still new ones dropping by every week, even with rumors about the brain-dead workers circulating aplenty. Scared people don't give a shit about consequences when there's only one hope for them."

I was so tempted to pull Hamilton out of the room and ask him if he could verify any of that—what suspicions I had in that aspect were mostly based on what he'd said—but cut down on that impulse. He likely wouldn't tell me, and it was a topic better suited for a briefing involving everyone else. None of that helped buffer the level of frustration and disgust that came up within me at Mike's explanation—if he was telling the truth, that was.

"Do you still have doses of that shit left?" He shook his head. "Any documentation?" More of the same. I let out a slow breath to keep from punching him in his face. So much for side effects. "So what you're pretty much telling me is that you deliberately shot up thousands of scavengers with some shit that makes some of them non-functioning and leaves the rest susceptible to all manners of shit that gets them addicted and coming back for more?"

A nod, and he definitely cringed away from my glare now, expecting retribution. "I swear, we didn't know at first, and then we had no choice."

"Just like you didn't have any choice with the prisoners?" I asked way too sweetly.

Mike's eyes widened as he realized that he couldn't win, but at least that didn't make him clam up. "I still remember some of the compounds he had me synthesize! And I know the recipes of the most common drugs by heart, too! Please, you have to believe me, if I knew more I'd tell you!"

I was tempted to taunt him that this was hardly enough, but then thought better of it. Straightening, I looked around, finally settling on a pad and pencil on one of the tables. "Don't you dare leave anything out," I instructed as I handed him both, abusing one of the tables to lean against—also to be out of his reach should he attempt to use the pencil for anything else.

"Sure, sure," Mike mumbled, already bent over the pad, setting to work.

I watched him scribble for a few minutes, the drawings easier to make sense of than his scrawl. The guys remained hulking over him like two threatening pillars made of muscle and hatred, but I didn't miss the vacant look on Nate's face that soon pushed away his general state of alertness. My own thoughts started to wander, stress and sleep deprivation doing its own to make it hard to concentrate—

So none of us caught the moment when Mike switched the grip on the pencil, and rammed it straight up into his skull through what used to be his left eye seconds ago. He was dead before I could do more than startle back into alertness.

The three of us watched as the body that used to be Mike sagged in on itself, a last pained gurgle leaving him. Hamilton leaned forward, grabbing a shoulder to make the head flop back, revealing the grisly display. I blinked, mostly irritated with myself for not having caught this, but also strangely fascinated. If not for Hamilton, I would have allowed myself to shiver as I wanted to—not sure why, but the eyes always got to me. It stood to reason that losing an eye rather than half of my fingers would have hampered me less, but maybe it was more a thing of familiarity versus fear of the unknown.

Hamilton's drawl finally made my attention snap from the idiot formerly known as Mike to him. "Fucked that one up good, didn't you?"

"Because it's just me in here, and I'm in charge," I pointed out, my annoyance mixing well with the intended sarcasm.

"Shows why you shouldn't be," Hamilton shot back.

Doing my best to ignore him, I pulled the pad toward me before Mike's eye goo could ruin what he'd scribbled. I half expected all of it to be nonsense, but I could decipher a few compounds—but none of it made sense beyond the obvious—MDMA, acid, ketamine. Except for the shared value where recreational use was concerned, they had nothing in common on the chemical side.

Glancing at the shelves around the room, I pushed away from the table and started perusing them. It was easy to verify that they had everything stocked here that Mike had written down. Maybe if we'd just kept him alive a little longer... but the point was moot, and besides, as far as their backyard-chemist approach to drug distribution went, I didn't give a shit whether they'd managed to synthesize the most pristine crystal meth or not—all I cared about was the serum.

Getting tired of staring at the corpse, Nate went to the door and called in the guards. Cole took one look at the dead body and burst out laughing, making me wonder just how sober he was—not that I could shame anyone in that department at the moment. "Damn, but that one didn't last long," he muttered, also oddly fascinated by the pencil sticking out of Mike's skull.

"This can't be the entire lab," I muttered after another look around. "Do you know where they keep the rest?"

Cole shook his head. "No fucking clue. But there's a supply room down the corridor."

At first I thought that this was a stab at our conjugal extracurricular activities, but when no acerbic remark followed, I let him point me in that direction. As expected, it was all crammed shelves, holding mostly white cardboard boxes and plastic containers—all still achingly familiar from my past life, but only so useful. I even checked the walls, hunting for a concealed door, but came up empty.

As great as it was to have Nate back, this whole endeavor got more frustrating by the hour. The latent sense of doom at the back of my mind—fueled by the knowledge that we were wasting time that we likely didn't have—absolutely didn't help. The storm raging on above us sure fit my mood perfectly.

Chapter 3

Scott looked up from the maps he had been poring over as we returned, surprised to see us. "That was quick."

I let Nate do the talking, instead focusing on what Scott had been occupied with. It looked like a detailed map of the citadel and entire camp beyond—nothing particularly interesting.

"He didn't know much," Nate offered, scratching his chin. "Dead lead either way."

I was tempted to speak up in disagreement, but since I'd let Mike kill himself on my watch, there was nothing I could do about that now. Damn, but Hamilton wasn't exactly wrong with his acerbic remark about me fucking that up. The fact that it didn't really bother me—except for giving that idiot a chance to reprimand me—was less disconcerting than how my body felt increasingly more sluggish, including my mind. Simply listening to Scott switch topics and prattle off a list of locations to check on was almost maxing out my mental capacity. The jitters were getting worse, and when I checked my forehead, my hand came away clammy. While Nate listened—or pretended to—Hamilton went to investigate the food offerings on a nearby table, heavily scrutinized by the Ice Queen, but she didn't reprimand him when he went for the stew pot and started ladling the contents with a hunk of bread. While I found the display disgusting on principle—and I didn't trust the pots here, even after they had been thoroughly cleaned—a couple of female scavengers at a nearby table got very interested. Hamilton didn't miss that, either, after slaking his hunger—and with a smirk in my direction sauntered over to the ladies to take care of another. I didn't suppress the harder shiver that ran through my body. Mutilating that bitch I could take, but Hamilton and his groupies? That was too much.

Only that when I turned around to join Nate, I found that he was about to leave the room through a different door, trailing after Andrej, who was keeping up a loud, animated, if one-sided conversation in Serbian. Looked like I was left to my own devices—and considering that Hamilton was holding court, I felt it was about time that I took my sorry ass elsewhere.

"Anything left on our agenda for today?" I asked Scott since he seemed to have somewhat of an overview of the situation.

He considered but shook his head. "Unless you want to have a chat with the freed prisoners and keep adding to your nightmares, not really." He gave me a small grin when I shook my head. "Thought so."

I was about to turn away when my eyes fell on his maps, the one with the building with the Chemist's workroom where we'd just been on top. "Say, is that all the workspace they had for the drug manufacturing? Considering that the assistant told us they were running a profitable business, they must have had a larger space set up elsewhere. That workspace had barely enough shelf space for small batches, which wouldn't have produced enough to keep the scavengers stoned for a single day."

Scott shook his head without checking. "Not that I'm aware of, but we haven't checked the warehouses and barns yet. Sounds promising?"

I considered for a second. "Something that won't tear down several buildings when it explodes? Sounds right to me."

I got a weird look for that assessment that made me want to ask him if he'd never considered why chemistry labs in schools were located on the upper floor or very end of a wing, but left it at a shrug. "I'll go check that out." I was sure buildings that size wouldn't be hard to find—and I had an inkling that I'd in fact already sneaked by them, right next to the barracks where the labor force was locked in. Somehow I didn't think anyone had been too concerned about what fumes they might have been inhaling.

I wasn't halfway across the room to the closest exit yet when Richards fell into step with me, signaling Cole and Hill to follow us. Since he ignored my annoyed glare, I let him tag along, figuring that it wasn't the worst idea to bring backup if I had to case the warehouses first. With three hulking soldiers in tow, it seemed unlikely that anyone would get any weird ideas, either.

"You're looking for the drug manufactory?" Richards asked conversationally as we made our way up the ramp to the ground level, getting closer to the incessant howling of the wind once more.

"Something like that," I replied, trying to sound like talking was the last thing on my mind. Hill chuckled under his breath, but while I was sure the three of them knew about how the interrogation had gone south, nobody asked for specifics.

Richards wasn't done, though. "Any leads yet?"

I shook my head. Stepping out into the storm, the wind hitting me hard enough to steal my breath away for a moment, saved me from having to elaborate. Nobody was stupid enough to venture out into the bad weather, leaving the broad road made of hard-packed dirt to us. I tried to avoid the worst of the puddles at first, and didn't mind when Richards sent Cole forward. Despite our gear, we were drenched to the skin by the time we reached the long, three-story buildings toward the northern quarter of the camp. Cole let me take point with a mock bow as I stepped into the first warehouse, letting my eyes accustom to the gloom before venturing forth. Just our luck that the building we were looking for was the third of its kind, packed behind the other two and what passed for a garage for the farm equipment around here. Having seen the laborers in the fields before had made me think they didn't have any larger equipment, but apparently they hadn't bothered bringing that out when I'd fled from the camp over two months ago.

I knew we'd hit pay dirt the moment Hill pulled open one side of the large gate, an acrid chemical scent tickling my nostrils. Hill, more intelligent than he sometimes pretended to be, paused immediately, clearly itching to run back for a gas mask. Squinting into the darkness inside, I spied some basic security equipment like gloves and coats by the door, but no full hazmat gear. So maybe they hadn't been cooking meth in here, after all. I waited a few more seconds to see if my eyes or throat would start burning, and when nothing happened, I stepped inside to get a better look.

Bingo.

"Don't touch anything," I warned the soldiers as I started down the open space on the left side that was mostly storage shelves. "If you suddenly start puking and bleeding from your eyes and ears, it's probably too late."

Nobody found my advice funny, but that was fine with me. Unlike the smaller workroom, there were fewer tubs of chemicals in here, but most of them were large enough that I would have needed both hands to pull them off the shelves. Next came a few tanks, some for liquid ingredients, but two also for what I presumed was storage of drugs. In the opposite corner, a part of the warehouse had been sectioned off, and it was outside of that cube that three bright-yellow hazmat suits hung, well-maintained but showing obvious signs of wear and tear. The others were smart enough to steer clear of that section, and I had no intentions of venturing any closer, either. Instead, I went looking for documentation.

Sure that no army of trigger-happy guards or doped-up scavengers was hiding anywhere, Hill and Cole retreated to the entrance, taking up position where they could check outside but were safe from the rain. Richards ambled along for a while, but after a few minutes got bored of watching me read labels and glance into drawers.

"What are you looking for specifically?"

I didn't halt in my so far fruitless perusal. "Anything, really. I think I have an idea what they used to make the crap the scavengers are snorting and smoking, but I don't really give a shit about that."

A sidelong glance was enough to catch his brief smile, but when I turned to fully face him, Richards was all closed-off professionalism. That, like me, he must have been riding the tail end of a massive high now drowning in withdrawal wasn't anything I could have read off his features. Asshole. Just my luck that every single man and woman in this blasted camp had less issues with that than me.

I paused when the next drawer was stuffed to the brim with papers, but most of that looked like notes from someone who needed their fingers to add up numbers from one to ten. They were in line with what Mike had explained, making me guess at first that they might actually be his notes—except for the fact that even at a glance I could make out three different handwriting styles.

"Looks like this was a team effort," I muttered, a new wave of annoyance coming up inside of me. "That lying piece of shit." It didn't really matter, since even having names and physical descriptions of the others wouldn't have yielded different results. They must have left with the Chemist—days ago.

Richards cleared his throat, making me look at him. He was still pretending to be Mr. Neutral. "Cole told me your interrogation didn't work out so well?"

"Depends," I offered. "He told us about the drugs they manufactured, and how they beefed up their farm-labor force. That's ten times what that bitch could deliver. But yes, he managed to get lucky and killed himself before I could get out the pliers."

"And how are you dealing with that?"

I couldn't help but smirk. "That I didn't have to torture another ass wipe to the point where pausing was a relief because he'd stop screaming? Not really bothering me a lot."

I could tell that Richards wasn't very convinced of what sounded like a lie even to me, but I had no intention of explaining further. When nothing more came from me, he dropped the point—and went straight for the kill. "And how are you dealing with everything else? You know, you can talk to me if—"

He cut off when I deliberately closed the drawer and glared at him. "Do you really think I'd do that, now that I have my entire crew back?"

Richards didn't look perturbed that I'd pretty much just told him that we weren't friends.

"Some things are easier to discuss with a virtual stranger," he pointed out.

"Which you aren't." I forestalled any possible response he could have given when his mouth snapped open. "Don't play games with me, okay? My patience is about maxed out by the very presence of your former commanding officer, and that's without the shakes, and the brain fog, and the fact that this entire place makes my skin crawl. From where I'm standing, I'm happy about every supporting hand readily lent, but I won't let anyone try to get between me and the people I trust." I also had no intention of shoving anyone away deliberately, so I waited until my ego let me back down a little. "We need to have a debriefing as soon as we know more, and plan what we'll do next—and who will be along for the ride. I can have more than two friends, don't worry. But right now I'm not really in the mood to talk."

Red nodded, if reluctantly—or maybe he was battling demons similar to mine. I turned back to my drawers, ready to sift through the next one, but he wasn't done yet.

"Hamilton and I talked last night," he offered. "As you can imagine, that wasn't a very elevating, light conversation. He didn't mention any specifics, but extrapolating from what he didn't say, I can imagine what's on your mind right now."

Strangely, the annoyance ebbed rather than flowed at his words, but that didn't mean our talk got any less strained. I made a point of catching his gaze before I responded. "And don't you think I will take all the things that might weigh on my mind that my husband told me to the grave, and gladly? No offense, but again: if I needed to talk to someone, it wouldn't be you."

Richards took my refusal to spill my guts with a curt nod. "I know that you both think that you can't confide in anyone—"

"I'd talk to Zilinsky if I needed to bawl my eyes out," I told him, adding with a not-quite nice smile, "Been there. Done that. And I know she will take my grievances to the grave, too."

A look of surprise crossed Red's features, something that I hadn't expected. "I didn't realize that you were that friendly with her." The way he stressed "her" made me realize the Ice Queen's reputation preceded her. That very fact made me grin in earnest.

"She's been Nate's right hand for longer than I've known them. After making sure I wouldn't accidentally kill myself with a gun, she started extending that same courtesy to me. I would talk to her if I needed to, and so would Nate. So unless you want to spill the beans on what Hamilton told you in confidence, or need someone to discuss private matters with, we're done here."

Expecting him to keep his tongue, I turned back to my drawer, but paused with my fingers on the handle when Richards spoke up.

"He's leaving command of our soldiers to me. Said he was done with the army. I would be lying if I wasn't at least a little concerned about his will to live, but when I was watching the three of you interact earlier, he seemed quite happy to be around. Looks like, indeed, he has become your problem rather than mine."

On some level, the fact that he was ready to confide in me felt good. His words, not so much, although I had been wondering about that already. Anger, coiled tight and impossible to disband, started roaring in the back of my mind but I did my best to ignore it, turning back to my drawer. More scrawled notes, no new revelations. The same was true for the next drawer. In the last, I found a basic organic chemistry book that had seen better days a long time ago. I leafed through it but the notes scrawled all over the margins seemed to belong to legions of students rather than give evidence of what they'd been up to here. It was just as bad as the books we'd liberated from that engineering department when Nate and I had been hunting for information on how to build electrical engines for the buggies.

It was that very thought that made me pause, then check the front of the book. The title page was gone where, without a doubt, the stamp or sticker of the library had been where it had lived before ending up here. That gave me an idea.

Ignoring Richards and his patient yet imploring gaze, I walked down the row of worktables to where I found a few boxes full of latex gloves. Someone had diligently unpacked them and stacked them, sorted by size, in the overhead racks above the tables. Looking inside the cupboards below the tables, I found them filled to the brim with plastic bags containing centrifuge vials of all sizes, again stacked according to size. I continued to open doors and drawers, skipping over to the central part of the warehouse—until, finally, I was met with brown cardboard rather than see-through plastic. And, wouldn't you know it—the box even had the initial address label where it had been sent to on top.

Not bothering with leaving the strangely organized state of the warehouse intact, I tore off the flap containing the packaging label and continued my search. In short order, I had a handful of torn cardboard in my hands, all of them coming from either of two addresses—in Texas. And while the companies didn't ring a bell, the street names sounded familiar. Definitely something to bring up in the briefing tomorrow.

"Found what you were looking for?" Richards asked when I looked ready to go.

"Not really, but I might have found something." When he kept eyeing me askance, I shrugged. "They must have had all their chemicals and containers from somewhere. Maybe that's where they kept working on the serum project." His utter lack of a reaction told me I was breaking new ground for him. "The Chemist's assistant told us that they were continuing to tweak the serum—that's what fried the worker bees' brains and made the scavengers come back. I need to check back with Harris to confirm that guess, but after Colorado, that's less of a surprise than I like to admit."

I didn't miss the latent horror crossing his face before he schooled his expression, which was yet another layer of confirmation. Too much, actually, and I turned away before more grievance could make me say or do something I would later regret. Yet Richards held me back, physically reaching out to touch my arm.

"Lewis, we are not your enemies," he insisted, withdrawing his fingers when he felt me tense. I stared at where he had touched me, then at his face, trying to gauge whether his expression of openness was real or fake.

"But you were the ones who started this," I ground out before I could stop myself. "You were there, in Colorado. You were there when your faction promised to take care of all the soldiers that had already turned into zombies in everything but the need to eat flesh." And my, didn't that have a sour connotation to it now. "Why are there still experiments going on? Why did hundreds—no, thousands!—of scavengers get infected and ultimately doomed to the very same fate? And don't you dare lie to my face and tell me this is the first you've heard of this. Is this why we went to France? So you could let the issues with the pesky scavengers take care of themselves? Is this what Emily Raynor has been cooking up in her lab for the past two and a half years?"

The storm howling around the warehouse was quite the dramatic backdrop for my accusations, but Red remained stoically calm.

"You mean because of what Hamilton said yesterday? That he'd been tasked to drop off the weaponized virus version here?" I nodded—no hesitation there. Richards looked doubtful, as if he was debating what to make of that himself, but ended up shaking his head. "Why don't we ask him, rather than throw accusations out there where they can easily get people killed?" When he saw my surprise, he laughed, and it wasn't a nice sound. "Don't you think that all of us are very aware that this camp is a powder keg, maybe more so now than before? The last thing we need is you of all people giving those drugged-up assholes even more of a reason to slaughter us on a whim!"

That accusation—and the mentioned consequences—made me draw up short, and it took me a few moments to work through my confusion. "You're serious?"

Under different circumstances, the exasperated look he shot me might have made me cheer, but today wasn't the best day to finally wear his patience thin. "Deadly."

It was then that I realized the reason why Richards continued to plaster himself to me—thankfully at more of a physical distance than yesterday, but still—was less because of ulterior motives, and more so the simple reassurance that came with my reputation. I tried to remember where I'd seen the soldiers mill around since Nate had officially retired the previous leadership, but couldn't remember. Somewhere with the Silo marines—who hadn't ventured far from our established headquarters, either, come to think of it. Only Harris and his scavengers had left the Citadel to roam everywhere and celebrate.

Huh. Maybe I should have paid more attention to this before.

Richards cleared his throat, actually looking a little taken aback, as if his brief outburst had left him thoroughly embarrassed. "Look," I started, not quite sure what to say. It fleetingly occurred to me that, maybe, he was trying this angle to get under my skin. Damn, but I hated that things had to be so complicated! "I appreciate that, for the second time, you and your men have risked your lives to help me rescue my husband. And yes, just between you and me, I do consider you as one of my friends, and one of the people I might confide in. Fact is, I'm having a really hard time hanging on to my sanity right now, and the last thing I need is this constant second-guessing. So let's not read too much into anything until we know more for sure, okay? We still have countless buildings to search and people to beat into submission so they'll share their nefarious plans with us. Then we'll have the next powwow, and we'll take it from there. Sounds good?"

He nodded without being an asshole and let me hang for the few minutes I probably deserved to squirm under his calm gaze. "Sounds good," he echoed. "Just, maybe, only accuse us of the things we're actually responsible for. Not the ghosts that you've already exorcised."

I couldn't quite suppress tensing up at the memory of where I'd first had to deal with that mind-destroying shit—Taggard's white-tiled cell. "Aren't you the least bit curious who is behind all this?" I asked as I turned toward the gate, only now realizing how dark it had gotten outside.

"Of course I am," Richards offered with a tight smile that was more of a grimace. "Those were my soldiers who had to take the first hit. I knew nine good men who lost their minds to that faulty serum. Nine good men who had defended this country against the undead, and helped rebuild without complaint or a single day of leave since the shit hit the fan. And all just because they believed there was an easy solution to the constant danger they had been in the entire time. And I lost several times that number to scavenger raids since. Do you think I'm a saint who doesn't feel the itch to gun down every crazy-eyed, war-painted idiot who still believes they are fighting for their freedom when, actually, they are the ones who keep terrorizing the country? I'm not. But what I have learned is that, all too often, hardliners like Hamilton only exacerbate the situation, and without compromise, we'll all be dead in no time. And as you know, when you bite it, it doesn't matter what color your uniform was or whether you ever wore one in the first place."

I hadn't expected quite such a speech, but for the first time since I'd gotten to know him better at the base in Canada and our journey to France, I felt like I was talking to the man, not the officer. Again, the nasty voice at the back of my mind whispered that it was entirely possible this was just his latest strategy to play me, but I didn't believe it. He had little to lose and nothing to gain—except maybe make me realize I really needed to watch what I was saying and who was listening to it. Realizing that with Harris we had a strong ally who could not only get us into the camp but also help us overthrow Cortez and his people had made me feel kind of invincible, but I knew that was a dangerous liaison at best, and might come with them turning on us next at worst. I loathed Hamilton with a vengeance, and still didn't trust the soldiers as much as their actions around me maybe deserved, but they were likely the more reliable compromise. Add to that both factions of marines—who would drop away as soon as the army left—and that latent sense of security suddenly turned into the opposite. Just maybe I should have brought more than three people on my little quest to find out more about the drug operations—and checked in with Pia to let her know what I was doing.

I wouldn't be making that mistake again in the future.

Richards seemed satisfied with the following silence as we rejoined his men and started making our way back through the storm, the rain feeling even worse, if that was possible. We were getting close to the Citadel entrance when something occurred to me. Turning to Richards, I asked, "Exactly where do you know Zilinsky from?"

I got a borderline sardonic smile for my trouble. "You mean, besides her being the XO of the biggest pain in our ass since the shit hit the fan?"

I nodded. "Naturally. As much as I like to delude myself into thinking everyone believes that I've been running the show, we all know it isn't so."

Richards waited until we were inside, shaking himself like a dog before responding. "You do realize that, medical personnel aside, only three people have ever been inoculated with the serum who haven't been active service members of the army?"

I was about to negate that but realized I already knew the answer. "You mean me, Zilinsky, and Romanoff?"

I got a curt if satisfied nod. "I'm sure that for none of you, any records exist, but people talk, and the more horrifying the story, the more embellished it becomes. I presume you know their version of it?"

"Actually, I only know bits and pieces," I offered, feeling vaguely stupid. But one did not simply walk up to the Ice Queen and ask her why everyone and their mother perked up when her name was mentioned. "She told me that she'd been lost, and Miller helped her regain her sanity." Which was oversimplifying it, but as close to the truth as I could get without spilling what little I knew of her past—which I would also take to my grave.

It spoke volumes that both Hill and Cole were completely silent, listening with rapt attention. Richards snorted, without a doubt bemused at his men's reaction—or my statement. "Let's put it this way: not even the black ops branch of the army makes a habit of working with mercenaries that have rap sheets that make any manila folder trying to contain them burst at the seams. Unless said mercenaries can give the best of our best a run for their money, and come out laughing at how incompetent and nice we are. The story goes that not just one of our strike companies but also the search-and-rescue company sent after them got bogged down in a situation where both captains knew they and all their men were toast—only to be sprung by a small strike force whose only reason to be there was because they hadn't been paid for their last contract and were now demanding their price in blood. The reason why the two surviving members agreed to work for us was because they were promised more of the same, over and over again—and the shot that would allow them to keep raining destructions on their enemies even beyond the grave. Sounds familiar?"

I was tempted to shake my head but refrained. In a sense, I could see why Pia hadn't been lying when she'd told me that Nate had "saved" her when he'd given her a new purpose in life. Also, the fact that she didn't want her name right next to his on our scavenger company sheet took on an entirely new meaning.

Also, the fact that she'd managed to get five factions to the meeting to plan the assault on the camp, with only Dispatch backing out, made a lot more sense now. And that nobody had dared attack the California settlement, either. Sleeping dogs, and all that shit.

Suddenly, the idea that the scavengers would turn on us and shiv us in our sleep bothered me a lot less than a few minutes ago.

"Well, at least I keep interesting company," I muttered, ignoring the incredulous look Richards shot my way.

"Is that all you're going to say to that?" he called after me, quickly catching up once more.

"What else is there to say?" I asked, grinning. "You had me worried there for a bit, but I think I'll sleep soundly tonight." Which, I was afraid, was likely still wishful thinking, but a girl could hope! When Richards kept staring at me, I snorted. "You know, ever since Hamilton told us that Decker was still alive, I was afraid he would come after us because he wanted his favorite lap dog back at his side. Now I'm starting to think that everything that happened was a preemptive strike to prevent said lap dog's attack dog from tearing out anyone's throat who might even glance the wrong way at said lap dog."

"You do realize that she's just one woman, right? And not getting any younger."

It was easy to shrug off Red's comment. "So am I. And just consider how much of a nuisance I've become for you, and without even trying really hard."

Richards didn't have a rebuke for that, but I heard Cole mutter a succinct, "At least it's not going to be boring around here any time soon." Truer words had seldom been spoken.

Chapter 4

The storm continued to rage throughout the night, but much to my surprise broke the following morning. By midday, the rain eased up and let a few tentative rays of sunshine through the endless cloud cover. By afternoon, the world had turned into a humid, hot nightmare again, the few hours of respite between the extremes not enough to make me feel alive. The shakes had eased up, but that only made it easier for me to concentrate on how drained and miserable I felt. I'd figured the withdrawal would run a similar course as the first time, when I'd escaped and made my way to the settlement where Richards and his men had picked me up; reality was a long shot from that, the mental impact far stronger this time.

We'd wasted another hour with Cindy, but I'd held myself in the background, listening only while Hamilton did the talking—and surprisingly little punching. Realizing that what we'd done to her had broken her spirit only added to my pervasive sense of malaise, and I was almost glad for Bucky's presence as that meant I couldn't own up to this and let myself fall into that black, black hole at the bottom of my soul. Nate and Hamilton also talked to a few of the less insane former prisoners, but there was woefully little to gain from that in terms of information. Scott had in the meantime finished his maps, and the marines and soldiers together had compiled a list of possible assets we could use for whatever we decided to do going forward. My first impression of how the camp had grown to this size and managed to sustain itself—strength in numbers and a reign of terror that coexisted in a climate of utter incompetence—seemed to be truer than I was comfortable with. The scavengers turned out to be the camp's lifeblood, trading everything needed for drugs, food, and short-lived entertainment—and judging from the half-empty stores, they hadn't managed well on the food side of things. In hindsight, our triumphant victory turned somewhat stale when it became obvious that it had worked mainly because nobody before us had tried in earnest to overthrow the leadership—and the fact that not just the Chemist and most of his team, but also several of Cortez's lieutenants had disappeared just before the storm hit with us riding shotgun made it even worse. Ten people sneaking inside under the cover of darkness might have been enough to end the constant misery of a shitload of prisoners. In what used to be Cortez's quarters, the Ice Queen found a ledger with names—or what went for them, seeing as Cortez hadn't known the real identity of most of his victims—of arena fighters that had perished. Nobody had counted them, but the fact that the list spanned pages upon pages and didn't even factor in the women who had died in the kennels made me really sorry that Nate had killed that asshole so quickly. Those very numbers also made me suspect that the arena fighters hadn't been the only ones who had been fed a constant diet of disreputable protein sources. Considering that the livestock rounded up barely accounted for what the scavengers must be consuming in a few weeks, I didn't want to know what had sustained the farm workers.

With room for over fifty people needed so everyone could be part of our big planning session, the arena turned out to be the most suitable place for that. I couldn't help but cringe inside as I strode through the gates behind Nate and Hamilton, both outwardly calm but, without a doubt, not so on the inside. Hamilton had turned up later this morning with no sign of the women he'd vacated the premises with, but I presumed he hadn't eaten them. I hadn't slept much that night but as far as I could tell that was still a lot more rest than Nate had gotten, yet far be it from him to ease up on the pressure he put on himself to keep going. Our entire assault group was present except for a handful of people set up to guard the entrances, including the scavengers and a few others that Harris insisted should be here. Already, he seemed to have started weeding out the people he felt he wanted to work with, but his enthusiasm about running the show had markedly cooled off when they'd realized that food was about to run out, and everyone who had any interest in synthesizing more drugs was either dead or gone. Frankly, I was surprised that nobody had pulled me aside yet to take over operations, or at least train a replacement, but then people seemed to associate me more with being Nate's wife than a scientist. To say the arena felt just as ready to blow up as during the fight where I'd watched Nate tear out and eat that guy's heart was an understatement.

When the Ice Queen gave him a brief nod, Nate stepped into the middle of the loose circle we had gathered in, more or less split into groups according to our affiliations. "Thank you all for joining me here," he called out, doing a quick turn and stopping with his back to where Pia and I were standing side by side with Hamilton lurking close by. "Now that the storm has blown over, it is time for action." No cheers rose, but particularly from the scavengers I got a weird sense of excitement. "We've had time aplenty to gather what little knowledge there was to glean from the few people who used to be in command who didn't run away like the cowards they are, or died with little more backbone than that." I didn't miss the grim look of satisfaction on his face—well-earned, but also disconcerting. A round of cheers went up, but died down as soon as Nate went on talking.

"What we need to know now is simple: who was responsible for this? Where did those cowards that fled run to? And what are the consequences that we need to deal with?" He half-turned so that he was facing Harris and his fellow scavengers. "We said we were happy to let you continue to run the show here if that's what you want. We will need to take some of the ammo with us that we found and a limited amount of food, but the rest is yours to do with as you see fit. I hope you are still happy with that arrangement?"

A few of the scavengers looked less enthusiastic, but Harris inclined his head with befitting gravitas for a newly-minted mayor. "We will do our best to keep the operations running. It's anyone's guess whether we'll manage to get enough food from the fields to make it through the winter, but we won't abandon those poor, lost souls to their fate." He must have been referring to the workers. "You can count on us."

That last bit surprised me; not so Nate, who accepted it with a nod. "The first good news in a long time," he offered—and turned back to the gathering at large. "And likely, it will remain the only good news. Killing Cortez was necessary—and will forever be the kill I will feel the least conflicted about in my entire life—but it solves little, and changes nothing. As we have had to discover, that this camp exists and how it treated some of its denizens is the least of our problems." I was surprised when he turned to me next. "Bree, will you please explain to Harris and his people what exactly has been done to them?"

I had not seen that one coming—and would have greatly appreciated a warning—but my stunned look did a thing or two to ease some of the tempers that looked ready to explode amidst the murmurs that rose in the scavenger quadrant. At his wave, I stepped forward to join him, yearning for another mug of strong coffee to jump-start my brain. I could have done without the smirk on Hamilton's face, too.

Turning to the scavengers, I did my best to sort my frayed thoughts. "All that I can tell you is speculation, built on what little we've managed to extract from one of the Chemist's assistants. I presume you all got what you thought was an updated version of the serum?" Silence settled over the arena, hanging like the death shroud over us that I figured it was for some of them. A few of them nodded, and the alarmed looks on the other faces was confirmation aplenty. "As I said, it's all speculation, but I don't think that's a stable, safe version of the serum."

I'd expected one of the more vocal scavengers like Eden to speak up now, but she and Amos were like calm pillars of confidence next to Harris. It was one of the other leaders who got in my face. "Yeah? Well, we can't all be like you and suck the right dicks to get celebrity treatment!"

I was sorely tempted to inform him in no uncertain terms that he was sorely mistaken of how I had gotten my dose, but at least the resulting anger that came up inside of me helped my mind to focus.

Mimicking his tone, I narrowed my eyes at him. "Yeah, but you were with us at the Colorado base where I struck a truce with the very people responsible and forced them to admit that one of their rogue elements had infected hundreds of soldiers with that shit! What's your excuse to come knocking a few months later and ask to be next in line?" Deafening silence answered me, but I didn't feel an ounce of satisfaction at that.

Harris spoke up when nobody else would. "But didn't we do away with that asshole scientist who screwed over all those soldiers? And

I vaguely remember you blamed him for the outbreak of the zombie plague as well."

All I could do was nod. "Yes, we killed him. And yes, I thought he was the root of all evil and doing away with him would, if not negate what had happened, put an end to it continuing to happen. Soon after that I heard doubt from others, and it's obvious that, whether he was responsible or not, someone else has picked up the torch. I presume you know about how the mindless worker drones became what they are? Some of them are the soldiers from back then. Most are your people who have succumbed to the virus, only without fully turning into undead killing machines."

I expected the scavenger leader to get in my face again, but it was a woman standing a short distance to the side who spoke up now. "We knew the risks involved," she insisted, her words drawing a few murmurs but only until she silenced the others with a glare. "We knew, but most of us didn't care. Don't realize you're already dead versus being close to invincible? Even knowing what I know now, I'd get the shot all over again." Several others agreed with her, and even those who remained silent looked determined to have chosen wisely. Frustration didn't begin to describe what I was feeling.

"But how could you—" I started to say, only to be interrupted by my least favorite person on earth as Hamilton stepped forward to join me and Nate.

"Because they still have no fucking clue what they agreed to," he said, not having to raise his voice much to be heard clearly throughout the arena. His smirk remained directed at me for a few seconds before he turned to the audience at large, stepping a little to the left to put physical distance between himself and Nate and me. "And they are not the only ones."

This was getting better and better. I had the creeping feeling that I wouldn't like what he was about to say—which got a million times worse when, rather than address the entire arena, Hamilton zeroed in on me.

"How are you feeling on this fine day, Lewis? How real is your concern for your fellow scavengers? Or are you simply vexed that someone did something you disagree with and won't see reason even when you explain their own stupidity to them?" That didn't deserve an answer, and Hamilton barely left me five seconds before he went on, his tone turning even more nasty. "And when, exactly, did your snowflake ass turn into a master interrogator and torturer? I've heard that, on your crusade to Colorado to presumably kick our asses into submission, you weren't shy to dish out a few punches so they'd get some traitors talking, but pulling out a helpless woman's teeth? Tearing out her fingernails one by one? Cutting off her fingers segment by segment, particularly considering how that must have echoed with your own, personal trauma? Or should I say, should have? Let's not even talk about the fact that you can eat whatever you want without a hint of revulsion, or have a zombie's low-light vision."

My riling mind couldn't come up with anything to respond with—and I meant really anything; my thoughts were completely wiped clear, the only thing remaining a latent sense of dread that kept rising as he continued, staring at Nate now. "And don't get me started on your dietary requirements." He snorted, sending a sidelong glance my way. "You still think he just got a taste for it? Think again. I watched him retch up what normal food he tried to eat several times over the last two days. You would have noticed, too, if you weren't so damn lovestruck—or did you zone out a time or two and miss it because of that?"

The fact that Nate didn't even try to protest gave me the heebie-jeebies, but as such things went, it was so much easier to get defensive than to think clearly. "All that can easily be explained with the shitload of trauma we've been through. And you're not exactly a paragon of sanity, either."

Hamilton laughed, and I hated that it sounded awfully like agreement. "Sure as hell I'm not," he told me with what must have been the first borderline nice smile in my direction ever. I hoped I'd never see that again. "And why should I be different? Just like you, and him, and a lot of other people, I got inoculated with the serum, and I believed the lies that they told us. Not even lies—none of us knew any better. The fact, plain and simple, is that no single version of the serum was ever foolproof against the zombie virus. It just gave us an extension of life. But that first bite or scratch was all it took to sign our death warrants. Just like with anybody else."

I wouldn't have been surprised if a fanfare of doom-and-gloom music had started blasting from the speakers the arena was rigged with just then. It would have been the perfect baseline for how my heart started to race, loud enough to drown out all other sound—and there was quite the confused shouting going on all around us. I turned to look at Nate, sure that he would be full of the same denial that I was hanging on to with dear life—but only found grim acceptance. So back in Hamilton's smirking face it was.

"That's bullshit!" I shouted, loud enough to be heard over the din, which incidentally shut most people up. "Plain and simple! That can't be true."

Hamilton chuckled. "Just because you don't like it doesn't make it so," he jeered—and was only too happy to keep rambling on with his bullshit theory. "Some—those who were lucky and only had a few encounters with the undead—still have a few more years until their time runs out. Others—like you, and Miller, and me—got up close with the zombies way too often for there to be much immunity left. Well, you're possibly the worst, because I can't think of anyone else who actually started rotting from the inside out, but he's not that far behind. The signs are obvious, and I'm sure I've missed listing quite some more. We've had instances of unexplained instant conversion for years, and they have gotten awfully common of late. You were there in France when Rodriguez bit it on that blasted golf course and came back before anyone could put her down for good. How do you explain that?" He paused for a moment. "Don't trust me? Trust one of your own." He turned to the Ice Queen of all people, who stared back at him without a hint of emotion on her face. "Zilinsky, you tell her: how many of your people have turned over the past two years who shouldn't have?"

She hesitated, glancing at Nate for guidance, but answered when nothing came. "Five." Reluctance was heavy in her tone, and it took me a few moments to identify it as my own dread's twin. "Two could have been suicides. And a third might have died in the fire. But we had two instances of people dying in the middle of the night with no natural cause or explanation. And all of them came back."

My need for denial was so strong that it threatened to choke me, but there had to be an explanation for this outside of what Hamilton was alluding to. Maybe voicing it would make it obvious just how ridiculous his theory was? "So what you are saying is that the scavengers aren't slowly turning because the serum they got was faulty, but everyone who ever got inoculated is, only their version is acting at different speeds than ours? That makes no sense!"

The sardonic smile I got in return just added to the dread clawing at my throat. "Then why do you think they had me deliver a dose of the weaponized version we got from France to their primary testing facility?" Gears started spinning in my head, but not because his question was so hard to process—no. I hadn't expected him to be that outright and honest. I was still gaping at Hamilton when he turned back to the gathering at large, but mostly glanced Nate's way as if he was answering the questions Nate had posed minutes ago. "I can't tell you the why and how of everything that has been going on here, but a few things are obvious. Whoever is behind this shit has been using this camp as a real-time testing ground for years, with fresh-blood guinea pigs lining up faster than they could have churned out serum versions to test on them." I was certain his phrasing was deliberate, stressing the same term Cortez had used for the first-time arena fighters. I couldn't suppress a shudder at the implications. Yet when Hamilton's gaze zeroed in on me, I got the sense that he hadn't even gotten to the worst part yet.

"You think those brain-dead workers are the negatives?" he asked, and I was sure that was a personal question directed at me. He went on talking without waiting for an answer. "I say, there's a good chance that they are the independent alternate experimental setup." His stare, unwavering, continued to bore into me. "Remember my warning? Dying to save others isn't the worst thing that could happen to any of us."

It took me a moment to make the connection—and when I finally did, my previous dread paled in comparison to the phantom fingers closing around my neck. "You mean, someone is turning their own army of super-soldiers who will do whatever they are told because they no longer have a mind of their own to consider whether the order they are following is one worth following?"

The hint of annoyance creeping onto Hamilton's face didn't make up for his belligerent smile. "We have a needlessly convoluted winner."

It made sense—too much sense. And it was easier to focus on than the part that directly affected me. "And the drugs that they have been testing on you…"

"…is the shit that cuts through the extra protection of the updated version," Hamilton stated, finishing my sentence. "Whatever they've been feeding those weirdos is the large-scale, low-dosage trial run."

Maybe it was due to a certain level of cognitive decline, but my mind didn't even bother with useless denial and went straight to agreeing with him. And it did make sense—the drugs that Harris and his people had been giving me had definitely worked on me, but the buzz had been comparatively low. Cortez's men had shot me up with the undiluted shit, and the aftereffects of that still had me crawling up the walls. Anyone subjected to that who hadn't gotten the full serum protection would likely have died. So much for Cortez's interrogation plans that we'd crossed.

It all made sense—even though I didn't want it to. And not just the camp and the turning tide of the scavengers.

"He sent you here to die because you warned us," I muttered, too late realizing that I'd said that out loud when Hamilton's gaze turned hard, the taunting quality of before gone. "Decker, I mean. That's who we believe is running the show behind the scenes, right? You became useless, or more of a nuisance than you were worth, and they needed a candidate to run the full-scale experiments on. That you did them a favor and didn't just up and die only helped them with continued testing."

Someone else would have at least given me a hint of credit for that deduction. All I got was a sneer. "You think you're so fucking smart—"

"And she is," Nate interjected, coming out of his—definitely disconcerting—stupor that had been mildly disguised as attentive listening. "Cortez didn't know who I was, so, more often than not, I got the low dose." When he caught the confusion on my face, Nate shrugged. "I'm sure he'd figured that because I had the scavenger marks, I couldn't have been part of the project when they rolled out the update that renders us immune to the mind-control shit. Everything they pumped me full of screwed with my mind, but more often than not I managed to fight through the worst of the haze before the end of the arena combat. That's why the first time we ended up in the arena together, I managed to hold back from needing to kill him, and why around a third of my opponents went on to live another day. I had to turn it all into a massive, crowd-pleasing spectacle to keep myself alive, but that still means that more often than not I couldn't hold back."

I had a certain feeling that his last fight that I'd witnessed had been one of those, but didn't ask. Plausible as Nate's deduction sounded, it opened the door to another question. Turning to Hamilton, I couldn't help but scrutinize him all over again, but except for more vitriol I got nothing from him, closed-off bastard that he was. That forced me to ask the question suddenly burning on my mind. "That explains why you are still alive. But what's your excuse?"

I didn't miss the sidelong glance he cast at Nate, as if the fact that he hadn't killed him still amused Hamilton. Nate's expression turned guarded, making me guess that the silent exchange between them had sent another message that I hadn't caught. With his usual amount of scorn returning, Hamilton answered me. "Wanna know my secret? My one true super power? I have amazing self-control, which is what you owe your life to." I couldn't help but make a face—did he really think I'd buy that bull?—but he went on before I could call him a liar, his voice gravelly and low enough that it barely carried beyond where I could hear him. "Your asshole of a husband told you what happened before they shot us up? The moment I came to again, my entire world was consumed with the kind of homicidal rage that you will never come to understand. There was nothing and nobody that I wasn't ready to kill, and right that very instant. Yet because my reaction must have been the most predictable in the world, Decker had given me a warning just before they put me under; that if I didn't perform exactly as expected, and in fact keep excelling in every single detail, what happened would be child's play compared to what storm I'd call down. And that thought— that fear—was enough of a lifeline not to lose myself even when every single fiber of my being was screaming to let go. Maybe it's coincidence that they hadn't perfected their drugs yet, but nothing Cortez shot me up with tore through that iron grip that I've always had on myself, and that's the only reason why you're not a widow or plain dead yet."

A shiver ran up my spine, and not because of that last little detail. I got the sense that, for the first time—and probably the only time—I'd just gotten a glimpse at the real Bucky Hamilton, the man who Nate, on some level, still considered his friend, or at least worth keeping around until he stopped being useful. I'd never expected to say that, but I much preferred the asshole persona he usually rolled out around me. He was one of the few people who I never wanted to feel two things for: empathy and respect. What he'd just told me evoked something inside of me that came way too close to both for me to be comfortable with. Judging from how quickly his usual mask slammed back in place, he must have felt the same way, his smirk making me want to repeatedly wash myself.

Riding shotgun with that realization came a different, if no less uncomfortable one. "What you did at the base—and right up to our fun little training stint on the destroyer—that wasn't you actually trying to force-feed me the tools I'd need to keep a grip on myself and not convert on all your asses where you were locked in with me in a tin can of a ship, now, was it?" I didn't need any confirmation from him—and, in a sense, he had already given it in the past, only that he'd claimed that my hatred for him had been the one thing that got me through that eternity on the operating room table—but the way Nate's eyes widened, if only a fraction, told me I was right.

Hamilton, of course, had to answer with a derisive snort. "Self-important little shit as always," he drawled, his smirk now directed at Nate as he kept talking to me. "It was a win-win situation for me. Either he's stuck with you—which should have been the ultimate worst-case scenario for any guy—or I get a front-row seat to watching him having to put you down like the bitch you are, thus crushing that last thread of humanity he's been holding on to for ages. Nothing to lose for me, and everything to gain."

This was getting way too personal for an audience in the high double digits, but I couldn't help it; I just had to ask. "Is it me, personally, that you have issues with, or are you still playing some idiotic game that makes you think you have to come up ahead of him? Because, really, since it looks like we'll have to work together, I'd like to know if it's something I said or did. I know I have my share of much-deserved resentment present in this world, but I just can't figure out why you're always up in my business."

Hamilton's mouth twisted into something that in anyone else, under different circumstances, would have been a smile, but I knew that wasn't the case here. "Wouldn't you like to know?" And clearly, that was the last he was going to say on that topic.

In a sense, dying soon was maybe not so bad.

That sentiment was enough to switch my focus back to the people around us, and I couldn't help but single out the handful of my friends, who'd spent the brief intermission of the three of us tearing into each other in hushed tones having their own, much concerned discussions. It wasn't that much of a surprise that Martinez looked the most upset. Any single one of us—or maybe that was just me and Burns—in his shoes would have been gloating at least a little, in an "I told you so!" sense. He'd always been adamantly against getting the serum himself, and from what I'd heard, had to fight a battle of wills against Emily Raynor not to be inoculated when she'd done her best to fix his spine injury in trade for us joining the expedition to France. But with very few exceptions, he'd just heard all of his close friends getting a death warrant served, and he was the kind of good guy who wouldn't just shake that off. Santos and Clark, both in a similar boat with him in that aspect, looked perturbed, but since nobody was insta-converting right that moment and coming for them, they both bottomed out at appearing vaguely disconcerted. No surprise with the Ice Queen and Andrej, either—while he did look ready to ask for a bottle of vodka, nothing could really faze him, and she was her usual collected, hard self. Who was definitely breaking his usual MO was Burns, but then this wasn't exactly a joking matter. I had a distinct sense that he was mostly vibing off Sonia, who was whisper-shouting at him with increasing agitation, which seemed to upset Martinez even more. I couldn't hear what she was saying but I could guess. Somehow, this would be my fault, too.

The rest of our group—the former guards from the California settlement, the handful of old contacts Pia had called in, and Marleen—seemed more interested in watching the reactions around them than looked concerned for their own safety. My guess was that none of them had been exposed to either version of the serum. Marleen's attention did center on the three of us briefly and I didn't like the cool, calculating quality of her look before she turned it into a small smile. It was likely too much to expect her to be truly upset;

she was probably calculating how to stay out of the fray but not miss a moment should we, inevitably, turn and go for each other's throats.

The scavengers, while alarmed in general since my explanation, took it in stride. A few of them even looked calmer than a few minutes ago. Part of me wanted to feel insulted, but really, I got it—we were all in the same boat in the end, and some might see that as fair.

That left the bunch of army soldiers. I hadn't expected any of them to show much more emotion than our command huddle, and they didn't. Richards was maybe a little white in the face, but that could have been due to the withdrawal symptoms. Cole was just whispering something to Hill that made the hulking soldier's shoulders shake. Neither of them seemed very upset or surprised. Two out of the group whose names I didn't know were standing a little more at attention than the rest, making me guess they'd been part of the serum project as well, but since their lieutenant was keeping it together, they didn't seem to have a reason to be nervous.

So it pretty much boiled down to me, Martinez, and Sonia losing our collective shit. I hadn't expected that, striding into the arena.

Maybe it was my stunned silence. Maybe he'd simply been biding his time, letting Hamilton and me have it out so he could spare himself having to sort through that. Whatever it was, Nate took that moment to whistle loudly, immediately shutting down all conversation, drawing all attention to him. Unlike in the tunnels inside, he no longer looked uncomfortable with that intense focus, but in fact seemed to stand just a little taller for it. No, it was something else, I realized; something that I'd stealthily gotten used to, and never realized it had gone missing when he'd decided to take the backseat.

The man standing beside me was Nate Miller, unquestioned leader of this chaotic assembly, and pity the man or woman stupid enough not to recognize that.

"Whatever the impact on our personal lives, this doesn't change much, if anything," he called out, speaking loud enough that the last straggling conversations easily faded into the background. "If you disagree, you are free to leave now, no hard feelings. But we have gathered here to hunt down the people responsible for all the shit that has affected us, and I for one won't rest until I have their heads on a pike, rotting in the sun."

No surprise there—the scavengers loved that statement and gobbled it up like… food that instantly upset my stomach all over again, as resilient in that aspect as it usually was. I swallowed hard, instead focusing on the other factions. None of them showed much enthusiasm, but there was grim determination on more faces than I'd expected—just as if he'd said what had been on their minds.

Nate, picking up on that very fact, went on. "We have few clues and even fewer names, but that won't hold us back. We know that Cortez's Chemist has been the driving force behind the experiments going on here, and he's the first we will track down. Depending on what we find and what he will tell us, we'll start working up that list, one by one."

The male scavenger who was convinced my survival solely depended on my performance in the sack spoke up, looking quite enthusiastic about potentially sticking people's heads on pikes, but less convinced about the details. "How are we going to find one guy in a huge country?" His gaze flitted to Hamilton, his eyes narrowing. Maybe he and I would become friends after all, judging from the dislike on his expression. My standards were pretty low these days. "And, correct me if I'm wrong, but I'm getting the sense that more than one individual is a turncoat here."

Hamilton didn't look fazed, but neither did Nate. "You could say the same for me, actually," Nate pointed out. "Only that I switched sides before the shit hit the fan. Others may have needed a little longer to see the light." He got a smirk from Hamilton for that, but no answer. Apparently, I was the only one who got steamrolled with those. Nate even went as far as to look at the gathered soldiers and marines before he went on. "What I'm calling for isn't all-out war on any faction. I'd very much like for everyone who survives to be free to return to their people, or do whatever else they want to do after we're done. This is not going to be an operation like the crusade that my wife kicked off three years ago. This will be a series of near surgical strikes—a few people only, doing what must be done."

Harris took it upon himself to ask the pertinent question. "And that is?"

"Kill a man who goes by the name of Decker, who we believe is responsible for everything," Nate explained.

A few people reacted, but mostly with confusion. The army and marines groups gave us little, making me guess that the name either didn't ring a bell, or was something not talked about by those in the know. Not for the first time I marveled at how anyone could build such a reputation, and no less by mostly flying under the radar.

Suspect-Blowjob Guy voiced what most of the others must have been thinking. "Who the fuck is that guy?"

"A phantom, mostly," Nate said, his voice hard. "He was working under the cover of recruiter for the army, but he's been heavily involved with PSYOPS and most black-ops jobs none of you will believe our military has been conducting for the past decades. The serum project was his baby, and considering the events since I dropped out from under his patronage, I strongly believe that he's one of the powers that is responsible for the apocalypse."

That made even me do a double-take. Nate ignored my imploring gaze, instead glancing at Hamilton, who, if not outright agreed, had a neutral look on his face that could mean anything. The crowd succumbed to speculations for a few moments, but hushed immediately as Nate spoke up once more.

"I'm not saying that turning the world into a free-for-all for his creations was beyond him, but I've talked to several of the people who have had dealings with us, and all of them have agreed that it's a possibility. Look at the evidence—the serum that is so close to the zombie virus. The fact that whenever one faction tries to thrive for stability, things end up going terribly awry. And don't even get me started on the operation that Cortez has been running here. It all makes sense."

Maybe to him. To me, it still didn't, and I wasn't afraid to voice that. "How can one single man be that powerful in a world where getting from one town to the next is a gamble? And you did hear about the part where none of us is as invincible as we'd like to be?"

Hamilton responded rather than Nate, making me wonder if they'd discussed this between themselves. "Easy. He's not controlling anyone's actions directly. That seldom was his MO in the past. He set it all up, and then he kicked the game into motion. We're all pawns, inadvertently doing his bidding because it's often the only chance we got."

"That's—" Ludicrous, I was going to say, but Pia, very uncustomary for her, interrupted me.

"That makes more sense than a lot of other theories," she offered, her voice drawing equal attention to Nate's. "We have tracked down the traces of his plans and machinations all over the place. We found the scientist who developed the weaponized version of the virus. We found—or, mostly, heard about—the people who distributed the contaminated food. There's evidence aplenty that someone meticulously took out the handful of people who could have worked against the plan, or even now possess the knowledge to do something about it." Not incidentally, she looked at me for that. "And we've had dealings with the rogue faction who has been working on the mind-killing version of the serum—Taggard and his people, who kidnapped you, and now this operation here. It all depends on relatively small command groups working independently—and presumably, unknowingly—of each other, each following orders that they must have had for months, years, maybe even a decade ahead of time. The outbreak of the virus is the only part about it that could have happened spontaneously if humanity had been absolutely fucking unlucky. The rest? Splinter cells working off their task lists, one by one."

I could have done without that explanation—and by someone other than the Ice Queen. It suddenly sounded way too plausible for the paranoia raging anew in my mind.

"Still doesn't explain our failing immunity," I pointed out, feeling stupid when both she and Nate—and Hamilton, with a second's lag—looked at me flatly.

"Collateral damage," Pia drawled. "Hamilton is right when he says that we are pawns. We are. Some of us highly skilled, and in motion for a long time, but still. All of us are dispensable. And a lot of us must have overstayed our welcome by a lot, considering how the forces in motion have been gunning for us."

"You think he'd just throw thousands of lives away like this?" I couldn't help the incredulity in my voice.

Nate shrugged off my argument. "He couldn't have known that we'd eventually succumb to the virus. Now he's just running with it. He still got over a decade of good use out of us; two, in some cases. That's more than any of us thought we'd survive when we signed up for the serum project."

It wasn't the first time that I'd heard any of them say something like this, but maybe it was now that I was in the same boat with them that the real impact of that conviction hit home. I'd come to accept a lot over the course of the past years since the shit hit the fan—like that, not exactly altruistic as I usually was, I could see the worth in dying for others or even just a principle. But this was pushing it. Then again, working with the hand you're dealt and rolling with the punches? That I was all too familiar with.

"Why not go for Decker first?" I asked what I felt was the obvious next question. "If we are convinced he's behind it, why not chop off the head of the snake and be done with it?"

I knew I'd served myself up on a silver platter when I caught the gleeful expression on Hamilton's face. "That cognitive decline really is a bitch, huh?" he goaded me on, giving Nate a sidelong glance. "Still don't see how you can continue to praise her intelligence." Nate didn't react—which left me conflicted in so many ways—which prompted Hamilton to, finally, answer my question. "We would, if we had the first clue where the spider is hiding. I have been his top attack dog from the first month of the apocalypse until I got discarded here, and I don't have a clue in which state he's in, let alone the exact location. I doubt I stand a chance to weasel the information out of the people I have gotten my orders from, so hunting down one of his other enforcers is our best bet."

"The Chemist," I interjected before he could steal even more of my thunder. See? Not stupid at all.

"Exactly," Hamilton replied, condescending as hell.

I was about to take that small victory for what it was, until his actual words caught up with me. "Wait," I started, narrowing my eyes at him. "What do you mean by, 'from the first month' on? In the past, you told us that it was only during the spring of the year after—the year we started to clash—that Decker was back. Trouble keeping your lies straight?"

Two could play the squinting game, but for once, Hamilton sounded neutral rather than nasty as he responded. "I got my orders from somewhere, right? And while Morris thinks he did a great job pretending to be in charge, it's easy to look back and see who actually pulled the strings. When we had that conversation in the middle of nowhere in France, I thought it was a more recent development. I've since come to change my mind. Nobody—not even a conniving fuck like Decker—can overhaul an institution like the US Army in a few weeks only. It all goes right back to the splinter cell model. A few people in key positions were all that was needed to keep the show going."

That made a lot of sense. More sense than what he'd told us in the past, actually. It didn't help the paranoia roaring in the back of my mind one bit. That, in turn, made me wonder how I was still alive—but the answer to that seemed obvious. Hamilton's orders to make sure I didn't survive had been a trap, likely to see if his connection to his former friend was still strong enough to circumvent taking the one thing away from him that he would never forgive Hamilton for taking. It fit right into what Hamilton himself has said about Decker's motives—that my death would leave Nate vulnerable to be pulled back into the fold. That we agreed on that not being the case rankled, but I wasn't beyond valuing my survival over my ego. We could agree on one single thing. Well, two, if one counted killing Decker was a necessity now more than ever.

Nate waited to see if either of us was going to add to that conversation, but when we both remained silent, he addressed the assembly at large. "Now, if anyone here has any clue where the Chemist and his people went, or where they could be found, that would be great."

Murmurs rose, particularly among the scavengers—I figured most of them had been here days longer than us, and might have noticed a train of vehicles leaving—but nobody came forth with any information. Mike's untimely demise rankled all over again, but I doubted he would have known much since they left him behind. Frustration mounted, and for a few seconds I had to fight for control, the urge to scream—or attack someone physically—overwhelming. I managed, leaving my body open for another round of shivers. Fucking drugs! Maybe I should look into what exactly that Glimmer shit was that Harris and his people were so fond of? Going cold turkey seemed to be more problematic than a tapering-off approach, maybe…

It would have been easy to blame the withdrawal symptoms for my momentary forgetfulness, but it was only when I looked around to where Richards was lounging that I remembered that we actually had found something in that warehouse. Fishing around in my pants for the strips of cardboard I'd torn off those boxes, I squinted at the addresses printed there before holding it out to where Hamilton could read it.

"That maybe ring a bell?"

His usual smirk was already in place, ready to blow whatever suggestion I had solely on the grounds of it coming from me, but as soon as his eyes skimmed over the print on the second, it dissolved into a slight frown. "That's one of our black site labs," he offered gruffly, clearly annoyed I had brought up something useful. "Where did you get that from?"

I couldn't help but bark a harsh laugh. "Seriously? You go to the length of having black site labs, but you send supplies to that very address? That's just fucking stupid!"

Hamilton snorted. "You'd know, since it was people like you who must have ordered said supplies. That's from something you found here?"

I nodded, my momentary excitement surpassing the need to keep my glare game on par. "Yeah, in one of the warehouses, where they produced the drugs large-scale. They could have grabbed that shit from any lab or supplier's warehouse, but I figured, if you ferry new serum versions around, you may get lenient and just grab what's already in stock to send along with the next guinea pig trial."

Hamilton didn't give me the satisfaction of telling me that I'd done a good job, but Nate's nod was all I needed. "That's as good a starting point as any," he declared. "Let's see if we have any means of verifying that, but it makes sense." He did a brief calculation in his mind. "That would also be close enough to keep samples refrigerated, I presume? One way must be around eight hundred miles, and doable in just a few days."

I nodded. "In a small liquid nitrogen tank, no problem."

Nate turned to Hamilton. "Would be great if you could give us a list of all the other black site labs you know of. And generally, all the installations that could harbor our possible fugitive."

Hamilton's mirthless smile in return was a thing of beauty. "Are you seriously asking me to betray my people?"

Nate scoffed, rather amused. "We're your people now. Get that into that thick skull of yours. The only way that you get to survive is if you help us—all in. No more bullshit about keeping anything back. There's a good chance that before this ends, we will be with our backs against the wall with an execution squad in front of us, and you never know which small tidbit might be the one that makes a difference." He waited for Hamilton to nod his agreement—which he didn't, but his stoic staring seemed to do the trick—before he turned to the other factions. "The same goes for you, although I won't ask you to give up your fall-back bunkers and hiding spaces. If you know anything you can reveal to us, please do so. It can be confidential between you and me and my wife only, and I promise you, we won't turn you into betrayers of your people's trust unless we are absolutely convinced that it's necessary. I can't stress this enough. Contrary to what propaganda will have you believe, it was never my intention to go toe-to-toe with the army or anyone else. All we ever did was retaliate, and try to ensure the safety of our people. If I can, I will minimize the fallout to as few people as possible. All we want is Decker's head, and to cauterize that hydra for good so that more heads don't keep popping up."

Neither Blake nor Buehler seemed very disconcerted at Nate's request, making me guess that Wilkes had sent them with instructions about how much of the Silo's secrets they were allowed to divulge. Scott gave us nothing, but then I hadn't gotten the sense that he and his marines were involved in any part of this in the first place, and had just shown up to help since they found us incapable of resolving the issue alone. Richards was the only one who looked slightly taken aback, but when Nate's attention turned to him, he stood a little straighter. "I'm happy to provide an updated list of our bases from what Hamilton can provide," he offered. "We have had a lot of trading opportunities with the scavengers that haven't tried to blow us to smithereens, so most of that won't be news to most people present. We are here for a reason, and that is still the same as for our joint mission to France. We want to ensure the survival of as many people as possible. Nothing else has ever been our intention."

Before our conversation in the warehouse I would have found that speech a little unnecessary and rather boastful, but the way most of the scavengers kept squinting at him and the soldiers spoke a different language. Nate himself didn't seem reluctant to believe him, but he also didn't say so out loud, making me wonder exactly what kind of game he was playing. Going on the fact that he'd trusted Richards with our location during our hiatus, I'd have figured that same trust went a lot further, but maybe recent developments had changed his mind. That he trusted Hamilton made that even more peculiar—until I realized that, with Hamilton gone for a year, Richards was a prime candidate for having filled his slot. The ramifications for this were giving me hives.

And all that mixing with dread from the realization that we were all going to die soon as a constant droning in the background? Not exactly what I'd figured my life would look like when I'd gotten my hands on my husband again.

"I think that about concludes this meeting for now," Nate declared, cutting through my internal musings. "We will work out an action plan today, and tomorrow morning, we decide how exactly we will proceed and who will be heading where. My second-in-command will take applications for the hunt for the Chemist. Please be advised that this will likely turn into a suicide mission, so don't approach her without being absolutely certain that you're up for it." He went as far as to briefly nod in Pia's direction, as if anyone would be stupid enough to confuse us.

With that said, murmurs rose once more, heavy debate starting among the scavengers, but also the so-far stoic factions. I watched them for a moment, but was quite happy to drop that when Marleen stepped closer, giving Pia a token, curt bow. "I'm coming with you. Don't even think about trying to send me home with the supply train."

The Ice Queen accepted that with a wry smile. "Wouldn't dare presume otherwise." When she caught my frown, she gave me a tight-lipped grimace. "Most of us will be going back to California to raise as much support as possible for what's to come, and get our civilians to safety. And I'm not looking forward to informing another fifteen people that they'd better say goodbye to their loved ones sooner rather than later."

There was no need to explain that remark, although she still didn't seem fazed by Hamilton's revelation that all of us were running on borrowed time. It was very like her to accept what couldn't be changed, and instead work hard on finding solutions instead. Me? Not so much, I realized, when the first thing I blurted out as Nate stepped up to me was a somewhat panicked, "You knew?"

His grin bordered on a grimace and was gone a moment later, but the general ambivalence of his body language spoke volumes. "I may have suspected something like that," he admitted, low enough that his voice didn't carry much beyond where Pia and Marleen were standing close to us. Hamilton was already leaving, following Andrej, likely to hunt down maps for that list he would compile.

"How? And why?" Had I really been the only one to be so oblivious? And it went without saying that I still didn't buy Hamilton's claim of the signs I was supposedly showing.

Nate shrugged, ending the motion with crossing his arms over his chest—a tad defiantly. "Small things, mostly. Things that keep adding up. There are other explanations, of course, but when there's a much simpler reason, it would be foolish to ignore that." When I just looked at him, silently imploring him to elaborate, he chuffed. "Hamilton's not the only one who had his issues with keeping the raging storm inside at bay over the past months. And, don't forget, we've all dealt with people before who converted, long before the virus turned people into undead nightmares. I've had to shoot more than one of the men under my command because shit went sideways on a mission. You've seen it happen with Bailey at that factory. You never forget the signs, particularly when you're looking for them. With some, like Bates, you don't miss the actual moment of death, but one instant conversion happening right in your face, and you just know."

His claim made me wonder if, just maybe, Hamilton was wrong as I was still one oblivious, happy bunny, but the nasty voice at the back of my mind just laughed at me. So much for that—but then I'd known for a while that my denial game was strong. I really could have done without that unease, twined with my paranoia, riding shotgun.

Then again, knowing I was going to die wasn't exactly something unfamiliar for me—and yet, I was still around and kicking. And going on Nate's assessment of our next mission, I'd have to survive first to be able to turn into a shambler on the spot—and, as usual, the chances of that happening were likely worse than my happy, carefree mind liked to contemplate.

See? There's a silver lining in everything.

Chapter 5

As soon as I was back in the tunnels, I felt dread start to claw at the back of my throat. Since falling apart right then and there wasn't an option—or not one I considered valid, at all, for the time being, or ever, if I had a say in it—I did my best to keep busy. It took Pia all of one look in my—probably pale as death—face to send me toward our makeshift armory to help with selecting gear and stowing away everything else that she wasn't ready to cede to the scavengers. My less-than-stellar grip might not have made me the perfect person to pack crates and drag them outside to where cars had been readied in two disjointed trains—the larger one bound for California, the much shorter one for our mission. I would have preferred a sparring lesson—or maybe even doing sprints—but I had to stop every so often to steady myself and try not to puke up my guts again, so it was likely for the best. Nate disappeared within the first five minutes—and thankfully, so did Hamilton—leaving me to my menial if not meaningless task. It was easy to shake off Martinez, who tried not once but three times to pull me aside for what I knew was a well-meant but not-appreciated chance to talk.

Or so I thought, until the hulking form of Burns stepped in my way to pluck a crate from my arms and add it to the stack some unfortunate schlock was dragging along who'd been walking behind me. I longingly stared after my burden before I forced my attention back to my friend, surprised not to see his plus one in tow. "Are you even allowed to be here on your own?" I snarked, hoping that would get me enough scorn that he'd decide to let me stew in silence instead.

No such luck, as it turned out. Burns deflected the blow with a bright—and rather knowing—grin, still physically blocking my path. "The missus graciously granted me an exception," he let me know.

I shook my head, hard-pressed not to add my opinion on that—but then figured, why the hell not? "I never thought you'd be that pussy-whipped guy who needs permission for anything," I tartly told him.

Again, my blow didn't hit home, although his grin turned a little sardonic. "What can I say—meeting the right woman changed me."

It was only then that I realized just how much he was screwing with me. The moment he saw my frown, his smile turned into a shit-eating grin, followed by a loud peal of laughter that made a few heads turn.

"You're such an asshole," I muttered, but couldn't hold back a grin of my own. "But you have to admit, you've been rather distant since our reunion."

Burns shrugged, unperturbed. "Takes two to tango, you know?" he reminded me.

I let a shrug be all the agreement he would get for that. It seemed to be enough. Silence fell, but, as usual, not for long. He was still grinning, but it now took on a hard edge as he continued. "So from one dead man walking to another—"

"Yes, please, ignore the fact that I have boobs and ovaries," I snarked, then corrected myself. "At least one ovary."

He went as far as rolling his eyes but dutifully didn't ogle my stashed-away goods. "You know what I mean."

"And there's nothing about this topic I want to talk about," I pointed out. "Did Martinez send you after me? I know it wasn't Zilinsky. She was only too happy to give me some menial task to distract me. And Romanoff would have come himself, likely packing a bottle of vodka. And I trust my husband to do the dirty work himself if he thought it was necessary."

Burns didn't try to deny our medic's involvement, although the last part of my assessment seemed to amuse him the most. "You know that he's talking shop with Hamilton? Or, more likely, shooting the shit as they must have run out of things to catch up on by now." I tried to keep my expression calm but was sure that mention drew a scowl from me. Since it was a near-permanent fixture on my face of late, I couldn't quite tell anymore. The snort I got for my trouble was affirmation enough. "And just how much does that bother you?"

"Bother? Not at all. It just annoys the fuck out of me, not that he cares." Meaning Nate. "But what else is new?"

Rather than rib me for my reaction—or point out that I had no business giving him shit for his relationship seeing how mine was devolving into baleful staring matches more often than not—Burns offered a good-natured chuckle as he slapped my back and physically pushed me toward our quarters. "Let's get some coffee into you, and then we'll do some good old denial therapy."

With nothing better to do, I preceded him, doing my best to suppress two series of shudders. Burns noted, his amusement turning grim. "That shit really did a number on you," he observed.

"No shit," I agreed, letting him push me toward an empty bench. He joined me a few moments later with two steaming mugs of coffee, not wasting any powdered creamer—a treasure we'd found in the badly stocked pantry—on mine. I watched him savor his drink for a while. "So how is Sonia taking the news that she'll be a widow soon?" I asked.

He shrugged. "I'm not sure the message has actually sunk in. Then again, I've been living for a while with the knowledge that I'm not going to gently fall asleep, surrounded by generations of my offspring, at the ripe old age of ninety-eight." He flashed me a sad smile that was more of a grimace. "But something tells me that between recovering from what should have been your deathbed twice over, and focusing solely on Hamilton's demise, you never got that memo yourself."

"I know you all think I'm the queen of denial—"

The grimace resurfaced, and he said a single word—"Nothing." I narrowed my eyes at him, which made him bark a harsh laugh. "Bree, no offense, but if you still think that any of us—and that includes your husbeast—believed that you just walked out of that bunker, unscathed, I can't help you. We chose to go with the narrative you carved out for yourself because it was the way of least resistance, but that's it."

My usual insistence that he was wrong—twined with frustrated need to explain that, of course, my escape from Taggard and his boys had been more complicated than that—died on my tongue when I realized that, in many ways, they were going by the same playbook regarding Nate now, and I was marching to the beat of the very same drum. Burns must have read that realization on my face but refrained from rubbing my nose in it—which, in a sense, annoyed the fuck out of me as I wasn't used to that kind of leniency and understanding. Then again, I had to admit that the months spent apart had let me forget a lot about the negative sides of being forced to get along with more than one person, who, more often than not, chose to do his own thing and was happy to let me do mine.

"It doesn't matter," I insisted. "In all instances. Yeah, so maybe coming to grips with a new shade of my own mortality may not have been my priority. But it doesn't change anything now."

He grunted. "Yeah, the way you look like you've just walked over your own grave makes that plain as day."

"Like knowing I'm dying is new to me," I grumbled. "And you forget, I stand maybe a one-in-ten chance of surviving what we're up to now. Honestly? I'll worry about what may come later if I luck out and actually am still alive next week so I can still worry. No sense in burning energy on something that likely won't happen."

I could tell that my nihilistic outlook on my future annoyed him. "You've survived so much shit that should have killed you, starting with the zombie apocalypse. You have no reason to be so pessimistic. Hell, the reason I keep hanging around you is because you're a veritable lucky charm!" he claimed.

"Don't you mean shit magnet?"

He laughed. "That, too, but somehow you still manage to come up ahead. I'm much more concerned about the people you bungle into than those that run with you."

"Together till the end it is?" I jeered.

His usual smile resurfaced, making me feel strangely warm inside. I had missed him more than I liked to admit—and probably should around Sonia. And, in a sense, his vote of confidence was exactly what I'd needed to hear—or something like that.

"Well, good talk," I said, already getting up, my coffee still untouched. "But I should get back to packing."

Burns didn't move a muscle—and neither did I when he said, in no uncertain terms, "Sit your scrawny ass back down, Lewis."

A million excuses ran through my head, but I ended up uttering none. Instead, I plunked back down on the bench. "What?"

Burns studied me for a few long moments, making me feel like an ant oblivious to the kid about to squash it. "Talk to me," he finally said. "I know you're great about ruminating about shit until it has blown completely out of proportion. Sure, sulking alone in the wilderness for ages may have changed you a little, but not that much. And if it doesn't help you, at least it will amuse me."

I felt like harping "har har," at that but left it at a—somewhat defeated—shrug. "Exactly why should I be optimistic? Ever since we met, it has always been one step forward, ten steps back and right into the worst of it. We survived the apocalypse, but a good chunk of our group either died or ended up worse off. We survived the winter only so Emma could kick us out and slam the door behind us forever. We tried to help others and ended up shot at and savaged by zombies. We get back at Hamilton and his asshole brigade only to find out I'm rotting from the inside out. I survive that, only to have to come to terms with the fact that I was the one to hand Hamilton the damn samples that are likely the basis for what will turn thousands of good people into mindless worker drones—or worse. How should going after the Chemist and Decker end any better? Sure, I can see why it's the right thing—and I absolutely hope to hell it makes a difference in the grand scheme of things—but on a personal level? Whether we die fighting, or die after it's done doesn't matter. Either way, we die. And some of us deserve it a lot more than others."

As expected, my gripes left him unperturbed. "My, aren't you a little ray of sunshine today?" When I didn't respond, he finished his coffee and swapped our mugs. "Look, I get it," he started after demolishing the better part of mine as well. "Things have been a little rocky for you of late. And I know how much harder it is to deal with someone else's shit than your own. You got pretty good with fielding the former. Now it's time to learn to deal with the latter. It sucks, but it's just another step in the road. And you know that even if we have to drag you on, kicking and screaming, we will do so. No whining or protesting will change that."

I was tempted to make a really bad joke about the level of consent involved, but just then Hamilton entered the room, crossing it without noticing us—a small mercy. I waited for Nate to follow, but apparently he had other things to do. Like avoiding me. And there I'd thought getting him back would be the hard part. I got the sense that when I turned back to Burns, he could read my thoughts right off my expression, but he wisely kept his tongue.

"You know, sometimes I wonder if any of us deserves to make it," I muttered. "I was always so proud knowing I'd end up on the right side of history. Hamilton's not wrong when he says that I've strayed a long way from that."

I got a sardonic grin for my efforts. "But he's also not right," Burns insisted. "Which you should be the first to point out. You can't take out the trash without getting your hands dirty. So what—and who cares? Just consider what being right—and wrong—has gotten us into. Yet here we are, all on the same side, fighting the same fight. The world doesn't give a shit what drives you. Sometimes not even how many bodies you leave behind. But what makes a difference is whether you flagellate yourself over every single wrong step taken along the way, or keep waltzing toward the big goal without ever looking left or right. So what if you end up being a little more tarnished than when you started out? I've never gotten the sense that Miller cared. If anything, he can deal with his own shit better knowing you're not brand-spanking new yourself."

"And that's supposed to be comforting?" I didn't try to sound less incredulous.

Burns guffawed. "Comforting? Hell, girl, I'm the wrong guy to turn to if you are looking for that. But as your friend I can assure you, nobody cares, and that should include you. Stop acting like you're carrying the weight of the world. That uppity demeanor really doesn't suit you."

"Just slum it with the rest of you like usual? Can do."

He grinned and slapped my back. I only managed to remain upright because I'd seen that coming. "That's my girl! No more moping. Leave that to Captain Broody McBroodface and his skulking sidekick."

I couldn't help but growl. "Don't remind me that we're stuck with him now."

"But see the positive in that! There's no more power gradient between you, and you get to do all the superior smirking that you want. It's not like the fact that every one of your punches at him will also hit someone else has ever held you back. And you were quite happy to hear that he's not dead yet just a few days ago."

That was true. "But the reality of having the evidence of that around all the time is a lot less fun than the idea," I pointed out.

"I don't know," he offered. "Watching you both clash in every possible way all the damn time is pretty hilarious to watch, particularly since I know how much you were burning to do the same when we were in France but couldn't. Isn't that spite enough to keep you going for another year at least? And I'm sure you'll find something else once all of that is used up." When he saw my frown, he returned it with a self-deprecating smile. "Oh, come on. Stop taking yourself so fucking seriously all the damn time. Hamilton is just one more asshole in an ever-growing collection of assholes that you've used to get ahead. He's no different than the others. And the same is true for that Chemist, and Decker, too. They've already thrown everything they got at you, and you're still around, kicking. Do you really expect that to change?"

"Except for the fact that we're all ticking time bombs," I objected.

Burns chuckled. "So you're over moping about the ninety-percent chance of biting it before you can convert? My job here is done." Still grinning, he finished his—my—coffee and got up. "Nice chat. We should do that more often. Who knows when the next time you'll decide to just up and leave and let us deal with the shit you left behind will be?"

"That's it?" I harped, getting to my feet. "That's all you got?"

He laughed but shook his head, turning just a little more grave when he grabbed my shoulder and squeezed. "Me? Sure, because come tomorrow, I'll be riding shotgun with the usual shit show. But not all of us will come, and some deserve a little more of your sweet, sweet attention. And if that wasn't obvious, I don't mean the physical part, because, girl, you look ready to barf the next unlucky guy who propositions you in the face. Let someone else stow away the gear. You have tomorrow morning to check that everything is where you need it to be. But tonight might be the last time you get a chance to not avoid those who won't be coming with you for various reasons, and we all know you'll regret spending it sulking around in the shadows."

I knew he was right, and neither protested nor tried to stop him when he left, likely to track down that prickly pear of a wife of his.

I found both Martinez and Andrej with the cars—where they were arguing with Nate, Pia a silent, if frowning, bystander. While the guys continued to argue as I drew closer, the Ice Queen focused on me, looking smug. So much for who had sent Burns after me. Traitor.

"You need someone who'll stay with the cars," Martinez was insisting, the frustration in his voice telling me that he was down to grasping at straws.

Nate shook his head, his visible exasperation letting me know he had already deflected that argument—or similar ones—more than once. "We need you with the support group more," he insisted, sending Pia a sidelong glance. "We have no idea how many will come after you when you leave here, and what they've set in motion in the meantime. With luck, you'll make it to the rest of our people without losing anyone else, and get the dependents to safety. Ideally, you will be ready with new gear and support to rendezvous with us after we hunt down the Chemist. I'd rather risk losing a handful of cars than one of the few people who has the knowledge to put us back together—and we will need it before the end. Our civilians need to be the responsibility of someone I can trust. The last thing we need is to serve Decker another target on a silver platter."

Martinez wasn't calling defeat yet. "What if one of you gets injured while hunting down the Chemist? If I wait with the cars, you can bring him back—"

"Then he dies," Nate said, his tone cold and very final. "Everyone who comes with us knows that we're going in without a safety net. Besides, chances are that either the injuries sustained are light enough that they can wait or we can fix them ourselves, or we'll need a bodybag, anyway." Martinez opened his mouth for another retort, but snapped it shut when Nate ground out a harsh, "Face it—you're a liability to us. Go with the people where you won't get in the way of their survival. Got it?"

I was more surprised than taken aback at his low blow, and while it definitely hit, I could tell that Martinez took it for what it was—Nate had reached his last straw, and nothing would change his mind. I would have gotten in his face for that; Martinez left it at a glare and snapped a sharp salute before he stormed off, almost colliding with me. I watched him go in silence, and when no one else would speak up, I turned to Nate.

"That was beneath you," I observed, more neutral than I'd figured I'd manage.

Nate's anger, unbridled, turned on me. "It was necessary," he snapped—and for a split second, I was afraid that he'd tell me the same counted for me. I raised my brow at him when he kept stewing in silence, making Nate narrow his eyes at me. "I'm not stupid enough to let you out of my sight," my dear husband said—quite in opposition to what he'd gotten up to since we'd liberated the camp. "What I need even less than Decker getting his claws into Sadie or her kid is for him to come gunning for you. But just so we're clear, I'd bundle you up and send you to the coast with Zilinsky if I thought I'd stand a chance of getting away with it."

I took that with a smidgen of satisfaction—until what he'd just said sunk in. I frowned at Pia. "You're not coming with us?"

She shook her head, her expression grim. "I hate to let you go after yet another asshole on your own, but getting our civvies to safety is more important. If need be, I will abandon the convoy to set out ahead on my own to prevent the worst." She paused, looking borderline uncomfortable for a moment. "I've also never been scratched or bitten. I show none of the signs of deterioration. Once the news about the serum spreads, there's a good chance they will not let you into the settlements, whatever you say or do—and I know that most of you may not even want to come inside anymore. I will do what is necessary, and I know I'm still capable of it. When we have gotten everyone settled, I will rejoin you. Until then, you're on your own." For just a second, a borderline proud smile flashed across her face. "I hear you've gotten quite used to that."

If Nate didn't like the fact that he was, once again, without his favorite second-in-command, he didn't show it. There was no need for Andrej to explain that he would be going with Pia, but he still nodded at the lead car of the convoy. "If we run into opposition, we may need someone insane enough to run interference. That's going to be my job. Lacking that, I'll get to play chauffeur again. Could be worse. Considering I can't run for shit, I didn't think you'd still find a use for me once you decided to finally set things straight for good. Kill a few assholes in my name and I'll consider it a victory."

I nodded, hoping I'd get a chance to later tell him all about it. Since there was nothing else to do here for me—the cars all looked packed up—I nodded back to the citadel. "I think I'd better go hunt down Martinez." Taxing Nate with a glare, I added, "To fix your mess. As usual."

My husband left it at a level look that was more of a challenge than I felt up to taking on right now, so I left. I had a feeling that, come morning, I'd soon get tired of being in constant danger and having to stay glued to him non-stop. Spending the evening with Martinez and whoever he'd found to bitch at us behind our backs sounded like a much better idea. Knowing him, by the time I'd tracked him down he'd be in much better spirits, anyway.

And, come tomorrow, it would be time to face the music.

Chapter 6

The next day dawned bright and early, and I almost hated to admit that I felt a little more like myself. Physically, I was still somewhat under the weather, but spending one last evening in good company and being able to relax—and eat as much as others told me I'd want to, if I knew what was good for me—helped. I still hadn't come to grips with our impending, serum-caused doom, but Burns making fun of my momentary lapse of optimism had helped somewhat. Likely it was just my inner underdog rearing its head to rebel against the expectation that I would die very soon in a very dramatic fashion. If nothing else, I wouldn't give Hamilton the satisfaction of existing in a world where I was gone, I decided.

I'd woken up a few times during the night, my brain too stupid to get the rest it needed—and wouldn't get again until we were back with the others, I was afraid. I spent enough time dreading taking our leave in the morning, but it turned out a busy, chaotic, and not very sentimental affair. Between diligent gear and weapons checks, I barely had time to eat and hug everyone goodbye who wouldn't be coming with us. Martinez chose to make himself scarce, avoiding facing Nate one last time, but the caravan had plenty more people and stuff to get ready than we did. We ended up bundling twenty-five people into seven cars, which was a lot quicker than a good hundred into more than I cared to count. As it turned out, while I had been busy trying to get drunk on moonshine with Martinez, Nate had been wrangling with the marines until both factions had found an uneasy compromise: Scott was bringing all four of his people in their two Humvees, while Blake's five guys had to split and ride shotgun with someone else as they only had one car that could keep up with our much faster pace and didn't need to recharge for several hours every day. I was a little surprised to see Richards opt for the same loadout as he'd used when they'd picked me up two months earlier—one Humvee, with Hill, Cole, and Gallager. After their boasting, I'd expected more scavengers to show up, but it ended up being Eden, Amos, and two more in the same car they'd used when they'd smuggled Richards and me into the camp. That left two cars for the six of us—me, Nate, Hamilton, Marleen, Burns, and Sonia—and since I refused to ride with Hamilton, and Nate insisted they had more strategy to plan, we ended up completely scrambling the seating order three hours into our trek at the first short break. Scott wasn't wrong when he pointed out it wasn't the smartest idea to split up according to factions if a single exploding car might wipe out one of those easily. After three hours in the backseat with Sonia glaring at me every once in a while, I was only too happy to switch over to the Silo marines vehicle, with Marleen tagging along. Sgt. Blake took it in stride, and the younger lance corporal who acted as his navigator seemed pleased to have two girls hitching a ride rather than broody, if equally stinky guys, which was fine with me and highly amused Marleen. The two of them started flirting as soon as we were underway again, making me wonder how long it would take her to add him to her collection. I hadn't really paid much attention who was hooking up with whom back at the camp, but I had gotten the distinct impression that Richards was avoiding both Marleen and the grumbling Sgt. Buehler, who, because of her injury, was forced to go with the caravan instead. This left me the option of watching the drama unfold on the other side of the car—or chatting with Blake.

"Still not quite over how we met at your home base?" I suggested when he spent a good thirty minutes glancing at me in the rearview mirror but not giving a single peep or grunt.

"We did lose a good amount of scientists because of you," he reminded me.

I shook my head. "No. The Silo lost some of its smartest because they were acting dumb. All of you should have been more cautious around a possibly infected corpse. They got too curious, so they got dead. It's as simple as that."

I could tell that he agreed with me but wasn't ready to admit it. Fine with me. I wondered if I should ask him about what had become of Petty Officer Stanton—who had gotten infected when she had tried to save the scientists, and ended up in the same Canadian base as me, if with less luck about what the virus had done to her. I decided against it, not sure if she'd tried to make contact with her former comrades. Disfigured and wheelchair bound, I could see why maybe she'd decided to stay there. Or make a one-way trip to the armory and call it a day.

Fletcher—the navigator—and Marleen continued to chat amicably, and at our next stop I offered to switch places with him to preserve his ability to use his neck come morning. Blake looked rather amused at how ecstatic the younger man seemed, if only where he couldn't see. It was going on noon, it was hot as fuck outside, and of course the car didn't have AC, which left me a lot less amused. Since only the three Humvees had any—and Nate had told them to shut off anything non-vital to preserve what battery power they had—it shouldn't have mattered, but I kind of missed riding with Richards and his guys. I would have preferred Martinez and his snazzy new ride, but beggars couldn't be choosers.

Using the route Nate and Hamilton had agreed on, we'd spend two and a half days on the road before we'd abandon the cars at the outskirts of our destination, from where we'd have to hoof it. That sounded simple enough—if one ignored the fact that the destination was downtown Dallas, and the aforementioned outskirts were what counted as one or two towns over to the north.

The level of idiocy it took to even consider heading into the Dallas-Fort Worth metroplex made the fact that we were all dead men walking pale in comparison. I had the distinct feeling that the true marvel would be that any of us stayed alive long enough to run out of time.

The bulk of the scavengers had definitely been smart to withdraw from the mission. That left me wondering what this said about us, the comparatively "sane" ones. And apparently, I wasn't the only one thinking along those lines.

"Are you going to address the elephant in the room, or keep pretending this isn't a suicide mission?" Blake asked downright conversationally, his eyes remaining trained on the vehicle driving in front of ours, one of Scott's Humvees.

"Well, since usually I'm the elephant, I feel out of my league to discuss this," I offered, trying myself at a bad joke—and even got a small smile for my effort, which surprised me.

When he saw my sidelong glance, Blake gave a one-shouldered shrug. "Figured you'd be used to both by now."

"I think you massively overestimate the amount of suicidal turns my life has taken," I muttered. "If it was up to me, I'd never risk my hide for anything."

Flirting with Marleen didn't keep Fletcher from interjecting from the back row. "Except for pretty much everything you did since the undead took over the earth, you mean?"

I didn't bother looking back as I flipped him off. "Most of that was simply trying to survive while someone else raised the stakes without asking me first." Yet even I could see why now was different—to a point. "But yeah, this shit isn't that outside of my usual MO."

Blake looked mildly scandalized, making me wonder if he was itching to throw a tart, "language!" in sideways—or his version of my reality varied greatly from my own.

Marleen apparently had also gotten bored of monopolizing Fletcher, now that there was something more interesting to do. "Is that a thing you do often, venture into zombie-overrun cities to hunt for black-ops labs?"

I wondered for a moment if she was kidding me. "More often than I feel comfortable with, actually." None of the other three said anything, but I could feel the tension in the air rising with curiosity. "Let's put it this way—this would be my third somewhat clandestine laboratory inside a crowded population center." I couldn't help but laugh, also at myself. "I really should start making better life choices. But in my defense, they were all built by the same people so it says more about their operations than my need to constantly risk my neck for science."

"I thought this was more of a manhunt?" Marleen asked, her voice carefully neutral. "Not sure I want to risk my neck for some stuffy formulas."

I could see how she'd come to that conclusion—as would everyone else in this car who wasn't me. "I'm not keeping my hopes up to find anything, but if we make it to the lab, and we'll have an hour or two, I'll check what they've been working on, pre- and post-apocalypse.

Call it wishful thinking, but I'm already risking my life getting there. I might as well spend some time trying to preserve it, too."

Blake gave a slow nod. "It makes more sense that Miller's taking you along, considering."

That made me chortle under my breath. "So you don't think it's romantic that my husband drags me into certain mortal danger just to make sure nobody can abduct me in the meantime?"

Blake shrugged. "Ever considered getting a divorce?"

Fletcher laughed, and Marleen was smiling slightly. All I had for them was a grunt. "Since we already did the death-do-us-part shit before we actually got hitched, it always sounded like a good idea to stick it out together until that's final."

"Ah, true romance," Marleen offered. I wasn't quite sure whether she meant that for real or sarcastically, but it didn't really matter.

"So you'll keep looking for a cure?" Blake wanted to know. "Not yet used to knowing you're about to die? That's nothing new for you, either."

I shook my head, chuckling under my breath. "Never quite loses its novelty. And no, I won't stop. I've never been one to accept conclusions that don't quite gel with my outlook on life."

"Good luck with that," Blake offered—and sounded like he meant it. I eyed him askance but he didn't add anything, instead concentrating on the road. With not much else to do—since we were driving in the middle of our little convoy, and someone else had taken on the task of pathfinder—I idly flipped through the maps that we had, none of them with the level of detail that we'd need to plan the last leg of our journey. I knew Nate had a bunch of better maps, and the first thing we'd do once we got to the Texas border was to hunt for more—but none of that gave me anything to do right now.

Which turned out to be a good thing, as staring out of the side window in frustration made me notice the light plume of dust far on the horizon. Grabbing my binoculars, I tried to get a better look at it, but it could be anything—a large group of grazing animals on the move, a zombie streak, or another caravan of cars. From what I could tell, it was heading in the same direction as we were, likely on rougher ground or with a lot more individuals. Experience made me rule out the animal option as Nate and I on our own had, at the most, seen three larger herds of cattle or deer in two years, and outside of hunting range. That left vehicles or zombies, and I wasn't sure which I preferred.

Reaching for the car's radio, I turned it to the general team frequency. "Miller, do you copy?" Nate was in the first car, either driving or annoying the fuck out of whoever was behind the wheel. Since it wasn't me, I couldn't care less, but suspected it would be Hamilton. "Did you see the cloud of dust to our one? Could be shamblers, or another caravan heading for the road we are on, or the larger one to the north that we're trying to avoid right now." Going ten to fifteen miles to the south of one of the established trade routes had sounded like a bright idea this morning as the entire corridor had, so far, been looted, leaving few obstacles on the roads or enterprising scavengers about. I'd seen firsthand how thorough the residents of the camp had been about scouring the landscape for anything useable, including dishes.

"I see it," came Nate's reply a few moments later, with enough of a lag to make me guess he'd had to check up on the plume first. My momentary triumph was a stale, short-lived one.

"Do we change course?" I asked when no further instructions came.

"I say we check it out first," Nate responded after an equally long pause as before. "If it's a streak, we'll see it long before they can come after us. If it's cars, we decide on what to do once we can identify their payload."

I made a face, about to ask what came of the stealthy approach he'd preached this very morning, but instead put the mic back into its cradle and switched the radio to receive only. The following silence in the car seemed deafening to me, but was likely just three pairs of eyes trying to catch sight of said plume. Since Blake was driving and the others didn't have a good vantage point in the back, that sounded reasonable.

Blake cleared his throat to make me focus on him. "You know, if you're that opposed to following commands, you're maybe in the wrong car," he noted, rather self-satisfied.

"I probably am," I agreed, making him chuckle but otherwise keep his tongue. I was surprised that none of them made an attempt to learn more about my animosity with a certain man I was less and less happy to see still alive, karmic backlash and all that notwithstanding. Maybe when I'd crooned about wishing Hamilton a long, long life to enjoy his daily nightmares I should have specified that happening far, far away, maybe on another continent. So much for being careful for what you wish for.

Eventually, conversation resumed in the back row, with Blake and me not-so-stealthily listening in as he kept driving. The plume continued to grow yet its spread remained somewhat contained, which limited it to a smaller zombie streak, if it was one at all. Nate and I had once seen one that dragged a haze that spanned the entire horizon behind it, churning dust up after a long, dry summer going into an equally warm and dry fall. That this had only been less than a year ago felt weird now, as if the raid on our tree house had somehow slowed down the time passing since then. For Nate, that must have been awfully true. For me? With my mind only now clearing up and the shakes still present, it was hard to gauge anything that went beyond my current withdrawal symptoms.

We took another break an hour after I'd first noticed the dust rising, driving the cars off the road and into the trees to make stumbling into us a little less likely. That left recharging with the portable solar panels impossible, but getting up to stretch our legs seemed more of a priority. I'd mulled over the possibility of switching cars, but one look at Hamilton sliding from behind the wheel was enough to decide that I did, indeed, appreciate the present company more. The one and only time I'd met Blake before, he'd been rather hostile toward me, but babysitting the pariah that everyone blamed for losing half of their scientists might do that to the most even-tempered man—and those weren't adjectives I'd assign to the marine sergeant. I was surprised that he was putting in an effort to let bygones be bygones. Or maybe I'd just hung out with too many assholes so that common, professional courtesy seemed downright friendly to me. Then again, Richards had never acted any differently, either. Looking back, Hamilton and Taggard had been the exception. Just my luck that I was collecting assholes like them.

With none of us expecting serious trouble until we couldn't avoid the urban areas any longer, everyone was happy to stuff their faces while rations weren't something we had to weigh the amount of ammo we'd be bringing against. From what I could tell, nobody found it strange that I wasn't riding with Nate—or Burns and Sonia—and the somewhat strict demarcation line between the different groups seemed to have gotten more blurred in just half a day of travel. I wondered if I should go hunt for yet another ride but the disapproving look I got from Scott when he saw me eyeing their Humvees made me decide that Blake was as friendly as it would get, unless I wanted to oust Gallager—or delegate him to the jump seat once more. The idea was tempting for a moment, until I realized that Cole and Hill would probably call me out on my ruminations on my own mortality within the first five miles, and my ego wasn't quite up for that yet. While the scavengers had turned out more friendly and pleasant toward me than I'd expected from what I'd been told before—and had seen firsthand before they realized Harris and I were friends—I wasn't keen on riding with them right now. Too tempting was the idea to try to stave off the withdrawal symptoms with a refresher hit of whatever they had brought along for the ride. Just because they appeared borderline sober today didn't mean the same would be true for me. If not for our mission and the overbearing energy expenditure I expected to come with it, I might have considered not eating a thing for a few days and subsisting purely on water to completely flush my metabolism, but we were far beyond that possibility. And, I hated to admit, the idea of putting unnecessary strain on my body that might just turn into a slippery slope right to insta-conversion gave me the creeps. Just standing in the sweltering midday heat, even in the shade of the trees, made me want to reduce the stress on my system.

Yeah, going into zombie-infested downtown Dallas really sounded like a bright idea!

We ended up back in the cars before I got a chance to chat with Nate, but since I had nothing to share and he seemed busy talking to Hamilton and Scott, that was fine with me. We switched up our driving order once more, with both of Scott's Humvees taking point and the army Humvee bringing up the rear. Conversation was either light or non-existent, which I didn't mind since the last few days had been, quite frankly, overwhelming on so many levels. I used to rib Nate about being able to spend days on end without talking; now that we were back in what counted for civilization, I realized I'd lost some of my constant need to exchange pleasantries. Looking back, Martinez had been leading most conversations that we'd had on the road. And damn, our reunion had been too short by years.

In the forest, we'd lost sight of the plume of dust, but as soon as we were out of the trees a few miles farther west, it was easy to find once more, closer now although we'd taken some quality time off the road. It was still moving, if at a weird pace. That was, until I checked the maps and, yup, as I'd expected, there was a larger road intersection in that direction. A caravan switching directions would leave a somewhat stationary cloud for a while. I was about to get on the radio and share my observation when I pictured Hamilton's reaction—to me reporting the fact that everyone else had likely come up with already. Latent anger was ready to flare but I did my best to keep a lid on it, and instead turned to Blake.

"Does Dispatch still keep track of convoys that have signed in? And before you ask, I don't know what Richards did when he picked me up and brought me to California, and our convoy back was, if not trying to fly under the radar, not advertising our position. I've been off the grid since last we saw each other."

His smile let me know that he'd been ready to tease me about my lack of knowledge—and really, I should have known the answer— but instead obliged my quest for knowledge. "The scavengers no longer sign in unless they are doing something highly official, which never happens. But some of the traders, particularly the larger convoys with extra guards, hope that the more visible they are, the safer. Why?"

"Just wondering," I mused, and picked up the radio after all. "Cole, how good are your hacking skills with the radio network?"

Chatter on the general frequency died, and it took the sour former Delta operator only a heartbeat to do what he did best— underline how little clue about anything I had.

"It may surprise you, but one doesn't have anything to do with the other," he let me know, not without mirth. I'd never get how being incapable of something could be a triumph for anyone.

"So you can't, I don't know, hack into the official Dispatch frequency network and splice us in so we can see if that plume over there is a sanctioned convoy and likely happy not to get too close to us?"

Muttering answered me, yet before Cole could get in my face again, a different voice responded—Richards. "I don't think he can. But the contraband transponder unit that we have in our vehicle can."

Part of me was annoyed, and not only because of the rebuke I'd gotten, but because on some level, I still identified more with the traders we were about to stalk than any other faction. Those had been my people, back when assholes had forced me to take sides. Hell, before there had been sides, even, considering Nate had set out in the first spring from the bunker to do just that—help get a little of the civilization that we'd all lost back to those who couldn't do it themselves. Look where that had gotten us.

Silence followed, until my impatience made me ask, "So, are you going to use it or not?"

Richards took his sweet time responding. "Are you just curious, or is there more to this?"

I hated justifying myself—particularly with everyone who was listening in—but this wasn't just on a whim. "We're trying to stay under the radar, at least until we are close to our destination? I think they just took a turn onto the road we're following, and considering how much closer we have gotten in the past minutes, I'd say we will show up in their rearview mirrors in less than twenty minutes. They must have seen our own dust plume, so switching roads will likely just make them question why we are avoiding them."

I'd hoped to keep the radio frequencies free of Captain Asshole, but he took it upon himself to cut in now. "And how is any of that of any consequence to us, Lewis? Except that you're bored and need to start shit, apparently."

I did my best to ignore Hamilton's interjection, but the way my jaws hurt from grinding my teeth, I was doing a shit job. That it was a valid question didn't help. At least nobody was speaking up in his favor, but I felt the silent agreement of the group close in on me.

Great—more paranoia. Just what I'd needed.

"Well, we are heading in a more or less straight line from our well-established, last known point of residence to our new destination. The people we are hunting will know where we might be headed if we are on their trail. Do we absolutely need to confirm that?"

I knew I was on to something when Nate responded. "If it's a convoy—and it looks like it, from the proposed direction change you mentioned—they have already seen us and likely reported us in. Where does that leave us?"

"Misdirection!" I maybe shouldn't have sounded so gleeful, but the idea that had just come up in my mind was too good not to be enthusiastic about it. Just then, the terrain after the next bend in the road fell away, opening up into a plain—and, true enough, I didn't need the binoculars to see the caravan of vehicles crawling toward the horizon. Or those were the most orderly-walking shamblers I'd ever seen. Roughly halfway to the last car I saw the intersection they must have taken. I stalled for a moment to take it all in and do a quick calculation how soon we would reach them. Half an hour sounded reasonable—unless we floored it. "Okay, I know this will sound crazy, but I have an idea that might work without much planning or chance of shit going sideways."

Hamilton couldn't pass that one up. "No planning? That does sound like you."

I couldn't help but bare my teeth at the windshield in a silent grimace, fighting hard to keep my cool—or at least a semblance of it.

"No worries. This one won't backfire in your face and require someone else to lay down their lives so you can get away," I bit out, instantly hating that I'd let him bait me like this. Before it could get any worse, I forced out the words I should have uttered in the first place. "We don't want to look like we're heavily armed, well-equipped, and on a clandestine mission, right? So we need to look like we have a reason to be on the road but not hunting down assholes. We can't do anything about the cars or our equipment, but we can absolutely do something about the optics."

I took a deep breath, which was too long, I realized, when the radio spewed out static—but at least it was Nate who asked, impatiently, "How?"

"We pretend that we're scavengers," I explained. No reaction followed, making me deflate for a second. "Which is easy, and a good plan," I went on. Still nothing. Blake beside me was grinning, but most likely because of me rather than the plan. "Oh, come on! All we need to do is let Eden and Amos take point—the paint on their car will be a clear indicator of what's going on. Add some reckless driving and a little bit of swerving, and we're all set. Maybe roll down a window and flip them off as we pass by." Still nothing. "Wanna know why it will work? Because they will apply the same snap judgment you just showed, and not question it after coming to the wrong—right—conclusion. Easy peasy."

It was a good plan, with barely a hitch possible and no flaw to be found. Nate, of course, had to disagree. "You do realize that half of our cars are military vehicles?"

"And?"

I could picture the annoyed look on Nate's face when I forced him to explain.

"That's a lot of armor plates for a scavenger group," he pointed out.

"And you know that from where exactly?" I asked succinctly. "Last time I checked, you had about the same exposure to their vehicles as I did. Maybe even less. I came into the camp in one of their cars. You didn't." Maybe not the best reminder, but I was getting near the end of my rope.

Nate didn't fare much better, although I doubted most of the others caught the hard edge in his voice. "And exactly how many Humvees have you seen them driving? Or stashed at the camp?"

That… was a good point. It occurred to me then that I had somehow missed the opportunities to ask both Hamilton and Cindy what had happened to the vehicles they had been driving getting close to the camp. Damnit! Yet far was it from me to accept defeat so easily. "You absolutely sure that none of the scavengers—all several thousand of them that are out there—have gotten their hands on any Humvees? I'm pretty sure nobody will 'fess up if I ask now, but all of the military factions must have, at one time or another, lost some of their transportation, or had a base raided. They managed to blow up the docks in New Angeles. Don't tell me they can't get their grubby little hands on a couple of Humvees."

More silence—until a wry, female voice offered, "Why don't you ask the scum directly how well they are doing in the transportation department?"

Eden's tone made me grin. "From what I've seen, quite well, but, sure. How are you doing?"

"Better than the traders," she drawled—which I could tell was the true point of contention. Looking back, her reaction toward me and the bunch of traders who had been along when we'd hitched a ride on the boat to New Angeles took on a somewhat new tint. It had been easy for me to discard them as the savages they so loved to style themselves as, but I could understand how losing all the privileges with the settlements—that the traders retained—must have rankled. "I'm not dishing intel about our troop strength, but we have, in fact, acquired a handful of Humvees over the past two years, and they are still operational. We have, more than once, also used them as decoy vehicles, so them not looking visibly different actually works for your narrative. Which is a good idea, Amos would have me tell you. I agree. Those assholes are very quick to discard us, and they will buy it if you sell it right."

Part of me was a little disconcerted about so much agreement coming my way; I wasn't used to that. Considering the scavengers seemed to be on board with anything as long as it was fun or violent—or, preferably, both—might have helped.

Nobody spoke up, so I did. "The plan's easy. You take point. My car goes last. The Humvees go in the middle. We sell it. They just drive. Sounds good?"

Blake looked tempted to ask how I intended to do that, but just then Richards interrupted. "We got into their open channel. They just reported in that a suspicious group is trying to catch up to them. They seem to assume that we want to rob them, or otherwise stir up shit."

That was better than I'd been fearing—and like they were already halfway to guessing what we wanted them to believe.

"Any way all of us can listen in?" I questioned.

"I can put them on the team frequency, but then we can't keep up this most enlightening conversation," Cole offered, his smirk plain in his voice.

I did my best to ignore that. "Do it. Eden, take point. The rest, just do what you usually do and either ignore them as we pass by, or look grim. Maybe brandish a rifle or two." Belatedly, I added, "Anyone got any objections?" meaning Nate, and expecting Hamilton to pipe up. Neither of them did, and Eden signed off with a whoop, just as their car started accelerating. I watched with amusement as the others let them pass, the way they inched to the side making the hulking, larger vehicles look like they were apprehensive of the garishly made-up smaller car. It had taken some discussion for them to do away with the skull-and-bones hood ornaments, but they'd refused to get rid of the bright red paint splatters on the sides. A little more rearranging, and we ended up as the tail guard of our little group, the column of six vehicles stretched out before us.

The radio gave a squawk as Cole did his thing, and unfamiliar voices took over. Someone was right now in the middle of a status report, rattling off road conditions and damage, making me guess it was still the caravan in front of us, talking about the unmistakable traces last week's storm had left. We'd had to work our way through several mudslides, drive around felled trees, and ford the odd low part of road where rain water had formed a temporary, shallow lake. The wry part of me mused that now that the camp was in disarray, nobody would go out there and clear up the damage anymore, like I was sure the raiding parties would have before. That made me wonder why the caravan was underway this close to the camp territory in the first place, but it explained their guess about our intentions.

Five minutes later and a good third of the distance to the caravan closer, a female voice that was vaguely familiar came on the radio again. It took me a few moments to recognize Tamara, one of Dispatch's initial radio operators. What felt like a million years ago, I'd spent a wild evening dancing with her and her sister. The next time I'd seen either, they'd been rather cautious about the lot of us. Now, I was borderline sure she'd shoot us in the face if we got down to talking distance.

"An update on the raiders?" she asked, sounding apprehensive.

The guy from before was back, answering. "They are catching up to us, no shit. But so far they haven't made a move to send us off the road with RPGs or some shit." He fell silent, making me guess he was studying us the way we were studying them. "Seven vehicles from what I can tell. Some armor but no larger transports. Looks small for a raiding party."

"You know that doesn't have to mean anything," Tamara cautioned. "But let's hope that Bo is right and they'll lose interest once they see that you can defend yourselves."

I would have expected Blake to appear grim at anyone accusing him and his people of ill will toward traders, but he still looked amused. When he caught my gaze, he chuckled. "I'm sure Scott and his grandstanders have their egos all up in a twist, but I frankly don't give a shit until they start shooting at us in preemptive self-defense. The Silo's never really been a part of the network. Sure, we've always welcomed traders and scavengers because they made our work easier, but that was about it."

"Unless they were disease-ridden, trigger-happy assholes, right?" I mused.

He gave me a pointed look. "We did let you in, right? And gave the rest of your group a cabin to live in while you ran your tests. Trust me, if you'd asked the same of Dispatch, Rita would have personally shot you in the head."

I had the distinct suspicion that he was right.

"You know that Stanton was giving us intel, right?" I asked after deciding that there was no harm in sharing that now, years later.

Blake didn't look perturbed by what was likely an open secret, at least to the command staff. "You didn't hear this from me, but rumor has it that Wilkes set his assistants to build—and maintain—their own networks of spies and connections, should the day ever come that the Silo required an additional layer of protection. Stanton used to be an army brat before she decided to join the marines. Doesn't surprise me she became the unofficial army liaison." He cast me a sidelong glance, as if to gauge whether the news that we'd been thrown into that same bucket would make me bristle. It didn't.

"So you never actually were with your backs against the wall?" I asked. "We got the impression that Hamilton was putting some pressure on you, or whoever was calling the shots."

Blake's smile turned wry, as if my reluctance to call the devil by his name was funny to him. He wasn't alone with that, I had to admit. "Exactly how cornered can you be when you're dug in like ticks in a decommissioned missile silo? You saw our surface extensions on your last visit. We've done an even better job underground. No need to advertise that by showing anyone our true strength. Unlike a certain group of show-offs, we're content to guard our own and prosper without anyone else the wiser of how much they are missing."

I took the snide remark for what it was, although a part of me wanted to bristle. It wasn't like my crusade had been a planned thing in the first place. Since I was sure he wouldn't tell me exactly how many people they were now, I didn't ask. That they were actively recruiting and training people was obvious; I hadn't tried to talk to the three assholes we'd dropped off there as potential spies, but from their demeanor I could tell that someone had taught them in the meantime how to be more than a ragtag band of scavengers. If anything, that underlined how little I still knew about what had been going on while Nate and I had spent some quality time driving each other insane in the middle of nowhere.

I couldn't quite quench my latent paranoia that this lack of knowledge would come back to bite me in the ass.

The guy from the caravan kept reporting in on our progress, which seemed tame enough in my eyes—until whoever was driving—likely Amos—suddenly floored it, shooting ahead of the next vehicle. Scott's marines were quick to catch up, the entire train of vehicles picking up speed in an unquestioned waste of resources. "You may want to buckle up," Blake noted, unnecessarily since I had been strapped into my seat the entire time—and he gave me quite the weird look when, instead, I unbuckled the seat harness and started stripping off the layers covering my torso. Not everything—and, truth be told, my sports bra more than covered the goods—but my sudden exhibitionistic exploits hit him right out of left field. "What the fuck are you doing?!"

I paused with my tank top partly over my head, grinning broadly. "Creating a diversion. Not for you—them. Please don't crash the car, I already have little enough skin that's not criss-crossed with scars, and I don't want to spend the next day picking pieces of the windshield out of my tits."

Blake dutifully looked straight ahead as soon as I reprimanded him, but the peanut gallery in the back was less inclined to do so. I did my best to ignore Fletcher repeatedly leering my way, although it didn't look sexual. More catch-a-look-at-the-full-freak-show style. Or at least that's what it felt like to me. Marleen, if anything, appeared befuddled. "Need some help?" she asked, holding out a small jar of black paint to me. I presumed it was for night-ops face paint camouflage purposes, but didn't question why she had it further.

"Never hurts," I offered with a smirk.

While I did my best to give myself raccoon eyes and some dramatic streaks across my cheek bones, Marleen peeled herself out of her outer, upper layers as well, although she stopped at the tight, short-sleeved shirt. I would have, too, if not for what had given me this idea in the first place. Good thing I had chosen this vehicle since it was one of very few that had windows that would roll down.

The scavenger car in front was maybe a hundred yards from the last caravan vehicle when I scandalized Blake one step further by not just rolling down my window but getting up into a crouch on my seat so I could partly climb out of the window, at least far enough that my lower back was fully exposed. A last check revealed that we were going close to fifty miles an hour, which might not have been that much—for roads that got regular maintenance, and weren't covered by years and years of debris and broken-down car wracks. The wind hit my face and torso with merciless pressure, whipping the loose ends of my braids against my shoulders and upper back. Last night I'd asked one of the scavenger girls if she'd help me get the mess on my head back under control, and I'd gotten more enthusiasm in response than I'd dreamed possible. A lot of negotiating had been required to make her braid it up right from the roots like I'd usually worn it when expecting no chance for personal hygiene but lots of running from shamblers. She hadn't budged on leaving the ends open to add a little bit of dramatic flair. Sure, I could have rolled the whole bunch into a bun, but when Nate didn't have a coronary when he saw me with a half-open, partly braided ponytail, I'd decided to go with it for now. In all the many too-close encounters with shamblers, somehow my hair had never been a good point to grab on to, and I kind of hoped that was still true. Besides, I had a bunch of hair ties, and a knife if need be.

By the time I'd straightened, the fingers of my right hand wrapped tightly around the oh-shit handle, the first car blasted by the stragglers of the caravan. Up close—and unhindered by the frame of the car—I could see that the last three cars were stuffed full with men in heavy gear who appear to be mercenaries or guards, bristling with weapons. Their attention was focused on the first two cars, still oblivious to me, which was a good thing since I needed some time to get my perch perfected that wouldn't end with me falling off the car and becoming so much road kill. The belt looped around my legs sure didn't feel supportive enough.

Marleen joined me in my endeavor to gain tons of road rash on the diagonal side of the car, instructing Fletcher not to let go of her legs, for fuck's sake! Smaller than me, she was likely standing straight. She took a moment to orient herself, but I saw the same silly grin tug on her face that must have been plastered onto my own. Insane as my endeavor was, it was also a lot of fun!

The guards noticed us as the car before us passed by them. We were close enough that I saw the eyes of one of the men go wide, and I didn't waste the opportunity for some crude hand signs after throwing my arms into the air and whooping loudly. Not sure if they heard the obscenities I was shouting their way, but they sure got the gist.

Ahead, Eden and one of the guys riding with her had picked up my idea and were now also leaning out of the car, laughing and shouting at the caravan. By the time we traversed from guard to cargo cars, a few of the guards were grinning if not laughing outright themselves, making me feel just a little less idiotic. The traders just stared, perplexed if not intimidated.

Whether it was feeling terribly exposed or the tension coming from being afraid to fall, the adrenaline pumping through my veins was making me stupid, turning my laughter—and some of the taunts I kept screaming into the wind—from forced to real to manic. I was fully aware just how idiotic my actions were, but there wasn't a hint of regret in my mind.

And then we blew past the lead vehicle and the road was empty and endless in front of us, and for a moment, I forgot all about the doom and gloom and threats and dangers, feeling alive and like myself for the first time in… way too long. I knew it was, at best, a momentary reprieve, but right then I didn't give a shit. I threw my hands in the air one last time and leaned into the wind, living in the moment.

Then I almost lost my balance, the momentary sense of vertigo slamming my heart into my throat and kicking my instincts into higher gear. I caught myself and quickly pulled myself inside the car, quite happy to be out of the wind and constantly getting pelted with dust particles that hurt way more than they had a right to. Blake was eyeing me carefully and seemed relieved that I was both whole and sitting next to him once more.

"Think it worked?" I asked rather needlessly since no shots had been fired and we were in the clear.

Rather than reply, he pointed at the radio. It was still tuned into the trader frequency, where the same guy as before kept insisting that it had turned out to be "Nothing. Just some tweaked-out assholes."

"Oh, come on! That's the worst they got?" I complained.

Blake grunted. "You missed the good parts. I'm sure someone else will be happy to recount them to you. I sure won't."

Since that sounded final, I didn't press on, and instead got dressed and belted once more. My mind calmed down a little once I felt the familiar pressure of the harness around my torso. Marleen was still snickering where she did the same in the back row, much to Fletcher's disappointment.

"I have one question," Blake said.

"Just the one? If I were you, I'd have several," I shot back.

He ignored me. "Why the strip down?"

I shrugged, unable not to smirk. "Let's put it this way—if I've learned something about this new breed of scavengers, it's that they love to have fun, and they don't give a fuck about the risks involved. Everything I learned about operational security is the opposite of fun. Wanna know who'd never get the idea to hang half-naked out of the side of a car? Exactly—the people who drive Humvees across the country on clandestine missions." I allowed myself a small laugh. "Besides, now that my tats have become legendary and even less of a security concern than when I got them, I might as well share them with the world—on my own terms. I've lost count how many people have forced me to show them my naked ass over the past years. If I can use that to my own advantage... You get my drift, I'm sure."

Fletcher seemed tempted to point out that I'd, in fact, kept my pants on, so technically, I hadn't been mooning the traders, but Blake's low, rumbling laugh took care of that.

"I think I'm starting to see why Buehler was so eager to join when she heard you'd be around," he noted.

"Yeah? Well, I'm sure she's not that heartbroken to be with the main group now—without me. That's generally the safer side to be on," I remarked, losing some of my recently gained levity. "Let's hope this turns out to be the most insane thing any of us will have to do until we find the Chemist."

Marleen chuckled darkly. "I somehow doubt that."

And my, wasn't that something to look forward to?

Chapter 7

We spent as many hours on the move as we dared, and it was still light out by the time we drove the cars off the road and went to seek shelter. That reminded me an awful lot of the time when we'd been a slightly smaller group with a lot more familiar faces. On the trek to the camp, the train that Zilinsky had put together was manned enough that we could camp wherever we wanted. Since we were trying to be more stealthy now, invisibility during downtimes was key once more. It was also a huge difference from how Nate and I had lived for so long, just the two of us, where the possibility to barricade our hideout had been the number one priority, since we would have had to light a signal fire to draw attention. It still bothered me that we didn't know for sure if the slavers happening upon us had been bad luck, or a concerted, well-planned effort. Since I doubted the executing—and now, likely, executed—party had had a clue about it in the first place, playing guessing games was useless.

Somehow I ended up without anything to do since none of the cars was mine—and it took only so many people to set up the battery recharging racks—and our rations meant no cooking was required. As usual I was scheduled for graveyard-shift watch, and I hadn't bothered with bringing a book, since entertainment seemed like the lowest priority ever on this mission. Usually, I didn't expect to need any since I could just talk to people. Only problem was that as we exited the cars, the different factions reassembled, leaving me with the wonderful prospect of either getting glared at for my antics by Sonia or my husband, or Hamilton's usual kind of hospitality. I would have considered joining the army bunch but both Cole and Hill were on watch and I could do without Richards's attempts at playing my own personal shrink. I also didn't want to overstay my welcome with Blake. The scavengers were the only ones who seemed eager to catch my attention, but I wasn't certain how that would end—and not just because of the drugs. My plan with the caravan had certainly continued to endear me to them, and while I wasn't hesitant to use that for my advantage, I also didn't want to risk it—or the uneasy balance our covenant here was hard-pressed to keep. It was hard to miss the way almost everyone was looking at the four colorful, not-quite sober individuals currently stuffing their faces.

Sitting in the car for so long had made my body stiff as fuck, and it made sense to withdraw to behind Nate's car to get some good stretches going on that the odd, bored male brain could perceive as a different kind of entertainment. Nate found me there not five minutes later, and for a moment I entertained the notion that, just maybe, I'd managed to catch the interest of the only male brain I enjoyed that kind of attention from. But I could tell that he was looking for a fight more than a fuck, which was disappointing—but also such a common occurrence that it alleviated some of my residual unease. He was mad at me because I'd been brilliantly stupid—what else was new? And because I knew that my resulting grin would annoy him even more, I let it fly as I shifted my weight to my other side, not giving a shit how much my tits or ass were sticking out.

"You think you're oh-so clever, don't you?" he remarked as he rocked to a halt in front of me, arms crossed over his chest.

"Yup," I replied, because it was true. "Was it stupid? Risky? Maybe needlessly so, on both counts? Yes. But it worked, and last time I checked, that's enough."

His glare expressed his disagreement, but surprisingly enough, he dropped the point. That made me immediately suspicious. "Are you done playing social butterfly now?" he asked, not bothering to mask his annoyance.

"You mean, am I being the adult here and trying to avoid giving your bestie the chance to be a royal ass wipe every chance he gets? He can't act up if I'm not there to receive his unwanted attention." Nate's eyes narrowed, but the fact that he didn't answer made me realize just how close to the truth I'd hit. That was unusual—and worried me a little. "Is he at least getting the same speech you're burning to deliver to me? I bet he had quite the opinion on the stunt I pulled with the caravan today and wasn't afraid to voice it."

A muscle jumped in Nate's cheek, but that could have been amusement. I knew he was capable of being both amused and offended for me at the same time. Did it rankle that, obviously, he hadn't gone off in Hamilton's face for that? Yes, but the opposite happening would have surprised—and disconcerted—me more. "A few comments may have been exchanged that I think you don't need to hear," he offered up succinctly. "But it wasn't a bad plan, or I wouldn't have let you go through with it."

Maybe it was just my general level of annoyance, but his phrasing—that he let me do anything—made my hackles rise. I would have loved to claim that it was simply my normal need to constantly push against my boundaries, but that missed the point. Intellectually, I knew that we needed a leader—consensus only worked so far, and in many ways I was glad to have him back to his confident self I'd gotten so used to in the early days of the apocalypse. Yet as I was the first to admit, rationality wasn't always my strong suit. It could have been something as simple as the lack of the people who usually reinforced the hierarchy and left no leeway. Not having Pia and Andrej around made it so easy to snap back to the mindset I'd cultivated over the past two years when it had been just the two of us. I hated to admit it, but having Martinez around to take my cues from and use as an emotional battering ram to tear down my stupid impulses was another factor.

I could tell that some of my ruminations—or the underlying misgivings—were mirrored on my expression, but since I could do nothing about that, and didn't necessarily want to pick a fight with Nate, I forced myself to ignore as much of that as I could. The patience he was showing as he kept waiting for me to go off in his face wasn't something I was used to, and it was tantalizingly easy to guess where it came from. So very like him to turn a lesson forced on him into a tool going forward. That thought made me shudder deep inside—just how much had Decker and his people fucked with Nate's mind in the past that his months spent at the camp were something he could just internalize and deal with, and move on with life? If anything, that hammered home that we really, absolutely, needed to put an end to all this.

He was still waiting for an answer—or some kind of statement or concession—from me, so I forced myself to back off my anger-fueled high horse and straightened from my crouch to bring us as close to eye level as we'd get with both of us standing there, in the middle of nowhere behind a beat-up, dirty car, barely out of earshot of the rest of our little war party. "Look, I get it," I lied, but tried to sound convincing. "For whatever reason, you think you need him along. Maybe because he is a good fighter, or he knows way more than anyone else, or because it's so comforting for you to have the single person in the world along that you feel can commiserate with what you have been through—your little trauma buddy, if you will." I should definitely call Bucky that to his face. Nate didn't move a muscle, neither in amusement or protest. Fuck, I hated his stoic side when it reared its ugly head like this. How could I bounce my indignation off him if all the possible blows just glanced off without any effect? "Or maybe he's just a meat shield," I went on. I sure liked that idea. "Wouldn't be the first time you used one of those. Whatever your reasoning, I am sure it is sound and you don't feel the need to share it with me. And I get that nobody else wants to sit beside him at lunch for so many reasons so you have taken it upon yourself to do that. But while I have to accept all that, I won't continue to subject myself to that bullshit. If you stick with him, I won't stick with you. I won't ride in the same car, and I sure as hell won't be in a fireteam with you. I don't think there exists a single person in this world I trust less with having my back then Hamilton."

Part of me waited for his immediate denial—and maybe a laugh to make fun of my grand stance there—but neither came, which made something inside of me run cold. Gee, some things I really didn't need a confirmation of. When he finally did stoop as low as opening his mouth to respond, Nate still sounded too level for his own good. "I see you've put some thought into this."

"Really not necessary," I retorted. "For that, snap judgment is enough."

That earned me a momentary grin, but it was a rather mirthless one. "Who are you going to pester instead? Blake will be wanting to have his marines work as the well-trained team that they are, and Burns, Sonia, and Marleen haven't expressed similar levels of resentment as you."

Way to make me feel singled out—but that was exactly what I wanted, right?

"I'll go with Richards," I decided, trusting that he wouldn't mind since we had already been in the field together—including underground labs overrun with super-juiced zombies. I didn't want to jinx it, but how much worse than Paris could it get?

Nate accepted that with a nod and looked pleased for a second, making me wonder if that had been his plan all along. It made sense from a tactical standpoint—both to even out the teams in number of people, and to spread what counted as the command crew out further. Then again, I was still surprised they'd all just accepted Nate's leadership like that since Scott and Blake were more than capable of running this ship as well, as was Richards, I figured. If the scavengers loved having me along as a mascot, they still hadn't overcome their starstruck awe at having Nate to stare at, so they were the faction I expected the least resistance from—and also the least discipline. I couldn't shake the feeling that would mean they'd have better chances of survival if my own still-alive status was any indication.

Burns interrupted what I only then came to realize was my completely derailed attempt at expressing my indignation by joining us, grinning at us both. At Nate's questioning look, he shrugged. "I'm here to ride to the rescue." When we both had just confused—or, in Nate's case, his usual stoic—looks for him, he laughed. "I saw you both stalk over here, bristling like cats. It's been over ten minutes and you're still not fucking each other's brains out, so something is definitely wrong."

While it was impossible to disband the wry smile from my face at his words, I couldn't help but be a little annoyed. "Do I get this right? If we try to hash things out like rational, normal people, something's wrong?"

"One hundred percent," Burns agreed wisely. "On your own, you may—sometimes—act rational, but you're never normal, and not when you're having one of your powwows. Not defusing the situation with sex always results in at least one of you stalking off mortally offended, and since this mission doesn't allow for this level of shitheadedness, let's hash this out in a more mature way, right now."

I wondered if Pia had set Burns up to babysit us. I didn't think it beyond either of them, if entirely unnecessary. Nate seemed to agree with me, but he still didn't rise to the bait. Since I was more than happy to do so, that was for the best. "What, just because I like to get naked and hang out of moving vehicles I'm immature now? You wound me." I cast a sidelong glance at Nate to gauge his reaction. Still nothing. He was starting to freak me out a little. I turned back to Burns. "But to answer your burning curiosity, we were talking strategy. I'm sorry to inform you that you're stripped of your usual babysitting-me-in-the-field duty. I'm going with Richards." Since he now had Sonia along, that was for the best, but I didn't voice that; I had no idea of her fighting prowess, but it was obvious that she would be his number-one priority. It only seemed to be my husband who let me roam free wherever I wanted—which was one of the reasons why he was my husband. Maybe for the first time ever, I considered how things might have been different if Nate hadn't gotten badly wounded right at the start of our fight for survival. I presumed he would have still left it up to Andrej, Burns, and Martinez to chaperone me and give me options aplenty to vent or cry on a shoulder when needed, but I doubted he could have kept himself from messing with me more. I was suddenly burning to ask Pia's opinion about that, knowing all too well that if I questioned Nate, I wouldn't get a straight answer out of him—and even less so an answer that I liked.

Burns took my words for what they were—a sound explanation, interwoven with lies everyone was aware of and nobody wanted to voice—and gave a brief nod, likely coming to the same conclusions, including Sonia, and my real reason for why getting constantly ribbed by Cole and Hill might be the pleasant alternative for me. "Doesn't explain why you're still standing here, talking."

Nate finally showed a hint of a smile—and turned to go. "I'm getting some chow. Feel free to keep ranting about me behind my back."

I stared after him for a moment before I turned to Burns—pretty much doing exactly what Nate had just accused me of. "Yes, I'm fucking annoyed, and more concerned than I like to admit, but it's not that outside our usual MO not to be all over each other."

Burns made a face. "When either of you is deeply traumatized, yeah. Guess that's been going on long enough that it's gotten kind of regular behavior for you now."

That statement should have given me pause maybe, but I wasn't going to indulge his badly concealed and equally just bad attempts to play shrink. "You know the company I keep. How is that still surprising to you?" I would have loved to continue trading quips with him but saw Sonia lurking in the background, glaring in my direction. "Chow doesn't sound half bad, don't you think? You can tell me all about my dysfunctional relationship if I still have one three days from now. No worries getting my panties in a twist when there might not be a reason for it if the shamblers eat us."

As expected, Burns found my optimistic attitude funny but didn't protest. Maybe it was for the best. And, if not? I really didn't have the mental capacity to care much about anything except our immediate survival.

We spent the evening in quiet contemplation, or as quiet and contemplative a group made up of seasoned soldiers ever got. There was food aplenty and we were in relative safety, so by everyone's definition, life was good. With one more day just like this to look forward to, it was easy to ignore what would come after that. Except that it wasn't, because the aspect of walking into a city the size of Dallas went beyond comprehension. We still didn't have the maps we needed, and I couldn't help suspecting that "winging it" would not just be our last, but only option. How some evil scientists and a handful of henchmen could have made that trek not just once but several times was beyond me. Clearly, they knew something that we were missing. But what?

I had the sinking feeling we'd either never find out, or find out way too late, and I didn't get my hopes up that this endeavor would go down any better than Paris.

Chapter 8

The next day wasn't exactly boring, but came and went without any noticeable events. Like every single time we'd traveled over a state border before, it was kind of anticlimactic. Keeping to small roads farther away from the trade network and going at a slower pace meant we didn't draw anyone's attention—that we were aware of. We finally got a chance to acquire some maps, and I spent the last two hours riding shotgun with Blake studying them. I'd never been to Texas before the shit hit the fan, but even so I was aware that the Dallas-Fort Worth area was one of the most heavily populated regions in the country. The heat might have been the only thing working in our favor, but I somehow doubted that it had driven the millions of shamblers out of the area. All former population centers had remained heavily infested, and I doubted Dallas was the exception. With buildings providing easy shelter and a river running through the city as a reliable water source, it wasn't a bad setup—for them, which made it very inconvenient for us. It was impossible to shake the latent unease that knowledge left, sitting deep in my stomach.

Dinner turned out to be a somber affair, the tension in the air palpable. I wasn't yet halfway done with my hunk of bread when Nate spoke up, making it a point to look at every single one of us—minus the guards out on perimeter duty—as he addressed the assembly. "I hope that as we get closer to Dallas, we'll manage to get better maps, but for now, these will do. This is the situation: we need to get into one of the buildings in downtown Dallas, and nothing less than up to several million zombies stand between us and our destination. Options and opinions, please."

At first, nobody wanted to speak up, until Amos cleared his throat. The tall scavenger looked as subdued as the rest of us, but the way his leg kept bouncing spoke of a need to burn energy that I decidedly didn't feel. "I guess simply not going there is not an option?"

"It's not," Nate agreed, a little softer than I was sure he would have with me. Amos nodded, but didn't offer anything else.

Since nobody else was speaking up, I went next. "Can we use the river that runs through the city and around the western and southern half of downtown Dallas? On the maps it looks like Trinity River has a nice, wide bed that's easy to follow."

I expected Nate to shoot me down. Scott took that over from him, instead. "I doubt it."

"Why—"

The marine leader grimaced. "I presume you got the idea because of how you went about your thing in France?" I was surprised he knew about that—including the details—but maybe shouldn't have been. Nate and Hamilton had spent some quality time with Scott and Blake both. It only now occurred to me to question why they hadn't included me in those meetings. Maybe I had been expected to join? Nothing I could do about that now.

"Won't work," Scott professed. "I've never been to Paris, but I presume the geography of the city and river helped. And that it was winter, too. We don't have any current data from the large cities in Texas, but we know they got hit hard by draughts and tornadoes. I wouldn't be surprised if half the city had burned at one time, and storms and rain washed all possible debris into the river. Think canalization, dead people, still moving dead assholes—you name it. It wouldn't have taken much to clog up the river, turning the water brackish and into a breeding ground for all kinds of critters and diseases. Even if we found boats and ways to get around everything that gunked together in the water, half of us would probably be too weak from fever and diarrhea to fight by the time we dragged ourselves into the city."

That made sense. I could think of a better way to spend my time than to drag myself through foul swamps. The storm that had come down on the camp had likely affected Dallas as well, if not directly then by sending water into the tributaries of the river.

"What about the storm drains?" one of Blake's marines offered. "Some might be clogged up, but if they have been washed free, they might be a way to get through some tight spots."

I continued to study my maps, but no drains or ditches were marked in there. "Or we could just walk right along the interstate," I proposed. "US-75 runs straight into downtown." Usually, highways were a no-go closer to cities, but since we could just walk around the heaps of rusting wrecks as we'd leave the cars farther back, it was an option.

I knew Hamilton was about to shoot me down—and dreaded what I was sure would be a great reason—but surprised the pants off of me when he agreed. "That was my idea, too," he said, pausing a moment to smirk at me. I just glared back. "In most parts, the highways are elevated and out in the sun. Only a stupid mofo of a zombie would be insane enough to be up there in the middle of the day. They must have stripped anything organic from the cars before the first winter. With luck, not too many of the overpasses will have been destroyed, but we'll bring ropes to get over any gaps." His triumphant smirk took on a really nasty twist as he singled me out again. "No worries for those who are climbing impaired. We'll just tie a rope around your useless carcass and drag you along with us."

Three of the scavengers laughed. Eden didn't, her eyes narrowing at Hamilton's attempt at a joke. She didn't speak up, but I wasn't the only one who noticed. Her attention flipped to me, and I gave her my best, "yeah, that asshole!" look. That did the trick and pulled a smile out of her, but it wasn't a pleasant one. I wouldn't exactly have called her a surprising ally—not after finding out how much the actual scavengers diverged from the tales told about them—but it was good to know that if I needed someone to hold Hamilton down when I finally decided to castrate him, she'd lend a hand. The male scavengers, too, I was certain, if only to be part of something bloody and brutal. Musing along those lines made Hamilton's assessment of my moral deterioration echo through my head, which was the last thing I needed to consider right now.

Nate ignored the glaring going on to instead voice his opinion of the plan. "That might work, or it will turn into a kill chute for us. I say we consider it but it needs further assessment as we get closer to the city." He glanced at his maps. "I say we try to drive the cars on US-75 as close as we can—likely north of McKinney. That way we'll have an easy time finding them again and we can use that spot as a fallback and rallying point."

I tried to gauge the distance. "That's, what? Forty miles from our destination?"

Nate nodded. "Give or take a few, depending on how many detours we will have to make. I expect it will take us two days to make it since we can't just waltz into there without looking left or right."

"Realistically, closer to four days," Hamilton corrected. "Unless we never need to find shelter, which I doubt will happen. A handful of people could maybe do it in one go, but a group as large as ours will inevitably attract attention. Depending on that, we will need to split up to maximize the chance that any one group will make it to our destination."

I really didn't care for the sound of that, but judging from the grim nods all around me, it didn't come as a surprise. Nate's attention turned to me, and I could guess at his question before he posed it. "Still want to go with Richards?"

Judging from how my gut was twisting in knots, I was far from certain, but I forced myself not to hesitate as I inclined my head. "Yes. Makes more sense from a tactical point. Besides, I wouldn't want to risk over two thirds of our chances for the propagation of the species in one fireteam." I didn't know why I added that—Nate certainly ignored it, as did Richards—but Hamilton gave an almost imperceptible jerk before glancing at Richards, then me. Oh, he knew. And now he knew that I knew. I stared back, the twisting, snarling beast of anger in the back of my mind growing cold, and for once there was no taunt in his gaze, either. It was so easy to forget that there was a reason why he'd been in the position I'd met him in, time and time again, and that hadn't been because he'd excelled at kissing ass. His brash demeanor, particularly toward me, made it so tantalizingly hard to remember that there was a ruthless kind of intelligence lurking behind those eyes that likely came close to rivaling Nate's. I absolutely didn't understand why Hamilton acted the way he did, particularly around me—but obviously, he had been snooping around the updated file that they had on me, and he knew about that note that Richards had told me about in his needlessly cryptic remark a few days ago…

And now was the worst time to let my mind get sidetracked with what-ifs and maybes, and letting what amounted to my arch nemesis see into my cards wasn't that smart. More to remind myself to prioritize than because I thought it was needed, I added, "Plus, I don't trust Hamilton not to knife me in the back." The moment passed—if it had even existed outside of my imagination; Hamilton was that good about shutting down his expression when he wasn't going out of his way to behave like an ass—and the possible culprit in question offered up a brief smirk and returned to mostly ignoring me.

Nate glanced from one of us to the other—and there was a certain warning in his expression that neither of us missed—before he turned to the group at large. "We likely won't get much use out of our coms as remaining as silent as possible will be key. Everyone up to date on their hand signals?" Kudos to him for not singling out the scavengers, but he did check in with them. Once everyone had nodded, he went on. "If you get lost, try to make your way to our destination, or if you're wounded or running low on ammo, retreat to the cars. I had a few possible rallying points underway in mind but since we have no idea how we will get into the city and be able to move forward, this is it. The idea with the highway is a good one—if it works. That will get us close, but downtown Dallas will be a nightmare every which way we look at it. These here are the exact coordinates of our destination." He prattled them off, also including the street name and number. It took me a little to find it on my map, particularly as it was lost in a cluster of buildings—and, if I wasn't mistaken, none of them would be small ones or easily accessible.

"How exactly are we supposed to make it there?" I asked when no one else posed the obvious question.

"Likely with very slow, very deliberate movements," Nate responded, showing humor that I really didn't feel. "But we may have one more ace up our sleeves that we didn't expect, and might explain how they managed to keep a lab running there." He pulled up a different map, this one crudely hand-drawn. Because of the position of the highways, I could more or less imagine what area it covered. Pointing at marks and connective lines drawn in red on the black and blue outlines of the city, Nate added, "Tunnels."

Danvers, Scott's second in command, perked up. "You mean the underground pedestrian network?" When most of us eyed him with confusion, he explained. "The city of Dallas built connective underground tunnels between key buildings to keep pedestrians out of the heat. A few sky bridges are also included. It's somewhat close to an extension of public transport access."

Nate shook his head. "We may have to cross through there as well, but I'd presume those tunnels are full of nesting shamblers since they give them shelter from all elements, not just the heat. No, I mean the closed railroad tunnels beneath what used to be the Santa Fe Freight Terminal. Luckily for us, the building we are aiming for was part of that at one time. They barricaded and walled off the tunnel entrances when the railroads went out of order decades ago, but I bet not all of them, or not permanently."

"Exactly how sure are we that this is the right address?" I asked. This was sounding more obscure by the moment.

Nate gave me a surprisingly acerbic smile. "Exactly how paranoid do you want to get?"

I already had plenty of that going on, but that was an easy answer. "Shoot."

Switching back to the street map he'd been using before, he circled four spots—three buildings and what looked like a parking lot. "Those are the sites that used to make up the Terminal. One building has been torn down and turned into a parking lot. One's in use by the federal government. One has been converted into apartments, and the last is a hotel. I bet that if the internet was still working, we'd find old listings for those apartments—but I doubt more than a few have ever been rented out or sold. That's the building we're headed to."

"What's the part about this that should make me all paranoid?" It sounded very convenient, yes, but France had been worse, really.

Nate flashed me a quick smile. "The Santa Fe Terminal Complex railroads have also been used to transport soldiers right from where they'd been recruited by the army for World War II."

And with Decker being an army recruiter himself, and the lab part of the complex…

"Exactly when did they start the serum program?" I asked, trying not to sound a little bit hysterical. "From what Alders said, I thought in the late seventies to early eighties, and it didn't go into full swing until the nineties."

"That's what I know, too," he mused. "But some things do make one wonder, right?"

While that connection—purely speculative as it was—freaked me out, it helped underline the theory. "Decker as a recruiter would have heard of that story, even if we are seeing ghosts where none are," I extrapolated from there. "And with the tunnels, it sounds like a good hiding place to weather out the first waves of the apocalypse."

Nate agreed with me. "That, and don't forget, there's still the possibility that it was never supposed to get that bad. Confusion, a few months of civil war, and nothing more was likely closer to the plan. Having access to a large city for possible looting should things continue on is a good contingency plan. And who would have bothered to go looking there? Even if things escalated further, Texas is a great hideout for the winter."

I looked at the tunnel map again. "Do we know how far out they extend?"

He shook his head. "That's what we found of the official, historic tunnels. I doubt we'll find any mention of any possible extensions, and even if we were to scour the archives at City Hall, I doubt we'd find blueprints of that. Since we have no way of knowing, we can't plan for that. It may make for a good exit strategy after we're done."

This was more information than I had expected to be able to go by. I did my best to memorize the hand-drawn map while Richards noted all the locations mentioned on the map I had been abusing before.

Once Nate had made sure everyone was up to date, he resumed the briefing. "It's as simple as this—we make it to the building aboveground, or we use what tunnels we know lead there, if we can access them. All of that depends on us getting into the general downtown area first, and not getting killed out on the streets. I don't need to stress how much depends on this. We don't expect heavy opposition once we are in the lab, but hiding in a former city of millions that are now guarding it is more of a defense than we can hope to overcome. We have no real numbers from Texas for the metro areas, but even the rural areas had over seventy percent conversion rate—which means they were hit hard at the very beginning of the outbreak." That could be a further clue that we were on the right track—and also meant that most people who had eaten contaminated food had turned rather than simply died.

"Anyone got any questions?" Nate wanted to know. "No? Good. Try to get as much rest tonight as you can. There's a good chance you won't get any shut-eye until we have made it to the lab and shut it down. Maybe not even until we're back outside the city."

Things looked about concluded when one of the scavengers whose name I still didn't know spoke up. "What should we do with the bodies? Of anyone who dies, I mean."

Nate cast him a sidelong look. It was Hamilton who responded. "There won't be any bodies. Whoever goes down will get torn to shreds."

My, didn't that sound lovely? I couldn't help but glance at the assembled clumps of people. Who of them would still be alive tomorrow by this time? And the day after?

Nate got up, officially ending our meeting. "On that cheerful note—make sure to pack your packs tonight so that whenever we need to abandon the cars tomorrow, you will be ready. We start out at sunrise. By the time we're out there, the sun will beat down on us mercilessly, so pack enough water and make sure you have your filtration systems with you. We'll be hard-pressed to find anything we can use that isn't foul from having something dead in it. Dismissed."

Finishing what was left of my dinner wasn't exactly high priority for me right now, but I made myself gulp down the nutrients my body would likely be screaming for come tomorrow if it didn't get them. Nobody seemed up for a chat, and those who had the last guard shift in the early morning were already hitting the rack. I tried to gauge if Nate looked ready for something—including talking but not necessarily that—but he continued to ignore me. Fine by me. It wasn't like we were walking into our near-certain doom or anything.

Annoyed more than angry, I eventually called it a night myself.

Sleep was hard to come by even though I knew I needed it and would miss it dearly tomorrow, but my mind was still in overdrive—mostly churning ruts around the sheer idiocy of our endeavor. I couldn't have dozed more than a few minutes at a time when Cole woke me up for my shift, and I forewent the coffee I usually got to make sure I remained alert. No problem with that now, but if I could catch another ninety minutes before we left, I wouldn't be devastated. It was cool enough to blast the tendrils of sleepiness from my mind, and I did my thing while I listened into the quiet night—or as quiet as the night ever gets when every damn nocturnal animal is out and about and screaming to get laid. Every animal but me.

It was close to the end of my shift when I turned, and suddenly Nate materialized out of nowhere. He'd always been a quiet, deliberate mover, but I'd noticed in the past days that he'd upped his stealth game. Part of me wondered if that was a byproduct of what Hamilton had mentioned—our unmistakable deterioration into the perfect, unnatural hunter. More likely, it stemmed from having been locked in for weeks with brief intermissions of violent unpleasantries of all kinds. Or he'd always been like this when it hadn't been just the two of us, and I only noticed it now because that had been a while. Whatever the cause, some subliminal part of me must have noticed him as I didn't startle, just stopped and waited for him to close the distance between us. The faint moonlight was the only illumination, the other guards with their flashlights far enough away not to impede my night vision. Since everyone present had heard Hamilton's assessment I hadn't bothered with bringing something that would more blind and hinder than help me—and I'd noticed that I hadn't been alone with that. Hill had been the only one of those who I knew were inoculated with the serum who had bothered with a flashlight. Theoretically, that should have boded well for the mission ahead, tunnels and all, but that was one detail I couldn't help but freak the fuck out about. Nothing much had changed for me since I'd woken on what should have been my deathbed, but that had been just me, and knowing that my blood must have been teeming with viral particles at the time. Nate's change had been easy to explain away with all the other small details he'd brought with him after we'd dragged him out of that blasted lab in Paris. But the others? As far as I knew, Burns, Richards, Hamilton, and Cole hadn't gotten bitten or scratched there. None of the scavengers had been with us, and they had no problems navigating in the darkness, either.

We were all so fucking screwed, Dallas or not.

Nate didn't say anything at first, just stood there and stared at me. I knew what he was doing—committing my face to memory. Why? Because I was doing the same, although my rational mind screamed at me not to—it felt too much like jinxing us. I couldn't help it. Losing him for an endless nine weeks once was too much. Deep inside of me, a different kind of resentment welled up that had been simmering for a while but that I'd managed to keep at bay until now. Damn it, but I'd only just gotten him back! A little tarnished and chipped around the edges, but I didn't give a shit about that at all. I deserved more time. We both did.

I opened my mouth to ask him… what exactly, I didn't know; somehow, "Wanna fuck?" went miles by where my head was, and other body parts as well. He shut me up when he brought his hands up and cradled my face before leaning in, the kiss passionate and deep but not the kind that urged for the prompt removal of at least some of my clothes. No conscious thought was required to join and lean into him, desperation clawing at the back of my mind that my body was slow to translate.

I was the one to break away first, and the words spilled out of my mouth before I could think about holding back. "Promise me that this isn't the end," I whispered, my voice hoarse and pressed. "Promise me that you will survive."

I expected him to laugh—or at least make fun of me—but while Nate hesitated, it wasn't from trying to be diplomatic. "I promise," he murmured back, the same desperation in his tone that I felt. I hadn't expected him to say that; it actually weirded me out on some level since his usual MO was to insist not to make promises he knew he couldn't keep. Maybe that occurred to him as well as a wry smile made it onto his expression. "Or I'll do my very best to make that happen. I don't think that this will turn into the last stage of our journey, and at the very least, I want to be around to see that miserable old fuck bite it." No need to explain who he was referring to.

"You don't think he's hiding out in there?"

He shook his head. "If he ever was there, I doubt he'll be there now. It doesn't matter. We have our mission, and even if the odds seem overwhelmingly bad in our favor, we've survived worse."

I wasn't sure about either, but didn't dare voice my doubt. Some things better went unsaid, particularly those where no one ended up alive to say "I told you so." Instead, I licked my lips, trying to decide what—and how much—to say. I was burning to tell him about my recent discovery, but now was not the time to bring up my possible fertility status, even though it felt weird to think that now three people in this camp were aware of it and Nate wasn't one of them. I told myself I'd have plenty of time to share the news—and very likely complicate everything—later, after we were back out of the hellhole waiting for us over the horizon. Instead, I went for a different kind of confirmation. "I know this is likely a very silly question, but I need to know this before we head out in the morning. You're not actively withdrawing from me, right? This is just you playing your usual underhanded game of manipulation, right?"

There was a hint of condescension in his gaze as he studied me, a wry twist coming to his lips. "I thought we were years beyond the point where I needed to—repeatedly—express that I'd lay down my life for you in a heartbeat, and there is nothing and no one in this world that will change that."

I hated how much I'd needed to hear him say that. "Why not tell me?" I waited for a moment, but then answered my own question since I knew he was about to offer up one of his favorite sayings—why ask when I knew, anyway? "You needed my authentic reaction. You needed me to strut around and throw a succession of hissy fits, particularly after how the three of us worked together interrogating our prisoners. But why? Everyone here knows that Hamilton and I will never see eye to eye, and I honestly don't know how I feel about knowing you wanted to delegate me to the B team."

Nate's expression turned hard, to the point where reading him was impossible. "Last time I looked, you and Richards did a great job springing both Hamilton and me, so it stands to reason you're not exactly playing second fiddle," he observed. Was that anger in his voice? And regret? Like he hated the fact that it was true? The notion was so strange that it took me a little to wrap my mind around it, but it made sense in a way—and there was something else. I hadn't missed how he'd pretty much growled Red's name. Far was it from me to accuse my husband of being jealous—and I was sure that it wasn't concerning romantic feelings in the least—but I figured, in a way that made sense, too. As grateful as he must be about the rescue—and he'd only ever been happy to see me grow more proficient and stronger—it must rankle that he didn't feel like the unbeaten, unchallenged top dog anymore. Considering what I knew about Nate's past, and how bitter and costly so many of his triumphs had been, it struck me as peculiar that he'd act like this now, but maybe that was just one more sign of just how thin his patience was wearing.

Either way, his obvious confidence in me was something that felt great to hear, and I hated that on some level I'd needed to know he was okay with all this. But that still didn't explain why the subterfuge.

"You know that I don't need much acting talent to make it look real that I don't want to be anywhere near Hamilton."

Nate sighed and looked away, making me wonder why he was avoiding me—until I realized that he was listening into the night, making sure that it was only the two of us here. When he focused back on me, his expression was a different kind of bland, speaking of underlying anger, tightly leashed until it was time to let it all out. "Someone betrayed your rescue mission and warned the Chemist. Since we have no idea who, we can't be sure they won't do so again."

"You think it's someone who's along with us?" With everything going on, I'd almost forgotten about that.

Nate shrugged. "No idea. Maybe not. Maybe their only job was to rat us out. They can continue to do that without a high chance of getting eaten."

"They?" I echoed. "You think it could be a woman? Not that many choices." My knee-jerk reaction was very focused on a single possible suspect, but I refused to believe that was true. "Do you really think Rita would betray you?" Just because she wouldn't help us didn't mean she'd sell us out.

I didn't like how dispassionate Nate looked when he responded. "Deliberately? No. But if this clusterfuck of a situation that we are in has reminded me of anything, it's that often good people end up in situations where they are forced to do not-so-good things." He paused, but then shook his head. "No, I don't think it's her. She wouldn't have needed to risk her hide leaving Dispatch to betray us. But as you keep reminding everyone and their mother, it's often a fatal mistake people make when they assume you're just a pretty face. I won't make that mistake." Another pause. "But no, I don't think it's a woman. Sadly, that only barely limits the pool of possible suspects. But it's another reason why I'm glad I can hand you off to Richards and his men. Then both of us can concentrate on something else other than looking after each other and getting killed because we're distracted."

I had to admit, I was glad that he pretty much confirmed that he still trusted Richards with his—and now, more pressingly, my—life. The fact that Red had felt the need for a detour before joining us again hadn't sat completely right with me, but he had explained that they had been on a mission before and likely had to get that underway before they could help us. And they had shown up, with backup and extra gear, and the second half of his group was now dutifully running wherever Zilinsky pointed. Or they were embedded where on their own they could never have gotten, in the perfect spot to tattle on us.

Why was I even concerned about the millions of zombies that, come tomorrow, would do their best to eat us? They sounded like the easier and way more predictable enemy for sure.

"Bree, I need you to promise me something as well." Nate's words made me frown at him, which was enough for him to go on. "I know you know this, and I know you've excelled in the past at ignoring this, but now I need you to promise me that you won't play the hero. I mean it. Everyone knows that your friends are your biggest weakness. I can't lose you because that's what you are to me—my weakness. If worse comes to worst, I need you to let someone else die for you so you can get away. So you can fight another day. And if that means that you're the only one of all of us who gets away, even if you have to walk from Texas to California or Utah, I need you to do that. Promise me." I already had my mouth open—to say what, I wasn't quite sure, but certainly not to agree—when Nate grabbed my arms, looking ready to shake some sense into me if need be. "Promise me!"

A million denials ran through my mind, starting with the point that it was unfair to expect anyone to die for me, and whether I'd even get the choice, but that was before the panic in his eyes registered. It was that small detail that fell into place like the last piece of the puzzle, and suddenly, his behavior since we'd taken over the camp took on a different meaning. The near-constant cold-and-warm behavior; how he could both seemingly ignore me and give me way more space than I needed, then turn around and give me concessions that surprised me because they almost went against his usual MO; the fact that he knew that I was highly competent and could take care of myself, but looked ready to beg me to wrap myself in layers of protective material so nothing could get close to me. I'd chalked some of that up to him dealing with all the shit that had happened to him and simply not having the mental capacity to factor in all my needs as well. Now I realized that I had been wrong: Nate was, indeed, factoring in my needs, likely prioritizing me way higher than was good for either of us—because he was scared shitless. Scared shitless of losing me; probably more of someone using me against him than me simply dying, but that was a very real possibility as well. Most other men would have been afraid for their own lives and sanities after what had been done to him, but if not quite taking that in stride, Nate was dealing with it in typical Nate fashion: accept that it happened and move on. Yet for whatever reason, something about that experience had turned his usually appropriate level of care and protectiveness for me into a manic bordering on hysteric need—and while I would have loved to shake it off as paranoia, I had the sinking feeling that the reason for that was that he was convinced that I was in real danger, and he couldn't live in a reality where what he was afraid might happen to me would come to pass. Considering both our rap sheets, that made a shudder run down my spine that had nothing to do with the—thankfully lessening—withdrawal symptoms.

Considering all that, it was easy to give my answer—and mean it. "I promise."

There was no relief on Nate's face, hammering down just how serious this was for him. A mere token promise of mine not to get myself deliberately killed wouldn't have done the trick. The fear clawing at the back of my throat was back, but now it had nothing to do with the danger we would be walking into come tomorrow. I didn't say anything because I knew there were no words in the universe that could bring relief. I also didn't try to jump his bones in an attempt to make myself forget, if only for the next twenty minutes or so. Nothing like feeling very small and oh so very mortal to act like a bucket of ice-cold water on my libido.

We could always catch up once this was over—if we were still alive.

"We should both try to catch what little sleep we still can," I proposed, grinning at the irony of me of all people saying that. Then again, I wasn't sure how many hours Nate had slept tonight, if at all. His wry smile told me he agreed—at least with the fact that me acting all mature was a novelty, and quite strange. Oh well. I was sure that, sooner or later, I'd get a chance to prove that was all just pretense.

"We should," he replied, but made no move to return to the campsite. A few moments passed, making me wonder if I'd read the situation wrong and he was looking to score, but then he signaled me to turn around as he stepped closer. I couldn't help but relax just a little as his arms wrapped around me from behind. We both stared up into the night where the Milky Way stretched, impossibly bright, across the dark sky above us. I couldn't count the many evenings we'd spent together, staring at the spectacle up there, and for a second, it was easy to pretend that the past two months hadn't happened, and we were still at our tree house, or maybe at the lake, or back at the caves, or one of our many other hideouts.

But that time was gone, and if I was honest, I was glad about that. Sure, it had been downright idyllic—but we'd always known that it wasn't for forever, and things would get way worse way faster than we could anticipate. That had turned out to be terribly true—but we were still here, still standing; still fighting. And I would be damned if I let anything in the world change that.

Chapter 9

The mood in the car was, frankly put, subdued going on graveyard, but I didn't find it within me to try to change it. I knew it was more than just bad practice not to sleep the night before what would be one awful tour de force, but at least the drugs had finally worn off, and most of the withdrawal symptoms were gone, too. I felt more like myself than in what seemed like months rather than the realistic week that it had been—which was great, seeing as being myself would be all the better if I got torn apart by the Dallas resident undead population. Red was driving while I was riding shotgun, poor Gallager again exiled to the jump seat in the middle of the back row. The soldiers seemed more somber than depressed, as if staring their own mortality in the face was business as usual. In many ways, it probably was. For me? Not so much.

We had our gear ready to leave the car on a moment's notice, but as it turned out, that wasn't necessary. Twenty miles outside of our designated drop-off zone we ambled onto the highway to start the agonizing and slow trek toward Dallas. Even that far outside the city, the road was jam-packed with car wrecks, and no clean-up effort had even started, let alone shown progress over the past years. I'd been aware of how much the trade routes had been prepped, but only after seeing the stark difference here did it hit home how much work and man hours had been put into keeping traffic up across the country. In a sense, that made me hopeful for the future, but it also underlined just how devastatingly destructive the events of the past years had been. Our country was fighting, tooth and nail, but with the chokehold of insanity slowly but steadily killing progress. If I hadn't had reasons aplenty for this mission, that realization would have been enough to make me dare the hike into Dallas ten times over.

Progress ground down to barely faster than walking speed, and we spaced out the cars farther and farther with every mile southwest, both out of necessity but also to attract the least amount of attention possible. The wrecks were abandoned for the most part but a few shamblers popped out of them whenever metal scraped on something, forcing us to mostly use the middle strip between the strips of tarmac, or the shoulders wherever not packed with mangled cars. There were traces of fires raging across the road and tornadoes hurling cars this way and that, which helped as much as hindered our progress. I thought the first few miles were bad, until we reached what I realized would be our final stopping point five miles outside what we'd hoped would be our drop-off, where a giant heap of metal blocked the entirety of the road. What seemed to have started out as a roadblock probably enacted by FEMA had turned into a barrier that nature had smashed cars on cars into, erecting a now permanent wall. Sure, we could have found a way around it and progressed forward, but it was too obvious a waypoint to ignore it. Even the smartest shamblers would have trouble overcoming that barrier while retreating humans could find ample cover. If we'd planned it, we couldn't have produced a better fallback point.

Nate's voice was clipped as he sent a brief command over the coms. "This is it."

Because we had the time and opportunity, the drivers arranged their vehicles in a pattern set for a quick sortie that would let them peel off should we come back with seconds to spare to get away from snapping jaws and grabbing claws. I waited until Richards shut off the engine before I got out, the heat of the sun immediately sending rivers of sweat down my body. No, I hadn't protested when I'd found out this morning that the assholes hadn't cut their AC out, but had taken the short reprieve for what it was. My watch showed that it was just after ten in the morning, so the heat would get massively more awful still. Nothing I could do about that, so I made sure my shades and ball cap were covering as much of my face as possible, leaving the scarf loose around my neck for now. Even out here, the stench was eye-watering, and I'd soon be glad to have something to cover my mouth and nose—but until I absolutely had to, I would leave the bottom half of my face bare.

Everyone knew what they had to do, and setting out turned into a surprisingly orderly procession. Like the cars before, we spaced out the fireteams to ensure that there was enough distance between us that if one group drew unwanted attention, not everyone else would die the very next second. Nate, Hamilton, and the rest of my people went first, with Scott's marines next. We were the second-to-last group, and by that time, Nate had turned into little more than a spec down the road, a good mile ahead of us. I'd been afraid that we would have over forty-five miles of duck-and-dash in front of us, but at least for now, as long as we went as silently as possible, we could walk, until someone roused a shambler out of its heat-and-sunlight-hours stupor. I'd debated for hours which main weapon to take with me and had finally settled on my shotgun, figuring that I was fucked anyway if I had to use it, but then close-quarter damage might buy me a few more seconds. I also had two handguns, and ammo for assault rifles, which, should I need it, I could likely pick up from someone else who couldn't use his any longer. The shotgun was on its sling now and my tomahawks were in my sweaty hands. I was praying that, like in the past, I would be able to use them moderately silently and efficiently.

I had the distinct feeling that, should I be wrong, I'd have very little time to regret my decisions.

Hours passed, the heat of the day getting worse and worse—and with the slowly dwindling distance to the city, the stench increased exponentially, soon making breathing difficult even when I covered my nose and mouth with the scarf. I'd expected it to get bad, but it was much worse than that. The tornado that must have created the roadblock where we'd left the cars must have done more cleanup than had been apparent, because once we traipsed into relatively undisturbed territory, I soon felt like we were trudging through a garbage dump. It wasn't even the stench of the dead so much as everything else and the terrible mixture that cacophony of stench created. More than one of our merry band ended up hunched over, retching as stealthily as possible. The heat and latent dehydration only added to that.

In short, before long, getting ripped apart by zombies didn't sound that horrible anymore. At least then I'd be rid of this misery.

During the worst of the afternoon heat, we hid wherever we found shade for brief intervals. As much as the hot daytime hours were safest for us from a getting-eaten perspective, none of that would help if we ended up dying of heatstroke instead. While feeling miserable, I was happy to realize I was doing moderately well, as were the other girls. One of Scott's marines collapsed mid-stride, forcing that team to take a somewhat longer break—which was easily facilitated by shuffling them to the very end of our procession, buying that poor guy another twenty minutes extra from that alone. Since we were making relatively good progress, Nate ordered everyone to keep hydrating, but to make sure not to end up puking from too much hot water sloshing in our stomachs. Even if we ran out and couldn't find a moderately clean source to replenish, we stood a good chance of running on fumes for a good two more days after the last drop was spent, but collapsing for good before that would be a death sentence—Scott's guy was a good warning for that. He was still looking queasy but was able to resume the journey after that little extra respite.

At least for the first ten miles, things looked moderately doable. A few times one of the teams met with some sluggish, rotten-down-to-the-skeleton opposition but overall, the highway was blissfully free of shamblers. The area surrounding the highway was more rural than I expected, with lots of free space. Beyond, homes and single-story stores started to cluster closer together—and I had no doubt that the ever-thickening maze of buildings was home to critters, particularly of the two-legged kind—but our route was, if not clear, passable on foot. Enough obstacles were piled up or haphazardly strewn across the lanes and surrounding area to make walking in a straight line for a minute or longer impossible, but there was no need to climb over or squeeze under anything. It was impossible not to notice that looting had virtually not taken place, making me guess that the outbreak had hit the city hard and fast, the only wave of looters present becoming food for the first zombies to spring back to life. Of the few doors we could see, most had been busted open—or were next to broken windows—typical of escaping undead ready to go foraging after devouring everything they'd been able to find wherever they had been locked in. While I was sure they had in the years since then scoured every inch of the city for edible things, there must be tons and tons of other things left that enterprising assholes like us could have put to good use. Maybe in a decade or two from now enough of the undead would have been killed or wandered off to reclaim some of those treasures.

Staying alert got hard past the six-hour mark, and impossible at eight. The sun was still blasting down on us, the hottest hours of the day just about over but leaving us no less miserable for it. Ahead, I could see an interconnected web of roads rise up at an intersection—that of the turnpike crossing our highway. A light level of trepidation started up at the back of my mind—shamblers loved tunnels—but as we drew closer, I realized that while there was inviting shade, little of it was permanent. I was so fucking glad to realize that Nate called for a stop once they reached the middle of the first overpass that I could have whooped, and almost did until my mind cut down on my accidental, suicidal impulsiveness. Right.

Scott's group behind us reached the rest just a minute after we arrived. I was honestly surprised that we were still at full strength, but our trip had, so far, turned out rather anticlimactic. I sure hoped it would continue like that, but doubted that would happen. Nate—having spent the twenty-five-minute rest wisely that he got until we caught up with them—was already on his feet while most others lounged on the dried-up grass or against a car wreck. Vain little me expected him to at least give me a smile but he went straight over to Cole, the two of them conversing in hushed tones. Cole looked less than happy from whatever he was told, but after stalling for a second he dropped his pack and, using slow and deliberate motions, extricated something from the very top of it. A small drone, I realized—what must have been one of the last still in existence. Or not; for all I knew, the army had bunkers full of them stashed away somewhere. They must have had that one along when they met up with us to storm the camp, but the terrible weather kept it from being useful. Now, in the heat without any noticeable wind blowing, it was much better suited for reconnaissance.

I silently watched as Nate, Cole, and Hamilton moved first away from us, then saw them climb one of the overhead passes of the intersection. The single lanes were split from each other, giving the entire intersection a futuristic feel—or the parts that were still standing. Two of the upward ramps lay in smashed hunks of concrete across the roads branching off from our highway, and the trio had to walk a good mile to get to an overpass that didn't look ready to join the others. I still didn't like having to watch and hope that I'd soon be a widow thanks to some static oversights. On the highest point, they stopped, partly hidden between yet more wrecks, and about a minute later I saw a speck zoom away toward the city, the drone doing its thing. The barely audible whine of its engine made my anxiety spike, but nothing around us burst from hiding spaces. I had no idea how fast that drone was flying, but sure didn't mind getting a little more rest for every moment that it was underway. A good thirty minutes passed before it returned, landing right up there on that overpass. Nate waved at us, signaling us to join them where the ramp on the other side touched down on the ground once more, so up and forward it was.

Using the mud-splattered hood of a car to unfold a map of the city, Nate gestured the fireteam leaders to gather around him. I knew that technically meant Richards, but nobody protested when I joined them as well. Pitching his voice to barely above a whisper, Nate explained the situation. "We're here," he pointed at the intersection, "and the roads are more or less clear until Glencoe park, here." He traced the thick line of our highway until close enough to downtown that my heart skipped a beat. It couldn't be that easy, right? Of course it wasn't. "It's only seven miles to our destination from there, but that will be one grueling stretch, even if we best it in the daylight and manage not to alert any squatters. We should start that stretch in the morning, as soon as the shamblers go underground, and hope for the best."

That didn't sound so bad—until I realized the implications. "You mean, tomorrow morning?" I whispered back, absolutely not liking a thing about this.

Nate briefly glanced at the others before giving a curt nod. "We can make it if we walk through the night."

I was already shaking my head, although less in denial than pure exhaustion. "We'll be too tired to run."

Hamilton, of course, had to interject there. "If we need to run, we're already dead."

He had a point there. Still…

"What's the rush?" I whispered. "We've been making good progress so far. A day won't make a difference."

Nate grimaced, but instead of answering he laced his fingers next to the car, nodding for me to let him boost me up onto the roof of the SUV. I hesitated but then accepted his offer, confused—until my focus fell on the stretch of road behind us. I'd missed it from where we had been squatting in the shade, but there was unmistakable movement behind us, enough to churn up dust. My immediate instinct was to jump down, but I accepted the binoculars that Nate handed me. Sure enough, a mass of zombies was drawing closer, stretched out across both the inbound and outbound lanes. They were still too far away to see details, but I didn't need to count them to know trouble when I saw it.

Back on ground level, Nate leaned in, murmuring into my ear. "Not sure whether they can smell us, or whether that's a pattern they follow on their own, but they are coming after us. We could hunker down in a building away from the road and hope it's the latter, but if it's the former, we're in deep shit. Still think my suggestion to walk us all into the ground is a bad one?"

I shook my head, gnawing on my bottom lip to keep from giving a verbal answer that was absolutely unnecessary.

Nate gave me a moment, then turned to the others. "Get your people ready. We move out in five."

Those five minutes felt more like five hours. It took a lot for me to try to remain calm and collected. Somehow, the knowledge that the only way now was forward, with likely no rest in sight until we had reached our destination—and cleaned it out, too—wasn't exactly comforting. I knew I could do it; I had pretty much spent a week twiddling my thumbs and sitting on my ass, and my body had plenty of reserves to burn. But guessing we might not get much rest was a different ball game than knowing we'd be lucky if all we needed to do would be more walking through the entire night. I tried to do a quick calculation in my head—if we continued at this speed and nothing got in our way, we'd reach our destination by late morning tomorrow. Somehow, the sea of undead building up behind us made me doubt it would work quite like that. Considering we'd already walked the ungodly distance of a marathon today, I wasn't even sure whether the shamblers would be the variable in this.

Nate hadn't explained to the others what was amassing behind us, but I was certain that by the time we set out, everyone knew exactly what was going on. He still had us leave in a staggered procession, but no longer were we spread out over more than a mile—more like a few hundred yards. The sun was in rapid decline now, sending long shadows onto the road ahead of us as the sky turned all shades of yellow and red. With maybe two hours until sunset left, and every fiber of my being screaming for a longer rest, even adrenaline wasn't quite enough to keep me alert and moving at a brisk pace. It wasn't long until I felt a new rush of energy flood through my body as the damn serum did its thing, mobilizing reserves I absolutely needed. Before Hamilton's big reveal I would have welcomed the rush; now, it made me fidgety, and not just because of my possible demise coming from that very sensation. If any of the others happened to turn now, a few guttural screams would likely be enough to send the entire resident population running for us. Gee, just what I needed.

I didn't protest when Nate signaled Richards that we would be group two, with Blake taking point. Scott remained our taillight, but a little bit of rest seemed to have been all his guy needed to not become a true liability. The first mile or two, it was hard to keep myself to an even pace as all I wanted to do was run. Every time I looked back,

I thought I could see movement with the naked eye, but knew that was impossible—unless a different group had found our trail. With my body gearing up for a fight—or a long night of playing hide-and-seek with the undead—I dug into my pack and forced myself to wolf down some of the provisions I was carrying. With luck, it would be an hour or more until I'd have a reason for more adrenaline to leak into my bloodstream, either from fight or flight, and I wanted some extra energy available by then—and me not ready to puke it all up from exhaustion. I couldn't exactly claim that I'd grown accustomed to the stench or that it had lessened in any way, but survival proved to be a great motivator. I wasn't the only one going for that option, and while the odd grimace appeared on a sweat-soaked face, nobody complained out loud. We were heading almost true south now with the sun disappearing to the west, the temperatures dropping a momentary relief—but not exactly welcome.

There was still the need to squint when looking to the right into the setting sun when the first growls and howls echoed through the dusk, reminding me awfully of the time we'd spent in Sioux Falls, way back when Bates was still alive and my skin had been pristine without a single tattooed mark on it. Only that city had been small enough to walk from one end to the other in hours, and we had been safe up on top of the hospital building. We'd also been stupid enough to catch super-juiced zombies to find out how to best kill them—not some of my proudest moments. Apparently, similar patterns were going on here with the zombies keeping a nocturnal lifestyle.

Just how much that was true was proven at our next waypoint up ahead—the junction of US-75 with US-635, a good six miles after our longest rest. We reached it around twenty minutes after sunset, only a few of the highest lanes far above our road still illuminated. I had no trouble seeing in the lengthening shadows—and that included what was lurking in said shadows, coming stumbling, crawling, and running into the lanes from the surrounding urban sprawl. I didn't need Red's warning signal to duck behind the next barrier, a small car so rusted that its previous paint job was impossible to guess at. Hill squeezed in behind me, with Richards, Gallager, and Cole disappearing behind a slightly larger limousine. The impulse to stay hidden was strong, but I forced myself to creep alongside the car to get a better view, and then skip on ahead to the next vehicle, and the next. While most of my body enjoyed the momentary stop-and-go, the soles of my feet didn't, and my mind wasn't too happy about the reason, either. As we kept inching forward, more and more shamblers came flooding in from all sides, making one thing obvious: if we waited much longer on this side of the intersection, it was anyone's guess how long we'd get bogged down. The next two groups were already catching up to us, our stragglers not far behind them, and Nate did exactly what I would have gone for: he gave us the signal to move forward, if need be on our own, without waiting for the rest of our team. I had no intention of abandoning Richards and his men, but signaled Red to spread out further. That way, a one-in-two chance of getting caught easily turned into one-in-five, or even one-in-twenty-five, if I considered all the others as well. Somehow I doubted Hamilton would run into a sudden lack of luck and be that one, but a girl could hope.

The last hints of light in the sky died as I reached the first lane splitting to the right which seemed to be the start of the zombie thoroughfare. Cars were crammed bumper to bumper everywhere, a lot of them closer as they'd turned into joint scrap-metal sculptures, but that didn't slow the shamblers down at all. The stench increased the closer I got, making me guess they loved to mark their favorite routes by defecating all over them—or maybe that just happened after years and years of following the same tracks. I felt myself gag and it took a lot not to start retching for real. To regain complete control over my body and senses, I paused, letting Gallager overtake me—which turned out to be a wrong move. For him.

I had just about time to tense when I caught motion from the side as Gallager stepped out of hiding behind one car to move to the next. Then, he suddenly wasn't there anymore. Growls and a cut-off gurgle came from farther to my left, mercifully out of sight. My mind screamed for me to back away and disappear, but instead I inched forward to where the zombies had tackled the young soldier. Sure enough, there was an empty patch of pavement, created by a truck slamming into several cars and pushing them aside, the gridlock around them preventing others from moving in. Roughly in the middle of it lay Gallager, back bent grotesquely over his pack, with one shambler tearing into his face, the other his neck. Already, three more were coming in, vaulting over the cars. Gallager's body was shaking but I doubted that he was still alive. The scent of blood that hit me was strong enough to be noticeable over the stench. The newcomers reached the site of slaughter and joined right in, effectively tearing the fresh corpse apart. More and more came, pushing through the group that had already found their hunk of fresh meat. In less than twenty seconds, there wasn't enough left that could have reanimated and fought, independent of whether Gallager had been inoculated with the serum or not.

Horror didn't quite cut it. The only thing worse for me would have been if something inside of me had started responding to that gore and blood with anything but revulsion, but at least I was spared that.

With the body rent asunder, the shamblers that continued to stream forward now started attacking those that were gorging themselves on the remains, either fighting for scraps or going for less-fresh but still edible substance. I realized that if I didn't want to get dragged right into that feeding frenzy, I had to move away, and quick. Forcing myself to turn my back on what was going on was hard—also because it was the most likely threat angle. Before long, I dropped down onto all fours to be less visible for the shamblers hurtling in the opposite direction. That brought me way too close to what the ground was littered in, but then the scarf was as good a splash guard as I could hope for. Being able to see even in the pitch black underneath the cars helped me pick out areas too crowded by cars for the zombies to choose—which worked well until I had to get up and climb over them in order to escape.

Glancing around me, I tried to gauge if the area ahead was clear, making me feel terribly exposed. That got even worse when I found no snapping jaws coming for me, and scrambled up and over the hood of first one car, then a second, immediately dropping into a crouch on the other side. The stupidity of that move became apparent when I had just a split-second to realize that the metal groaning behind me wasn't caused by me, and then the shambler was on me. Swinging with the ax in my left hand, I managed to bury the weapon between its opening jaws, forcing it to a halt, but the impact in turn sent me staggering back. The blade of the ax became unstuck as I keeled over backward, sending me into a fall. Rather than try to break it, I trusted that I'd survive and my pack would cushion some of it, and instead hacked at the zombie with my right hand. As predicted, it came right for me, ignoring the ax—which sheered right across its gangly, exposed neck, severing the head with one perfect swoop. The shambler went slack, but I had no time to notice it as that was the moment I crashed into the ground, the corpse landing right on top of me. Fowl liquid oozed onto me, hitting my shoulder and upper torso before I managed to wrench us both to the side, using the momentum to get up. Revulsion hit me but I cut down on the impulse to clean myself, instead dashing for the gap between two cars, and around the next. Behind me, I heard another commotion forming, but I didn't allow myself to look back, instead continuing forward. That shambler had been barely more than parchment stretched over bone, but still it seemed like a perfect source of food to others. I wouldn't have been able to push a strong, fleshy one off me like that—and those that had come after Gallager had definitely been more massive.

In my attempt to lose any tail I might still have, I kept weaving around cars until it got a little more quiet again. It was only then that I realized I had no fucking clue in which direction I was heading.

Fuck.

The lanes above should have been a clear giveaway, and my addled brain took a few moments of panic to realize that, but even so that only helped me so much. I was sure that my rough-and-tumble moment had turned me around to a certain degree. Finding a sign post might help, I told myself. I'd ended up farther away from the central part of the intersection, somewhere toward the shoulders of our highway, wherever they were visible now. The sky was dark, the moon and stars out now, not much help with directions. Asking on the coms was out of the question with any noise easily becoming a death sentence—and it wasn't like anyone else could help me since they didn't know where I was. The upside was that I seemed to be out of the worst of the zombie incursion, at least for the moment.

I tried my best to keep moving forward in silence, but progress was insanely slow. Five minutes, then ten passed, and still nothing. I finally caved, and after squatting next to a pickup truck for twenty seconds and not hearing anything close to me, I pulled myself onto the truck bed, shimmying toward the cabin to try not to turn myself into a broadly visible silhouette. Easing myself into a crouch with my hands on the roof of the cabin, I tried to get a better look around.

Bingo—somewhat off course but still up ahead I found the familiar outline of one of the buildings I'd noticed when we'd gotten closer to the intersection. I was a good four hundred yards away from where the highway disappeared into the city, and the ground between me and there was relatively undisturbed at the moment. The center of the intersection had turned into one writhing mass of bodies, not unlike a crowd at a concert. It was impossible to make out if there were people moving away from there as the streams still swelling inbound were too distracting—and I doubted any of my compatriots would be stupid enough to be seen at a distance. It was too dark now to see what was happening with the shamblers that had been coming up behind us, but the incredible din from the intersection was likely ringing the dinner bell for them as well. Except for unlucky Gallager, this might even turn out to be a blessing rather than a curse.

With a general direction now fresh in my mind, I made my way down from the truck and set out once more, pausing every few steps to listen. My progress was painfully slow, but I knew I'd still be faster than if I got eaten. That tended to get in the way of reaching destinations more than being cautious. It took way more energy to proceed like that—and do my very best to remain as alert as possible—than trundling along the highway, and my body was starting to show it. Despite what common sense might have dictated, I forced myself to slow down even more, including taking a break once to gulp down some water. More than once I paused just in time to see a shambler move past where I would have been had I moved on—and damn, those sneaky assholes were quiet. Like the one that had tackled me, all of them were emaciated to the point of not being able to fluently move any longer, but move they still did. I realized that they must have been the underdogs, usually hiding where they wouldn't become a meal themselves, now called forward by the promise of scraps. Even years in, I had no fucking clue how long it took for them to starve to death, or become too weak to be a menace for anything except carrion eaters. It was easy to guess that the strong ones were those smart enough to kill worthwhile prey, but what about the weak? Were they smart enough to eat vermin and bugs? That idea alarmed me to no end, because it would explain why they were still around—and would massively extend the lifespan of the entire undead population of the world. We could, technically, subsist on bugs only, so why not them?

And sheesh, now was really not the time to contemplate shit like that, but exhaustion, dehydration, and hunger—even if I couldn't feel it—will do that to the best of us.

An endless eternity later, I finally made it over the last access ramp and back onto US-75, and even found a sign telling me I was heading in the right direction. Behind me, carnage was still going strong, but what had sounded like battle or rallying cries had subsided. Did that mean that there was nothing left of the fresh meat they had found?

Or had they realized we were slipping through the cracks? I had no intention of finding out, and slowly continued to make my way toward downtown Dallas, hoping I would find someone alive before the dead found me.

Chapter 10

It wasn't so much me finding them as them almost tripping over me. With the howling continuing behind me, I could only pay so much attention to shuffling sounds happening around me, but when I did hear the scrape of something on concrete, I hunkered down behind a car—and something backed into me from the other side. I stepped back and raised my tomahawks, ready to slice into whatever was inevitably coming for me any moment now, only to find one of Blake's marines—wide-eyed and tense—about to do the same. I only lowered my arms after I was sure he'd recognized me—at least for one of our group, if not me personally—and he gave me an uneasy smile that looked more like a grimace. I looked around to see if there was someone else with him, but didn't catch anyone. He shook his head when I glanced back to him. He didn't protest when I signaled him that I'd take point and was quick to follow—or as quick as was possible, which wasn't much. Our overall pace had slowed down to little more than a crawl as an endless sequence of dash-and-duck will do to you. My heart was still hammering in my throat after escaping the intersection, but at least staying alert wasn't an issue for the moment.

It took me a while, but eventually I spotted two more people moving in similar fashion to us. A few hurled pebbles and some praying not to attract the wrong kind of attention, and we had caught up to each other. One was one of the scavengers, the other Danvers, Scott's second-in-command. I was happy to relinquish my position to Danvers and let him scout instead, not that it changed much. It took us a good hour to be out of earshot of whatever was still going on at the intersection, and by then most of my adrenaline was burned up. My arms got increasingly heavy and soon I had to be just as careful not to fall over my own feet as not to stumble into a suddenly appearing shambler—and there were quite a few of those lurking between the wrecks now, drawn out by the night and possibly the screams of their undead brethren. Whenever we could avoid one, we did, but more often than not we had to put it down. Even skilled at doing so quickly and nearly silently, that still caused yet more ruckus that drew others out of hiding. While we didn't catch up to anyone else from our group, the irregularly occurring thumps in front and behind us made me guess the others were working in a similar fashion. One thing was for sure: my timetable estimates had been wildly optimistic, at least for the nighttime hours. I couldn't be sure of the exact distance we'd managed since the intersection, but miles-per-hour wasn't in the measurements anymore. Nobody complained—or said anything, for that matter—but I could tell that I wasn't the only one overdue for a longer rest.

I would have missed Scott standing by one of the exit ramps but he flagged us down when we got close enough, the uneven motion pattern of our group enough to be spotted. He and Danvers did some whispering into each other's ear and some pointing was involved, making me guess someone had established some kind of gathering point nearby.

Leaving the relative safety of the highway made my skin crawl—even though it was populated, the broad band of lanes between concrete walls was good terrain to hide and move forward. The city surrounding it was one giant unknown. As we followed the ramp up, the terrain around us revealed itself, and I could see why they'd chosen to exit here. The broad roads were choked up with wrecks but didn't disappear into the urban jungle I'd expected. A swath of undeveloped land surrounded a creek that cut through it, and that was exactly where Danvers was headed. As soon as we descended into the shallow valley, I saw two more lookouts—Hill and Cole, to my momentary relief—silently pointing us farther down. Maybe half a mile along the creek sat a small, squat building, our destination if I wasn't completely wrong.

It turned out to be some kind of maintenance building, likely from a park authority or something similar. It had a lower level that was half underground, with only two small windows high in the low wall that let in a little moonlight. That basement was now full of dirty, sweaty bodies in different stages of cleanup efforts.

I felt more than a little elated to find Nate and the rest of my people down there, and not even Hamilton's presence could put a damper on that. Everyone looked okay at a first glance, although Nate had a nasty gash down one cheek that Sonia insisted needed at the very least cleaning up, which he grudgingly agreed to after he saw me step into the basement. From what I could tell, only two more people were unaccounted for—and would remain so, I figured, when Scott, Richards, Cole, and Hill were the last to file in after us, effectively barricading first the upstairs entry, and then the door to the basement on their way down.

Not giving a shit about anything except that we were safe, I let myself sag down onto the floor without even bothering to pull off my pack, glad to just sit there for the moment. Our hideout was ideal, not just coming with a basement but two entire shelves stacked with plastic water bottles—the big ones for those upside-down dispensers. A lot of them had burst or were caved in from years of heat and cold working their shit on the liquid inside, but all that mattered was that it was clean water. Nobody had escaped the intersection without getting a few more layers of grime caked on, and to get rid of that the water was still good enough.

It took me watching a few minutes of the somewhat frantic scrubbing the marines got into to realize it wasn't just personal preference. I also noticed that Sonia, armed with some clean rags, water, and bleach, wouldn't go near anyone until they had cleaned up. My confusion clearing up must have played out on my face as I caught Eden smirking at me across the room from where she was equally as relaxed as me where getting doused was concerned.

Giving myself a mental shake, I pushed my pack off and set to wiping zombie gunk off myself and my gear, which went much faster when Nate came to lend a hand. He remained at my side when I found a new space to park my tired ass against a wall, opposite the rest of our people. Burns gave me a lazy smile and a thumbs-up before he closed his eyes, looking tired enough to fall asleep right that second. Sonia and Marleen were still busy looking after scrapes and cuts, one of Blake's men getting increasingly agitated about a gash on his arm where something had torn his jacket. It looked more like he'd gotten caught on a sharp scrap of metal than a shambler bite, as Sonia confirmed soon after, but he wouldn't listen, continuing to mutter in low tones.

"Press your finger down on the bandage," I whisper-advised him. "What does it feel like?"

At first, I wasn't sure whether he'd understood as he kept staring nervously at me. Sonia, clearly at the end of her patience and energy alike, grabbed his arm and pressed her thumb into the center of the bandage she'd just applied, making him wince in discomfort.

"Hurts," he grunted.

I offered him a tight-lipped smile. "Then you're good. If it was infected, you wouldn't feel anything." Obviously agreeing with me, Sonia was already moving on, but the guy was now staring at me weirdly. I couldn't hold in a snort. "Trust me—I'm kind of the authority on getting mauled by the undead assholes and limping away from that to tell the tale. Never regained the sensation around the scars, either."

He looked slightly more at ease now but still awfully spooked. Nate allowed himself a chuckle next to me. "As I remember it, you weren't limping; you were driving like fury incarnate."

I slowly turned my head and gave him a deadpan stare. "Well, someone had to save your useless ass. I knew I was already dead. Might as well rescue those that weren't." Which reminded me of something I'd always wondered, and now might be the last opportunity to ask about it. Leaning forward and craning my neck, I found Hamilton slumped against a wall in the corner, right next to the basement stairs. He'd been watching the exchange in silence, and I felt a certain trepidation to get him talking, now that he was shutting up for once. "Hey, ass wipe—what exactly was your plan at that damn factory for the rest of us? As much as I always wanted to subscribe to the idea that you were incompetent enough not to execute Miller the second you had him cornered, I know that wasn't the case."

Hamilton grimaced, as if the mere fact I was addressing him was paining him. Good. I half expected him not to respond, but he did. "My orders were to bring him in alive. I would have shot out his kneecaps before that, to ensure transport security." If anything, Nate seemed to find that funny but remained silent.

"And the others?"

Hamilton gave a tired, one-shouldered shrug. "Of those we had captured already? I would have tried to reason with Burns. Zilinsky

I would have put down like the rabid bitch she is. Never should have gotten the serum in the first place, if you ask me. The others, depends on their behavior. After one of you assholes already turned himself into a living weapon by converting, not sure it would have been worth risking that happening a second time. All of them were fucked up enough to stay with you after they had a chance to jump ship when you got marked up. I'm not standing in the way of anyone's voluntary suicide."

I didn't miss that Richards, Cole, and Hill all kept a rather low, neutral profile. I still had no clue whether they'd been part of that operation, but I'd gotten the sense in the past that hadn't been the case. We might not have gotten away if Hamilton had more people with their kind of track record at his disposal. Then again, a part of me still marveled that we had gotten away at all, and while I didn't voice it, deep down I harbored the suspicion that Hamilton had let us get away. I hated having to admit it, but he was more capable than that, and, confusion and luck aside, they could have made it impossible for us to evade their trap after springing it. Hadn't he said in the past that it should have served as a warning to Nate? I didn't remember—which only upset me so much right now. I'd certainly waltzed all over that attempt with my crusade—but that had been after I'd been kidnapped and locked in that damn white-tiled cell, and half of our team had either died or been severely crippled in that ambush in the woods.

"My, it's such a relief to see that we're all one huge, happy family," Marleen piped up as she found her own spot against the opposite wall, next to where Sonia shimmied up to Burns—who had the presence of mind to raise one arm so she could scoot under and press herself against his side. How cute. At least I got to abuse Nate's shoulder for a pillow, and while he gave me a bemused look, he made no attempt to shove me off him. I might have, in his place, considering how lax I'd been in my cleanup efforts. Then my gaze fell on a bit of dried-up gunk on his thigh next to mine, complete with a clump of brittle hair sticking out of leathery skin, and I figured he couldn't throw stones. I considered unsheathing my knife to gingerly pick that piece of gore off him, but it was too much effort. It wasn't my leg.

With everyone settled down now, Nate did a quick head-count, coming up three short. Blake had lost two of his men, and Richards was one Gallager short. Since I'd seen what had happened to him, I reported that one in, hating how dispassionate my voice sounded. Sure, I hadn't exchanged more than a handful of words with the kid—beyond grossing him out with my fingers—but he'd deserved better than that. I was surprised when Cole spoke up as soon as I fell silent. "You couldn't have done anything for him," he assured me, his usual penchant for noting my shortcomings, if in a different way from how Hamilton did it, missing. "I was hunkering down behind a car a few vehicles in front of where you were. I saw him get up, and I saw the two zombies that took him down gear up to come for him. I couldn't prevent it any more than you could. Wrong move at the wrong time. Bad for him, but we got away. No sense in crying over spilled guts."

Something similar had happened to Blake's guys. One had died right at the beginning of the frenzy like Gallager, the other had bit it in the very middle of crossing the intersection. My accidental route to the western area had likely saved my life as the eastern parts had ended up the epicenter of the shambler incursion. I must have gotten turned around more times than I'd realized, accounting for why I'd ended up one of the last to reach our hideout. I was surprised that Hamilton didn't point that out but was instead staring blankly at the wall, not engaging with anyone. Fine by me—and pretty much what I fell into myself when exhaustion finally claimed its due.

We didn't set up any official watch, but since we were jam-packed into the room with only that single exit, there was not much sense to it. Tired as I was, I wasn't sure I would be able to fall asleep. That didn't matter much as simply being able to sit there with my pack between my knees, weapons in easy reach, and right now not about to get eaten sounded great. Once enough of the old, bottled water had been purified, it made the rounds and I forced myself to dig into my provisions to give my stomach something to cramp around, but exhaustion remained the general name of the game. After the last strip of jerky was munched down, Scott switched off the single flashlight we'd been using for illumination, turning our little bunker into even more of a tomb than it already felt to me.

I may have dozed off a few times but deep sleep was impossible. About two hours in, I felt my body shut down when the adrenaline-fueled kick of the serum finally dissipated. The exhaustion deepened but didn't knock me out as I'd wished for. At least that would make getting up in the morning a little easier, or so I hoped. Every few minutes I glanced over to the windows, trying to gauge how long until daybreak it still was. The irregular grunts and shifting sounds all around me made me guess the others weren't getting any more true rest, either. It didn't matter, really. Most of us were still alive, but I had no expectations that we would remain that way. This was, without a doubt, the stupidest undertaking of my life.

The sky started to brighten eventually, but nobody made a move to get up. It was only when sunshine glinted somewhere in the distance, reflected on a window, that Nate let out a low sigh next to me and, gently but insistently, pushed me off his side so he could get up. I remained sitting as he first straightened and stretched before starting the short trek to the stairs, stepping over feet and legs until he got to where Hamilton was getting ready himself. They both only took their melee weapons, leaving guns and packs behind to get a brief look around outside. I waited for my heart to seize up or some shit, any indication of loss or whatever, but all I felt was exhaustion still clinging to my body and soul. As long as I didn't need to get up, I might not even have cared if a shambler had started gnawing on my boots. An eerie silence settled over the basement, as if everyone was collectively holding their breaths, waiting for the inevitable scream, or just the heavy thump of a body hitting the ground.

Nate returned a good twenty minutes later to get the rest of his things and tell us to get going. He barely more than glanced at me because his pack had remained next to mine, and he was gone as soon as he had strapped it on. I went through my gear cross-check with Richards, which made more sense since our fireteam was now down to an even number. While we waited for the others to finish getting ready, I ended up idling next to Eden, who looked a lot more chipper than most of the guys strapping on their gear. It took me a second to realize why—she was smirking at the guy who'd almost lost it last night because of that scrape that he continued to prod now, still wincing. She didn't outright call him a baby, but it was hard to miss the message. I couldn't help but agree with her.

"I get it now," I whispered to her, leaning close to make sure the sound of my voice didn't carry since the doors to the outside were open now. "What your people said when Hamilton shared that crap about the version of the serum that you got. Why that still wouldn't have changed your minds."

Her smile got a little twisted at my words, but her shrug was a light, offhanded one. "You're worrying too much," she murmured back. "None of us will be alive long enough for that shit to kill us. So why give a shit?" Her gaze fell on my gloved hands, and if I wasn't mistaken, on to my left thigh where that landscape of scars was. "None of that would have happened to you if you'd gotten the shot earlier—but all those things made you who you are. Maybe you would have bitten it in the very first week of the apocalypse because you'd have trusted you could survive easily? Or you wouldn't have dared to be brave in the face of certain death. Complacency kills more fools than anything else."

I snorted at the fervor—and hint of reverie—in her voice. "I can one-hundred percent say that everything I've done that you'd call brave was fueled by fear or stupidity."

"If it works for you, why change now?" she quipped. Great—now the crazies were giving me life advice. What did it say about me that I kind of agreed with her?

Sanity was definitely overrated.

Five minutes later, the last of us stepped out of our hideout into the bright sunlight of late dawn, the distinct knowledge hanging over us that by the time the sun would set once more, not all of us would still be alive.

Chapter 11

I t took us a good twenty minutes to make it back to the highway.
The rising sun did a good job chasing away shadows, but there
was still movement going on occasionally between the cars.
I'd been afraid to find it completely overrun, our retreat from the
intersection somehow drawing streaks of shamblers after us. Whether
we'd gotten lucky there—or terribly unlucky to run into them in
the first place—nobody knew. Looking around, I noticed more
destruction in these parts—cars not just mangled from accidents but
windows smashed, hoods and sides dented as if someone had used

them for anger management and failed. The odd cadaver—animals, for the most part—lay torn apart between the wrecks, some still buzzing with flies, others years old. Most were smaller than humans, making me guess they'd been beloved family pets at one time. Out there, in the small villages, most critters had escaped relatively unscathed, leading to a rising population of wandering—if mostly shy—packs roaming through their own kind of paradise. That here the shamblers had been skilled enough to hunt down dogs and cats made the hair at the back of my neck stand on end. That didn't bode well for us—but then, what else was new? Gallager could attest to their hunting skills. Seeing a partly torn-down sign at the front of a supermarket made me wonder if they'd been smart enough to realize what bounties lay in there. Likely, since we'd more than once had to clear out a store we'd raided before we could check on food boxes. Cereals and rice were often the last non-canned goods left, their plastic packaging keeping enterprising shamblers from smelling the contents. From what I could tell, the undead masses had raided the houses in suburbia as well, or maybe just used them for nesting. As much as those details burned on my curious mind, right now wasn't a good time to dwell on them. Skipping from cover to cover took my entire focus, and although I felt more rested than last night, it was still a physically demanding task.

In record time, the heat of the day caught up to us, drenching me in new layers of sweat before long. We made progress, but for every longer dash we managed that brought us closer to downtown, we ended up having to wait for a moving corpse to either get close enough so we could kill it easily, or let it pass by. We were the third team from the front today, and before long Richards split us into two parts—Cole and Hill doing their thing, and me getting stuck with Richards. I let him take point for the time being, but when he tried to wrest that privilege from me again after a quick break, I quickly signaled up a storm of threats, although he may have had trouble interpreting half of them from the quizzical look that crossed his face. I honestly couldn't give less of a fuck if me threatening to slash his throat came out more like an offer for a hand job. He should have gotten the meaning in context. We ended up switching every thirty minutes, although I felt like every time he followed behind me he seemed extra vigilant. It took me hours to realize that, very likely, I wasn't the cause of that, failed pantomime or not. I had ended up arriving at our temporary shelter long after the others, and I didn't put it past Nate to have been a thread away from literally tearing Richards apart for losing track of me. How that translated into him getting anxious when I was taking point, I didn't quite get, as lagging behind him had done the trick last night. I wasn't vain enough to think that my dirt- and gore-caked ass bobbing up and down in front of him was making Red nervous. That seemed highly unlikely.

Hours after we'd set out for the day—and a good hundred dead shamblers later—we got to the marker Nate had identified the day before that would become our exit point. The reason became obvious a mile earlier. From what I could tell, there must have been some construction going on right next to the road. That, or the fire that had raged through the charred remains of the skeletal building must have burned hotter than usual. Then again, what did I know about fires? Maybe the fire had come later, and the upper two thirds of the building had ended up across the highway due to an earthquake or tornado. It certainly had created a lot of rubble.

How wrong my assessment was I only found out when we trudged up the last exit ramp before the highway block, and realized that it wasn't just the building, and the overpass right next to it that had sealed the highway up for good. It was the entire area around the former building in a radius easily five blocks in every direction, the epicenter of the destruction somewhere east of here. Everything was reduced to rubble and charred black, the years since it had happened doing little to let nature reclaim what had been taken from her.

If Richards hadn't pulled me behind the wreck of a truck I would have ended up standing there in the middle of the road, gaping.

Signaling to lean close, I asked in as low a voice as I could manage, "What the fuck did that? Gas main bursting?"

He shook his head. "They must have bombed the city." When all I had for him was confusion, he mimed what I realized was supposed to be a fighter jet with his fingers, dropping bombs. The resulting explosion didn't do the actual destruction visible any justice, even though he gave it his best.

I didn't even try to suppress a shudder. I hadn't seen any movie-magic light silhouettes where people had been downright evaporated, but I doubted everyone had already been dead when the bombs hit. We'd seen little to no signs of well-executed evacuation so far, and the car wrecks that were even closer here than farther out proved that.

Theoretically, I'd been aware that the larger cities must have been true hellholes in the first days of the outbreak—underlined by the fact that I'd barely heard of anyone who'd been in a larger population center surviving. I'd seen the destruction caused in L.A. firsthand on our trip through the rigged maze on our first journey into the city, and few people would have been surprised to hear a city in California crumbling down because of an earthquake or ravaged by fire. In fact, the new settlements had already had to fight those very same disasters, as my friends had filled me in on what I'd missed. From what I'd picked up from group chatter on the way to France and back, and the marines in the camp, all branches of the military must have had a hell of a time mobilizing their troops, and just like the first responders, they were mercilessly decimated once the undead rose in force. No one had confirmed this for me yet but I had a certain feeling that a lot of the bases had been prime epicenters as well since they had been picked as targets ahead of time—just like the larger cities. Most military personnel that had survived had been on leave, and had been stationed in more rural areas. Maybe it shouldn't have come as a surprise that Texas of all states had tried to make a stand, but damn, I hadn't needed to know about that.

Picking our way through the rubble wasn't an option as years of rain and storms had done their own to add to the utter destruction. From what I could tell, the epicenter of the bomb drop must have been farther to the east, but that still meant that the highway was devastated for a good two miles, judging by the distance to the next taller building that was still standing in that direction. It was hard to judge at the very edge of the zone of devastation, but it looked like the blast had hit a residential area.

It was only that when we veered off the road and into the rabbit warrens of streets on the other side of the highway that I noticed what could have been manually erected barriers, obliterated by the blast wave that had turned a part of Dallas into a blackened pockmark on the face of the planet.

Getting out of the huge ditch that the highway had been sunken into came with one advantage—more shade. Not quite noon, the sun was beating mercilessly down on us, already bad enough to make the air flicker and warp. Maybe it was a simple illusion, but I felt like it was a few degrees cooler as we stepped into the smaller streets, with buildings ranging from one to maybe five stories in height. Only the very middle of the streets wasn't ankle-deep shit, glass, leaves, and other debris—where it wasn't covered by yet more cars. On the highway, they had remained more or less in orderly rows; here it must have been each man, woman, and child for themselves, the cars creating a worse maze than the city itself.

Spread out as we were moving forward, it took us a good three blocks to realize that we were far from alone.

And we learned that lesson too late for the last two people—Danvers, and another of Scott's marines, the guy who'd gotten some heat stroke issues yesterday. Richards and I were a good block away so I didn't hear a thing—not at first. Not when both men were tackled by shamblers that must have been watching us from the second Hamilton stepped into the street, and somehow managed to coordinate an attack ranging across both sides of the corridor we were walking through.

Neither of the men managed to get out a scream, and they went down far enough away from any car to hit that.

What I did notice was the heavy pounding of feet when Scott and his remaining two guys came sprinting forward, running at full speed ahead of what must have been close to fifty shamblers, who were quickly closing the distance.

Unlike my gape-induced freeze a couple of minutes ago, my body didn't shut down but jumped right into action. My first impulse was to start running—particularly when, from the very edge of my vision, I caught something stirring on the other side of the car I was right now squeezing past—but before I got more than two steps forward, Richards grabbed my arm and hauled me toward the next building to our right. There was no door close but the ground-level windows were all busted, so I hurled myself through one of those, praying that I didn't choose a room full of nesting undead. I got lucky, only crashing onto a desk and bringing two flower pots down with me as I rolled onto my feet. Dried-up plants aside, it was better than Richards, who overshot the thin shelf underneath the window he was coming through and ended up tumbling to the floor, hitting his shoulder hard in a bad roll. I grabbed his other arm and pulled, helping him stumble upright. He stopped swaying a few steps later as we hastily retreated deeper into the building, away from the windows. A brief slap on my shoulder from behind told me he had my back while I was on the lookout for what may have been lurking in the apartment. Something had been, at one time or another, but all the feces and gore I saw at first glance were dried up, months or maybe even years old. The entrance door was gone, leaving the doorway a gaping maw into a dark hallway beyond.

Hill poked out his head from the adjacent apartment just as I stepped out of ours, quickly reuniting our fireteam. I hesitated for a second, but when Richards practically gave me a shove forward, I quickly made my way farther down that hallway, only pausing briefly to check what lay beyond the other doors. I was almost at the very end where it branched off in two directions—toward the street, where I expected the building entrance to be, and toward the back—when something burst into the apartment three doors down, where Hill was bringing up the rear. I didn't need another push to make me round the corner and move toward the back as fast as I could and still secure the hallway as much as that was possible. There was no exit there but a stairwell instead. In a pinch, that would do.

I didn't quite run up into the first floor but took the single steps as fast as I dared. The way up was partly obscured by a trashed bookshelf and two chairs that someone must have hurled out of an apartment. Two shamblers were standing in the hallway that led to the front of the building, just now turning toward the sound of my footsteps. There was one more floor above this one, and since the stairs looked clear enough, I pushed on upward rather than tried to tackle the zombies. Let someone else—like Hill, with his sledgehammer—take care of them. There was even more furniture blocking the stairs up and I dislodged at least one piece as I scrambled over it, hoping that Richards behind me would be quick enough to evade. I was still three steps and half a shelf away from the top when a shambler came hurtling toward me.

In a bad movie, I would have been able to simply duck and let it pass by me. Sadly, they were more agile than to always bullrush us, and too smart to try, either. I managed to brace myself with one shoulder against the wall as it came for me. The impact still forced me a step down, and my left arm went numb for a few seconds, forced to take the brunt of the impact. Snapping jaws clacked in front of my face, but this once my lack in height was a plus, keeping my head out of reach without me having to duck much. As soon as I found my balance, I pushed away from the wall, up and to the side, forcing the zombie toward the rails of the staircase. It didn't resist much since I was following along.

Then Richards was there, shoving his weight into the shambler, and off it went over the rail and down the stairwell. I was breathing heavy enough from exertion that I wouldn't have tried to talk if being stealthy hadn't still been imperative, so I gave him a thumbs-up—that he ignored as he vaulted past me up the remaining stairs and right into the next shambler that came toward us. I took a second to make sure the stairwell was safe before I followed, ax at the ready. Richards caved in the skull of that one, leaving the next one for me. More and more undead kept pouring out of the doors, a heap of ten or twelve at our feet as the last one went down. I remained in the middle of the hallway as Richards checked the apartments closest to us. Cole and Hill joined us, both breathing heavily and covered in equal amounts of bodily fluids as I was. None of the shamblers had been super smart or strong, but even so they had used up a good portion of my energy reserves. But that seemed to have been the last of them up here, as our more thorough check revealed.

Stepping up to the window at the front of the building, I checked the street first. It was once more looking abandoned, but from my elevated vantage point I could see a few shamblers creeping along behind cars and pressed to the side of buildings. They ignored each other, so clearly, we were what was on the menu. The opposite building was only a single story tall, giving me a good view toward the highway and the destruction beyond. From up here, it was even worse than it had appeared on the ground. Damn, but the Texans didn't mess around.

Richards came out of another apartment as I returned to the hallway, signaling us to come closer.

"You saw the stragglers on the street?" I whispered.

He inclined his head. "Yeah. Even more lurking on this side. There's a row of balconies on the southern end of the building. Next door is another apartment building, a few stories higher. I say we try that and see if maybe on the other side or to the west it's more quiet."

We were already through the next two rooms and getting close to one of those balconies when I realized what his plan was—and I didn't much care for it when I saw Hill get a grappling hook and rope ready.

At least if I broke my neck trying to get from one building to the next, it would be quick.

Under different circumstances—say, if I still had ten fingers and full grip-strength—I would have gone first, but Cole got that honor now as the second-lightest member of our team. Agile like a monkey, he had no problem crawling over the balcony railing and onto the rope, hanging suspended from it for a second before he had his feet up and wrapped around it, and over the street below he went. A few equally measured motions and he was on the balcony of the other building, unhooking the grappling hook to secure the rope with a few knots. Richards went next, proving that the knots on both ends held well, and then it was my turn. Because we were already attracting enough attention by hanging suspended in the air, three levels up, I didn't dare ask Hill about advice, but he gave me a supporting thumbs-up as he pushed me toward the balcony railing.

We'd had a rope in the bunker in Wyoming that the Ice Queen had forced me to scale on a daily basis, even after my upper body strength was at a point where I could do ten pull-ups without dying, but that was a long time ago. I was, without a doubt, stronger and lighter now, even with my pack, but climbing hadn't exactly been my priority over the past two years. Did I regret that negligence now? Yes, but there was absolutely nothing I could do about that, and stalling seemed more likely to get me killed, so I forced myself to just go for it.

Unlike the two men before me, I didn't choose the dramatic "dangle from veiny man-hands" tactic but instead sat on the rail—with Hill steadying me—so I could get my ankles wrapped around the rope first before I trusted my hands with it. I was a little surprised when my fingers managed to hold on without my grip slipping, the extra weight of the pack considered. Around one third across they were already hurting like a bitch, and while my left hand was doing moderately well, my right was becoming troublingly weak. I did my best to shift my grip as far into my palms as possible as I pushed myself forward, agonizingly slow. And that wasn't just my impression, judging from the growls and howls coming from below me. I was starting to become a liability for my team, and that was absolutely the last thing I wanted weighing on my mind. Well, actively getting one of them killed was worse, but that was usually the consequence.

I stopped for a moment to let the rope slip into the crook of my right elbow to take the strain off my hands, and made the mistake of looking down. A small mob had formed below me, which was bad but to be expected. What I also noticed—and what disconcerted me far more—were a handful of shamblers that broke away and aimed for farther down the building, where I expected the door to be. Damn, but if they had learned building architecture, we were screwed.

The need to share the news more than fear gave me a new boost and made me shimmy forward, doing my best to use my leg muscles as much as I could. As soon as I was close enough to grab, Richards and Cole hauled me the last foot or two, also keeping me from some more embarrassing and time-consuming scrambling. As soon as I was off the rope, Hill jumped on, although with less bravado than I would have expected. Whatever he was doing, it was damn efficient, and he reached us in half the time it had taken me to cross the gap.

We left the rope where it was and moved inside, the interior slightly cooler than the outside. My eyes needed painfully long to adjust to the gloom inside—the downside of great low-light vision. The apartment had been a more upscale place than what we'd been wading through in the other building, but little of that remained now. The stink of death and fecal matter made me gag, and I didn't protest when Richards signaled me to get to the door and out as soon as possible. Something was nesting in here—or had been a short time ago—and there was no need to alert them to our presence.

After fighting without having to watch my every movement, making sure not to stir anything or even breathe too loudly now as we sneaked through the busted door and into another dimly-lit staircase grated on my nerves, my heart still beating a mile a minute. Cole went first, followed by Hill, then me and Richards. My ears picked out sounds of movement from deeper into the house, but the howling outside easily distracted from it. Not knowing whether that came from the undead residents or another group, we did our best not to alert anything to our presence as we aimed for the central staircase—and found it occupied. With the rest of us waiting in the hallway, Cole went forward to check, and almost immediately halted and signaled us to turn back. So into a different apartment we went which was in a similar—and thankfully also empty—state as the one we'd come in through. Richards opted to check the balcony that went out into a small yard between this building and the next, as far away from the street we had been on before as possible. It looked clear enough that the next rope was knotted to a railing, and down the outside of the building we went.

Chapter 12

Cole went first again, but this time they had me go next. Down was easier than across, mostly because I didn't need that much grip strength and could let gravity help along— which would have been fatal ten minutes ago when we'd made it across the gap to this building. My palms hurt like hell from slight rope burn, gloves or not, but I managed to get down to ground level without cracking an ankle or breaking my neck. As soon as my boots hit the asphalt, Cole and I spread out to secure the area.

Since the front road was a no go, we skipped around the next building and made for the next parallel street, hoping to find it abandoned. It wasn't—at least not completely—but the shamblers there seemed to be less intelligent than the pack that had ambushed us. These stood, if not quite in the middle of the street, easily visible out of cover, and with lots of patience and deliberate movements, we managed to slowly make our way past them without alerting them to our presence.

We were three blocks further down the street when the howling finally died down. I hoped it was due to the shamblers having lost interest, and not because they'd hunted down enough food to satisfy them. With the parking lot of a supermarket ridding us of cover to the right, Richards signaled us to try to detour to the road we'd previously followed, and maybe luck out and find one of our other teams.

The road looked as deserted as when we'd started on it earlier, not a scrap remaining of the two people we'd lost. With the lanes blocked and cars wrecked into those that had been parked on the sides, it would have been easy to hide anything back there—as we'd learned the hard way. Richards had us break into our previous two-and-two formation again, and within moments, I'd lost sight of Cole and Hill both. The heat was unbearable, even with the odd cover throwing shade, and I felt like our progress ground to a halt.

If not for a hand suddenly shooting out from behind a truck, I wouldn't have noticed that someone was hiding there until after I'd passed by, and maybe not even then. I wasn't too happy to find out it was Hamilton, but that Sonia and Burns were with him and still alive was good news. While I did my best to get some rest crouching between two mangled wrecks, I watched the road nervously as Hamilton and Richards had a quick, near-silent conversation before we set out once more. Cole and Hill remained out of sight until an hour later, when they dropped back to report that the marines were taking a break ahead of us. All the while, we'd slowly gravitated away from the highway, and if we'd made it more than three miles, I'd eat my despicably stinky socks. Being forced to constantly duck and run for cover with intervals of crouching in between was hell on my hips and knees, and with no chance of a reprieve ahead, the idea of getting torn apart by zombies lost more and more of its inherent horror with every minute that passed.

Ahead, the haphazard maze of buildings evened out momentarily at a patch of green—the spot where the marines were supposedly waiting for us. My stomach sank when I realized that it was a cemetery. Theoretically, not the worst place in the zombie apocalypse since those that were dead for good remained that way, but it meant a lot of open ground. Taking a stroll among the tombstones sounded like a great way to make that our permanent residence. Lo and behold, neither Scott nor Blake were stupid enough to make us all crawl across the overgrown lawn, and using the small mortuary at the eastern end of the cemetery for a gathering spot wasn't that bad of an idea. Like the shed where we'd waited for the morning to come, it was a small building that nobody had bothered to loot, and it came with an intact door—at least for one of the rooms in the below-ground level in what used to be the morgue, or whatever you'd call the room where the dead were kept before being displayed in one of the two somberly furnished rooms above. There were some signs of carnage downstairs, making me guess that someone had gotten their dead loved one to the mortuary quickly enough that they had reanimated here—but otherwise the room was mostly clean.

Shirking my pack without a word and lying on my back to stretch out my aching limbs seemed like a damn good idea, so that's what I did. Rest, water, food—it really was a very short list of priorities. I did a quick headcount as the remaining people came filtering in, coming up one short; the scavengers had lost one of theirs, but I hadn't bothered memorizing his name. None of the others looked more or less shaken up than before, but Eden had stopped with her over-the-top, cracked-up routine. Withdrawal ebbing, if I had to take a guess. Unlike last night, nobody seemed to feel the need to clean up, and what words were traded were few and far between.

I checked my watch—three more hours until sunset. If yesterday was any indication, that would give us less than four hours until we turned back into the city's main attraction and all-you-can-eat buffet.

Nate gave us twenty minutes. Then we were off again. In my head, I cursed up an exhausted storm but obediently took my place in the single-file exit line.

Not surprisingly, nothing had changed in the time we'd spent underground. The city was still stinking to hell, the air was hot enough to create flickering mirages over the pavement, and in every dark doorway some thing or other could be lurking.

From the slight elevation of the cemetery, the highway was visible once more where it turned true south, the zone of utter destruction coming to an end. About a mile down, part of it branched off to the west. Our destination was maybe four miles away—an easy one-and-a-half-hour walk in the past.

The few hundred yards over to the highway took us a good thirty minutes. Closer to downtown, the entirety of the roads that led to the highway were jam-packed with vehicles, which was a blessing and a curse. A blessing, because without the cover that provided, we would have been dead in no time. But it also worked like that for the shamblers.

I had been the seventh to leave our hideout, only Scott and his remaining marines and my fireteam before me, with Richards remaining plastered to my side. Having paid for the lesson with blood earlier, they fanned out and remained as close to the ground as reasonable, every motion deliberate and as silent as possible. Neither Hill nor I could replicate that level of stealth but Cole had managed to sneak further ahead to test the waters. Since we stirred up no extra attention, I thought I was doing reasonably well.

That was, until a shambler made a grab for my ankles, and a hard jerk later, I was sprawling on the cracked pavement, only the suddenness of the maneuver—and the hard impact that drove the air from my lungs—keeping me from shouting in surprise. If it had been smart and launched itself at me, I wouldn't have had a chance against the shambler, but it tried to pull me underneath the car instead, fingers like claws digging into my calf hard enough to make me afraid they were already tearing into my muscles. The undercarriage of the SUV it had been hiding under was certainly far enough from the ground that I would have fit underneath. Thankfully, they weren't intelligent enough to account for the bulk of weapons and packs.

Instinct had me kick out with my free leg, but I didn't manage to get much force behind that maneuver while my mind was overwhelmingly blank. The pain jump-started my adrenaline, sudden clarity wiping away the fog of confusion. I had maybe three seconds until I would be dragged far enough underneath the car that my pack would get my torso stuck, thus halting my progress but also leaving a lot of fleshy thigh and juicy ass for the undead to get interested in. I was partly on my side which greatly hindered the usefulness of my arms, but since hurling one of my tomahawks under the car—and possibly chopping off what remained of my foot in the progress—didn't seem smart, that wasn't much use. My best bet was to wait until most of me was closer to the snapping jaws and then make the next kick count.

Instead, I slammed the heel of my boot up against the back door of the car, hoping that it wouldn't give, which would likely end with a stuck foot and dislocated hip—which I'd have maybe five seconds to enjoy before becoming zombie chow. Rather than lock my knee to try to remain in place, I pushed as hard as possible, trying to get away. That did nothing to dislodge the shambler, but it got me a few inches back into the glaring sunlight—enough for Richards to grab my pack and left shoulder, and pull.

One giant heave was enough to get me free of the car, but that left the shambler still clinging to my leg. I felt one clawed hand's grip loosen, yet before I could kick it off, it sank its fingers back into my leg, closer to my knee now. Ignoring the sun, it started pulling itself farther up my body, the other hand now digging into my thigh. Since it wasn't my left, mostly numb leg, that hurt like a bitch—but also brought the shambler close enough that I could jack-knife up from the ground and slam one axe into the skeletal arm that was attached to the claw that was trying to strip my thigh of vital muscle and fat.

Honestly, part of me was surprised just how well I hit, and that I didn't narrowly amputate my own leg. It wasn't a perfect blow that sliced off the limb or shattered the bone, but it distracted the shambler and made its grip ease up. As soon as he'd felt me move, Richards had let go of me, and now used the opportunity to kick at the zombie's head where it had just cleared the vehicle, putting his boot right through the softer bits of what remained of its face. I had to wait until he cleared the space before I could use my ax again, and this time the damaged arm split apart, leaving the hand and a few inches of bones attached to my leg. Richards must have done some real damage as I felt the grip of the other claw lessen, and when I pushed myself farther out into the sunshine, he finished off the shambler with a second stomp that reduced the zombie's cranium to so much mush and splinters. Gore splattered all over my legs but I didn't care, scrambling backwards onto my feet as soon as I could. From the corner of my eye I saw movement coming from underneath another car, making me whir around to face it with a second to spare. Coming full-frontal for me as soon as it could clear the vehicle, that shambler was easier to fend off, but two more came after it, making me start to back away. Richards picked off one of them but then got busy fighting off yet another that came vaulting over the hood of the car underneath which I'd almost ended up. And as if the sounds of fighting off the undead weren't bad enough, they took that moment to howl for backup, making the entire blocked street around us come alive.

No, I didn't really need Hamilton sprinting by me and giving me a clap on the shoulder to realize that it was time to run.

Richards and me getting bogged down momentarily had one advantage: in the meantime, the scavengers and the rest of Nate's team had managed to sneak by. That left Blake's group behind us. I didn't dare check on them as I forced my body into forward momentum, giving up any pretense for stealth in favor of what speed could be gained scrambling over rusting cars. Richards caught up with me quickly but remained just behind me, giving me the odd boost when a car ahead seemed a little too large or high for me to get over it on my own. My ego howled with rage but the smarter parts of my brain didn't protest, instead paying him back for his efforts by often halting long enough for him to clean an obstacle—and hack at what came after him when he seemed a moment too slow to make it unhindered.

In front of us, the street continued over the highway and into the charred remains of the houses on the other side, but just like Marleen and Burns sprinting ahead of me, I aimed for the ramp leading to the highway instead. Somewhat sheltered from the blast, the cars across the many lanes had been pushed together but no longer to the point of turning them into one giant mass of scrap metal. Maybe three hundred yards farther downtown, I could see the lanes of the branch-off leading to the side, and at least the two innermost lanes leading downtown were somewhat less of a chaos of metal and rust. I saw figures bobbing up and down between the cars there, hoping that it was our vanguard and not more shamblers already jumping up in anticipation of their next meal.

Fletcher and one other marine sprinted by me, making me guess that Blake's people were catching up to us. As soon as I managed to squeeze past the cars permanently clogging up the ramp, I did my best to aim for the inner lanes, using every inch of free room to get there faster. The howls cut off but there was still movement aplenty around us, which kept me pushing myself as hard as I could. My lungs were screaming for oxygen, making me slightly woozy, but I knew that if I slowed down, I was toast. The leg the shambler had been clinging to gave a few uncomfortable twinges but soon got drowned out by the other signals my body was sending.

Whether by accident or because he decided his life was worth more than mine, Fletcher cut me off as I tried to vault over a limousine's hood, forcing me to bounce off the side of the car to halt my momentum. I cut off the curse that I wanted to scream at him, instead taking a step back to gain enough speed to slide across the car after him. Rather than a normal—or even scrambling—landing, Fletcher disappeared out from sight, giving me a split-second to wonder what was going on. Then I was coming off the hood myself, legs first—and right on top of the two zombies that had grabbed Fletcher and were doing their best to haul him underneath that very same car. I felt a little like a late-comer to a huddle in a football game, and since directly underneath me was only animated dead flesh, I blindly hacked at heads and hands where I could reach them. Too fast to slow down or avoid me, Richards came barreling right into me, incidentally—or maybe not—shoving me off the heap of bodies.

Staggering to regain my balance, I whirled around and went right for the closest shambler, and within moments, Richards had pulled the other off Fletcher to give him room to breathe—but not before the one I was about to kill reared back and went straight for the marine's neck. My ax bit into the back of the shambler's skull a few seconds later, but the damage was done, bright-red blood spurting when I kicked the zombie off Fletcher. His eyes were impossibly wide—likely more from pain than panic, but that would come soon enough—and when I leaned down to offer him my arm, he was quick to grab it so I could pull him to his feet, never mind my gore-covered tomahawk at the end of it.

Richards pushed me aside—or gave me a shove further down the highway, it was impossible to tell which—and pressed a wad of fabric against the wound on Fletcher's neck, his scarf as I realized. Fletcher's whole body shook as he switched his own hand for Red's, and then both men came bolting after me, Richards quick to deflect another shambler that tried to come for Fletcher. Figuring that I was no use to anyone if I got eaten because I didn't pay attention, I forced myself to face forward, my pace quickening now that the vehicles were far enough apart that I could swerve around rather than needing to go over them.

Whether by intent or accident, the marine had likely saved my hide, and now had less than forty-eight hours of his own to enjoy.

I much preferred running until my lungs felt ready to burst and the muscles in my legs were on fire to contemplating that.

I fully expected to keep running on the southward-bound branch of the highway—particularly since we'd all gone right past the lanes leading in the other direction—but just where the ramp coming from over there merging onto the highway came up, Hamilton had stopped, signaling us to turn right. Knowing that danger lay behind us, my mind wanted to balk at the idea of partially turning back, but as soon as I whipped around and started toward the ramp, I realized that it was a smart move, whether I wanted to admit it or not, coming from that jackass. For whatever reason, there were far fewer cars broken down there, leaving us enough room to sprint, unhindered, at full speed. My body protested but I forced it into compliance, then pushed myself more until my entire focus narrowed down to the open patches of road and where I could force my body through. I flew past a few of the others, catching up to Marleen and Scott where they were running almost at the top of the now gently curving passover. Below, I could see the last of our people—Hamilton and Blake bringing up the rear. Ahead, I caught my first real look at the skyline of downtown Dallas, but my mind was too preoccupied with keeping me alive to appreciate it. What caught my attention wasn't that, but instead the tunnel the highway seemed to be leading into. From up here, I couldn't tell if it was just for a few yards or a longer stretch. The cars were piled up almost on top of each other leading there, so it didn't look like the best way to go.

"Where to?" I asked Scott, hoping that he had a better idea. He did, wordlessly pointing to the very right of the highway where another lane, once separated by a low cement boundary from the rest that was mostly gone where several trucks had plowed right into it. Rather than backtrack, I jumped over the blocks, running up the lane toward where the skyscrapers hulked over us.

Nate caught up with me before I got to the top of the ramp where it merged into a huge intersection right above where the highway disappeared into the tunnel. Rather than turn to the street that led between the skyscrapers into downtown, he pointed at the park-like space above the highway, quickly signaling me to hide there. "Get lost" was more like it, I figured, when I glanced back over my shoulder and saw a good hundred shamblers coming up the upward-turning ramp I had just left, hot on the heels of the last of our people. I didn't mind Hamilton getting eaten, but it would be a shame about Blake and Fletcher.

It was a real park, I realized, complete with sculptures and benches along what I figured must have been well-kept grass and trees. There was debris and junk everywhere that the wind must have carried with it that had been caught between the obstacles, turning it into a giant hide-and-seek stage. Scott and Marleen were right beside me as I disappeared into the green-brown maze, doing my very best to stop making so much noise. My strained muscles and lungs might have been happy for me to slow down, but my lizard brain was still in full-on flight mode, my instincts screaming at me to go for the open spaces where I could run faster.

What must have been a children's playground appeared ahead and to my right, not much of it left except for the partially broken-down remnants of some kind of monkey bars and attached tower. It wasn't great cover, but unlike the trees, it was something I could scale unaided, and it was far enough out in the open to see that it wasn't inhabited. With a running start and some praying, I launched myself at the structure, feeling the hard wood shudder underneath my weight but hold. Crouching down in the corner, I held my breath until I started to see spots, forcing my breathing to slow down. I was still partly exposed, but with luck no shambler would check up here or see me if I didn't move. The remains of the formerly bright red plastic slide on the ground, now bleached a light pink, were far more distracting than my tan-and-black gear.

Marleen took inspiration from my move and climbed one of the trees with branches hanging low enough so that she could reach one to pull herself up, and Scott disappeared deeper into the park. On another walkway maybe a hundred feet from me I saw his remaining two marines make their way through the maze. Maybe half a minute after them, Sonia came hurtling down the path I had been following, with Burns behind her. The sound of running steps slowly abated and silence settled—all the better to hear the clamoring of thousands of undead coming from virtually all directions around us. The sun was still in the sky but sinking slowly, turning the world into a kaleidoscope of yellows and reds—not that I could appreciate it today.

A few shamblers came roaming into the park, but they seemed to be wandering around aimlessly rather than following a lead. They kept bobbing their heads up and down in what I realized was some kind of sniffing maneuver, but how they could have caught our scent over the abominable stink of the city was beyond me. Life on the road—even if it had only been days since we'd left the camp—didn't exactly come with perfect hygiene practice. They didn't halt near Marleen's tree and also skipped the playground, only pausing when they saw a different group come around a cluster of trees to their left. Some silent snarling later, the two groups turned away from each other, searching elsewhere. Far was it from me to make observations about their hunting patterns, but that looked tantalizingly like small packs of predators to me, like a pride of lions.

Fuck, but I hated being prey.

With us spread out over who knew how many square feet now, I checked that my com was on, but no orders came over the line. From time to time I picked up some static, making me guess that Nate had his on sending, not just on receiving. The first fifteen minutes of waiting were tense but felt good after running as fast as I could. But then my paranoia got the better of me, and the fear of getting caught out in the open for the night got stronger and stronger. The influx of shamblers didn't stop but it also didn't get worse, making me guess that we had done a good job throwing them off our trail. Judging from the fact that the park was less heavily defecated on than the highway we'd left behind, the shamblers must usually avoid the somewhat open spaces. And why not? There was the densely packed labyrinth of downtown Dallas mere minutes away, and a lot more hiding spaces in all other directions as well, not to mention the highway tunnel underneath the park. Why risk exposure—to the elements, but also other hunters—when you could lurk in the dark? And from how the late afternoon sun was still beating down on me, I could definitely say that they were much smarter than us in that aspect.

I was just about to consider easing myself down from my perch when more static crackled over the line, followed by Nate's voice. "We need to move out, unless we want to become zombie chow come sunset. There are four streets leading into downtown across the length of the park. Unless impossible for your position, the fireteams will take them in this order from east to west." He quickly rattled off the team leaders. My group was called for the east-most, which wasn't ideal since I could tell I was much further west than that. I considered speaking up but decided that I'd head toward the closest road and backtrack in the direction Nate had just assigned to me. I wouldn't have been surprised to find Richards hiding somewhere close by so he could materialize out of thin air as soon as I moved out, to go with the theme of sticking with me like a dug-in tick.

Nobody acknowledged—or objected—but I still waited another five minutes before I got back down to the ground. Call me an asshole, but if the shamblers were laying in wait for us, I wanted someone else to traipse into and spring that trap. I felt refreshed enough to easily run a few more miles, which told me I was actually dipping into my reserves and on the far side of exhaustion.

Red didn't step into my way, but I saw Eden and Amos, and later Blake and Fletcher move just outside of what would have been shouting distance, each group heading in a slightly different direction. Paranoia made my skin itch as if a million eyes were following my every move but I forced myself to ignore it. As long as said eyes weren't attached to snapping jaws coming right for me, they could watch all they wanted.

It took me a nerve-wracking ten minutes to reach the mouth of the street I had been assigned to, which was, of course, the street I had wanted to turn to before Nate had sent us hiding in the park. Pressed against the side of an overturned car that had ended up blocking the sidewalk, I waited for twenty endless heartbeats before I stepped around the obstacle and started my way down the street, doing my very best to blend in with my surroundings as silently as possible. The street was wide and completely choked-up with vehicles, but that was still better than the sidewalk where debris and dried leaves had gathered, making silent passing virtually impossible.

Something rustled behind me and to my right, making me duck and freeze. The sound didn't repeat itself—and it could have been leaves or paper rustling in the light evening breeze that still felt like furnace exhaust—but I didn't dare rely on it. Through the windows of the cars next to me, I couldn't see anything, so I crouched down to peer underneath the vehicles. Since the shamblers had been hiding there before, it sounded like a good guess. I didn't see any of them, but just as I was about to come up again, I caught motion ahead and to the right of me—a pair of boots. I waited, and a few seconds later, I saw them again a few feet further south. Bingo.

I didn't so much try to sneak up on whoever was making their way forward but ended up almost scaring the shit out of Hill when I stepped into his path between two crashed and mangled trucks. He narrowed his eyes at me in silent reproach—and gave me the finger

where his hands were firmly wrapped around his sledgehammer—
before a jerk of his chin told me to precede him. I couldn't hold back
a smirk as I followed suit, telling myself no harm, no foul. Ahead,
beyond the next intersection, lay the fourth block since the park,
making me guess that we were half a mile closer to our destination.
So far, so good. I didn't have my hand-sketched map out but I
figured we must be getting close to where the southbound highway
continued on that we'd left before the park. Everything was slowly
sinking into deepening shadows as the sun dipped closer and closer
to the horizon, night coming early in the concrete-and-glass ravines
of the city.

I got ready to cross the street but hesitated when the hot wind
carried a particularly foul note right into my face. At first I thought it
was coming from up ahead—closer to the highway. But when I waited
and listened, I realized I could hear low, shuffling steps coming from
my left—a lot of low, shuffling steps. With dread crawling up my
spine, I crouched further down—to keep a low profile—and I peered
around the hood of the car closest to the intersection, trying to catch
a glimpse of what was lurking to the east.

I stopped counting at thirty and went right on to rough
estimates—at least two hundred shamblers were swaying down the
street, like molasses oozing between pebbles, slow yet impossible to
stop. Pulling back, I deliberated for a moment, then signaled Hill that
we needed to get going, and forward was likely not the best option. I
hated the idea of turning right and having that at my back until the
next intersection, but crossing right in front of them sounded like an
even worse idea. Hill took one glance over the car and gave me the
go-ahead, looking worried himself.

I forced myself to keep moving slowly and deliberately, even with
every single fiber in my body screaming for me to break into a run.
That would get me hunted down and killed in no time, I was sure,
but that didn't change anything about my hard-wired instincts. The
parallel streets were running in close proximity here so it was not

even a long block to the next intersection, but every second that passed felt like an excruciating eternity. I was halfway there when I saw two figures sneak between the cars—Amos and Eden, if I wasn't mistaken. I wondered if they'd lost the third member of their group since nobody else followed.

Two steps further, and Hill's hand suddenly clapped down on my right shoulder. I glanced back at him, but before he could signal something, I realized what was going on—the shambling mass must have caught on to us, as I could see them surge into the intersection where we'd turned off behind us. My pulse kicked into overdrive, and while I tried my very best not to make any noises, I increased my speed to a weird kind of hopping and weaving around cars.

A loud howl behind me told me it was a wasted effort.

Hill sprinted past me, sliding across a car hood to cross half the distance to the other side of the road. Under different circumstances, I would have been annoyed to be passed by and left to the shamblers, but with his larger frame he had a harder time remaining hidden, and any attention he could draw away from me was something that worked in my favor. I sprinted forward, in seconds making it to the intersection—and kept going straight while Hill turned after the scavengers, who still followed their ordered path. The houses on the right were all sky high with glass fronts, but there was a multi-level car park on the other side, so I switched over to run alongside that. Peering into the semi darkness of the ground level, I tried to make out whether it was infested or not, but when the howling reached the intersection behind me—and much quicker than I had hoped—I realized I was out of options. Forcing a burst of speed out of my aching legs, I ran to where the entrance and exit lanes of the car park left a wide hole in the concrete facade of the building, and ducked inside. My mind screamed for me to keep running, but all I did was duck and inch back alongside the first three cars abandoned there, hoping that any shamblers on my trail would surge ahead further into the level. That turned out right, although most kept streaming by outside, from what I could hear where I did my best to hide alongside and behind a pickup truck's front wheel.

I forced myself to count to a hundred—hoping that would end up being around a minute of too-fast seconds—before I checked on the exit. A few shamblers were still coming inside but most looked confused, more like they were following because the one coming before them had turned, not because they were actively hunting me. Peering further into the building, I saw a good fifty lurking this way and that, none of them coming in my direction. A few snapped at each other, making me guess that the newcomers were mixing with the resident population. I needed to get out of here before they realized they had a common goal.

Returning to the exit was a no go, so I aimed for the ramp up to the next level. I had no intention of taking that but hoped to find a staircase close by. Doors were often problematic for them. Also for us, considering creaky hinges, but I figured I could always slam the door and hide to lay a false lead.

Sadly, the staircase turned out to be not an option, since it was on the other end of the level—where there was a huge chunk of the building missing where a crane had crashed down on it, tearing through the four levels above and leaving the ground level a giant heap of cement rubble and bent rebars. Sunlight was streaming in from the side, turning it all into a devastatingly beautiful landscape of light and shadow.

To say the effect was lost on me was an understatement.

I chanced a glance over the cement balustrade that was between me and the street. I could have crawled over that, but since the street outside was teeming with shamblers, that wasn't a good idea. Maybe trying the street Hill had turned down would be better? Since it was the only direction that I could head in where I had cover, that sounded like a good idea. But it turned out as much of a bust as the other since a good third of the pursuing zombies had made their way down there as well.

Fuck. Looked like the field of rubble it was after all. With luck, they wouldn't see me as they were still avoiding the sunlight, and I could make it to the other side and escape that way. The only upside of so many shamblers around was that the sound of a misplaced step or scrape against a car didn't draw much attention since, en masse, they weren't exactly silent themselves.

It was due to that very fact that it took me more than a minute to realize that I wasn't the only one hiding in here. Moving alongside the balustrade at the very outer edge of the car park didn't help with getting a good overview, but when a few of the zombies startled for the third time, I managed to get a sense of direction. Pausing for a few seconds did the trick, and I caught sight of a head popping up behind a car hood for a second. Extrapolating from there, I caught him again a few cars further down—Cole. And Richards right behind him, if I wasn't completely mistaken.

I considered trying to signal them but didn't want to risk it. Now that I was aware of their presence, I managed to track their progress easily enough. They were moving parallel to me yet on the other side of the level, and would arrive at the debris field maybe a minute ahead of me.

Something caught my attention a few cars farther down my track—something glass or metallic reflecting the sunlight at the other end of the level, beyond where the crane had bisected it. Since there were plenty of cars remaining there, that wasn't out of the ordinary. But then it glinted again, and again, and I realized that someone was signaling with a mirror or some other reflective surface. And when the next instance pretty much blinded me for a second, I got the sense that they'd seen me, too. I could have done without losing my vision for a few priceless seconds, though.

I blinked furiously until I could see clearly again, making sure I remained out of direct line of sight until I caught the signal again. Then I raised my right arm and flipped them off. Two quick flashes made me guess they'd caught that. Awesome.

I scampered forward to the next car and found myself face to face with a shambler that had been waiting there for me. Well, the upper half of a shambler since it ended in shattered hip bones, its entrails dragging on the ground behind it. It had been a while since I'd seen one still around that was this damaged. Judging from the fact that I could see where it had been dragging itself underneath the car, it was probably a recent injury, maybe even from one of the others. Fucking great. At least I could permanently dispatch it easily enough with one well-placed ax swing—but not without alerting half the undead population around me to my presence.

First, one started to growl, then five more picked it up, partly hidden by rows of cars as they were but coming closer. My first instinct was to keep going but another flash of light made me hesitate. I was crouching right next to a flat-bed truck that looked fancy enough that I figured it had been a vehicle of vanity, not necessarily use. With the shamblers preferring to hide on the ground, up was always an option. Casting around, I saw no immediate danger, so I grabbed the side of the truck bed and hauled myself up, immediately flattening myself against the dusty metal. If they'd seen me, I was busted. If not, they might get distracted by the dead shambler on the ground.

Closing my eyes for a few seconds, I forced my breathing to slow down as I did my very best to relax. Listening to the undead draw closer wasn't very conducive to relaxation. Feeling the adrenaline pumping through my veins, neither. I still managed to even out my breaths, at least until their stink drew closer. Then I switched to shallow breaths through my mouth only, and hoped for the best.

Staring straight up, I caught a glimpse at the very top of the heads of two shamblers to my right—where the dead one was. They paused and keened at each other, close enough that if I'd reared up, I could have sliced at them with my ax. A step closer, and all it took for them to see me would have been a turn of the head. But they didn't look to the side, instead dropping down, and a moment later the telltale sounds of flesh being ripped from bones made me want to grimace.

Good for them—and if it kept them focused on their meal, good for me as well. At least until the sun set completely, and we'd all be caught out in the open with nowhere to hide.

Yeah, that wasn't going to work so well.

Thankfully, before I could consider whether the shamblers were distracted enough with eating that I could ease off the truck bed on the other side, I heard cement grate on cement, followed by the sound of pebbles rolling away. Red and Cole must have made it to the rubble and were using the momentary commotion at my end to make their way out into the open. The shamblers next to me stopped in their feeding frenzy for a moment but almost immediately resumed, a sure meal more important than uncertain anything.

The damn light hit my face again, but this time I didn't mind so much as I recognized it for what it was: a signal for me to get moving.

In reverse effect to before, I had to will my muscles into action, instinct locking down my body. Yet unlike the damn rope climbing, this was something I knew how to do. Nate and I had spent a lot of time on what had started out as a mix of yoga and stretching to keep all the parts of me limber that weren't in prime, untarnished condition—and said activities had often evolved into a rather different kind of movements—but had eventually taken on a dynamic of its own, based on the fact that we had no equipment for strength training beyond our own weight. Suffice it to say I'd never expected to master that kind of control over my own body, and it had seemed more like a fun novelty to perform than actually useful, besides keeping my core engaged. Now, I was grateful for every second that I'd spent doing all kinds of plank variations, up to completely balancing my entire body on my arms only. It may have taken me a good five minutes to slowly ease myself off the truck bed and over the side, but it beat dropping down with a thunderous crash that alerted every shambler in the city to my presence. But damn, my nerves were frayed once I felt the soles of my boots touch down onto the ground with the ease of a feather landing.

As much as the countdown to sunset clamored in the back of my head, taking my time came with one advantage: Richards and Cole were halfway across the debris field by the time I could check on their progress, and while it was slow going, they easily outpaced the shamblers that kept trying to rush after them. Throwing caution to the wind, I started toward the gap in the building myself, my left shoulder almost brushing against the cement balustrade. Fifteen cars, ten, then five, and finally I reached the last vehicle. By then, the other two had almost made it across the rubble field. My turn would likely be faster and easier since there were more intact pieces of concrete on this side, but a different problem was looming. As I pushed myself forward and into the debris, the last rays of sunshine started to recede, leaving me scrambling at the very edge of darkness. I only realized just what a difference that made when, almost immediately, the shamblers all over the building surged forward—and after me.

Throwing caution to the wind, I did my very best to gain speed—and keep my backsliding to a minimum. I gave up checking behind me after a few moments when I realized that I lost momentum, and if they caught up to me, I'd be dead whether I saw it coming or not.

I was halfway across the gap when the sunshine disappeared.

The howling and growling behind me increased in pitch and volume almost immediately. I tried to tell myself—quite rationally—that I was just imagining things, but it must have been more since I felt an almost visceral shudder run through me as the baser parts of my brain responded. Exhaustion was still weighing my limbs down but I managed to increase my speed further, jump farther, and get to the finishing stretch quicker.

There was only one problem: on this side, the crane had pretty much buried the ground level completely, and there was a huge gap between the highest part of the debris and the next level up. I'd never hated my lack of physical height, paired with my other limitations, that much in my life.

For a second, I considered diving into the darkness beyond that gap and hope I didn't spear myself on a rebar. Maybe there was a way out on the other side, and it might make for a good place to hole up. Yet ending up wedged in the opening, ready to be plucked up by the shamblers, didn't sound like so much fun, and neither was the idea of fitting through with several of them following me. No, the only way was up, even if it looked borderline impossible. I still had around fifty feet of distance to traverse to come up with a plan.

Just my luck that Hamilton turned out to be my best bet for survival.

Movement in the shadows beyond the ledge that I had to reach drew my focus. Two hulking figures materialized into people—one of them Burns, the other Hamilton. I had no attention left to check whether he was sneering down at me, but I would have been more surprised if that hadn't been the case. Thirty feet, and I realized that I only had one chance, and couldn't be picky or demanding. I was sure that Hamilton hadn't volunteered for the job but they must not have had anyone else to spare for it. Part of me still hoped that Richards would show up next to him, but this once my knight in shining armor left me hanging—hopefully not literally, I prayed… and jumped.

The last three steps I got lucky and had good, stable footing, so I could launch myself forward and upward at maximum momentum, pushing myself off the concrete with as much power as possible. I knew from the moment I left the ground that it wouldn't be enough to reach the ledge and pull myself up, but both men were crouching down, ready to reach for me. My arms were already halfway up and I strained my body to reach higher and further, fighting for every fraction of an inch—

And slammed into the ledge, torso first, the impact hard enough to leave me disoriented and scrambling.

Strong, sure hands grabbed my arms and pack, hauling me up against inertia and gravity's pull. My stomach revolted, and then I felt as if I was airborne again when their combined effort to heave me onto the ledge proved stronger than necessary for my weight. Still half locked in their grasp, I had no way to evade or cushion my fall, but Hamilton's body did a great job providing a buffer between me and the concrete.

Neither of us looked very happy with the result, I might add.

He let go of me the same moment as I pushed up and Burns gave my pack another hard pull, ending with me pretty much flying off Hamilton's prone form. Staggering against Burns was a much better outcome, even if it might have earned me a nasty glare from Sonia. I couldn't tell as I was much more preoccupied with getting away from the ledge and the surge of undead below than to see if she was even around, let alone her reaction. A moment of elation was all I got; then Burns gave me a shove toward the back of the room, just a few more feet away. The crane had taken out the ramp, but the staircase looked intact enough where Cole was keeping the door open. Below, Richards was playing lookout, and as soon as he saw me stagger down the rubble-strewn steps, he took off running down the street at breakneck speed. Why became apparent the moment I staggered out of the staircase, and found masses of shamblers waiting for us. For every stupid one that was still trying to brave the debris, five smart ones had simply followed the streets running alongside the block made up by the building.

I didn't think. I didn't question how intelligent it was to try to run away from them, or where we were headed. There was an alive human being running in front of me, so that's who I followed. The three men caught up to me, but seeing Hamilton push past me gave me an extra smidgen of energy, helping me not to fall behind more than a step or two. Ahead, Red careened through an intersection without checking and took a hard turn right, Hamilton following in his steps. Not bothering with good form, I stumbled onto the sidewalk and through the remnants of what used to be a FEMA roadblock, this cutting a good three feet of distance from my route.

The road ahead was empty but I saw shamblers trickle onto it four or five blocks away. Richards did another turn, back in our initial direction—south. One block, two, and then more shamblers came running and screaming toward us, an entire wave of them from how they suddenly filled out the street. Yet Richards pushed on, running right toward them, missing the last possible route away from them as he ran straight across another intersection. My instincts were screaming for me to take the turn he'd missed but I forced myself to follow and only concentrate on catching up to him.

With half of block of distance to the shamblers left, Richards suddenly hurled himself onto the sidewalk and through a small portal barely broader than a normal house entrance. In the deepening shadows, it looked more like a dark maw into hell, but turned out to be a short staircase, less than ten steps deep. Beyond that was a ramp just about broad enough for a car, although obviously meant for pedestrian traffic only. One of the entrances to the Dallas pedestrian underground tunnels, I realized—not quite what we were headed for, but the next best thing, and better than getting torn to shreds by the undead.

My shorter legs cost me a few feet of distance down the stairs so Hamilton managed to catch up to Richards in the meantime, with the three of us following. Not a bad turn, I realized, when Richards hesitated at the first intersection yet Hamilton barreled right on, heading straight, then left, and straight again, as if he had a map of the pedestrian tunnels memorized. That was likely what was happening, I realized, as I followed him blindly, not looking at any of the side tunnels that we didn't take.

On and on we ran—and we were far from alone in the tunnels; more than once, a huddle of shamblers lurched toward us, but they clearly didn't belong to the hunting mob we had encountered on the surface, too slow to be much of a menace to us. We must have run well over a mile when Hamilton picked another ramp upward, leading us back to the surface. I had just enough time to feel my animal brain react to the stench my nose must have picked up before my mind noticed it; then we were crashing into a crowd of shamblers, out onto another street clogged with wrecks. I almost went down but a strong hand grabbed my arm and pulled me forward, and down the street we went with the confused undead coming after us. My vision was swimming with patches of color as hypoxia set in, my lungs incapable of drawing enough air. I knew I had maybe a minute of this in me, two tops—

But it turned out, all I needed was another fifteen seconds before Hamilton launched himself into what looked like an ordinary entrance to a building's underground parking lot. With mounting panic I realized that it was a dead end—until a sudden shock of bright light revealed an exit where there shouldn't be one, at the very back left corner of the level. Nate and Blake were waiting for us there, urging us on with silent gestures. Needing no incentive, I staggered through the gap in the concrete, slipping through easily while Burns had to actively squeeze himself through. As soon as Cole was the last to get in, Nate and Blake pulled what looked like a rusty sheet of iron across the gap, effectively sealing it shut. A locking mechanism engaged, and not a second too soon as the repeat sound of bodies slamming against the other side of the barrier proved. It didn't budge or give—or even shake, really—way sturdier than it looked.

Hunching over, I did my best not to fall flat on my face as I sucked air into my lungs, feeling like my entire body had just gotten worked over by a sledgehammer. The guys didn't look to be in much better shape, although Hamilton was trying to hide it. I honestly didn't give a fuck, as long as I was safe from the undead for the moment. Beyond what little illumination Blake's flashlight provided, I could see the other surviving members of our team huddled together, equally happy to be alive. My earlier guess had been correct, it turned out—only Eden and Amos were left of the scavengers, the other two members of their party gone. Considering what the last two days had been like, it was bordering on a miracle that any of us had survived, but I couldn't help but feel that special kind of frustration rise inside of me that I'd gotten awfully familiar with over the past few years: that senseless loss of life when really, we couldn't afford to lose anyone. I tried to console myself that it wasn't any of my friends—and least of all Nate—but couldn't ignore the bitter taste it left on my tongue.

"We move out in five," my dear husband grated out, the first loud words any of us had uttered in what felt like ages.

I glared at him between pants that made me sound more canine than human, but didn't protest. We'd made it to the abandoned railway tunnels. Our destination was less than two miles of hopefully mostly straight paths away. That was enough time to catch my breath. And, soon enough, we'd find out whether we had risked our lives for something worth risking it for, or all the senseless deaths had been for naught.

Chapter 13

We did not move out in five, as it turned out. That order had come before Nate had gotten a chance to realize how badly wounded Fletcher had gotten, and that Scott's two remaining marines were both pretty beaten up and needed some rudimentary checkups and bandages. Sonia could easily take care of that, but even before she hesitated with Fletcher, Nate told her to steer clear of him. I would have preferred to sit this one out—literally, since my lungs and legs were still protesting after the recent abuse they had suffered—but all the tall, hulking guys seemed to think that cleaning savage bite wounds warranted a woman's gentle touch.

I was still wheezing with laughter as I pulled off my gloves after rudimentarily wiping gore off my arms, and set to work. And my, having my mutilated fingers right in front of his face—the unmistakable price I had paid for getting infected and having the audacity to survive— seemed to upset Fletcher's stomach greatly. Or that was just the onset of the virus-caused flu symptoms. I tried to remember how long it had taken for my body to start deteriorating, and realized that Fletcher was a tantalizingly close match. I didn't tell him that as I first got rid of all manner of gore and dried blood before checking the wounds themselves. The shamblers had gotten him good, but not to the point where they'd managed to tear out chunks of flesh. Around the bite marks, the skin was swollen and red, and he definitely needed stitches where it was damaged enough to start bleeding as soon as I was done with cleanup. I was happy not to have to deal with that when Blake whipped out a small pouch and extracted a plastic syringe, handing it to me.

"You still have reserves of the glue?" Last I remembered—which had been around the time I had gotten infected, actually—the Silo scientists had been working on upgraded versions of the booster shots and the glue, a wound coagulant that could knit together tissues well enough on the surface, and was great for deeper wounds yet needed removal later as the surrounding flesh could turn necrotic. One of my fondest memories of that still remained when, right at the beginning of the zombie apocalypse, Nate had managed to get speared by a rebar and Martinez had sealed up the wound with that shit, only to tell me two days later that I was the only one qualified to cut it right out of him again. Thankfully, the assholes hadn't shared with me that Nate was fully conscious during that makeshift operation, or could have torn my head clean off had he died under my scalpel and converted. Fun times.

"Aren't you supposed to tell me something along the lines of it not being as bad as it looks?" Fletcher asked, his voice scratchy.

I paused, taking a moment to catch his gaze. "Like, 'just a flesh wound,' you mean?" He nodded, even managed a slight smile. "Yeah, the problem is, you are right now the poster boy for newly infected with the zombie virus, and while I can very competently give you a timeline of what's up next for you, I'm not sure that will help."

I didn't miss the dejected look on his face even as I worked on spreading a thin layer of the glue across the deepest cuts. While I couldn't use the rest in the syringe on half of our team, there was no sense in wasting it, so I wiped the top with a tissue doused with alcohol, closed it up, and let it disappear into my pack.

"How long do I have, doc?" he asked. I wondered if I should clarify that he wasn't that far off from my qualifications with that moniker.

"To live? Probably another thirty hours, maybe even going on fifty. But you won't be lucid or able to fight in five, six tops. Unless we are super fast with the cleanup of the lab, you'll get to guard the back door that we'll use to get inside, and that's it." He didn't look too disturbed about the news. I couldn't hold it against him. He was quickly succumbing to what felt like real influenza on speed; that wasn't exactly a great condition to go all-out Rambo on anyone's ass.

"Guess that's it, then," he muttered, wincing as I finished slapping a bandage on my work.

I hesitated for a moment, but then went for it. "You know, there's a good chance they'll have some serum samples in that lab. Maybe the original, or the upgrade, but even if it's just the variant that the scavengers got—it's a lease on life that adds months, if not years to your existence. More than enough time to finish this mission, and get to cash in on all the favors anyone still owes you." Saying "to bring all your affairs in order" sounded too much like a death sentence— even if it was just that.

Fletcher shook his head, the way he regarded me turning almost shrewd. "No, thanks. I saw the horror plain on your face when Hamilton broke it to you that you're already more than halfway into zombie territory. I hate knowing that next week I won't be around anymore, but then none of us could have seriously expected to survive this mission. I'll go on my terms, when my time is up—and without becoming an issue to my people." I must still have been bad about reining in my features as he cracked a small, if pained, smile. "What, you really think that our scientists couldn't have reverse-engineered that serum shit if they'd wanted? When Hamilton dropped by that summer when you and your buddies went all ape-shit on his ass, the army even offered our squints stocks and the entire documentation. They declined, but I know they've been in contact with the USAMRIID R&D branch ever since. If you ask me, they knew they were dodging a bullet, not saying no to an opportunity of a lifetime. Bet you didn't know that, huh?"

I didn't, but it wasn't that much of a surprise, particularly since, far as I knew, Petty Officer Stanton had remained with Emily Raynor in the Canadian base, both because she probably continued to need medical attention that no other place on earth could give her, and to act as a liaison. We'd seen ourselves that Wilkes, the Silo's commander, was more than happy to cut deals with everyone if his people might profit, and he could keep them free and alive in their little facility. My bitterness only stemmed from the fact that I personally was banned—or had been; considering that Blake, who'd had to serve as my personal watchdog on my last visit, was now working with us, maybe Wilkes had changed his mind. Then again, the list of places where I wasn't allowed to enter was probably longer than that of where I was welcome, so it wasn't like Wilkes was singling me out that much. Wilkes had more reason than most of the others, even though it hadn't been my fault that his scientists had been stupid enough not to make sure that asshole guy I'd infected was dead for good. Complicated shit, and simply banning me was the easiest solution.

Fletcher looked annoyed when I gave him a wry grin. "No, I wasn't aware of that, but since I've likely met all people involved, I'm far from surprised." When he kept staring at me weirdly, I couldn't hold back a laugh. "I hate to break it to you, but where the safety of people—and a possible cure for the fucking zombie virus—is concerned, I try very hard to keep my personal quarrels and ethics out of the game. I didn't exactly volunteer when Hamilton dragged me across the globe and almost got my husband killed in Paris, but I still spent the entire way back going over the notes we found there and doing my best to contribute my expertise to their cause. And that's also the reason why I'm here now. I, personally, have long since given up on getting vengeance, or satisfaction for anything anyone has done. All there is for me in this game is to hope we can prevent worse from happening, and to stop the shit that's already in motion. So, good for you if you look forward to blowing your brains out later tonight when you realize you'll soon be too frail to do it yourself if you wait much longer than that. If you need help, I'm happy to lend you my shotgun."

After cleaning my hands again, I straightened and set to putting my gloves back on, finding most of our illustrious bunch watching me. Ignoring them, I checked on what Sonia was doing. She looked about finished herself, so I grabbed some water and jerky from my pack and did my best to fuel up my body since it would have to last me a while longer still. Part of me waited for Nate to check in with me, but I wasn't terribly disappointed that he didn't. He and Hamilton were busy poring over their maps, and since that very knowledge had just saved my life, I couldn't really gripe about it.

It turned out, the group that had left the park on the westernmost street had made it here in almost a straight line with minimal resistance. We had them to thank for finding the iron door that had blocked the entrance to the tunnel, just as the second group had come running, chased by a few shamblers. That would have been those we'd run into once we'd made it out of the pedestrian tunnels. All in all, it had only been my fireteam that had, rather successfully, landed in deep shit and had needed help with the extraction. Hill, following Eden and Amos here, explained that they hadn't even realized the depth of the shit the three of us had landed ourselves in. One wrong turn and a seemingly smart decision will do that to you, I figured.

With everyone patched up as well as could be expected, we finally set out. The zombies on the other side of the iron door had quieted down somewhat, most likely having wandered off. Since the area here was surprisingly clean—for railroad tunnels that had been abandoned long before any one of us had been born, but the shamblers did manage to destroy and stink up a place in no time—I hoped that these tunnels had somehow remained undisturbed, at least the part here leading to the lab. There were no signs anyone had come through here before us beyond where Marleen and Scott had scouted ahead so it couldn't have been the entrance the Chemist and his people had frequently used, but simply not getting tackled and chomped at for the rest of our journey sounded damn good.

As Nate told us to get ready—this time for real—it got quite apparent that our previous fireteams didn't make sense anymore. The Silo marines were still at four people but Scott's group was down to three, same as the Army bunch, and of the scavengers only Eden and Amos remained. To me, it would have made sense to combine these groups two and two, but I was clearly the only one who thought that way. You wouldn't have believed the instant animosity that arose when I offered up that suggestion, just as if we weren't locked in underneath a mega city teeming with the undead. While both the scavengers and army guys were happy to cooperate with me, they glared bloody murder at each other, and the marines amongst themselves still hadn't buried their hatchet, either. Nate looked mostly amused at my frustration, probably having anticipated shit like that to happen. Very diplomatically—and very unlike his usual self—he instead suggested that his group split up, moving Marleen to Scott, Sonia and Burns to Blake's people, and the two scavengers would do just as well on their own as he and Hamilton would. I had to admit, I was happy to stick with Richards—particularly if having Bucky breathing down my neck was the alternative—but it still irked me to realize nothing much had changed. Then again, why should it have? Just because our people were dying like flies, and, likely, the worst was yet to come?

Since the cat was out of the bag about the side effects of the serum, it made the most sense that Nate, Hamilton, and my fireteam went first, going ahead of those that would need flashlights to navigate in the pitch-dark tunnels. It wasn't like any of us could see in complete darkness, but the illumination behind us would likely be enough and preserve most of our low-light vision. Hamilton took point, smirking as he stepped past me into the tunnel, for whatever reason. I was too exhausted to give a shit, really.

I hadn't bothered to ask if this was the entrance they had planned to use or a different one. Since we were definitely on the right track, I didn't do so now. I had to admit, I had expected something different. "Train" always made me think of those endless Amtrak things— or the good old steam engines from Wild West movies. What we found here was neither one nor the other as, for one, the tunnels weren't sized for full-on modern trains with twenty cars. From what I'd gleaned overhearing the others, the network had been built to distribute goods and serve as an alternative to the clogged-up overground traffic routes. It made sense to go for smaller cars then that could be loaded with cargo quickly and moved to and fro without much ado. But all of that was gone now, at least in this part of the network, except for the rails. It was all a little underwhelming—just endless, dark tunnels interspersed with abandoned freight elevators. The tunnels must have been open to the surface in places as the air wasn't too dank and the sound of water dripping echoed around us, and the odd rodent scurried away as we got closer. They still made me jump, but I much preferred them to the shamblers aboveground.

I was surprised when, less than an hour later, Nate signaled us down what looked like an off-shoot side tunnel, announcing we had arrived. Disappointingly, there was no sign announcing "secret lab" or anything similar. All I could see was another dilapidated freight elevator next to a metal frame and door that had seen better days even when the railroad had still been active. What was also missing were any signs of recent usage.

"Are you sure about this?" I asked. "We are presuming that the Chemist and his buddies fled to here, right? Doesn't look like anyone came in this way."

Hamilton was only too happy to enlighten me. "As we said before, this is the back door. Presumably, they've arrived days ago taking a different approach." His expression turned belligerent. "Need me to sketch you a diagram?"

I shook my head, hating that I'd run straight into this one. "How sure are you that this leads anywhere?"

"Guess we'll find out soon," was all I got from him.

I had to admit, I felt a little vindicated when, once everyone was ready, Hamilton tried the door and it wouldn't budge. No amount of force worked. What a shame. I knew better than to articulate any of that but couldn't help but smirk. At least until Hill dropped his pack and got out the C4.

Cheaters.

I shouldn't have been surprised that they came prepared, and considering that Nate and Burns were both bona fide pyromaniacs—sadly, not a talent you got to use much when civilization goes belly up—and even had certification for that, I could have counted on it coming in handy sooner or later. That apparently they'd found another enthusiast of all things that could go boom in Hill was just perfect. The fact that Sonia also sported a somewhat annoyed expression made me wonder what explosion-related shit I'd been missing while Nate and I had been hiding in the middle of nowhere.

All of us retreated to behind the last bend in the tunnel when it was time to set off the charges, with only Hill and Nate remaining behind to do the deed. The resulting "boom" was loud enough that I was sure zombies over in Houston must have heard it, too, and I felt the shockwave even with that much distance to its cause. On our return, I found the entire door gone and what felt like a whole city block of pulverized dirt in the air, making me cough and my eyes sting. Great—just how much asbestos had been in that? Maybe that would kill me before the serum had a chance to do the trick.

Massive as the explosion had been—and successful as well—it only helped us so much as the door might have been gone, but there was one at the other end of a short connective tunnel just like it. Rinse, repeat. With that gone, we still weren't more than pulverized bedrock and thirty feet farther, at the next door—but this one was an improvement, relatively speaking. It looked much newer, came with an electronic keypad that was working, seemed even more massive than the other two doors, and there was a camera—trained in our direction—above it. I looked straight at it and waved, figuring that after two massive detonations, playing coy made only so much sense. I doubted they'd simply let us in if we lied and claimed we were selling girl scout cookies. Nate gave me a vexed look before he went to investigate the door closer.

"Oh, you're just annoyed you can't use your boomstick for knocking down these doors," Cole accused as he joined me off to the side, grinning at my shotgun. The tomahawks had been useful—and necessary—for the shamblers, but if I could avoid going into melee from here on forward, I was all for it. Shotguns still produced enough gore and splatters that I'd have that aspect covered. I didn't reward his statement with an answer.

"Try zero-zero-zero-zero-zero," I suggested. Nate and Hill ignored me. Burns chuckled under his breath. Hamilton grimaced—but tried it nevertheless. The keypad gave an indignant beep, the indicator above it flashing red. "One-two-three-four-five, maybe?" I helpfully provided. Hamilton, still smirking, looked tempted, but Nate knocked his hand away when he reached for the pad again.

"We have no clue what happens when we guess the code wrong five times," he suggested.

"You mean, like poisonous gas getting released?" I figured it was a valid guess. "Or are you afraid the two detonations weren't enough to alert everyone of our presence?"

Nate ignored me in favor of looking at Hill's pack. "How much more do we have left?"

Hill shrugged. "Enough for this door, if it's not too heavily reinforced. But that's it."

"Then let's do this."

Already familiar with the proceedings, the rest of us were about to file out when Cole spoke up. "I know I'm the first to give Lewis shit, but try nine-nine-nine-nine-nine." Nate gave him a deadpan stare, which made Cole shrug. "Wouldn't be the first time that some admin or another got annoyed with his people constantly forgetting the current passcode. Shit, I know I've done it. Not with anything this simple, but—"

Nate had already turned around and was hitting the keypad, which emitted five identical beeps—and then the door swung outward. I wasn't the only one that jumped, which might have been satisfying under different circumstances. Thankfully, no one's head got blown off. That had to count for something. Nate and Hamilton shared a look, then Hamilton eased the door open with his assault rifle, ready for anything. I'd expected another door—because that would have been hilarious, if really bad for us—or some high-tech shit, but instead we were greeted with something that looked like a mix between a decontamination chamber and a foyer. It only took a minute to clear the room which meant I got to explore it soon enough. The hazmat suits I'd expected were there all right, but at a closer look they were rather different than what I was used to. "Are we sure that this is a bioweapons lab? Because that setup looks more like what you'd use for radiation decontamination than viral warfare."

Nate shrugged. "They likely overhauled it during the Cold War. They must have expected that atomic bombs would be more of an issue."

It turned out, the next door we encountered was a plain old wooden one, no explosives required. With no idea whatsoever how the facility was structured—and how many levels there were—Nate started dispatching us one fireteam at a time, slowly leap-frogging away from the entrance. What I presumed was the lowest level was mostly storage, we quickly found out, and abandoned from the looks of it. The lights didn't work, and there was no hum of a ventilation system. If not for that third door, I would have presumed it was abandoned, but that one had had electricity. We also encountered some kind of guard room and a few offices, but all paper files that must have once been stored there were gone.

After the hell aboveground Dallas had been, it was weird to be all alone in here—and not in a good way. My paranoia got worse with every turn we took, and still we found nothing. Whoever had been watching the feed of that camera above the door must have alerted their security forces, but we hadn't heard a single footstep that wasn't caused by one of us.

We managed to clear the entire level in a little over thirty minutes. The most exciting thing anyone had come across was a candy wrapper, but since it had a production date from 1999 printed on it, that wasn't necessarily a lead. Blake's group had cased the elevators and set a guard at the staircase, but reported back that the sticker from the last maintenance overhaul was also from the last century. Frustration was spreading among us, except maybe for Fletcher, who looked like he was nearing the barf-your-soul-out stage. Nate took in the reports and then did the only sensible thing: told us to check the upper levels.

The second level—still below-ground, judging from the lack of windows—wasn't very promising, showing equal neglect. While I was still part of the search party for that level, Nate sent Scott's team further up the stairs to see if they could find anything at a glance. They joined us once more when we were done down here, the slump in their shoulders already telling me what I didn't want to know—

nothing. Well, not nothing, exactly; the building seemed to be the right one, with the other floors turning out to be apartments, and not quite empty from what they'd heard. I felt my heart sink. Somehow, finding nothing was an option I hadn't thought would be on the menu. This was, after all, the very same address that the boxes full of lab equipment had been addressed to. Had it all been just a front?

Worse, had someone set that up, expecting us to get eaten in the attempt to get here? That would be really depressing.

I was trying to come up with a suggestion—witty or not, right now, any idea sounded good to me—as Nate and Hamilton started discussing whether it was worth risking going back to the tunnels and trying for the city hall next. That building had also been part of the underground railway system, and might hold blueprints.

Blueprints. Why did that set off something in my mind?

Turning in a quick circle, I tried to both orient myself and see whether anything caught my attention. That corridor over there was right above the one through which we'd come in. And that over there led to what were the offices downstairs. That's where Blake and his people had searched, and that over there our quadrant. Only that…

"Who here has the best spatial awareness?" I asked. The murmurs around me dropped off as hopeful attention turned to me.

It wasn't without misgivings that I glanced at Hamilton, but he shook his head with equal disdain. "I'm great at memorizing maps, but that's it."

No one else spoke up, until one of Blake's marines cleared his throat. "What exactly are you looking for? I'm pretty good with those three-dimensional puzzles where you compare turned-over silhouettes to each other and select the one that makes sense." That explanation didn't, but it sounded like a useful skill—and exactly what I was looking for.

"Check the layout of the rooms on all levels. Does anything outside of what you'd expect jump out to you?" When Nate was still frowning at that, I clucked my tongue at him. "What if the real lab is in one of the other buildings, like an annex? Maybe even underground, too. You said it yourself—they've been using this whole building here for almost a century, and eventually they gave it up and turned it into condos. Why leave the lower two levels as is? They could have converted them to parking spaces, or a gym. They also didn't wall them off. What's the thinking there?"

People turned around and started staring at the walls—except for Hamilton, who was now squinting at me. Yet rather than call my idea the most stupid thing he'd ever heard, he offered up a low grunt. "It will be in the lower level." When he saw my questioning look—and likely also the surprise that he hadn't called me or my idea fucked in the head—he barked a brief laugh. "It makes sense, since they did list this as one of our black sites. One level off the street is too easy. But see that staircase? It's wide enough for some unlucky bastards to drag all kinds of shit down to the lower level. That's exactly how they must have gotten new stocks in. If everyone knows your secret hideout is a secret hideout, that's a great recipe for getting bombed into the Stone Age."

It took our marine a while to familiarize himself with the floor plans, but then it was just a matter of fifteen minutes and some pacing, until he stopped in one of the offices. "That wall's three feet further into the room than the one above," he reported. The fact that Nate and Hamilton had both spent the last five minutes also investigating that very room made that guess sound legit. I doubted I would have noticed the difference, and even now it looked like a plain old wall, without any drag marks on the floor or possible hidden shelves that could swing to the side.

Nate started tapping on the wall, looking for hollow spots, but then gave up, instead asking Hill for his sledgehammer. The lot of us stood back, watching him take a swing, then another, plaster raining down onto the unremarkable linoleum floor—until he hit something more solid. One more powerful swing, and an entire panel—previously hidden well under the plaster—came off the wall, revealing a recessed door. It had an electronic lock but didn't seem too sturdy—whoever had designed it must have expected that the panel's concealment was the better defense—and one more swing was enough to smash the entire locking mechanism. A kick, and the door flew inward—

A salvo of assault-rifle fire raked the room we were all standing in, lined up like the imbeciles we were.

Bullets whizzed by my face but somehow managed to miss me. I dropped into a crouch and threw myself forward, hoping that a lower profile would do the trick of minimizing myself as a target. Landing on my side, my shotgun was already up, and I blindly fired back through the door, sure that I wouldn't hit anything but suppressing their fire was more important right now. Someone was screaming—and someone else shouting orders—but disorientation from surprise and the terrible noise of weapons discharging turned the situation into the worst kind of a mess.

That was, until Nate hurled himself through the door, sledgehammer a-swing, and somehow managed not to get shot in the back by all of us.

I scrambled to my feet and pushed myself forward, immediately taking up a defensive stance as I cleared the door. Two men lay on the ground, both bleeding profusely and very obviously dead. At least I guessed the second had also been a guy, judging from his body size. His head was a smashed ruin, what was missing from it currently dripping from Nate's sledgehammer. Hamilton, Scott, and Marleen came in after us, taking up forward positions, which let me check on Nate. Straightening, his face was locked in a grimace of pain, but he shook his head when I tried to reach for where blood was leaking from bullet holes in his side and left thigh. There was no spurting blood, so that was something, I figured, but really didn't like the feeling of dread settling into my stomach.

No other assailants were hiding in the room or the adjacent corridor which was a great place for us to set up quick defensive positions. No one was stupid enough to linger in the possible direct line of fire from anyone moving toward us from that direction. Everything was clean and white, and while only every third panel that looked like recessed illumination was turned on, it was a lot brighter than our flashlights had managed in the other part of the building. This looked way more "high-tech laboratory" than the sixties nightmare before.

A quick roll call revealed that the damage done was limited. Nate and Hamilton, standing directly in front of the door, had both been hit, but mostly by strafing fire. Sonia quickly confirmed that only the bullet lodged in Nate's side had caused a real wound, but he insisted it wouldn't hold him back for now. One of the marines had gotten hit in the upper arm, taking him out effectively for assault, but we'd need someone to guard the entrance, anyway. The only real casualty turned out to be Fletcher. The fever had left him too slow to react, resulting in three full-on torso hits. He was dead—bloody spittle and wide, staring eyes included—before we'd secured the room beyond the door. I turned away when I saw Blake bend over him, a knife aimed at his neck to sever the spinal cord. It was debatable that the infection had had enough time to spread in his body to achieve reanimation, but the last thing we needed was a zombie chomping into our backs now.

Steps sounding ahead made everyone stop what they were doing and snap to full alertness. At Nate's nod, Blake sent his fireteam forward, Richards and the three of us right on their heels. I barely managed to leave the corridor last and press myself against the opposite wall before bullets hailed down on us, stopping seconds later when Blake's people mowed down the opposition. Cole and Hill went after them with Richards and me providing cover. Again two men in good gear, but not military grade. Blake took point, then us again, making it through five rooms and a short corridor until we got to a T-shaped intersection. As soon as Cole checked around the corner, bullets whizzed through the air, narrowly missing him although he had been cautious. Hill reached for a grenade but Richards signaled him to wait. Calling back to the others to take cover in the last room before the corridor, Richards had Cole check a few more times, with the same result every time.

"Did you see how many?" Richards wanted to know.

Cole shook his head. "I'm not even sure it's a manned station. Could be some automated machine gun or similar. That, or they are paying way more attention than is healthy for us."

Richards turned back to Hill. "Have at it."

Flashing a brief grin, Hill switched places with Cole, and after two checks in the hallway to get a sense of the situation and the timing right, he hurled the grenade down the corridor. Five seconds later, the corridor around us shook with the detonation. When Hill checked again, the gun remained silent.

Cole and Hill did a silent round of "me or you first" that ended with Cole stepping into the corridor. Nothing. As soon as he sprinted down the hallway, one of Blake's marines did the same in the other direction, both men halting at the respective bends in their corridors. It turned out, Cole had been right. Hill's grenade had reduced the machine gun set up behind a low barricade to so much scrap metal, and no body was in sight. I didn't like the idea that they had motion-sensor-activated weapons here, but it couldn't be that many, considering we'd already encountered four human defenders. Pushing forward in a slow, methodical manner was definitely the way to go.

Another intersection—this one with three corridors leading away, but two of them ending in empty storage rooms—and another, longer corridor later that had my skin crawling with the utter lack of cover for over fifty feet, and our corridor opened up into a much larger room, several hallways, doors, and two staircases leading away from it. Richards had us wait for backup. My legs might have appreciated the brief respite but my nerves absolutely didn't, the adrenaline in my veins making me want to keep moving. A few minutes in, Nate's voice—clear and strong, much to my relief—came over the com, ordering everyone in our direction. The other corridor apparently ended in a small suite of rooms but was a dead end and a bust. As soon as the last team—Eden and Amos—caught up to us and Nate got a chance to check on the room, he sent us forward. He, backed up by Burns and Sonia, would secure the large room and staircases while the rest of us scurried into the corridors, continuing our search.

It was obvious that this level was meant for storage, mostly, as besides the odd windowless office, all we found were storerooms. A few had boxes stacked in them, but it was all just random equipment, like latex gloves and plastic vials—exactly like those I'd seen at the camp. I couldn't help but feel that whoever was guarding this complex wasn't very good at it; all they'd needed to do to throw us off would have been to make the staircases look defunct and not hurl any guards at us to shoot, and we might have given up. Well, probably not that easily, but the complex looked large enough that a hundred people could have hidden easily, particularly as they'd already had a good two hours of warning since we'd breached the first door. Had they really expected that we wouldn't find them here?

I wasn't the only one voicing the suspicion that we were walking into a more elaborate trap that hadn't been sprung yet, but there wasn't exactly anything we could do to avoid that, if it was true.

Using one of the rooms adjacent to the hall with the staircases, Nate ordered us to take a short break to refuel. I would have loved to leave my pack there since it felt weighted down with stones by now, but I knew well enough that this was a stupid move. Chances were, we wouldn't be coming back this way, and might even exit onto the street. While everyone except the guards got busy stuffing their faces, Sonia did a more thorough check on Nate's wounds, forcing him to peel himself out of his outer layers so she could assess the entire damage. Glued shut, his thigh didn't look too bad, but the bullet in his side hadn't left an exit wound, so it was still lodged in there. Sonia wanted to dig it out so she could properly clean and close the wound. Nate shut her down and insisted that she just seal the wound up.

I'd have expected the staircases to lead onto a shared landing, but as it turned out, each was the access point to a different wing. The one to the left, viewed from our entrance corridor, seemed to lead to shared common areas at a first glance—including a cafeteria, as Scott reported five minutes in. The right wing was labs and server rooms, so that's where I went, obviously. We encountered another two of those automated machine-gun setups—that Cole forbid me to call "gun turrets" however much I begged—but no other opposition. From the other wing, we heard a lot more gunfire and grenade explosions as they met with heavier opposition. As much as I liked not getting shot at, I was frustrated as hell when every new door we burst through revealed yet another lab… that hadn't been used for pretty much anything since I'd taken basic chemistry in high school. The air processing system had kept them mostly dust-free, but sticky labels were peeling off everywhere, their adhesive long expired. I randomly checked containers, and while it would have all been a gold mine if we could take the reagents with us, it was all inorganic chemistry shit, set up for analysis but not production of anything useful—except maybe meth, but we didn't find anything hinting at drug production. We didn't find even a single room that was set up for anything beyond biosafety level one, which meant nobody had worked on anything more dangerous than the odd E. Coli batch in here. Anything to do with the serum project—and potentially highly-infectious viruses—would have been BSL-3, even if they didn't give a shit about safety. Getting any results would warrant keeping the workspace and samples clean, and you'd need the environment for that.

We also didn't find another exit, or an elevator or stairs to a separate level. Richards went as far as sending Cole up into the vents in the ceiling to check on the ventilation system. From what he could tell, it was contained to this level only. After we radioed our findings in, Nate told us to come join the others in the cafeteria.

We were back in the larger hall and aiming for the stairs to the other wing when the lights went out, the sound of the ventilation system shutting off moments later.

Chapter 14

It took minimal fumbling to get the flashlights out, but Richards had us wait another five minutes before we went up the stairs, mostly to listen for someone trying to sneak up on us. Blake's team—who had been with us in the lab wing—went to join the others right away. Soon after we followed, we could hear the voices of the other teams, finding half of our people in the cafeteria. It was the first room I encountered that had seen use in this century, also evidenced by the three dead bodies stashed in a corner, close to where their blood had spray-painted part of a wall. I didn't pass up the chance to refill my water bottles and grab some provisions, but made sure to keep them separate from what was left of those that I'd brought in; just because ten other people had already eaten them and hadn't ended up dead didn't mean I fully trusted them. No further casualties on our side, but three more wounded and down for the count—and one of them was Sonia. A bullet had strafed her high up on her thigh. While I took the fact that Burns was joking about "her juicy ass saving her life" as a good sign, she was limping heavily and in no condition for the duck-and-run routine required to keep pushing forward. Amos had a sprained ankle and damaged knee from getting into a physical tousle with one of the guards and regaining the upper hand too late, and the remaining marine from Scott's team that wasn't Scott himself had gotten chewed up by another of the auto cannons but was still well enough to drag his sorry ass from one corner of the cafeteria to the other. His face was white as a sheet, and while Sonia had done her best to patch him up, I could tell that his life was definitely hanging in the balance. If it had been up to me, I would have ordered Nate to stay with them, but nobody asked me.

The tally on the other side was more grim. Twenty dead, and not a single one surviving so we could beat some intel out of him. Nate and Hamilton checked up on all of them, and from their grim looks I could tell that they recognized a few—former guards from the camp. At least that meant we really were in the right place.

With thirteen people able to still move freely, it made no sense to keep our fireteams up. Nate didn't protest when I told him I was coming with him and Hamilton now, leaving Richards, Cole, and Hill to fend for themselves. Burns opted to stay with Blake and his two remaining men, while Eden attached herself to Marleen and Scott.

Our team took the lead as we proceeded to the staircase at the opposite end of this wing, the farthest point away from the central hall and the direction we'd initially come from, if my spatial orientation hadn't completely forsaken me. "Staircase" was a bit much for the two sets of ten steps each leading upward, bringing it roughly to street level. There was only one paranoia-inducing corridor, though, and then more steps went back down to the lower level. I halted between the two sets and stared at the wall there, making the others halt, Hamilton the only one looking annoyed. Using my knife, I pried away one of the wall panels, and was greeted with what I'd expected, although they'd tried to hide it: three feet of layered shells, making up the outer cocoon of any self-respecting high-level lab in the world. We'd likely find another, similar if smaller construction further in if they had a BSL-3 and BSL-4 setup.

The lights were still turned off, but when Cole checked one of the cables he dug out of another panel at the bottom of the stairs, he reported that it held an electrical charge. Since we hadn't found a computer room or guard station—just defunct banks of servers that had never encountered an iPod—it was likely in this part of the complex as well.

The corridor leading away from the stairs was only twenty feet long, ending in another T-crossing. Cole was the first to reach it and did a quick spot check, coming up empty. The corridors leading away were both a good hundred feet long with a single corridor leading off about two thirds of the way to the end. There were airlocks on both ends, from the looks of them leading into lab clusters. It wouldn't have made much sense to build an airlock for a maintenance room.

Nate signaled to Richards to come with him and chose the left branch, leaving the other for Blake and Scott. As I'd expected, the corridor at the intersection was a much longer one, leading deep enough into the building that the flashlights barely reached the other end. Nate signaled Richards to stay there and went to the airlock, Hamilton and I trailing behind him. Unlike the lab complex in France, there were no retina scans required to get the lock to cycle. From the lack of warning signs, it was an area that didn't require a hazmat suit. It took Nate and Hamilton both to breach the two parts of the airlock since someone had either gone to great lengths to seal it, or the electricity working it had been shut off with the lights. With them already in front of me, it made sense to let the guys go first, so I waited impatiently until Nate whispered back that the air was clear. Clean, too, I realized as I stepped into the workspace—that special kind of clean that required HEPA filters that had only very recently been turned off. The main room of the workspace looked just like that, but both rooms at the back contained two laminar flow hoods for working with more dangerous shit, an autoclave each sitting between them. To the right was a small office, looking like every office I'd ever had the great fortune to call my own—full of stacks of papers, the shelves overflowing with more.

Ignoring the main workspace, I went to the office first to get a quick idea what they might have been working on. I wasn't familiar with any of the proteins mentioned, but from the names of the publications it was immunology stuff—viruses, yes, but not those ranging into serum-program territory. Most papers were from the last five years before the shit hit the fan, but more reviews and overviews than single-topic publications. It looked like someone might have been working on cross-checking effects, or just setting out to breach a new specialty. That guess also fit with what I found when I checked the two cell-culture rooms—bare-minimum set-ups to run the odd experiment, but not have four people running a million different trials at the same time. They only had a small incubator and a fridge, not even a nitrogen tank for keeping frozen samples.

In short, interesting for me personally, maybe, but not the reason why we were here.

When we returned to the others, Richards had already sent Cole and Hill forward to go snooping into the rooms ahead and secure the corridor to where the next cluster of lab rooms was, again to our left, putting it right adjacent to the office of the first lab. No airlocks on this one, letting us see right into the rooms through the rows of glass panes. The massive metal doors to the right—to the middle of the complex wing—led into storage rooms, filled with the usual equipment of large centrifuges, freezers, and my beloved nitrogen tanks. Hamilton frowned at me when I unscrewed the lid of the first tank and peeked inside.

"Ha!" Three pairs of eyes shot to me, making me snort. "The tanks are topped up. Someone's still using them. Those in France were half empty, and that was years ago. Someone is still refilling these."

Rather than pull the rack inside out, I went to check on the inventory book where the samples were marked. I didn't see any dates but several different styles of handwriting, and none designating the samples as anything that jogged my memory. I left the room after that, figuring that finding someone—alive—would be easier in order to find out what they'd been up to.

Scott radioed in that they were making their way through equal setups—which made sense as most labs were built in boring, symmetrical ways. In case of an emergency, it made no sense to confuse people.

Once it became clear that the labs were pretty much useless, Nate sped up the process, only checking for possible nooks and crannies rather than letting me get lost in perusing the research itself. Scott and Blake were even faster, reaching the end of their corridor ahead of us. That way, they got shot at when they checked the corridor continuing on from the middle of the lab spaces, but not where that turned into another, similar two-pronged layout beyond.

Hearing gunfire jolted me alert immediately, but my body was more sluggish to spring into action, making me stagger when one of my feet caught on a table leg. I managed to catch myself before I could face-plant on the floor, but didn't miss Hamilton chuckling under his breath as he pushed past me to check on what was going on ahead. Nate was already outside with Richards and the others, so it was just me. Cursing under my breath, I sprinted after them, trusting that we had been thorough in our check.

That's when I came face to face with the fatigues-clad figure right now crawling out of the open floor panel.

If I'd had a moment to think, I would have tried punching him out instead, but the shotgun was in my hands and he startled me, so he ate a slug before my mind could get smart. Looking behind me down the corridor, I saw four other guards, all in different stages of coming out of the floor. If I'd had a rifle, I would have considered spraying them with bullets, but the shotgun lacked range, and by the time I'd have fumbled the dead guard's rifle from the sling across his body, I would be shot and dead myself. So I sent one slug toward the closest guard, whipped around, and ran, hoping that by the time any of them got ready to aim and fire, I'd be around the corner.

"They are behind us! In the floor!" I shouted, trusting that someone would hear me and get ready to guard our rear and flank. I almost collided with Marleen as I careened around the corner. She quickly sidestepped, letting me slip into cover before she glanced into the corridor. She only got five shots out before the return fire made her pull back.

"Got one," she shouted over the din of the bullets smashing chunks out of wall paneling everywhere. "One's down, and one's on the ground but still shooting."

"That leaves one," I summed up, getting ready to reduce that number to zero as soon as he was close enough to pulverize his brains.

"You got this," Marleen told me and ran to the other corridor, immediately drawing fire when she checked on that. "Five here!" she called over before she set to decimating them.

Unlike the automated guns, the human opponents weren't as quick in shooting when I glanced into the corridor, finding the single standing guard still a little far away. The shooting at Marleen's side was loud—and near-continuous—enough to make me chance it, though. No sense in waiting for a kill shot here if I got gunned down from the other side in the meantime. To steady my aim—and present less of a target—I crouched down before I stepped into the corridor, aimed, and shot. A good call, it turned out, as he was still hitting where my head had been on the check before, ending with him dead on my second shot, and the one I'd wounded before down on the third.

The guard Marleen had killed was close enough that I risked wasting a few moments in favor of going for his assault rifle and the two spare magazines in his MOLLE vest. Not bothering with the one currently in the M4, I ejected it and slammed a fresh one in, and went to back up Marleen.

"Two down, three to go," she told me as I patted her on the shoulder, letting her know I was ready. "You up, me down, on three!" I had barely enough time to register what she meant as she dropped to the floor and started her countdown. Without bothering to aim, I took a step into the corridor and shot everything at shoulder height that moved. I was almost surprised when her ploy worked and we killed the remaining guards before they could return the favor—or rather, pay it forward. My brain didn't much care for me taking the risk, sending a shake through me that didn't feel very pleasant. But we were still alive and mostly unscathed, so who cared?

"We need to catch up to the others," I told Marleen, and after a last look in both corridors—finding them still empty of new dangers, and positively chewed-up from weapon fire—pushed on forward. Immediately, the acrid scent of too many weapons getting discharged without proper ventilation in too little space tickled my nostrils. It was easy enough to catch up to the others since they'd only managed to make it to where the long corridors started, needing the two corners on each side for cover. Two bodies were on the floor but still alive, clutching makeshift bandages—Blake and one of his guys. Marleen quickly joined them, walking backwards so she could keep an eye on what might be coming behind. I did the same, going in the other direction.

"They're using the maintenance shaft in the floor," I shouted at Nate as soon as I reached the corner. "We killed nine and it looks clear, but we need to check our six better." He didn't react but I presumed he'd heard me. Sending another volley down the corridor seemed more important. "What's our opposition?"

"Two of the automated guns, and three or four men behind that. We already took out one gun, and killed two," he explained.

Just then, Hill got ready to pitch another grenade down the corridor, making the others flatten themselves against the walls to avoid any shrapnel hurtling back toward us. That reduced the number of auto-guns to one, and soon to zero after two more grenades. He'd already used up all he had been carrying—very smart, considering he'd also been our C4 supply—and I offered him the two from my pack when he looked around for more to scavenge. The other group must have resorted to similar tactics since I heard two explosions go off there as well—followed by an eerie silence settling over us, only the low crackling of something flammable catching on fire audible.

"Go!" Nate hissed, and Richards sprinted down the corridor. Glancing over my shoulder to the other group, I saw Scott disappear as he did the same, the others getting ready, except for Marleen who was kneeling next to Blake, doing her best to help him to patch up a wound on his leg. As soon as she was done, she helped Blake pull himself closer to the center of the corridor so he could aim his rifle into the section behind us.

I was the last to leave, only needing to step over scrap metal and dead bodies as we made our way forward. As heavy as the opposition had been, no backup arrived, allowing me to chance a glance into the lab spaces—from the outside only as all of them were fitted with airlocks, and nobody made attempts to pry them open for me. Inside, it was all orderly cell culture with lots of incubators—production and high-throughput testing spaces, unlike the labs we'd passed before. The last two even went a security level above that, the three separate lab spaces only accessible through more airlocks, and the hoods I saw inside were closed glove-boxes, making me guess those were makeshift BSL-3 setups. Now we were talking, but no way did I have any intention of stepping in there without extra protection. I was already infested with enough shit that was killing me slowly. No need to add to that. Not just because of that I was happy to see that the security glass of the inner sections looked unaffected by the bullets and even grenades, built to withstand far worse. The corridor was littered with shards, crunching unhealthily under my boots.

Like in the other part of the wing, the corridors merged into a single one again—only this one was fitted with not just an airlock, but also a security checkpoint and heavy steel doors beyond the airlock, making me guess that we'd reached the innermost sanctum—the BSL-4 part of the building. It occurred to me that we still hadn't come across the central control room, and we had been thorough about searching for it. Whoever must have figured it was worth setting that up inside the bomb-proof cocoon that likely housed plenty of viral shit that was way more likely to kill everyone than a nuclear strike must have been one paranoid fucker.

It absolutely fit the bill, but meant that we needed to get through that checkpoint.

I felt like joking to Cole that I'd known there was a reason why we let him tag along when he got out a laptop and somehow connected it to a cable that he pulled out of the wall, minimal sparking required. Hill and Scott meanwhile worked on prying the airlock open, but it was a heavier one than those we'd encountered before, needing four people in the end. Nate wasn't one of them, staying back, turning his body so the others didn't see how he pressed one hand against the bandages in his side, grimacing. I caught his gaze, giving him another wide-eyed, semi pleading "stay back!" with my eyes, which he of course ignored. I used the opportunity to dig into my pack and get the extra rifle ammo out that I'd been lugging with me for such opportunities as the one that had presented itself in the form of my new M4. The others had already searched the dead and relieved them of their spare ammo. Not knowing what opposition we'd be facing, we had packed heavy, and nobody was running empty yet—also due to the fact that we were below half strength now, manpower-wise.

"Ha, gotcha," Cole muttered with a triumphant smile, typing even more furiously. "Sure, why upgrade your cyber security when you're sitting three levels deep inside a bunker? I should have the lights back in three… two… one…" It actually took five seconds longer, but then the illumination panels all around us came on with a random series of flickers, quickly followed by the low hum of the ventilation system.

It was the latter, probably, that got Scott to halt and glance back to me. "Hey, Lewis—you're the biohazard expert here, right?" I nodded. "Just how much junk did we breathe in since getting to this level?"

I shrugged. "Not much more than you'd get on any shooting range." When he eyed me quizzically, I grinned. "You mean because of the labs? The ones with the airlocks likely have their own, closed-off systems that weren't affected by the shut-down. The hot lab we presume is behind that door? That has its own entire ecosystem, including waste management and air. Nothing comes in, nothing goes out. Until you go through the decontamination chamber, you won't get anywhere close to the shit that will kill every single one of us." Or so I hoped, but there was no sense in spreading my personal brand of paranoia around. I could guess how much of that was based on reality; the others couldn't.

Burns stepped up to me, still looking around alertly but a little more relaxed now that we were stuck here in a position that wasn't that hard to defend—for now. "Do you ever get tired of ending up in places like this?" he asked, allowing himself a small chuckle. "This is now how many times that I've asked you if you get nostalgic about no longer working in high-security labs?"

"Fuck you," I told him succinctly, answering his grin with one of my own.

"Any progress on the locks?" Hamilton wanted to know, still busy on the second half of the airlock, calling right over our chat.

Cole glanced up for a moment, then back down at his laptop. "Give me a sec," he muttered. "I need to crack the security override first. Because you went all ape-shit on the outer door, it won't let me disengage the system." That said, the inner doors gave a squeal, followed by the mechanical sounds of getting pried apart. The heavy metal doors swung inward as well, making everyone standing idly by raise their weapons. Cole cursed but didn't explain why.

No guards greeted us. Also no automated machine guns, nor a pack of mutant dobermans. Just the boxy complex of the BSL-4 lab with its impressive banks of air filters on top, surrounded by gray-tiled corridors, and two separate partitions on each end that were likely for maintenance or offices. Whoever had built this hadn't bothered to make the inside of the security cocoon look pretty, leaving concrete and metal struts exposed.

"Two remain here," Nate ordered, singling out Eden and the last Silo marine. Eden looked ready to protest, but a look at Nate's face had her close her mouth without a word coming out. The rest of us—eight, minus Cole staying behind with his laptop—went through the open airlock and doors, quickly separating into two groups to cover the open space around the lab as quickly as possible. With the others paying attention to everything except the lab, I allowed myself a few lingering glances through the few viewports. Unlike most BSL-4 labs I'd seen, this one was more closed off. It was also larger, about double the size of the already substantial lab of the Green Fields Biotech complex where I'd been working until Nate had to bring down the sky on it. I could only guess at what they needed the extra space for. It was hard to tell, but what equipment I saw looked outdated if well-maintained.

Nobody shot at us during our entire circuit of the lab complex. If anything, that seemed to make all of us even more jumpy than we already were. I was surprised to see that on the other side, at the back wall, was another heavy metal door, like the one with the airlock. Nate explained the situation to Cole on the radio. Cole tried to get the doors open but gave up after five minutes. "They're locked out of the system. My guess is you'll need to flip a switch in the control room to open them. But I can put a temporary lock on the controls so that they can't disengage them unless they have a hacker around who's better than I am."

"Do it," Nate said, then took a look around before focusing on me. "Which end do we bust down first?"

Glancing at the ceiling, I tried to judge whether one sectioned-off part looked bigger than the other, but they seemed identical. "You choose."

Since we were standing closer to the left one, Nate chose that, setting Scott and Marleen to guard the other for now.

Because of the required height of the cocoon, the single door to the section looked comically small although it was as broad as the airlock. While nobody had bothered to build a ceiling to hide the air recycling system, they had bothered with a floor; else we would have had to traipse across the sewage system—not a good idea, under any conditions. Nate hesitated, which gave Hamilton the perfect excuse to go first. I might have considered shooting off the lock; Hamilton tried the door first, finding it unlocked. We all watched, weapons at the ready, as it swung inward, revealing a normal-sized room. Even before I could more than catch a glance inside I knew that something was wrong. The scent of blood was so heavy that it tickled my nostrils just from what air filtered through the door.

At first, I thought someone had made the questionable interior decorating choice of painting the walls red. That must have been my mind blocking off reality because it was beyond what I'd come to encounter. But then I saw the bodies on the ground, dropped where they had been standing, most facing away from the door. It was over twenty, and only one was clad in dark fatigues. The rest were all in either scrubs or plain clothes, some wearing formerly white lab coats that had done a stellar job soaking up the blood—the scientists who must have been working in here. The blood was still fresh but had started to congeal, making me guess that they'd died over an hour ago. Since we hadn't heard any shots, whoever had executed them must have done so while we'd breached the outer doors with our charges.

I'd thought I had seen it all, but the sheer amount of senseless slaughter horrified me in a way that nothing else had. Maybe some of it came from the fact that, however much my life had changed, it was still easy for me to see myself as a part of them.

I wasn't the only one thus affected. Burns cursed under his breath, and even Hill had nothing disparaging to add. Everyone seemed loath to step into the blood, as if our proximity would somehow desecrate the space even more. From just inside the door, it was obvious that the room had been some kind of mixed office and recreational space, a sofa in the corner the only thing substantial enough that anyone could have hidden behind it, and since it was pushed against the wall I doubted that was possible.

Hamilton was the first to tear himself out of his stunned stupor and checked the sofa after all. I followed—not because I hadn't already seen enough to give me new nightmares, but to check if I recognized any of the faces, where enough of them remained to identify anyone. I was praying that I wouldn't, but no such luck. I didn't remember the name of the young woman ten years my senior, but she had been part of the lab in Aurora, that blasted Kansas town where we'd gotten inked and officially ostracized by what remained of society. Two other men also looked familiar, likely from the same place. Since one of their people—a young scientist named Ethan— had ended up with Taggard's merry band of kidnapping and raping assholes, it wasn't that much of a surprise, mostly an unpleasant one. Ethan had ended up skinned alive and hung, his zombified self trying to eat us even so. At least these bastards had died in a quicker and more merciful fashion, although I didn't allow myself to make a judgment call on the level of insanity involved. None of them were from the Silo, and as Hamilton's search confirmed, also not from among Emily Raynor's minions.

It was the very last body, slumped in the corner as if he'd been trying to hide behind the others, that made me pause, then shy away as if burned. Nate noticed, immediately training his rifle on the corpse, but it wasn't active danger that had made me back away. He frowned down at the body, then looked at me, confused.

"Don't you recognize him?" I asked, my voice flat going on hollow. When Nate shook his head, I looked down at the body again, just to be sure. No question, it was him. "That's Walter Greene. Biotech pioneer and a long-time runner-up for a ton of awards, down to a possible Nobel Prize. Co-Founder of Green Fields Biotech. Gabriel Greene's father."

I was almost glad when two pistol shots rang out from the direction of the BSL-4 lab. That was something my mind had far less problems wrapping itself around than finding one of our age's most brilliant scientists here, of all places.

Chapter 15

Having been at the opposite side of the room, I was the last to make it back out through the door. By then, Burns and Richards were already sprinting toward where we'd left Marleen and Scott outside. Since Cole immediately reported in that the checkpoint was still secure, it made the most sense to check on the heavy steel doors in passing, but they remained untouched as well. From halfway around the lab I already saw the door to the partition on the other side open, but my attention was drawn to the figures on the ground. Two guards were dead a few steps away from the door behind which they must have been hiding. More worrisome, Scott lay on his back, blood spurting from a wound in his neck, while Marleen tried to do CPR. The amount of blood on her hands spoke of more wounds on the marine commander's torso. She gave up just as Burns reached her, her head whipping around with frustration. "One of them got away!" she shouted. "He ran toward the door to the lab!"

Being last meant I was also the quickest to switch course and turn in the direction she indicated. I thought I saw someone disappear behind a corner, but that could have been just my imagination since I didn't hear the slap of footsteps—but that was easily masked by our own pounding. Nate was right there with me, overtaking me with the entrance to the lab in sight. Hamilton pushed past me just as Nate flung open the door, forcing me to slow down a little. The good news was I had no need to case the two rooms they rushed through, and could fully concentrate on the blood smeared across a doorframe, alongside a wall—and the red light above the decontamination room just as it flashed back to green, indicating that someone had just entered and the airlock was ready for the next person or group to do so.

Hamilton saw it as well and rushed toward the door. My mind told me to shut up, but as much as I wanted to see him dead, this was different.

"Don't!" I shouted before he could reach the door.

I was certain that in any other environment, he would have ignored me, but apparently around deadly viruses, my word counted for something, even with an asshole like him. It was still more anger than respect that I read on his face. "Why not?"

"It's not like he can get away," I offered. "This is the only way in and out of there. I doubt they'll have a bomb hidden in there that will kill us all on detonation. Short of that, there is no fucking reason for any of us to deliberately kill ourselves. I mean, who does that? Bring two bags full of C4 into a BSL-4 lab. Present company included." Nate smirked but said nothing. Hamilton scowled but I could tell that my message was getting through to him. Just to make sure that was the case, I added, "Plus, you two both have open, bleeding wounds. Even if that lab has been unused for years—and I have a feeling that this is not the case—you will contract something, even if it's just vapors remaining from the last cleaning cycle. Give me ten minutes and I'll have three suits prepped. Then you can waddle in there and behave like as much of a blundering ass as you like."

"Do it," Nate said before Hamilton could reply. I immediately set to work, right after dropping my weapon and pack, and tearing off my gloves to replace them with two sets of latex gloves.

"If we dare risk overheating, we can stay in our gear, but the packs are too much," I called back over my shoulder. "No knives or sidearms, either. It's too risky as they could tear the suits, and you won't be able to use them unless you carry them in your hands, anyway." I felt like snarking that Hamilton knew his way around guns and hazmat suits since he had brought one into the hot lab in the Paris complex, but following the previously routine steps that had dictated my life for years seemed more important.

In no time I had the first positive pressure suit checked and set it aside, watching from the corner of my eye as Nate and Hamilton got down to T-shirts and pants. "Boots, too," I advised, continuing in the meantime.

The door to the changing room outside opened, admitting Richards. "Need help?" he offered.

"Help them with taping their socks and gloves, and then to get in the suits. And then do me." Maybe not the best way to phrase that but I was otherwise occupied. I didn't miss Red's smirk, which disappeared as soon as he went to follow my instructions, coming face to face with a rather glowering Nate. Richards used the distraction that offered to give us an update on the situation.

"Scott is gone, as are the three guards—we found a third one inside the room. Marleen said one got away, wearing civilian clothes, so he's likely a scientist."

It wasn't my most thorough checkup ever, but I figured that the suit integrity and the general setup was enough to keep us safe. Contrary to what people may have believed, hot labs produced surprisingly few infections. Work accidents usually involved animal bites or blunt force trauma of people bumping into shelves and tables. Unless, of course, someone shot at you, or you tried to tear your suit off because you were hallucinating, thinking that scorpions were crawling all over your body underneath the heavy-duty plastic. The latter had almost cost me my life and job when my supervisor effectively poisoned me. I'd never gotten a chance to ask her about her motives, but the theory that she'd done it to save herself from having to murder me was the one I chose to believe. I doubted that the scientist we were after now had that answer for me, but who knew?

"Let's try to catch him alive," I said as I finished with the second suit and handed that to Nate. "He's wounded, without a suit, so I doubt he'll survive, but that doesn't mean he won't talk if we threaten him."

Hamilton laughed harshly, pausing for a moment in zipping up his suit. "Exactly how do you threaten someone who knows he's as good as dead?"

Not bothering with actually looking at him, I shrugged. "Lots of shit in there to hurt someone. I've always wondered what would happen if you dipped someone's hand too long into a liquid nitrogen tank. Simply getting that shit on your clothes burns, but it evaporates too fast to leave more than red skin. I wonder if you could break off fingers like that."

Hamilton continued to laugh, mumbling something that sounded like "psycho bitch" under his breath. Yeah, I'd realized how that sounded as I'd said it, but any filters I had still left had gone to shit somewhere across Dallas. A glance at Nate revealed that he wasn't bothering to give me any emotional feedback in favor of getting his suit on. I didn't miss the dark stains all over his shirt, most not sweat, particularly around the tears and bandages. I told myself that he would be okay since he could still move fluently enough to get in the suit—and run faster than me, too—and the bandages weren't soaked through yet.

I hated that I needed Red's assistance with taping up the pair of fresh socks I grabbed from a rack, and the gloves. Zipping up the suit only underlined how fucking useless my hands had become, muscle memory still in my brain not working any longer with several digits missing. By the time I connected the suit to an air hose to inflate it, Nate and Hamilton were ready, piling all available weapons that they could carry and use at the same time into their arms. As soon as I dared, I unplugged the hose and lumbered into the decontamination room, waiting for the others to follow before I cycled the airlock.

Call me jaded, but I went first, unarmed, trusting that handguns would not be my end in here. Because he hadn't bothered with a suit, the trail of blood—smeared on walls and corners, but also in droplets on the floor—made it easy to follow the path the scientist had taken. I still checked the signs around us to get a feel for the layout of the lab. Two of the closed-off parts with no viewports were labeled "Test 1" and "Test 2" respectively. I didn't want to venture a guess why, but it seemed ominously obvious—including the heavy locks in an environment that had a lot of doors that closed tightly, but didn't lock from the outside.

The trail led deeper into the lab, past animal processing and a handful of work rooms. Without my suit connected to the air hoses, it heated up in record time but this way I heard a crash coming from up ahead and to the right before I saw the blood smear veer off in that direction. I had a certain inkling that turned out to be true as I passed from one hallway to the next, reaching the heart of the lab: the viral vault.

My first instinct was to head right there but instead I grabbed a hose to at least top up the air supply inside my suit—dying of carbon dioxide poisoning wouldn't do me any good, and neither would getting dizzy or barfing before that. Getting shot sounded about as pleasant, so I signaled the guys to go ahead. After all, it should pay off that they were lugging around their weight in weapons.

Hamilton went first, shouting at someone to stop doing whatever was going on. A crash followed inside, making me guess he was disobeying, and maybe scrambling for cover. Hamilton repeated his barked order, louder now, and he and Nate disappeared through the door. Allowing myself a last moment of feeling the blissfully cool air run up my body, I disconnected the hose and followed them.

What I noticed first was just how fucking huge the vault was. The ones in my old workplace and the lab in France had been the size of a small office maybe. This vault was easily ten times as large, holding way more than the ten or so liquid nitrogen tanks that I'd expected. I had no idea how large the storage vaults at the CDC were that held samples of all known diseases, but this one looked sized to easily rival that. Most of the tanks were undisturbed, lined up in neat double rows easily but likely not often accessed. A single man was half crouching in front of, half leaning against one of the tanks toward the wall in the third row from the door, four tanks seemingly at random open with their racks removed, currently lying discarded on the floor. The crash I'd heard must have been the last of the racks. Bloody handprints showed his progression from the first row of tanks to the open ones, with an extra trail along the third row—over to where an autoclave was starting up, already locked and well into destroying the samples likely dropped into it for disposal.

The man looked familiar but it took me a few moments to jump-start my memory. The connection to Gabriel Greene—and my old workplace—finally did it: Brandon Stone. Gone was the ill-fitting suit he'd so loved to wear around the Green Fields Biotech complex, but he was still tall and gangly, and the pained smirk he directed at us reminded me of the disdainful ignorance he'd—mostly—viewed us scientist worker bees with. His hair was longer now, grown out of the stylishly tousled business cut he'd maintained even after the world had gone to shit—when I'd last seen him, in Aurora, Kansas, where he'd pretended to head up the lab there. A job that he'd offered me, and that I was glad—now more than ever—I'd never seriously considered taking. At least I'd always presumed that it had been pretense only. What had a lawyer-slash-economics guy had to do with running scientific research? Maybe that had been the pretense. Somehow, I didn't buy that Cortez and his flunkies at the camp had been relying on a seventy-plus-year-old geezer. But a late-thirty-something?

Damn, but was every single person I'd ever met in my life going to turn out to be a lying, scheming, murdering asshole? I was expecting that with Nate, but me?

A glance at Nate and Hamilton confirmed that they definitely recognized him—and likely not from where I remembered him if the open hatred was an indicator. I stepped closer to them but made sure to remain at enough distance so they could bring their arsenal to bear on Stone if the need arose. I idly wondered if I should tell them to be careful should they discharge a gun in here so that a possible ricochet from a tank or shelf didn't kill us. I figured they were smart enough to know.

I would have loved to strike a pose, arms crossed over my chest and cocky as hell, but the suits kind of made that impossible. Connected to an air hose, it was even worse. Standing there with my arms hanging by my side wasn't quite the same but what I had to go for instead. The face shield of the suit probably concealed half of my features. There was an obvious reason why interrogations were usually not performed under these conditions.

"Fancy meeting you here," I offered in as even a voice as I could manage. Not sounding tired as hell was a feat, and being angry for what they'd done to Nate only went so far now that I was running on fumes only. Not even Hamilton's proximity was enough to give me a certain edge. Judging from how much more leaning than standing Stone managed, it didn't look necessary, to be honest. "What should

I call you now with all your recent career changes? Should I go all friendly with Brandon, or do you still fancy Dr. Stone although you haven't done shit to deserve that title? Then again, the Chemist does have a certain simplicity to it." I could tell from the light jerk that ran through Nate when final recognition set in, but that was all he gave.

Stone flashed me a bloody grin that turned into a wheezing cough, blood bubbling out of his mouth. My guess was that he had a perforated lung. Too bad, really. As long as he could still talk… which I hoped he could. Otherwise this really was a bust.

"I should have expected you to show up here," Stone ground out, making me just a little happy—both with his words, and the fact that he was still able to answer.

"That's what you get for making shit personal," I pointed out. "I would have been happy to live the rest of my life in the middle of nowhere, hunting deer and skinny dipping in the summer." Sure enough, Hamilton had to grunt at that, which was audible even with the suits and all. I ignored him, my focus remaining on Stone. "But you can't expect to kidnap the person most important to me and use him as a guinea pig and not call the wrath of me down on yourself." Maybe I was laying it on a little heavily, but who cared? Stone looked bad, but not die-within-the-next-minute bad. I'd limped away from way worse myself.

I didn't care for the nasty grin appearing on Stone's face. I really had liked him better when I'd thought he was just a sleek paper pusher. "You do know that's not all we did to him, right?"

I waited for either of the guys to say something, but Hamilton seemed for once content to let me do the talking—with running grunt commentary, of course—and for Nate it wasn't that unusual. Glancing from Stone to the arsenal they were both toting, I shrugged as I turned to my husband. "May I borrow your combat knife? For whatever reason I'm suddenly overcome with the urge to ram it up his ass, blade first."

Nate had to turn around so I could catch his smirk. "Be my guest."

Stone looked alarmed for a second—which should not have been this gratifying but sure was—but relaxed when he realized I wasn't about to lumber over to him so I could sodomize him with an edged weapon. Maybe later. Instead, I did my best to sound diplomatic, although I felt anything but. "How about we at least attempt to remain civil? We're all intelligent people here. This doesn't have to end in needless bloodshed." Since that had already happened—and there wasn't much else to do except deal with Stone—I felt that wasn't even a lie. Stone didn't believe me, of course, proving a different kind of smart.

"You're too late," he offered, sounding tired yet vindicated. "Everything you have been looking for is already destroyed."

My gaze flitted over to the autoclave, happily continuing doing its thing. "Honestly, unless there's a cure for the zombie virus in there, I'm not interested. For that, I'd maybe try to shut that thing off and rescue whatever possible, even if it's denatured shit by now." I narrowed my eyes at him, although I wasn't sure whether he'd even see that. "Do you have the cure? Unlikely since I doubt you've been looking for it, but I have to ask. For my inner peace, and shit."

Stone blinked, torn between being irritated with me, and confusion. "Why would you not—" he started, then cut himself off. "No, there's no cure. You know that." His expression turned shrewd. "You do know, but that's not what you meant, right? You know that you're a dead woman walking, don't you? Whatever you do, the serum will soon kill you."

It was surprisingly easy to shrug that off. What a difference a few days made—that, and bone-deep exhaustion. Permanent death to escape the painful weight my body had gained wasn't sounding that bad right now. "Which just makes me twice as deadly and ten times as dangerous, to you," I stressed, following that up with a jovial gesture as I spread my arms. "Let's be civil. You tell us everything you know, including what you've been doing here and why you thought murdering every single scientist working for you was a bright idea.

And maybe I kill you quickly, without finding out first whether I can freeze off your dick with liquid nitrogen."

Stone didn't seem perturbed by the threat. Maybe I should have held out on my musing until now, or offer up a repetition? Nate had other plans, though, coming out of his glowering stupor. "You could start by telling us where Decker is."

Stone smirked, leaning back against the tank that was the only thing holding him upright now. "Ah, wouldn't you like to know?"

"We would," Hamilton answered. "And if her rambling has given you any wrong ideas, we have absolutely no qualms beating the answers we seek out of you."

"Oh, I trust that you don't," Stone said, his grin spreading. I wondered briefly whether he was having a psychotic break. I could see how people still underestimated me—stupid move, but it happened—but he knew damn well who my companions were, and what they were capable of, and he didn't seem to suffer from any delusions that he would get out of this alive. A smart man would have tried to bargain for a quick, painless end. His situation was the definition of nothing left to lose.

"What do you know that we don't?" Stone's attention snapped back to me but he didn't answer. "You could really profit from appeasing us, whichever way possible."

He pursed his lips, still deliberating. "Actually, I think he'd want me to share this with you. Oh, yes. It would be quite the reunion. Too bad I won't be there to see it." He briefly glanced at Nate, then Hamilton, but continued speaking to me. "Sadly, I have never been informed of where his hideout is. You could consider that the best-kept secret in the world right now. But I have a feeling that he will find a way to reach out to you, now that you've proven to become a prime nuisance. Please, ask what you want to know and I shall answer it to the best of my knowledge."

Very gracious of him—and I wasn't going to look that gift horse in the mouth. Not yet, at least. "Why kill the scientists? With Walter

Greene you had a veritable legend locked in here. Why the fuck would you murder him like any useless gutter rat?"

"Orders," Stone offered, ending with a wet cough. "I had them. The guards had them. And I'm sure several of the scientists did, too. The only reason why I'm still alive was because I was chosen to be last."

"Because you're so damn important, huh?" Hamilton goaded him on.

Stone's grin resurfaced. "Because I'm expendable, and because I'm about as fucking useless to you as they come." His attention turned back to me. "Walter Greene was a true visionary. The serum project wouldn't have developed in the direction it eventually took, and our efforts would have been fraught without him. Leaving him alive for you to brainwash him into helping you and thus destroying his greatest creation? Impossible. If we hadn't offered him a merciful death, he would have done it himself."

That answer didn't sit right with me on so many levels. One certainty was the feverish tone it was delivered in. Another, the sheer senseless loss and stupidity of the idea. But what really made bile rise in the back of my throat was that it reminded me an awful lot of the speech Dr. Alders—the mad scientist we'd found in NORAD, who had been one of the founding brains behind the serum project—had given that had made exactly as much sense: none whatsoever. Maybe that shouldn't have come as a surprise as it seemed the next step to connect the dots and throw them all into the same pile of assholes that deserved to die...

And still, something didn't add up.

"Let's suppose I believe that—"

Stone cut me off with a snort. "You'll have to take my word for it, seeing as I'm the last man standing." His head snapped in the direction of the red room. "And you must have seen the evidence with your own eyes. So why doubt me?"

Why indeed? Sadly, the truth didn't do shit to set me free in this case.

"What exactly have you been doing here? The scientists, I mean. I'm starting to understand that you've only ever been the face of everything that's wrong with this world, but not bright enough to be directly involved."

If that hit him, he didn't show it, his amusement only growing. "What exactly have we been doing?" he said in a musing tone. All that was missing to turn him into a movie villain was a small mustache and his fingers stroking his chin. "Ah, right," he went on, as if he'd just remembered. "We were busy working on wiping the vermin off the earth, and in a way that even the most idealistic, stupid moron couldn't refute the evidence anymore." Somehow, I got the impression he was talking about me specifically with that.

"You mean the scavengers?"

He snorted, as if that suggestion amused him. "Nothing but pawns," he insisted. "It would have been a waste not to sweep them off alongside seeing as the opportunity presented itself." I was suddenly glad Eden wasn't in here to hear that—and I hoped that Hamilton would manage not to spill that can of worms first chance he had. It was bad enough that thousands of good fighters were doomed. No need to rub their faces in why since there was nothing they or anyone else could do about it.

"You mean the serum project, and everyone who's gotten inoculated with it," I offered up next. Stone smiled, as if I'd morphed into his favorite overachieving student. I couldn't help but frown. "How does that make sense? The serum project is Decker's baby. Personal resentments aside, why kill thousands of capable soldiers who have more than done their duty?"

Stone cocked his head to the side, studying me. "And what duty have you performed, Dr. Lewis? Besides becoming a huge pain in the ass to some, and a real menace to those you profess to care about. What makes you deserving of the advantages the serum conveys?" He let that sink in for a moment—or needed to pause because breathing was becoming increasingly harder for him. "You, like few other people, symbolize why what we do is necessary. The serum was always meant for the elite few who proved worthy of it. Instead, thousands have received it who did nothing but squander this amazing chance." His focus dropped from me to the men at my side, and his smile took on a nasty lilt. "It was a mistake, but one that proved hard to correct. As you know, this is one of those matters where it takes one to eliminate one, and yet, you are both still standing, after several attempts to correct that."

Neither Nate nor Hamilton reacted—not even to trade glances with each other—but I couldn't keep my trap shut about that. "What do you mean? Obviously, we know that Miller spent a while in fallen-from-grace territory. But we know that Decker wants him back. Why else would either of them still be alive?" If nothing else, Stone had just confirmed for me that, whoever had been in charge for real at the camp—Cortez had just been a figurehead on the power trip of his life—had known exactly who they'd had sitting in their prison cells.

Stone gave me a look as if I had deeply disappointed him. "Are you still not getting it? Every single clash that has happened between the both of you was a chance to prove yourself worthy of being welcomed back into the fold," Stone declared. His tone then turned disdainful. "And what you did was squander it. Giving Hamilton the rescue mission when we knew for a while that the Green Fields Biotech lab would get hit? Sending Miller's misguided ragtag band of misfits right into the trap at the factory? Leaking the position of the Colorado base, knowing full well Miller would easily pick it out of any possible lineup of destinations? Giving Hamilton the chance to cut Miller's one weakness right out of his life?" Stone's attention snapped to me. "You really proved more of a nuisance than anyone could have expected, Dr. Lewis. How you made it to Emily Raynor's lab is beyond me, and how nobody caved in your skull in France or on the way back will forever remain a mystery—particularly as someone had very specific orders about that and a lot of opportunity."

I was less surprised to hear that than the bark of laughter coming from Hamilton. "Well, someone must have reasoned that if a very specific thing is that important to a certain entity, why not let them take care of it themselves?" Or make that the fact that he could communicate in something other than grunts and insults.

Nate took a step forward, which seemed to be more of an involuntary reaction than intent. "This all has been a game to him, to see which of us would be the more ruthless and kill the other? His best friend and only rival?" Stone didn't offer a verbal response, but his expression said it all—Nate had just hit the nail on the head. "Why?" Nate asked, but more to himself. "I gave up that race a decade ago—and Decker knows it. I threw in the towel, and he accepted it. He was disappointed, but the day I asked to be assigned from strike force to search and rescue, he agreed he'd misjudged how some of his methods might backfire, and that this was the logical step in the right direction." I didn't exactly know what he was talking about, but the time frame made sense—what happened with Bucky's sister definitely broke Nate's back and shifted his moral compass; or maybe even made him remember that he had one, in the first place. He'd more than once stressed that Hamilton had been damn ambitious and only too happy to kick Nate off the number one spot. From what I knew, Decker had mercilessly played the two against each other whenever and wherever possible to force them to one-up and outperform each other, but that seemed to have ended with them both entering the serum program. A good leader knew when to push, and when too much would just break useful tools instead, and Decker had definitely known when to back off, particularly as that left him with two top dogs still in play rather than one, broken by the other's loss.

It wasn't Stone who answered but Hamilton instead. "The old man never forgave you for letting me win," he remarked, sounding less snide than usual, and almost pensive. "I think that was the real betrayal for him. Not that you changed your mind, wanted your old job back, and then found a way to completely screw him over. That you pulled that off likely gained you some of his admiration. I've always wondered why he didn't send me after you before the shit hit the fan. He knew that I was suicidal enough to get the job done and not care whether I made it back or not."

I wondered if there was something in the air supply that made people spout bullshit they'd otherwise never admit to. Nate went as far as turning toward Hamilton so he could see the look on his face. Hamilton gave a shrug, as if to say it was all the same to him whether that cat was out of the bag now or not. That, in turn, brought up a different question in me that I just had to ask. "What changed?" That something had changed was obvious. His hatred for me aside, Hamilton had passed up a lot of very good chances to give up, least of which had been the arena. And yet, he was still standing, and right next to the man he'd decided to turn from his best friend into his nemesis.

Hamilton considered, surprising me yet again when he gave what sounded like an honest answer. "I'm not sure I can say, exactly. At first, I thought it was the certainty of him biting it after we left you assholes standing in the middle of that overrun town. That first winter was rough, and we had so much to do that I almost forgot about it. Then I got the news in spring that not only was he still alive, but he'd managed to assemble an entire team made up of the rejects and dipshits that he'd collected along the way. I expected that would rekindle my animosity, but I honestly didn't give a shit anymore. I had my orders, and I followed them to the best of my abilities. Not my fault if some of you proved more resourceful than expected." He shrugged as if to say he also didn't get it but it was all the same to him. He turned to Stone then. "Decker really thinks he can somehow select who'll be a part of his new master race, or some shit? If history taught me anything, it's that shit like that never works out. I maybe get why he'd take some pleasure from watching the two of us beat each other to death, but that's personal. The serum project isn't, and never was. Every single member was painstakingly selected, and a lot of good men and women washed out ahead of getting the shot. He was damn proud of every single one of those who made it." He paused, casting me a sidelong glance. "Even though I don't get why she was elected to be worthy of surviving, he must have had his reasons. I've never met a single person where that wasn't the case. So why the change of heart now?"

It was strange bordering on insane hearing Hamilton say that—about me, specifically, but everyone else as well. It also cast Decker into a very different light from the image of him that I'd formed in my head. Hamilton's tone bordered on reverent, and considering what that monster had others do to his sister—and how that had destroyed everything in his life just as much as in Nate's—that was saying a lot.

Unlike me, Stone looked less impressed with our powers of deduction. "As I said, I'm expendable," he reiterated. "And I'm by far not important enough to have all the answers." He opened his mouth to say more but succumbed to a bloody coughing fit that went on for over a minute. His skin looked deathly pale, and not just in contrast to the blood splattered across the lower half of his face. "I'm afraid we will have to cut this conversation short if you insist on torturing me still. Even if that is no longer the case, I've about outlasted my usefulness. If there's nothing else—"

Not so fast. "What was the intent behind testing out all the components and variants you tested out on these two, and the others in the arena? Drug trafficking might have been of great benefit for Cortez to keep the camp running, but you had a purpose beyond that."

Stone looked vexed, as if he had to explain something simple to a child—again. "To find something to break the serum's hold on someone," he said. "Waiting for all of those undeserving to fall over and die might take a decade or more. Might have come in handy as an incentive for others to join him in his cause as well. You and those miserable bastards you collect and drag around with you still see it as a blessing, even when you can't avoid facing that, to all of you, it will only ever be a curse. Ask your friends from the Silo how much they would have appreciated a tool to strip you of the danger you present. Ask any of the settlement citizens."

Now he was sounding like Emma, Sadie's mother, who'd kicked us out of the bunker and later the Wyoming Collective because our cooties might rub off on someone. That this had backfired colossally and cost her spending time with her own daughter and grandchild was just one more sad fact in our lives. I wasn't quite sure what to make of all those grandiose claims. Oh, I was sure that Stone believed them wholeheartedly—but both Hamilton and Nate had proven to me repeatedly that, where Decker was concerned, it seemed impossible for people to get a real grasp of the situation.

"Anything else you feel like sharing?" I asked, then turned to my companions. "Because if not, I'll consider this done." If Nate was surprised about that, he didn't show it. Hamilton shook his head, as if to say that he was just along for the ride.

Stone cast me an incredulous look. "That's it?"

I shrugged, as far as that was possible in the suit. "As I said, we didn't come here to get anything except information—and maybe revenge. Old habits are hard to shake, so I bet I will find what I need in the lab journals your scientists kept—and you said yourself, you have no clue what their day-to-day work was. You don't know where Decker is, so there's that. I'm content to watch you useless piece of shit bleed out in here. Maybe not the most satisfying ending, but somehow, real life seldom gives you those grandiose movie finales."

I did another check-in with the guys. Nate, changing his mind, cleared his throat. "How did you get here without losing half of your people every single time? I presume the scientists only got here after you cleared a path."

Stone seemed amused, and I already knew I wouldn't like the answer, even if it might prove useful to us. "You presume correctly," he snarked, looking downright nasty. "We haven't had a single casualty in transport in over a year now. How does that compare to your experience?" I was considering how well pistol-whipping would work with the positive pressure suit I was in, but Hamilton, surprisingly, jumped into the breach.

"All in acceptable range," he provided. "And last I looked, we will be the last ones standing, while you did our work for us. Tell me how exactly that's a bad outcome?"

Stone narrowed his eyes but continued to prove jovial with the answers he was ready to provide. "The tunnels," he offered. "If you go through that airlock over there, you'll find our vehicles at their charging stations. The tunnels leading north from here go up well past the Dallas city limits. The exit is in a storm drainage system up in Plano."

For the first time since we'd entered the facility, I felt like swearing up a storm. If I had my Texas geography right, that put that exit only a handful of miles away from where we'd left our cars. So close, and we'd lost so many people for nothing!

"That does it," Hamilton muttered, me probably the only one close enough to hear it. He then turned toward me. "Let's end this." Since we'd already reached that conclusion, I didn't feel like protesting. He glanced at Stone, then back to me. "Exactly how does the cleaning system in here work? I remember you babbling something about cycles, back in Paris."

It was probably too much to ask for him to ditch his penchant for verbal abuse even once, but right now I didn't feel like jumping at his throat for it. "Pretty much like the decontamination shower, only on a widespread level. Vaporized formaldehyde and shit like that, plus hours of UV radiation."

"You can activate that from the outside?"

I nodded. "As long as the inner door of the decontamination shower is closed, the cycle is activated with a simple push of a button. And you can override it."

Hamilton looked pleased. "We can lock that door, too?"

"When the other side of the airlock is open, it's on auto-lock—and you can't override that." I paused, although I had a good idea where he was going with this. "Why?"

Hamilton gave me a nasty smile. "Sounds like a fitting end for a rat, wouldn't you say?" He turned back to Stone, raising the pistol in his left hand, but not like he was going to shoot. "This is way too good and easy for an asshole like you."

I would have panicked at the idea of biting it like that, but either Stone hadn't fully grasped what was going to happen to him, or was beyond caring. "The only regret I have is that I won't be there when you come face to face with Decker and realize that your entire world just went to hell."

I might have shot him for that claim but Nate and Hamilton exchanged one last look and then turned to go. I considered lingering for a moment—and maybe taking the index of the tank samples with me, for later perusal—but decided against it. I hadn't been lying when I'd said we weren't here to get anything, and I couldn't exactly decontaminate that shit. Stone watched us leave, his skin color so pale now that he didn't contrast much with the beige wall next to him. The last to exit, I pushed the vault door shut with a satisfying click.

Nobody said a word as we made our way back to the airlock, my interest in exploring the rest of the lab squashed for good. We suffered through the chemical onslaught of the decontamination shower in equal silence, but that was also due to the fact that I hadn't bothered with handing out the suit com units, and the torrential rain coming down on us was too loud to allow normal communication. We exited the shower once the inner door unlocked, and I welcomed the sweet relief of the world having me back as soon as I could tear open the zipper of the suit. Richards was still waiting for us, eyeing us askance but was happy to help us out of the suits first. Hamilton didn't bother with anything except getting the suit open and the top half flopping behind him as he stepped up to the control panel, and after a moment's perusal hit the—clearly-labeled—button to start the lab cleaning cycle. Through one of the viewports I saw the lights change as the normal illumination powered down and the violet UV lamps came on. I held my breath, listening for movie-magic screams, but realistically, there was too much space and reinforced walls between us and Stone to make that possible. Hamilton had a certain satisfied expression on his face as he set to getting out of the suit. I mostly felt empty. Nate—surprise, surprise—gave me nothing as he pushed Richards aside so he could help me peel off the tape around the socks and gloves. If he noticed the downright caveman behavior—for Nate's standard—Red didn't show.

"You got whoever fled in there, I presume?" Richards finally asked when nobody volunteered any information.

"Yup," I offered. "And also anyone else who could have been hiding in there." That said, I still checked on the number of suits, finding all accounted for. It was theoretically possible that someone had taken a backup suit in, but I doubted it. Stone had made it sound as if the scientists had all been on board with their suicide pact, however idiotic it had been. I was sure Stone had performed a final head count before he'd given his firing squad the go-ahead. Somehow I didn't think he'd gotten his hands dirty with that, personally.

"Anything happen while we were gone?" Nate wanted to know.

Red shook his head. "We checked all the corridors again. No stowaways as far as we can tell. Cole's taken over the control room, but he already reported that what data storage they've had, they completely wiped. Maybe we'll find a flash drive or two among their personal things, but I doubt it."

"They left paper copies," I pointed out. "If we have time, I'd like to go over some of that."

Nate looked amused at the notion that we were on a running clock. "Let's retreat and regroup. The cafeteria sounds good. The medical station is close by, and it's easily defendable. I for one could do with some sleep myself. We'll decide later how long we need to stay here, but a day or two for recovery won't hurt."

I couldn't help it. My gaze dropped down to the wound in his side. He still held himself upright but there were more bloody splotches visible on the gauze now, and I wondered how close to simply keeling over he really was. If anyone was stubborn enough to keep that from happening on his will alone, it was him, so I didn't ask.

I also didn't ask myself if this had been worth it. That had never really been the question—and not my main concern, I realized, when I watched Nate and Hamilton both trot out of the lab in front of me, tired as hell but their heads raised high.

Chapter 16

Since I was among the less wounded, I got first guard shift—four hours of leaning around, listening to the ventilation system drone overhead and not much else. Nobody shot at us, we had food and water aplenty, and no zombies anywhere in sight—it was as close to a vacation as things could get. Exhaustion kept my mind mostly blank of guilt and curiosity, and when it was time to hit the sack, I crashed as hard as I dared—which turned out a full five hours of comatose state that didn't feel refreshing, but at least my body and mind were functioning again once I pried open gritty eyes.

To make sure that no ninja guards were still hiding anywhere, Nate set a patrol pattern through all parts of the complex, but Cole confirmed from the camera feeds—and there were a lot more of them than we'd expected—that except for us, the corridors and rooms were empty. The first—and only—good news came from him as well, a few hours later. He not only managed to crack the last airlock where four electric cars were waiting for us—no. He went as far as checking the SatNav systems for all of them, and after comparing years of data, came back with a single location all cars had been to at least three times where, as far as we knew, nothing was located. Nothing as in no settlement, no town, no base—from after the apocalypse happened and before. It could be nothing—or something as simple as a navigation point to get anywhere else—but Nate and Hamilton both agreed that it was too good a lead not to follow up. A good two days of driving south of Dispatch, it would be easy to justify swinging by there either way.

The sight of the cars annoyed me for the most part, even if it was, in fact, a huge advantage. If Stone had told the truth—and there was no reason to think he hadn't; the SatNav data also confirmed the entry and exit vectors they had taken in the past—we'd be out of this hellhole within hours, and we'd scored four additional vehicles that were perfectly fine to keep. There was no way we could have known about how far the tunnels reached or where exactly the exit was. People who killed themselves just to keep vital information from us were unlikely to have left someone behind who we could have pounded the information out of. But, damn, what a colossal waste.

Sonia was still busy patching people up, but thanks to the cars we would be able to take everyone with us who made it. The fact that we didn't need to find a much less pleasant solution lifted some of the weight off my chest. Getting torn to shreds by shamblers had many disadvantages, but at least it didn't leave anyone behind who was suffering and needed absolution. Gunshots weren't so merciful.

We did a thorough search of the personal quarters first, but all too soon I felt myself gravitate toward the lab spaces deeper into the complex. Richards offered to tag along—and Nate made sure to tell the patrols to check in with me whenever they passed—but, frankly, I was glad to have some time on my own. Anyone could go through personal shit and raid the pantry; they didn't need me for those tasks. And since it only took me two hours of searching in Walter Greene's office to happen upon the documentation of everything they'd sent to the camp and tested out on the scavengers and prisoners, I could also provide a list of chemicals someone could pick up from the older labs that hadn't seen use in ages. It was a short list—and the things Nate confiscated because they could be used to craft more explosives was miles longer—but it was something.

When Cole managed to establish a satellite link for communications, I knew that list was too important to let it burn a hole into my back pocket.

Nate and I debated how much, if anything, to share—not because we were super paranoid but because there was real danger lurking out there, and the last thing we needed was to flag anyone previously operating under the radar. There were two obvious exceptions to that—the Silo and Emily Raynor.

We contacted the Silo first since with Blake we had someone who needed to report in, anyway. I went as far as to suggest leaving the room as not to scare off anyone at the other end of the line. Nate cut that attempt at diplomacy short right there but agreed that the three of us—including Hamilton—were better off lurking in the back. The radio tech looked surprised to get a call over video, and wasn't alone in that, judging from the peanut gallery of people assembling in the back where they thought the camera might not pick them up any longer. Commander Wilkes made an appearance in under five minutes, and while I was sure he noticed us, he didn't react.

"Sgt. Blake, good to hear from you. Considering your surroundings, I take it your mission was a success?"

Blake looked somewhat astonished by that assumption, and started by delivering the bad news that his team had been reduced to half strength. One of the techs in the back ran out of the room, making me guess that he'd been close to someone they'd lost. Wilkes took the news with the same stoic expression as the recount of the mission that followed. Blake ended it with a quick explanation why we were still here—to check up on possible resources, and information that I was looking for.

"Anything I should ask our squints about?" Wilkes asked when Blake was finished.

Blake cast a sidelong glance in my direction. "I'm afraid I'm not qualified to answer that," he replied. "Dr. Lewis remains the resident expert for these things."

Wilkes grimaced, but it was less like he'd bitten into a slice of lemon, and more of the "here we go again" kind. "Then why don't you let her relieve you, Sergeant? I will inform the relatives of the deceased." He paused as if he was ready to walk away, but then turned back to the camera. "I presume you will want to stay along for the ride?"

Blake gave a curt nod. "Unless it is of vital importance that we personally deliver whatever we take with us from here, I would like to rendezvous with Sgt. Buehler and her people. We have a vested interest in seeing that Miller and his people succeed."

Wilkes looked amused by what sounded a lot like a reminder of a previous conversation between the two of them. That made me wonder how much convincing it had taken for Blake to agree to work with us. Buehler had always seemed friendly toward us—and her enthusiasm in getting to work with Zilinsky had been undimmed, getting shot or not—but Blake hadn't been my biggest fan in the past when he'd had to babysit me. Apparently, he'd changed his mind.

Just then, two familiar faces appeared behind Wilkes, giving the commander a good excuse to leave. Dom and Sunny hadn't really changed since I'd last seen them—an eternity and several appendages ago, I remembered, not without an unhealthy shot of wry amusement. Blake looked ready to bolt himself so I took pity on him and stepped forward, trying for a diplomatic exchange. Before we'd been banned from the Silo, I would have considered them friends, but considering the shit that had gone down since then—with and without my involvement—I felt like I was skating on thin ice again.

I needn't have worried, I realized, when they both looked a little anxious but decidedly happy to see me. "Hi, Bree, how are you doing?" Dom asked.

Ever the diplomat, Sunny had to follow that up with, "We heard a lot about what you've been up to in the meantime."

Hell, but I was glad I was still wearing my gloves. I was aware that his utter lack of tact was part of the package with Sunny, but I'd never be able to look past the fact that he'd been annoyed with my inability to deal on a rational, scientific basis with the results yielded from him dissecting the unborn child I'd thought Nate had buried behind that fucking motel.

"None of that's as interesting as what I've found earlier today," I said, then cut myself off to change tracks. "I presume that, although your people are damn glad they didn't get inoculated with the serum because of the unexpected side effects, you'd still like the data on that, if only for scientific purposes?"

Sunny nodded impatiently as if even having to ask was unreasonable, while Dom frowned. "What side effects? They did tell you that you'd all end as viral walking bombs before they shot you up, right?"

"Hard to miss that since it was one of the perks, not a bug," I offered acerbically. "But none of us was aware that the immunity to the zombie bites was only temporary. By now, there's not a single one of us around who hasn't been bitten, scratched, or worse." I figured there was no sense in singling the Ice Queen out, particularly if her immunity was still at a hundred percent.

Dom looked horrified, giving Sunny the opportunity to take over. "What news do you have to share?"

Bless him. "Blake has updated you on what's been going on with the scavengers, the drugs, and that damn camp altogether?" Dom nodded, still too stricken to regain his voice. "Turns out, we now have the master list of the changes made to the serum, and another list of substances that have been confirmed to cut through the protection the serum provides. Since we believe it's practically useless as a weapon but might save lives when used responsibly, we are happy to share that with you."

That they knew about that shit—and how it had been verified—became apparent when both men glanced at Nate then, who did a great job ignoring their curious expressions. I figured that pretty much concluded that topic.

"Need anything else from a moderately well-stocked lab that won't go bad in the heat? I checked—they didn't have much in terms of antibiotics, but your everyday lab chemicals might be in stock."

"Nah, we're good," Sunny was quick to reply. "Wilkes is regularly sending out the marines to go raid everything they can carry. We have stocks that will last into the next century." Dom gave him a vexed look that made me guess this hadn't been knowledge to be shared, although I didn't see the harm in it.

"Good for you," I told them. "That's it from us. Unless you want to know anything else?"

Dom shook his head, but Sunny piped up. "I'm really curious how bad the necrotizing—"

That's as far as he got. Before I could give Cole the cue to cut the signal, the screen went black. Cole barely glanced in our direction as he muttered, "Oops." I had to admit, I was surprised by that unexpected show of... whatever that had been. Respect? Loyalty? Disdain for someone's nosiness he liked less than me?

Emily Raynor was next. Not without some amusement we shuffled Richards in front of the camera, who looked like he would have much rather been anywhere else, including the streets of Dallas above us. As it turned out, none of the soldiers had actually been stationed at that base for much longer than it took to grab us and leave, and they'd only returned for the debriefing. Hamilton only had a deadpan stare for me when I asked where they had been in the meantime, and his silence got the other three to clam up for good.

Masking this as a call between friends wasn't the worst of ideas, although I figured that if Decker managed to trace it, he'd already know what was actually going on. All the operator who appeared on screen needed to hear was Richards rattling off his rank and name, and the call was immediately transferred to the medical wing. Emily Raynor appeared, a completely alienating smile on her face—that took all of a second to freeze and turn into the perpetual frown that I was much more familiar with.

"Ah, I should have realized that this was a ruse," she drawled, her British accent as present as ever. "No need for that, of course. I'm more than happy to directly talk to your superiors, honeybun."

I'd seen Richards squirm before, like when at the meeting before the assault on the camp he'd realized that with Marleen and Sgt. Buehler there were two former bunkmates of his around, but that was nothing compared to how red his face got now, leveling the difference between his skin and hair color. Neither Hill nor Cole pretended not to be a step away from crying with laughter, and I was hard-pressed not to join them. Red's only saving grace was that Nate and Hamilton one-upped each other in who could pull off that neutral-going-on-hostile non-expression, so I couldn't very well roll on the floor, laughing.

Damn, but we probably all deserved to be called honeybun.

"Fancy seeing you again," Raynor quipped in our direction. Hamilton barely got some hostile side-eye. I remembered her disdain for him all too well. On paper, she and I should absolutely get along with each other—if not for the fact that I couldn't stand her. Nothing had changed about that in the two and a half years since I'd last talked to her. That she'd saved my life—and kept what remained of my body functioning—was beside the point. Richards took that moment to flee, much to everyone's amusement. "Not that much of a surprise," she conceded. "You'd both set heaven and hell in motion to drag each other back out of whatever hole someone tried to throw you into." So much for whether Richards had already given her an update after we'd taken over the camp—or she'd heard the story from a different source and had just used an uncannily accurate figure of speech. She then glanced at Hamilton once more. "But you I didn't expect to see alive. How did you convince her not to kill you first chance she got? She's clearly armed and you're distracted right now—how are you still breathing?"

Bucky offered her a bright smile that creeped me the fuck out. On second thought, I didn't mind his constant scowls that much. "Looks like someone has more sense than you and deduced that I'm still useful for something."

I could tell that Nate was already getting annoyed on my other side—making me realize that he'd actually given up on hoping Hamilton and I would bury the hatchet, but as long as we were not literally at each other's throat, that was enough—and that didn't change when Raynor pointedly glanced at him. His voice held a certain edge when he responded, making it plain that he liked her even less than I did. "Turns out, common enemies can make for great neutral ground."

Raynor smiled, and I was sure she knew all too well that he included her in that group as well. "Always good to know. But telling me this can't have been your reason to mortally embarrass Lt. Richards. You are all so terribly fond of him, after all. Or have allegiances shifted there as well? Nine weeks can be a very long time."

I almost jumped when Hamilton let out a roar, going from stoic to slapping his thigh in moments. Nate's glare promising nothing short of deadly violence got him to shut up again, but not before he shook his head and muttered something under his breath about lost causes. Raynor looked annoyed by that outburst, but it was enough for her to drop the point—something I was glad about. I knew this was my chance to cut to the chase before this could deteriorate—and if I actually liked Hamilton coming out of this conversation, I'd eat my boots. I still needed them, so that wasn't a smart course of action.

"We contacted you because we found some data here that might be of interest to you—provided you didn't lie to my face and are still actively searching for a cure," I offered.

She scrunched up her nose. "I make it a habit of always telling the truth."

I knew for a fact that she wasn't, but I was beyond bothering to clarify that now. "I have a list here of the substances they tested that made it through the protection of the serum, and I also have documentation of how they continued to tweak the serum, for whatever purpose—possible mind control, maybe, or simply to send anyone interested in it into an early grave." Considering Stone's great speech about too many having received access to it, that sounded more plausible than before. "I've already shared the data with the Silo," I pointed out, just so she didn't get any weird ideas. "I will also send paper copies of the report I'm compiling to every independent settlement that I can reach. The least the scavengers deserve is to know what is happening to them—the same as to the rest of us. I presume you know about the faulty immunity?"

Raynor looked surprised that I brought up that point, but in a different sense than I'd expected. "Why do you think I wanted you out of my wing as soon as possible? I gave you a less than thirty percent chance that the serum would take and halt your inevitable conversion for long. Frankly, when you didn't return to the base, I'd figured you had realized that you were already well past the halfway point and chose to live what little time you had left on your own terms." Her gaze flitted to Hamilton briefly. "And he corroborated that story—for both of you, I might add."

This was getting better and better—and I still didn't know how to handle the fact that Hamilton had repeatedly chosen to help us do our thing. I knew it wasn't as a favor to either of us, and likely the only way he had been able to rebel and bend orders he didn't want to follow for whatever non-altruistic reasons, but it still freaked me the fuck out.

The man himself only had a shrug in response to her accusation. "As I said, I must have come in useful somewhere," he offered gruffly.

Raynor ignored him. "Yes, I want that list. I want everything you can give me. I presume biological material is out of the question?"

I shook my head. "Stone destroyed what I'm sure were all the useful samples they had in storage before we got to him. We have no way that we could get anything to you that wouldn't end up destroyed in the heat." Liquid nitrogen kept shit cold, but it also had a tendency to evaporate in warmer temperatures. Without one of those nifty special cases that Hamilton had had with him in France—and the cold of winter—that wasn't an option.

"Stone? Brandon Stone?" Raynor asked, not trying to mask her incredulity. "What does that weasel have to do with any of this?"

"You knew him?" I asked, not bothering to hide the fact that he was dead.

"Of him," she pointed out. "He was the figurehead leader of the laboratory in Kansas. No competence whatsoever. Apparently, I stand corrected."

"Not necessarily." I quickly brought her up to date with our recent encounter. "Is that lab still operational?"

"Not that I'm aware of," Raynor said. "I was offered three of their people but declined. I like people to have to put actual effort into getting spies into my lab." When she saw me grimace, her expression turned shrewd. "So it is true. They were the source for Taggard's misinformed undertakings."

Shit, I hated when she and I agreed on something. "You know that for a fact?"

She deflected my question with a shrug. "There have been rumors. Very few survivors, from what I have been able to gather. Whoever set them to their task made sure none of them could flip and make it easy for us to undo the damage." She paused, her gaze going to Hamilton once more before she went on. "I'm sure that Cpt. Hamilton has filled you in on the fact that we did our best to attempt to break the serum's hold on all affected soldiers who got the wrong versions, but we eventually had to give up since nothing short of killing them would have done the trick? That's how that abysmal camp got started. It sounded like a good idea to let them be useful in food production so they could provide for themselves, under supervision of course. That did not turn out as expected."

"You could say that," I muttered. Stone's connection to the camp suddenly made a lot more sense. If he'd been a part of the faction that was working on the wrong serum versions, it must have been easy to keep track of what happened with the affected soldiers—and then keep adding the scavengers to the mix. Complete insanity in a world that had already lost billions too many, but that didn't seem to matter to a lot of people. If I'd learned one thing, it was that.

"I can read you the report now," I told her, done with that topic. "Should I find anything else, I will update you on that."

The interesting part of our conversation concluded, most of the others turned to focus on something other than two scientists prattling overly complicated chemical terms at each other—for the second time tonight. Nate and Bucky left for the cafeteria, with only Cole, Hill, Marleen, and Eden remaining, the two women mostly because they weren't done with the game of cards they had been engaged in since we'd gotten started. I was damn exhausted when I finally signed off, but at Cole's question if I wanted to hail anyone else, I paused.

"Get me New Angeles on the line. Greene himself. And tell them he will want this to be a private conversation." The least I could do was tell him about his father's demise. I considered calling Nate back, but didn't figure that necessary. All I wanted was to see Greene's reaction, and I wouldn't need anyone's help to interpret that if it turned out to be what I expected. Hoped for, really, or else we were more fucked than ever.

Unlike the other calls, it took a good fifteen minutes to get someone on the line ready to listen to us in the first place, and I'd almost given up on this when Greene, sitting in his secure office, appeared on the screen. He was staring at me expectantly. "I'd say it was a pleasure to receive a call from you, but judging from that pinched look on your face, you're jonesing for a fight, and I'm absolutely not in the mood to oblige you."

Two could play that game.

"I'm sorry to inform you of your father's death," I said. "Since he was directly involved in the drug trafficking to the labor camp, the infection of thousands of scavengers with a serum variant that kills them sooner rather than later, and doing his very best to find a way to cut through the protection of the working version of the serum itself, I'm not sorry about his death."

I felt a smidgen of relief when Greene's eyes widened at the mention of his father. Obviously, he hadn't been aware that Walter had survived the end of the world. He quickly regained his composure after that.

"I presume you had something to do with his demise?"

I shook my head. "Not directly. The guards killed the scientists while we were breaching their compound. The only one left standing was Brandon Stone, who'd been acting—yet again—as a figurehead for a much more nefarious organization." Putting my hands on my hips, I glared long and hard at him. "I always assumed he was your spy at the Aurora, Kansas lab. Your spy and liaison to the army. It was he who leaked the location of the Colorado base to you, that you later gave us when we came after them?"

To his credit, Greene hesitated less than I would have before he replied. "Yes, he was my spy, until he wasn't. He did all that, and more, but soon after your crusade was over and you disappeared, we came to realize that a lot of his intel had been bad, costing many good people their lives. I hope you at least had something to do with his horrible, gruesome demise?"

That made me feel a little better about the whole thing. "Hamilton suggested we leave him locked in the hot lab. He turned on the lab's cleaning cycle. I doubt Stone manage to bleed to death before that. Not a way I'd want to go myself."

Greene looked pleased, but I could tell that the news didn't make up for the damage caused. "Good."

I considered offering him the same information as I'd already shared, but figured it would be less useful to him—and he likely already had someone on a line who was painstakingly writing it all down. Maybe someone from the Silo would send down a flash drive to spare them the weeks it would take to make sense of it all.

I knew I should have signed off then, but for whatever reason, I felt myself reluctant to do so. It wasn't like Greene and I would ever become friends, but I couldn't help but feel that if he was actually as much of an asshole as I loved to pretend, he would have turned on me by now. Pretty much everyone else had, including a bunch of people who I'd have sworn never would.

I wasn't quite sure why, but on some level I felt knowing that most people currently alive were likely going to outlive me by decades mellowed down my need to get into everyone's face somewhat.

While I stood there, unsure what to say or do, Greene kept studying me, going from leaning forward with his arms crossed on the desk to reclining, much more at ease. "I presume someone has by now told you that the serum isn't quite what it was cracked up to be?" he questioned.

"That's one way of putting it," I grumbled. "Why didn't you tell me when we were hitching that ride together on the boat?" I presumed it really wasn't recent news.

He shrugged. "Honestly? I figured you knew. You are actually one of very few people who has a clue what that shit does and why. From what I've heard, accidental conversions have been going on from the very beginning of the outbreak. Since there's usually nobody left standing to share the details, we have no clue about the unofficial numbers."

"And the official ones?"

"Somewhere between one in three to one in five," he offered, his tone surprisingly gentle.

I swore under my breath, incapable of holding the words in. Greene's grim expression was as close to a sincere declaration of condolence as I was likely ever going to get from him.

"Most people still don't know," I stated once I had myself back under control. "Why?"

Now a smidgen of his usual condescending attitude returned, but after dealing with Hamilton on a daily basis, it was easy to ignore. "And escalate the shit storm that has been raging for the past two years even further?" He shook his head. "How would you even get the level of confirmation needed for it to be more than rumors? Even with Cortez and his camp infecting hundreds of scavengers, most affected still got the original versions. I know you likely don't want to hear this, but the army has been bleeding manpower more than any of the other branches—or maybe it's a simple fact of having been better organized because of you amped-up assholes that they've remained more visible. Who knows? Since the marine corps didn't systematically single out their members, it's hard to tell them apart from the rest."

I couldn't help but grin, despite the grim topic. "If you check out the odd scavengers, you'll see a lot of them carry around a different kind of easily identifiable ink, besides the single marks on their necks." I paused. "Do they still do that shit—mark us up?"

He shook his head. "Not since the winter you disappeared, pretty much. Dispatch still requires the marks, but I hear they have a flourishing black market outside their gates to account for the people refusing to enter."

"Good."

Now it was his turn to snort. "People were scared—can you fault them for that? Now consider what would happen if all their worst fears got confirmed. Anyone with three marks would be shot on sight, and likely a lot with single marks as well. Traders would refuse to deliver goods to settlements. People would die of starvation again. What little we've regained of civilization would go up in flames quicker than you could go off in my face. Nobody wants that to happen. So you're safe for now. Or as safe as you'll ever be. You have a penchant for finding yourself in the worst of places."

I had to accede that point to him—in part. "Could have been worse."

Greene pursed his lips. "You mean, you could have been at that very lab you're standing in? Stone did offer you their little satellite office in Kansas. And you were always kind of an overachiever."

I would have loved to refute his claim, but the words refused to make it over my lips. "Your father was their leader," I choked out. "He was as much a part of why I signed that contract with his company as Raleigh Miller was. I don't know what it would have taken for me to realize what was going on, but there's a good chance that it would have been way too late to undo the damage."

If I'd expected him to throw me a pity party, he'd have disappointed me right then. "That still makes you one of the better people in the company you keep," he remarked wryly. "Speaking of which—why is it just you here, talking to me of all people, in the middle of the night? Shouldn't there be at least one asshole hulking in your direct vicinity?"

"Maybe I needed a break from that," I offered, laughing in spite of myself.

"Don't we all," Greene mused, growing pensive. "That old cooter. Never thought he'd survive the apocalypse. Sure, I joked a few times that there's a good chance he's locked away with the elite in some doomsday bunker, but I never expected to be right about that."

"Do those even exist?" His eyebrows shot up at my question. "Doomsday bunkers, I mean," I clarified. "Sure, small remodeled basements like where we spent the first winter are easy to set up. But beyond that I haven't heard of anything else, if you ignore all these super-secret laboratories."

He flashed me a quick grin but his eyes remained distant. "You must have toured all of them by now."

"There's still the official CDC installations," I pointed out. "But if I found out they were connected with this as well, I'd give up." I wasn't even joking about that. "I can take on megalomaniac assholes, but not the people actually sworn to protect us from shit like this happening."

Greene shrugged as if it was the same to him. "I'd have expected things to work more efficiently if the CDC had been involved," he admitted. "The FEMA blockades and camps got a lot of first responders killed, but they also saved a shitload of people. They did what they could on short notice that was a fraction of the most pessimistic contingency plan in existence."

Silence fell as we both got lost in thought. More on a snap-judgment decision than because I actually believed this would lead anywhere, I got out the piece of paper where I'd scrawled the address down that Cole had retrieved from the SatNavs. Prattling it off, I asked, "That ring a bell?"

Greene laughed, which irritated me as much as it set off the sirens in the back of my mind. "You're joking, right?"

"Let's pretend for a second that I'm not," I offered, trying for a neutral tone.

I must have failed because Greene sat up, his eyes narrowing as he squinted at his screen. "Stop screwing with me, Lewis. It was kind of funny when you did it with Decker's name, but this one's just stupid."

It was only that mention that made me remember that—back when I had been fishing for intel—Greene had mentioned that his father and Decker had been tight. Just one more piece in the puzzle that fit perfectly.

"Indulge me," I begged. "Please?"

Greene harrumphed but finally did. "You were joking about doomsday bunkers just minutes ago? Well, there you have one. Or not. It turned out to be one of the biggest scams of the last decade. Apparently, a lot of people way too wealthy for their own good had bought into it, but an investigative journalist debunked it all."

I'd almost forgotten about Cole idly cleaning his fingernails with a knife at his computer station, but that made him perk up. "Yeah, I remember the documentary," he threw in. "The progress updates were all filmed on green screen, or some shit. A friend of mine was pretty impressed, saying that was blockbuster movie level of CGI that they used. Apparently still cheaper than attempting to build the real thing. The documentary even featured footage from the construction site. In five years of work, they'd barely done more than required to pour the foundations of a house."

That did jog my memory, but since it had been long before I'd found anything related to survivalism interesting, I'd mostly ignored the hype. "But what if the documentary was the real ruse?" I suggested. "I feel like we've been chasing ghosts for fucking forever. Adding a ghost bunker to the list really doesn't change much."

Greene didn't look convinced, and now that the topic had come up, Cole seemed less enthusiastic about his own investigative powers. Since Greene and I were pretty much done weirding each other out by not being at each other's throat, I signed off. Cole excused himself to go check on the cars once more. I didn't hold him back, but mostly because I was sure he hadn't been wrong in the first place. Even with the communications center here making not just audio but video possible to the handful of other places like it—which would probably include that doomsday bunker—it sounded highly unlikely that they'd be able to make do without physically sending people this way and that. A simple three-page report about experiments was hell to discuss over the radio. I doubted something as involved as Greene's father and Stone had been running here was possible without a lot of direct interactions.

I was overdue to hit the sack but I knew that this new realization would make sleep impossible, so I decided to make myself useful. Eden and Marleen were still playing cards, likely waiting for Cole to call it a day so they could return to the cafeteria together. Since they had to walk by the labs with the airlocks, I'd join then. I'd already scoured the offices adjacent to the BSL-3 labs and I was too tired to bother with suiting up now—even if it was just disposable scrubs with some protective gear instead of a full suit—so I went further back to the lower security labs. I still hadn't checked on three of them. Considering how many scientists we'd found dead in that room, a substantial number of them must have been working there as well.

Because the bright lights hurt my eyes, I didn't turn those in the lab itself on, leaving the corridor illumination to do its thing through the large window panes instead. It didn't take me long to find several volumes of black, bound journals filled to the brim with scrawled notes, print-outs, and the odd dried gel on thick paper directly glued in. From the very first basic chemistry lab on I'd always been required to keep detailed notes of what I'd been up to, making it second nature to keep doing so even for the most routine shit. The scientists here hadn't been any different, although they hadn't kept notes for later needing to reference anything for publication. Knowing what they'd been up to suddenly put a very different spin on the seemingly disconnected mix of disciplines showing up in the different lab suits. The one I was in now was full of neurobiology stuff—brain chemistry for the most part, with an extra emphasis on pain management around. It made sense—the serum definitely screwed with neurotransmitters, and I doubted I would have survived on Emily Raynor's operating table if I'd felt the effect of every cut and scrape to its fullest extent. I still didn't know how much the serum itself dulled pain, but the virus sure did a number on the receptors, and not just at the direct infection site. Being able to replicate that effect must have been a neat little trick, although like a lot of things concerning the serum I felt like it had been a lucky side effect, and then scientists had scurried to explain how and why it must have been deliberate.

I got so lost in reading—and my own acerbic commentary in my head—that I didn't realize someone had snuck into the lab behind me until I felt a sharp pain in my lower right torso... before my world exploded in agony.

Chapter 17

The pain should have kicked my body into overdrive, but while my mind screamed, my lungs didn't comply. My pulse slowed although it should have skyrocketed. I tried to whip around but barely managed to catch myself on the workbench, and even so my control over my muscles was slipping away quickly.

My first guess—as much as sluggish ideas managed to cut through the pain—was that we'd somehow managed to miss one of the guards. No, scratch that—of course my first guess was Hamilton, but while emotionally that made sense, what disjointed information my body managed to give me as it systematically powered down made it obvious that it couldn't have been him. Whoever had just knifed me in the back—figuratively and literally—was shorter than me… which left only a single possibility.

Marleen.

The moment that name came up in my mind, I heard her coo into my right ear, from where she was standing behind me, straight while I was hunched over the lab journals on the workbench, my legs barely holding me up. Her grasp on the knife was the only thing that kept me from slipping to the floor, making the blade slice deeper into me. I tried to scream but my throat had completely shut down, not even letting me swallow.

"This is too easy. When I accepted the contract, I expected it to be at least some kind of challenge, not a walk in the park."

Her free—left—hand grabbed my shoulder and pulled me upward and back. I tried to tense but my muscles felt like goo, my body folding in on itself without any resistance. I recognized that sensation all too well from the nightmares that still plagued me sometimes—that fucking paralytic shit! Marleen managed to keep the knife right where she'd stuck it into me to the hilt, crouching down behind where I ended up almost kneeling on the floor, only her hold on the knife and her hand on my shoulder where she eased me against her torso holding me upright. All that jostling sent the pain levels up another few notches, but my tear ducts refused to work. I tried crying out again but that didn't even produce a croak—or any sound, for that matter.

Fucking hell—

"I presume you are asking yourself right now, what the fuck is going on?" Marleen sing-songed, sounding way too chipper for what she was doing. Or maybe not. Obviously, my new friend Marleen wasn't someone who actually existed. She let out a low chuckle. "I do hope you can put two and two together now, but I'm afraid it's too late for you. I'd say I was sorry but unlike someone who just thinks he's a bad guy and cut out for this line of work, I'm not capable of that sentiment, and really, it would be a lie. I accepted a challenge when I took that contract seven years ago, only that now my golden opportunity is a real cake walk. Too bad."

She paused, the hand on my shoulder squeezing ever so slightly. "You know, I love to hear myself talk, so I'll wait another couple of minutes here. Rushing gets you caught, you know?" She sounded like she was smiling. I itched to punch that smile right off her face but couldn't even keep the drool from dribbling down my chin.

"You're probably asking yourself now, why is this happening?" she went on chatting. "It's nothing personal, really. You're technically not even my mark. Your husband is, although I have orders to keep him alive a little longer. First, he has to suffer, and only after that comes the legendary 'to the last breath' part. Although, this could just do the trick. A shame, really, but seven years of complications is long enough."

She waited, as if I was capable of responding. I tried, but the paralytic had completely set in now, to the point where I couldn't even close my eyelids or move my eyes. I hadn't felt a needle's pinch so she must have coated the blade of the knife in it. Warmth continued to spread across my lower back and over my ass, but I wasn't fooled—that was my blood, leaking from the wound. The fact that I could feel my fingers and toes go cold as circulation shut down at the end of my extremities lent more evidence to the loss of blood.

"My initial plan was to kill Zilinsky as she seemed the only one close to him, but she's not someone you just surprise," Marleen went on, her tone still conversational. "Same goes for Romanoff. I took an immense risk, pretending to flip so they could turn me—but as I said, having a soul in this line of work is always something that holds you back. Not sure if you're the jealous type, but trust me when I tell you that I only fucked Miller because I knew that would take my perceived threat level down a few notches. You wouldn't believe how many guys that move works on." I felt her shift, as if she was trying to get a look at my profile. "Or maybe you do. I didn't really bother finding out more about your background since you were so quick to both let me close to you, and to hand me that golden opportunity on a platter. Really, telling me directly who you'd expect to kill you in exactly what way, and it fits into the overall framework of the job? That's too good to pass up. A shame that I had to clean up a few messes along the way, but hey, lives are cheap these days."

A shudder ran through my body, twisting the knife awfully, but none of that was voluntary. Marleen let go of my shoulder to check the pulse at my neck. I could feel how slow it had gotten where her fingers pressed into my skin.

"Not much longer now," she whispered, her tone comforting although it couldn't have been intended as such. She resumed her prattling. "I didn't want to kill Scott; he was a good man. Ruthless enough to deserve to make it. Such a shame. But when I realized that Stone was trying to make a run for it, I had to act. Sadly, Scott threw off my aim and thus you could have your little chat with Stone in the lab. Was it enlightening, I wonder? He doesn't know enough, so I'm not concerned, but that mistake's on me, him even getting the chance to make a last stand. Eden, now, I didn't mind killing her; she's been almost as annoying as you. If she'd just followed Cole to the cars like she's tried before and sucked him off while he did his thing, she'd still be alive. Not really a waste there, but it did take me five minutes to drag her carcass over to the dead scientists so nobody would find her too soon. Not that it matters. You were still here, doing shit you're not supposed to do. I couldn't have snuck up on you like that if you'd been doing what any warm-blooded woman would do after surviving shit like this—fuck her husband. But no, you had to go review what the scientists have been up to here. Maybe I can't even fault you for that; not sure I'd want to have sex with a guy who's probably thinking about which parts of me he could eat in the meantime." Again she halted, considering. "Too bad I won't be here to see this play out. I wish I could watch, but the fact that you've also gotten the serum has complicated my life immensely. I could have just killed you and staged it as a revenge job by someone else, but overwhelming you might have gotten problematic. You really saved me with your rampant paranoia, you know that? And Hamilton made it so easy for me to steal his knife when he went into the lab with you. I wonder why he kept it all these years if he hates Miller so much. It was a gift from him, you know? I'd hold it up so you can see the engraving to prove it, but if I pull it out now, you'll die too quickly and the paralytic won't shut down your body as you reanimate. It's a messy way to go, and needs so much great timing."

She checked my pulse again, which was just as well as her silence let me hear my own sluggish thoughts. I could see her plan unfold now—make it look as if Hamilton had killed me. Nate wouldn't take that well—and it stood to reason that none of the three of us would make it out of here alive.

I had to give her that: it was a good plan. Only too bad that it hinged on my demise.

"It really is a shame that I couldn't mortally wound you the conventional way," Marleen simpered on. "The impact would be so much worse—and maybe I could have made it look like I'm innocent so I could have stuck around a little longer. See the entire drama unfold, you know? I might miss the end now, and maybe we won't even have the great showdown. Too bad, really."

She seemed poised to go on but then halted. I strained my ears, praying for footsteps, but whatever she'd heard was too far off for me to catch. My heart sank when she relaxed.

"My time to go," she explained as I felt her shift. She left the knife in as she pushed me off her, making me flop over onto my side, my body alight with new waves of agony. The floor was cool underneath my cheek except where my blood continued to spread, soaking into my clothes. I saw one of her legs step into my field of vision as she leaned over me so she could twist the knife, both doing more damage and making sure it stayed in. Then she turned around so her face was above mine, leaning down to me like a young girl would to a puppy. "I know you won't make it. But in the off-chance someone finds you and you don't die of blood loss now but from your single remaining kidney shutting down because I just shredded it to hell, tell them this." She smiled, but now I could see it for the mask it really was. "Decker sends his regards."

Without another look back, she stepped away from me and left, her light steps almost immediately swallowed up by the roar of my pulse in my ears. The bloody latex glove that had covered her knife hand she took with her, not even leaving that clue behind. I thought I heard her voice a few moments later, coming from further into the complex, toward the hot lab. A male voice answered her but it was too low for me to catch—Richards? But I couldn't be sure. I tried to scream, or just make any sound, but I couldn't even blink when blood started seeping underneath my cheek and to the corner of my eye.

Simply trying to move was getting incredibly hard. My pulse was down to around one beat of my heart where there should have been five. Then, ten. I felt the gloom of the room around me deepen but had the feeling it wasn't from the corridor lights dimming.

I was bleeding to death, on the floor, and it was anyone's guess how long it would take for someone to find me. Hell, maybe they wouldn't even come looking, and once the paralytic wore off, my reanimated corpse would stagger aimlessly through the corridors in search of food—

At first, I chalked up the thumping I heard to what my struggling heart was producing, but then I felt something rhythmic against my cheek—steps, coming closer. Heavy steps, from someone not trying to be stealthy. I heard muttering next, too low to make out words but I'd recognize that voice anywhere—Hamilton. The spark of hope that someone might find me in time flickered, about to die, but I forced my mind to focus. Yes, there was the possibility that he'd just stand there and watch me die, but for that, he had to find me first, and that was also the first step to my possible survival.

Dipping deep into what little remained of my energy reserves, I concentrated only on making a sound. A single sound—a croak, a grunt, anything would do. My jaws were partly slack and my lips open—it should be able to get out, if I just managed to get my throat and lungs working under my control. The paralytic wasn't wearing off by any means, but I felt more aware than on that damn operating room table. Maybe it was because they'd given me the serum just before getting me in there, versus years later now. Or maybe the fact that my body was slowly but surely pushing toward the end results of the serum meant that the paralytic couldn't as fully claim me as before. My world narrowed down further until all I could see was the patch of floor in front of my face as I strained and pushed, but that was all I needed to see—as right behind the corner of the workbench was one of the two doors to the lab, and I'd see anyone stepping in here, just as he would see me.

I couldn't tell whether I succeeded, or whether it was luck that brought Hamilton to the door to glance inside, but it didn't matter. His focus was higher up as he scanned the room, looking for someone standing in there, or maybe sitting on a chair. The whooshing sound in my ears was so loud that I almost didn't understand him, only fragments coming through, "errand boy" and "better things to do" among them. Seeing nothing, he turned to step out again, which made my frustration and panic increase tenfold. Always did he have to get in my face, and this once when it would do me any good, he managed to ignore me? Rage boiled up inside of me, overwhelming and loud, turning the low vibrations in my throat that I could feel but not hear into a growl.

Hamilton jerked to a halt, probably because what had made it out of me sounded a lot like what a shambler about to charge might utter. His casual stance snapped to full alertness as he listened, slowly turning his head to catch a repeat sound. I tried—oh, did I try!—but the sudden surge of hope nixed the anger, turning me back into a lifeless husk on the floor. Hamilton's head continued to swivel, and when he couldn't see into the last row at the back, he took three slow, deliberate, utterly silent steps—and then he froze.

He was standing far enough away that even at the weird angle that my cheek was pressed into the now-bloody floor, I could see up to his face. Recognition lit up his expression as he quickly took in the scene. I could only imagine what was unfolding in front of him—my limp body, twisted on the ground, lying in a spreading pool of my own blood, with a knife sticking out of the lower right half of my back. Two agonizingly slow heartbeats he simply stood there, considering. If I could have screamed, I would have done so, more out of frustration and helplessness than anything else.

"Ah, screw it," he muttered, and a moment later, he was kneeling by my side. He was smart, hesitating a second to see if I moved. Only then did he check my pulse, and when that must have been inconclusive, he held a hand in front of my mouth and nose to check whether I was still breathing. I did my very best to push air out of my lungs to make it easily detectable, but my body was hell-bent on shutting down. Hamilton's eyes narrowed as he stared into my face, likely disappointed that I didn't sneer back at him—either alive so he knew I was still in there, or dead so he could finish me off. He prodded my shoulder but I couldn't react. His expression twisted into a deeper frown, concentration pushing away his usual look of misgiving as he must have been running through a few mental checklists.

"Something's not quite right about this," he said to himself. Sadly, I couldn't give my opinion—also not when he reached out and grabbed my breast, and he really did get a good feel. None of the mental protest made it into a physical signal, not even my indignation managing to rekindle my anger, also because the move made no sense. That was, until he got his flashlight out and directed it right into my eyes, making a different agony explode in my head. "Thought so," he muttered as he clicked it off almost immediately, dropping it mindlessly on the floor. "You're chock-full of paralytic. Your pupils don't even contract. No way you wouldn't have come for my throat for doing that." And we both knew he didn't mean searing my retinas to the point where I was still seeing weirdly colored patches.

"Let's see about that," he went on talking to himself, doing a quick check on me but coming to the conclusion that the knife wound was causing the leak all over the floor. I felt him gingerly push away fabric and prod the area around where the blade had sunk in—and my, that was not pleasant—but left it where it was. I heard him curse then—he must have realized that it was his knife. "Asshole trying to frame me with that, too, huh? If I didn't know it's impossible, I'd guess you did this to yourself, just to get back at me." He wasn't uselessly sitting there while he talked but pulled his jacket off, followed by his shirt, which he grabbed in one hand. With the other, he went for the knife and pulled it out, immediately pushing the wadded-up fabric against the wound.

And then, he froze.

A sound very much like the growl I'd uttered came from the direction of the other doorway. It was only when Nate came stalking—and I really meant moving like a tiger on the prowl—around the workbench to where he was in full view of the scene that I recognized him. I felt Hamilton tense, but, if anything, he pushed the shirt tamponing the wound even harder against me to staunch the blood flow. "Tell me that this is not what it looks like," Nate uttered, his tone as hard and menacing as I'd never heard it before.

"It's not," Hamilton said, his voice pressed but calm—a first for him. He definitely realized what conclusions Nate must be jumping to, and did his best to deescalate the situation. "Just think—if I ever went for her, it would be in her face, because I'd humiliate her before I chose to finish her off. Or not, to rub it in yet again that she's no match for me."

Nate's eyes narrowed, his hand dropping to the side of his thigh and the knife there, strong fingers wrapping around the hilt. Hamilton swore under his breath and tried again.

"If I really wanted to kill her, why stab her in the kidney that's not there anymore? You know her diseased, scarred carcass better than anyone else. You know that the worst of her scars are on the opposite sides of her body—her left leg, the back of her torso at the right. Where they removed her kidney, part of her liver, and her useless-as-fuck ovary. Whoever did this got his hands on the falsified report that switched the torso scars to the other side. Trust me, she can verify this for you, because I have it on good authority that Richards read the real one, too, and blabbed about a different detail to her that's been omitted from the false report. But for that, you need to back the fuck off now so we can save her life. She likely knows who did this, too. She's weak, but her vitals are still going strong. She's pumped full of paralytic and some shit that slows her heart down so it takes longer for her to bleed out fully—don't ask me why. Maybe so if we hadn't found her, she'd turn while she was still paralyzed, and could have torn your throat out while you held her in your arms like a baby and bawled your eyes out. Fucking think, man!"

Nate was still standing there, staring down at us, his face frozen in a rictus of hate. I could see how much it cost him not to give in to the rage boiling inside of him; not to launch himself at Hamilton and slice him up or kill him with his bare hands—and I'd die in the time it took him to do so. I realized then that this was what Marleen must have meant with the outcome she couldn't stick around to watch—Nate losing his shit, killing Hamilton, and either being pushed too far to rein himself back in or wounded too heavily not to die himself. Either outcome would end with three super-juiced, freshly converted zombies—or at the least two, if Hamilton's skull got smashed too badly for him to turn. Nate alone would likely be enough to kill the remaining members of our group, and the paralysis delay might lead to me finishing off whoever wasn't completely dead after he was done. It was a brilliant plan, based on Nate's biggest weakness—his love for me.

Quite frankly, I was impressed with the range of that, but not so the situation it had thrust me into. Hamilton kept crouching over me, the wadded-up shirt never moving, and I wouldn't be surprised if I'd get bruises from that alone.

Five seconds passed. Ten. Nate took a step forward, and I knew Hamilton was getting ready to let go of me so he could defend himself—but the moment passed, and rather than try to punch Hamilton's lights out, Nate dropped to his knees next to him, taking over. Hamilton scrambled to his feet, his boots squeaking on the floor, and he was off toward the cafeteria, hollering "Medic!" at the top of his lungs.

It took maybe five minutes for Sonia to limp into the room, with everyone else who could move in tow, Burns lugging her kit for her. Nate spent the entire time almost motionless, putting even more pressure on the wound than Hamilton had before if that was possible. He didn't say a single word out loud, but I heard him whisper a barely audible litany of, "Don't die. Please, don't die." He didn't touch me anywhere else, but considering that any jostling of my body felt as if someone was trying to squeeze what remained of my blood right out of me like juice from a ripe orange, that was probably for the best.

As soon as Sonia stepped into the room, a flurry of activity broke out around me. Hamilton must have filled her in already but repeated his recount of how he'd found me while Sonia barely seemed to listen, first cutting away the soaked fabric so she could better get to the wound, and then setting to work. I had no fucking clue what she did but it hurt like hell. Not being able to do anything, not even wince, made it a million times worse for me, but I knew it let her get the job done quicker, and likely better as well. Moving patients were a bitch for doctors and nurses everywhere. Lucky me, indeed.

"That's all I can do for her right now," I heard Sonia's tired voice proclaim eons later. "The glue will help heal up the tissue around the stitches. She's damn lucky that the knife didn't rupture her intestine. If she'd still have had all her internal organs, she would be dead. I'll have to open her up again tomorrow to remove the glue and check on the stitches, but she should be out of the woods now." I heard her pause. "It'll be better if we let the paralytic wear off on its own. The less she moves now, the better for the wound healing."

It was impossible to miss the glare Nate sent her. "Do you have something to counteract it?"

"Yes, but—"

"Then give it to her right fucking now!" he shouted, loud enough that Sonia physically drew back. When she didn't comply immediately, Nate looked ready to come after her, but managed to explain instead. "I can guarantee you that she's living her worst nightmare right now because there's no way that the trauma from back when she lost said organs you were commenting about isn't catching up, full force, to her now. She also can't tense, or move herself into a slightly more comfortable position, or even fucking grit her teeth or scream in pain to try to take some of the pressure off. I can see how analytic medical thinking may lead you to believe that you're doing the right thing for her, but you are not."

Sonia glared at him but went rooting through her kit. "Suit yourself, asshole." Damn, but I really wanted to grin so badly right then. And scream. Yeah, scream first, and maybe grin a thousand years from now.

I expected her to do the dramatic needle-in-heart thing now but realized she wouldn't when all that followed was a quick, barely noticeable prick in my left thigh. The effect wasn't immediate. Sonia was pretty much done gathering up her things by the time I managed the first voluntary muscle spasm—and no, that didn't feel good. Done, she lingered, but gave Nate as much space as she could.

Slowly but surely, my body returned to my control. Moving anything hurt like hell, and after spending almost an hour with my eyes and mouth open, it took some extra time to get those working as they should once more. I didn't try to sit up, Sonia's protest enough of a warning for me. Besides, they had moved me away from my own pool of blood and Sonia had cleaned me up as best as she could around the tatters of my clothes. She'd left those on after verifying that I had no other wounds that needed treatment. Nate was quick to slosh a sip or two of water into my mouth as soon as I could swallow on my own again, and left a wet rag over my eyes until I grunted for him to remove it. Speech seemed a million miles away, and by the time my feeble croaks got closer to intelligible words, whoever wasn't involved in treating me had already gotten busy scouring the entire installation for intruders.

My, was I happy to rain on their parade now.

But screaming first.

It was more like a series of whimpers as I finally managed to curl up on my—left—side, grunting through the red fog of pain until I could breathe again. It wasn't exactly fear of appearing weak that made me lock my jaws, but I'd be damned if I gave that fucking bitch the satisfaction of bawling like a little girl, now that she hadn't managed to kill me. It was irrational, and maybe even stupid, but my stubbornness had gotten me through hell and back what felt like a million times, and today wouldn't be the exception. As soon as I managed to relax as the pain ebbed a little, Nate leaned in, trying to catch the words my sluggish tongue still had issues with forming. Behind him, I saw Sonia still glaring at him, not hiding her misgivings one bit.

It took me six tries, but I finally managed to grunt out, "Marleen."

Nate leaned back enough so I could see the frown of confusion on his face, but already something dark came lurking back into his eyes. Oh, he was giving her the benefit of the doubt all right, but he also wasn't dismissing the fact that it was likely whatever I uttered first that would be the name of my attacker. He knew me well enough that my first utterance wouldn't be concern about anyone else—but might be about someone kidnapped, or some shit.

"Did… it."

Someone in the back cursed, and Nate looked as if someone had shot his favorite dog, if only for a second. Then his expression hardened. I never wanted to see him look at me like that. Hamilton, who'd chosen to linger as well, back in his jacket sans shirt now, snorted, but it was a grim sound. "Sounds like your assassin turned out to be someone else's assassin. Or would-be, at least."

Nate made a move as if to get up—likely to give the order to scour the complex with a more specific target in mind—but my hand shot out before he got far. I had to squeeze my eyes shut and breathe through the pain—sinking my fingers into his arm helped a little— before I managed to get the next words out, but he needed to hear this.

"Said... Decker sends his... regards."

Nate and Hamilton both froze. Under different circumstances, it would have been funny to observe, but the humor was lost on me right now. Bucky was first to regain his composure, and when he saw that Nate was still staring down at me with horror, he turned to the others. "Check every fucking nook and cranny of this blasted lab and find that cunt. Go in teams, and check in regularly. Get the damn coms first. Report anything you find. Anything. Bring her back alive if you can, but take her down if that's not an option." Nobody protested his orders, and Sonia looked a lot less interested in leaving all of a sudden. Burns remained to guard her—and us—and after someone returned with a portable radio, Hamilton joined the search party as well.

There were a million things I needed to tell Nate, but my body had about enough—and all of it could wait until tomorrow. I had no doubts that Marleen was long gone, scurrying back to wherever she had come from. I could tell that Nate was blaming himself, but I had no energy to attempt to alleviate his guilt. Part of me wanted to be resentful, at least for now. Low-grade anger burning in my stomach was a much better companion than the wave of desolation threatening to crash into me.

Chapter 18

Marleen was nowhere to be found. Also gone were her pack and weapons, a substantial amount of provisions, one of the electric cars in the car park behind the airlock—and Richards. Almost immediately, discussions broke out about whether he was her accomplice or not, but the fact that we hadn't found his body hinted that he was still alive. I didn't want to believe that he had betrayed me—well, us, but it was personal, too—and I abused my injuries to push that decision off to another day.

Eden's body turned up exactly where Marleen had told me she'd stashed it, but there were no further casualties. Cole had, accidentally and narrowly, avoided getting stabbed to death—like Eden—or shot—like Scott—by choosing the right time to return from the garage, and taking the corridor that didn't run right by the lab that might have easily turned into my grave. We even knew that as he'd run into Hamilton at the intersection at the end of the tract, and had told him he hadn't seen anyone around.

How Hamilton had turned into my most unlikely savior was slightly more deliberate. Apparently, I'd lost track of time in my perusal of the lab journals, and had missed reporting in for deciding whether I wanted first or second watch. Since Hamilton wanted to catch some sleep badly enough, he'd ventured into the labs to hunt me down and tell me to get my lazy ass back to the cafeteria. To think that if he'd been more annoyed and walked faster, he might have prevented all this—or I'd have sent him away while Marleen had bided her time, and her plan would have unfolded flawlessly.

Nate ended up carrying me from the lab to our makeshift camp in the cafeteria after Sonia gave him the go-ahead two hours after patching me up. I got two saline infusions and what felt like a pound of meds, but considering what we knew about the effects of the serum now, I was happy not to need a blood transfusion. I had lost a lot of blood but less than I'd thought, leaving me feeling frail and in a lot of pain but on the fast track to recovery. Nate stayed next to my makeshift hospital bed for twenty minutes but then left, using the ongoing search effort for an excuse. In the past, I would have been hurt, but I could tell that he needed to move and do something to avoid going insane. He'd spent nine weeks physically locked in a cell, and I could tell that now his mind was caught in a mental prison; if pacing more than five steps in one direction at a time might help, I was happy to see him go.

He was back the next morning to help me take a shower, made possible by the still-running generators that powered the lab. My skin was still deathly pale but my energy was slowly returning. Another day, and I'd be ready to leave, if that meant sitting in a car and not having to run for my life. Nate was reluctant to make the decision whether we should stay longer, and I was glad when Hamilton—staring me in the face and willing me to protest—declared that we would leave as soon as possible. He was right that the fact that I was stubborn enough to chance it likely meant I was ready for it as well. I hated that Nate seemed so passive, but since he had no problem coordinating everything else, I let it slide without a comment.

After that first night of being mostly awake because even the idea of tossing and turning hurt like hell, I followed Sonia into the infirmary that had been part of the complex. It had already been raided down to the bare necessities—and sadly, not only by us, but we had still acquired a gold mine of supplies—except for Sonia's kit. I refused Burns and Nate's offer to hold me down while she cut me up again, instead opting to tough it out myself. As every single thing anyone had done to me in the past five years, it was way worse than I'd expected, but I forced myself to push through the pain and not kick Sonia into a bloody pulp. She was surprised how well the wound had healed already, which meant she actually had more cutting to do to get the glue out. The staples and stitches would remain in, hopefully to dissolve all on their own. If not, it didn't really make much of a difference, considering the general state my body had been in before this shit had gone down.

While I lay there, trying to relax but of course tense as fuck, fighting tears and screams and curses, I couldn't help the dark twist of emotions that kept swirling through my mind, making me physically sick—although that could have been from the pain just as well. The only upside to Marleen's actions was that I'd quickly gotten over the morose frustration left by losing so many people all over again. I still remembered all too well how much losing Bates had cut me up, but it had gotten easier to move on. Whether that was a side effect of trauma, or coming from the fact that those close to me were still up and running, or because the serum had eroded what was left of my empathy and compassion, I couldn't say. It bothered me, but not as much as all the questions kicked up by the assassination attempt.

I had no way of knowing whether Marleen had been lying when she'd held her endless monologue while waiting for me to bleed out. She had no reason not to tell the truth to her would-be victim, but that didn't mean anything. I had to admit, I'd almost preferred the lies.

Knowing that she'd spent almost a decade working under cover—and leaving him absolutely none the wiser—hit Nate hard. He didn't admit it, but I could tell from his latent anger, barely contained by the constant need to move. The fact that Hamilton didn't even once taunt him with his oversight somehow made it worse. It was the confirmation that nobody had seen it coming. That it likely meant that we were on the right path only helped so much. Me, at least, it left feeling frustrated and paranoid as fuck. If we couldn't trust people who we'd been working with for years, who was left?

But it wasn't those thoughts that left me anxious and wound up—nor was it the fact that I'd almost died, and was likely another step closer to my early grave thanks to the recovery my body was going through. It was connected to that, sure—and I knew that, soon enough, both would haunt me, but not right now. We were, once again and now more than ever, standing with our backs against the wall, and the only thing that kept clamoring through my mind was the thought that if I'd died, I'd never have had a chance to find out if I could have gotten pregnant again and could have added a life to this world before ours would inevitably leave it.

It made me feel incredibly selfish and like I had no business leading anything or anyone if I couldn't even have my own priorities straight. I also had no fucking idea where that obsession came from, particularly as, all the things I'd lost considered, my ability to procreate had been the least of my issues. Maybe it was a byproduct of my mind finally catching up to the fact that the serum was killing us, slowly but surely. Or maybe it was Hamilton's remark about the falsified report, which pretty much proved that Raynor had temporarily rendered me sterile. Maybe it was the aftershocks of seeing Baby Chris, Sadie's little girl, and inevitably remembering that, a million years ago, I had the chance to end up with one just like her. Maybe it was the not-so-latent fear that our people—including Sadie and Christine—weren't safe, and now, more than ever, possible targets. It was easy to say that Marleen must have been the mole, or her and Richards, and chalk all of our near-misses and losses up to that. But what if there was someone else secretly reporting and not-so-secretly acting against those who depended on us?

What if, what if, what if...

"What exactly is your qualification?" I heard myself ask Sonia more than decide to question her, particularly when I realized how easy it was to misunderstand the question. Nate's behavior hadn't endeared me any more to her than I'd managed all on my own.

Sonia laughed, and it wasn't a happy sound. "Wouldn't you like to know?" I was sure it was just my perception, but the next time the needle went into me, it hurt a little more.

I closed my eyes and waited for the pain to lessen, counting down from ten. "I didn't mean it like that," I offered through gritted teeth. "You're doing an amazing job. I was just wondering what else you can do besides battlefield surgery?"

The next suture was just as bad, but Sonia's tone was gentler, almost mollified. "Most routine things," she offered. "We do learn that shit in nursing school." Yup, turned out she had been an EMT in a former life, working on becoming a nurse. Also, a bartender, a call center operator, insurance inspector, and a million other shit things she didn't feel like sharing with me now. Burns had told me some of it last night, after she'd gone to sleep and I'd needed ten minutes to get to the toilet and back again—housed in the adjacent room.

"Like checkups?" I wasn't even sure why I was beating around the bush. Whatever else she was—to Burns or anyone else—she was a professional.

She chuckled, as if she had a good idea what I was working my way up to—which was, of course, wrong. "I didn't find any antibiotics specifically for the many things that might make your lady bits itch, but if you're worried about genital warts, they have the equipment here to freeze them off."

Laughing out loud while you are getting stitched up is never a good idea, but I couldn't hold back a chuckle. "Did you just seriously refer to my vagina as 'lady bits'? Fuck off."

"If you want to split hairs, vulva is more like it," she tartly informed me. "I take it this is not about your coochie-coo being all itchy-itch?"

"Fucking stop it!" I half pleaded, half snickered, not helping my general predicament. Grabbing the padded bench I was bent over harder and waiting until the worst of the pain had subsided made it bearable again.

"Almost done," Sonia said, her tone neutral for a moment and not without compassion. "I should probably not tell you this as it might dangerously inflate your ego, but you're quite the trooper when it comes to this. Half of the guys I had to sew up before you made three times the fuss, and usually on lighter injuries."

"You say that like I have a choice," I offered, letting out a sigh of relief when she started to apply the bandage. "But, yeah. I've had worse."

After she finished, I pushed myself into an upward position and gingerly rotated my torso, trying not to howl with pain. Sonia went to the freezer on the other side of the infirmary to hand me an ice pack. As it turned out, it really took the practicality of a nurse to find a way to soothe pain for those who were immune to painkillers. I was sure that Martinez would have thought of that, too, but since he wasn't here but Sonia was...

"So what is it that you need checked?" she wanted to know after she'd helped me fix the ice pack in place.

I considered how to broach the subject but then just went with it. "I presume that, by now, someone has told you all the things they removed when I almost bit it?"

She nodded. "And from what I can tell seeing your insides firsthand, everything looks like it healed up well."

The joke was almost bad enough to have come from Burns. Maybe there was a reason they got along so well, after all.

Exhaling my exasperation, I went on. "They also removed my right ovary. With the miscarriage, the infection, and what everyone kept saying about the serum, I figured that was the official end to my reproductive capabilities. Never had my period since then, or any PMS-related shit."

Sonia's expression turned pensive. "They don't have an ultrasound here so I can't really check up on what happened to what's still there."

I shook my head. "Of course not. But you can check for strings." She looked confused, making me explain quickly. "After we liberated the camp, Richards pulled me aside."

She interrupted me before I could get to the important part. "You mean, your buddy, the traitor."

"I'm not convinced he is, but that's besides the point. He beat around the bush, but I think what he was trying to tell me was that there's a chance I can still get pregnant. The likeliest explanation is that they inserted an IUD while they were busy removing half the organs from my torso. It would explain the lack of periods but mean it's reversible."

Her forehead creased as she considered the possibility. "You were conscious the entire time during the operation, right? Remember them putting you into stirrups and asking you to shimmy your ass farther forward?" she joked. When she saw that her humor was lost on me, she turned to look at the shelves. "I know I saw a box of disposable speculums somewhere here, so there's that. But if they didn't insert an IUD the conventional way, there might not be strings going outside of your cervix. Or they could have used any other kind of hormonal contraceptive."

"Richards hinted it was something that someone with medical knowledge could find. And if you're just trying to be nice about it, yeah, I'm aware that if you have to pry my cervix open, I'm likely going to scream my head off. I'm almost at the point where I can say with full conviction that I've been there, done it, and didn't even get a T-shirt."

She still seemed reluctant but then went to search for what she'd probably need. In hindsight, we should have done this before she cut my back open and sewed it shut again, but I hadn't considered the ramifications. Even before she slapped on a new pair of gloves, Sonia hesitated. "Are you sure that you really want to do this?" she asked, quickly raising her hands when I looked at her. "Just saying, your body is in a shitload of stress right now. If it's just an IUD, it's a quick five-minute procedure that can be done pretty much anywhere, anytime. You may want to have life-affirming, scream-in-the-face-of-possible-death sex soon enough. I've known you for only a little over a month, and I can blindly tell you that your chosen lifestyle isn't exactly conducive to getting knocked up and waddling around for the last few months of it."

Her words made my heart sink, but not because I hadn't considered all that and she'd just given me a much-needed reality check. Sitting up again, I fixed her with a serious stare, dropping all the joking and posturing and shit. "Sonia, if you were me, what would you do? I know that I'm dying. Maybe not today, and hopefully not tomorrow, but Hamilton was right with a lot of the shit he flung in my face. The same, if not more so, is true for Nate. Sure, if we had the time I'd say we forget about all this for now and bring bloody, violent vengeance down on those that have wronged us, and after a nice holiday afterward we'd maybe talk about it and plan our future together. But I don't have that luxury. I may not even have enough time to bring a possible pregnancy to term, even if I get knocked up this week—and, yeah, I don't quite see that happening with all the shit we keep stirring up. But if I want that chance, I have to jump on it now. Does it make me want to shit my pants? Hell, yeah, but all that pales in comparison to the likely chance that neither us will be around to raise the kid. It breaks my heart, and it makes me feel like crap that I'm going to have to foist it at someone who'll likely resent me for it—"

I had to close my eyes for the last part and didn't manage to finish the sentence as my throat closed up with all the grief and frustration the very idea brought up inside of me. I'd been through so much, had suffered through more than I'd thought I could possibly survive, and now this? Now the only thing that had kept me alive would keep me from what should have been my right by nature? Angry tears sprang to my eyes, but somehow I managed to blink them away. When I could focus again, I found Sonia staring at me with a weird look on her face, something I hadn't seen there before and didn't know what to make of—

The next moment, she was hugging me, hard enough that a pained wheeze left my body. She quickly shifted her grip upward to my shoulders but kept on squeezing. When she let go, she only did so to have me at arm's length, still holding on to my upper arms. "Bree, you can be one stupid twat for a woman with that level of intelligence, and I say that with all the love I can muster for one of my husband's best friends." She followed that up with a real, surprisingly warm grin. "You won't be alone, whatever happens. And you will have lots and lots of people who will help you. Even if the worst happens, your child will be loved and grow up with legions of aunts and uncles ready to teach him or her whatever you would have, and a million things you'd rather they keep to themselves. That should be the least of your worries." She smiled. "Now lay back and spread 'em like you mean it."

"What's that even supposed to mean?" I harped, but didn't get an answer.

For the first time in forever, something went better than expected. A cough and a quick if uncomfortable moment later, Sonia informed me that in this one aspect, Red hadn't been a deceiving liar. I stared at the IUD for a second before I told her to get rid of it, quickly getting dressed once more when an old, deeply buried horror came knocking at the backdoor to my soul again. I was more than ready to leave, and Sonia didn't look ready to protest but halted at the door when I called after her.

"Wait. One more question." She eyed me askance, so I went for it. "Why do you hate me so much?" Considering what we'd just gotten up to, I felt like I could stick to the real deal without the cushioning.

She frowned, and for a moment I was afraid she'd give me the most useless answer in the world—either that I should know, or that she didn't, which was technically two answers but really, the two sides of the same coin—but then her expression evened out. She didn't try to smile, and the way she gave me a brief up-and-down left me feeling vaguely uncomfortable—and judged.

"Do you want the truth?" she asked, her voice carefully neutral. "You have earned some of my respect, so I offer it to you, if you think you can take it."

Spreading my arms—carefully—I muttered, "Let me have it."

"As you wish." She thought about what to say for a moment. "Do you have any idea how weird it was getting accepted into the community that your people built at the coast?"

I noticed all too well that she didn't refer to it as my community. It hurt, even though I knew it was the truth and I had no right to freely include myself, even though all of my friends had welcomed me back with open arms. "They can be a rough bunch sometimes, but—"

"No, no," she was quick to correct me. "All it took for them to welcome me was Tom telling them that I was here to stay. They are good folks, and they went out of their way to make me feel at home. It wasn't anything they did. It was what was missing." I had a certain feeling where this was going but kept my trap shut to get this over with quickly. Sonia was only too happy to oblige, crossing her arms over her chest as she went on. "Every once in a while, someone would tell a story, funny or sad, and suddenly shut up, with all the others acting strange but alike. I've seen people avoid opening up old wounds often enough to guess that it was grief over lost loved ones. But it didn't add up, you see. Like how Zilinsky kept refusing to officially assume leadership. Or that half the comments that made everyone shut up were about possible future events, not something already long over. It wasn't exactly hard to get the stories they didn't tell from elsewhere, and then I started to realize what was actually going on. It wasn't that their friends and leaders had died, no. They were hiding somewhere for whatever fucked-up reason, leaving an entire community bleeding and hoping for an event that wasn't likely to ever come, while at the same time dreading that, one day, they'd get the news that it had all been for naught and you're fucking dead. You didn't just forsake them—you left them hanging, incapable of finding resolution. And then, one day out of the blue, you come waltzing in, expecting to find everything just as you've left it. You prattle off your half-hearted excuses and expect everyone to just buy them and forgive you. And they do, because that's who they are. But do you thank them for it? No. You keep doing your thing and you keep all of them at a distance whenever possible. You didn't even stick with our team on the way in but jumped at the chance to get chummy with your army buddies. And the marines. And the drugged-up assholes. You even became best friends with a random stranger who—surprise!—ends up almost killing you. And the worst thing about it is the way you're staring at me now, as if this is the first time you've heard this or even considered it. So, hell, yeah I think you're a cunt, and you don't deserve the loyalty my people are showing you. You may have earned it once, but you have done nothing since to keep it. Maybe think about that sometime. But, sure, they'll keep helping you, and if you have a kid, they will lovingly raise it with stories of your heroic deeds. Maybe consider how much of that you can take into the great beyond with you. But no, I don't hate you. I just don't see what all the buzz is about you."

I was still standing there, dumbfounded and with my mouth hanging half open with the response that my brain refused to formulate, when the door swung shut behind her.

Fuck, but sometimes I really could be an idiotic piece of shit.

Chapter 19

"I'm taking the wheel." Nate looked at me as if I'd sprouted a second head. I glared right back at him, not budging an inch.

"You just bled through your bandage," he told me, his voice tight, nerves obviously at the end of the rope.

I offered him a humorless grin. "Yes, and it hurts twice as much as you'd think. Which means I can't concentrate, and I can't aim or hit for shit. But I can mindlessly accelerate and brake in sync with the vehicle right in front of me. If our intel is bad and we need to exit the car, I'm dead, anyway. If we get overrun, we'll do a quick switcheroo and you'll drive us out into sweet, sweet freedom. Until that happens, I need something to do to keep my mind off the pain. I'm taking the wheel."

Surprisingly, Nate gave up after that. I doubted that he'd let me drive past the first leg of the journey—or whenever we'd take a break—but right now I was happy to run with any victory I could get. Our car was the smallest one, which afforded us the luxury of being just the two of us, the spare room stuffed to the roof with things from the lab. Our gear was already stashed away, and there was nothing left to do but get in and wait for the others to signal that they were ready.

I felt a certain kind of satisfaction as I climbed into my seat, and a hell of a lot of discomfort. Sonia had packed me a small cooler filled with the ice packs she'd found that would likely last me through the tunnels at the very least, and maybe even until tonight. I very much looked forward to the mix of heat and agony that waited for me after that.

Nate was silent and somber as he strapped himself in, doing a quick weapons check as if he expected we'd need them any time soon. I sure as hell hoped not, but better safe than sorry. Even with all the ammo we'd needed to clear the complex, we were taking enough with us that I was glad we likely wouldn't have to walk. Provided we found our cars still where we'd left them, we'd be able to keep this vehicle to ourselves, and there wasn't much need to double up for the others. We might even need to take a few breaks so those driving alone in a car could catch their breath. The plan was to get on the radio as soon as we got a secure line and see if we could rendezvous early with the rest of our people, or maybe ask for some of them to hang back so we could catch up. Vehicles would come in handy whatever we'd do next, and we'd paid for them with a lot of blood.

Since it looked like the others would take a while longer, I fished out a bag of nuts and chewed them meditatively, belatedly remembering to offer Nate some. He stared at the offending nuts with a grimace. "You have to eat something if you don't want to make their work even easier for them," I offered. No need to explain who I was referring to.

He hesitated and pushed my hand away. "I've… taken care of that."

My first impulse was to ask "Who?" but I managed to swallow that. He looked tense enough that it didn't sound like the smartest idea to possibly set him off. My, wasn't I being all mature and diplomatic today? Sonia's talk still sat vividly in my mind, making it a little easier to keep my trap shut—for now. "Glad you did," I said instead.

Nate gave me a look that was one third surprise and two thirds guarded hostility, as if he had geared up for a fight and was now disappointed I hadn't offered him the opportunity. If I'd felt a little less like death warmed over, I might have changed course now but instead kept munching on my nuts.

"Aren't you going to ask who ended up on the menu?" he asked acerbically, leaning close enough that I could smell the fresh mint on his breath. Toothpaste—one of the few staples of the apocalypse we were still not about to run out of, and likely not for the next hundred years considering that baking soda made a great alternative.

I pointedly ignored him while I chewed and swallowed, then slowly turned my head to face him. We stared at each other from up close, and I couldn't help but smile. No, the world wasn't all roses and sunshine, but we were still standing, and right now, that was enough.

Also, very boring, so I flashed him a grin and asked, "Was it a juicy bit of ham or did you go for organ meat, maybe sliced liver?"

He answered me with a heavy sigh that did nothing to hide his amusement. "You are insufferable."

"And that's why you love me," I quipped. "So, who was it? One of the guards? They were the last to go down. Lots of relatively fresh meat."

Nate paused, and I could tell that, joking aside, he wasn't quite comfortable with the subject. "Actually, more like crispy chicken," he offered. "That's probably the best analogy, considering we used to douse them in chlorine, too."

It took me a few moments to make sense of that, and I wasn't quite sure what to make of the news. "You went back into the hot lab and ate Stone?"

He didn't look at me as he replied, instead pretending to check on the progress of the other vehicles. "I needed to confirm that he was dead for good. Which he was, and no sign of reanimation. I figured, possible other contagion chance aside, that would be my best bet, except for eating one of ours—and unlike what you love to accuse me of, I have a moral code, and that's outside of even my boundaries."

"Fair enough," I conceded. "I just wish you hadn't taken the risk of possibly infecting the others with some shit from inside the lab."

I got a less perturbed shrug for that. "I left the body in the decontamination shower after washing and slicing it up in the bathroom by the changing room inside the lab. I made sure to cook the meat to well-done before I ate it, using one of the Bunsen burners from the other labs. It tasted like shit but must have been enough since I stopped wanting to tear into anyone who happened to cross my path. I'd hoped I'd manage to hold out until we were back in the wild and try with some freshly killed game, but I didn't want to risk it."

As gruesomely fascinating as the entire topic was, that last part made me frown. "When exactly did you do this?"

He paused before admitting, "Last night." Which accounted for some of the time he hadn't spent attentively doting on me.

"Smart move," I said, more because I figured he'd need to hear it than actually believing it.

Silence fell and quickly turned uncomfortable, making it easier for me to start blabbing my mouth off. "I have something to tell you as well."

Nate cast me a sidelong glance. "If you'd wanted a slice of asshole instigator, you'd only have needed to ask."

"Eh, I'm holding out for a juicy one, thanks," I retorted. "Stone was too skinny for me. Maybe we can fatten one up just for that?" And because my mind got weird fast these days, the very idea gave me the creeps—but not because of the cannibal angle. "No, it's something else. It's something I should probably have asked you about before making the decision, but then it's kind of my problem, really, and you're the one who can, mostly, avoid it, if it goes completely against your grain."

When I checked Nate's face, I found him frowning at me, confused and not exactly happy about it. "I'm a little too strung out to play your bullshit games right now," he said, and it came out somewhat as a warning. Something inside of me wanted to make the warning bells go off, but I quickly reminded myself that I wasn't the only one who had a reason to be mentally past their breaking point.

"Aren't you curious about what Hamilton meant about the falsified report?" Nate kept staring at me, the intensity of his gaze willing me to just spit it out, so that's what I did. "Raynor did exactly what he said. She switched up the physical orientation of everything that hadn't been damaged before, or so I think. That's why Marleen managed to give me a good scare and some great new scars on top of scars, but surprisingly little damage. What Raynor left out was that they fixed me up with an IUD. Don't ask me why—maybe to use it as an incentive for blackmail or some shit. Or, more likely, she had orders to sterilize me but her scientific soul couldn't go through with it as the idea of us possibly procreating in the future was too tantalizing."

"That woman doesn't have a soul," Nate muttered. I wasn't surprised that was the detail he chose to respond to.

"Anyway, Richards hinted at it, and when I made a passing remark about me possibly reproducing, Hamilton gave a start, pretty much confirming my guess. And since Sonia already had to have her hands inside my body, I asked her about it, and, well. Surprise! Or, really not that much. No idea if anything can, or will, come of it," I explained. "But, yeah. Because we have no other worries in our lives and I have all my priorities absolutely, perfectly lined up, there's that possibility now that I can get pregnant. I kind of thought I'd freak out about it when I realized what Richards was trying to tell me, but just like with that damn serum killing us, I think I'm getting pretty relaxed about all that shit. Chances are I won't make it into next month, so even if you did manage to knock me up before that, we'd never know. The upside of that is, even if you don't, I'd likely not get my period before that, either, so that's a bonus."

Nate kept staring at something slightly past me, thinking, and I felt myself deflate. Springing that on him, now, might not have been the best of ideas, hence my rambling. I opened my mouth to make a joke—any kind of joke, which would likely just make it worse—but he silenced me as he leaned in, a finger softly brushing my lips as he caught my gaze and held it. Yes, there was fear in his eyes, but that was not the only thing I saw there now.

"I'm not mad at you for making that decision without asking me first," he said, barely loud enough for me to hear, as if he wanted this to stay just between the two of us, our shared little secret. "Actually, you telling me that we might have another shot at making a baby is the best news I've heard all week."

Nate using phrases like "making a baby" weirded me the fuck out, and judging from his goofy yet twisted grin, I wasn't alone with that.

"And there I'd thought me surviving would do the trick," I snarked.

Unlike what I'd expected, he didn't take the bait, instead turning serious. "Bree, I would not have heard anyone pronouncing you dead," he said, his tone hard, his eyes boring into mine. "You have no fucking clue how close I was to tearing Hamilton apart when I saw you lying in your own blood with him standing over you. And the urge didn't go away even when I rationalized that it hadn't been his fault. The only thing that saved him was the fact that you would have bled out in the meantime if I'd chosen to come after him, and even if you hadn't, the others wouldn't have managed to get to you through us before it was too late. And it all came roaring back at twice the strength when you told me it had been fucking Marleen who tried to kill you."

He swallowed thickly, licking his lips. I exhaled slowly, trying not to listen to the voice of panic screaming in the back of my mind. "That's why you went looking for food," I surmised. "You were hoping that slaking one thirst might quench the other."

I got a jerky nod from him. "I didn't dare try one of the guards. Chances were high that they'd gotten the serum, and I didn't want that to possibly add to my own fucked-up biochemistry. Same with the scientists. I know that most of the serum project staff had been inoculated to cut down on possible work accidents, so they weren't safe. That left Stone or one of ours, and I told myself, if he really was that insignificant, he would have been clean."

"Well, otherwise you'd have found him shambling around the viral vault, still knocking over tanks because he didn't manage to make his way out from between them," I wisely pointed out.

Nate made a face but let my failed attempt at being funny slide. "Either way, it worked. I wouldn't call myself calm and centered, but Hamilton's not the only one with a good measure of self-restraint."

I just had to interject there. "You mean, unlike me?"

I got a deadpan stare back that was one-hundred percent Nate— and more reassuring than anything he could have said. "Just maybe try not to get stabbed for a minute. You know that I don't give a shit about your scars, but it might be nice if our kid didn't come shooting out of your uterus already put back together three times over."

I made a face, and not just because of the mental image his words created. "I'll try, but I can't promise anything. I don't go looking for trouble nearly as often as it finds me."

"That's something," he muttered before turning around to face forward again, leaning deeper into his seat. I watched him for a few moments, waiting for more, but now he seemed content to sink into one of his endless silences. I considered using Sonia's diatribe for an excuse to bail and let someone else suffer endless boredom instead of me. I wondered if I should share the joy of what she'd told me—valid, yes, but also unfair; and Nate deserved at least half, if not more of the blame than I'd gotten. I decided against it. That was a conversation for another day, or maybe never.

"So your former lover and sometimes help is working for your former mentor who's trying to wipe us all off the face of the earth now," I summed up our most recent findings. "Guess we're in for an entertaining summer." Nate scowled at my description of Marleen—or so I thought, until he didn't stop. "Why, what am I missing?"

He took his sweet time answering, and when he did, his voice was less sure than I would have expected. "Something about this is rubbing me the wrong way." My mouth was open, ready for a snarky remark about that maybe being connected to them almost getting me killed, but he forestalled me. "Just, listen to me explain and then you can get in my face about it, okay?" he offered, unfamiliarly hesitant.

"Sure. Shoot."

He did some ruminating before he finally let me have it. "On the surface, it all makes sense. I can see that, mostly because you haven't uttered a breath of doubt. It's my gut feeling that's telling me that can't be it. Or not all of it. And yes, I'm aware that I'm not omniscient and can be—and frequently am—wrong. But this is Decker we are talking about, and he has never been anything but methodical. If I look at his purported motives now, they don't gel. There's something that doesn't fit, and it's larger than us not having all the details. I've spent over a decade of my life learning to think and act exactly like he wanted me to, and even though I might not like it, his machinations should make perfect sense to me. But they don't."

"Could it be because he's a manipulative asshole and just made you think you can read him that well?" I suggested. "I mean, we are talking about the guy who thought it was a brilliant idea to break both of his top guns by having one's sister raped and forcing them both to watch it happen."

Nate's smirk was brief, but strangely self-satisfied. "Case in point. Take away your moral blinders, and see that for what it really is. He'd spent years of his life grooming and molding two independent, highly competent killers and was about to give them near unlimited capabilities, as close to superpowers as we have. He knew we would become the ultimate weapons, and because of our training and skills even more deadly than the men we were supposed to command. That's not something you do lightly, and you make damn sure that you will retain absolute control over them. They're both dedicated, and you trust them in that, but one wildcard remains—what if someone else can pull those strings? For me, it was easy. All I had for family was an asshole, ambitious brother who was a step away from estranged from me, and a mother who likely would have found the entire psychological side of it deeply interesting, maybe even enough so to forget who said subject was to her. I'd formed zero attachments to any women I'd had relationships with, if you could even call it that. But Bucky? He had an entire family, and while he is still the first to tell you that he couldn't give less of a shit about his parents, his sister was a trigger waiting to happen. He was lying whenever he insisted she meant nothing to him. I knew that, and Decker knew that, and Hamilton himself must have known that as well, but I think he trusted that his act had been convincing enough. And then she ruined it all by showing up there, and Decker had his confirmation—and the perfect tool to teach his disappointing student one more lesson. He miscalculated, and that's why he later let me switch tracks when he had to realize that his warning misfired. It made me grow a conscience and got Hamilton to lose all sense of self-preservation. A perfect tool needs to be always ruthless but is only useful when you can use it again and again. Decker rolled the dice and lost, but cutting his losses still got him a lot of good use out of us. Is it, without a doubt, the most fucked-up thing in the world to analytically plan shit like that? Absolutely. But his reasoning is right there, written all over it. Kicking off the apocalypse? Perverting the serum? None of that makes any sense. Not in the framework I'm looking at, or anything I can relate to that."

I couldn't say that was enough to make me agree with him, but as much as my skin was crawling with revulsion, I couldn't wholeheartedly dismiss Nate's concerns. "So what do we do now?" I asked. "Is your gut feeling enough to change our plans?"

He shook his head without hesitation. "No. We regroup. We do our best to weed out what moles and possible traitors we can. And then we come after that miserable old bastard and resolve this, once and for all. Whether we'll find a bunker at that nav point Cole dug up or not, we will eventually pick up the right leads. They won't get a jump on us again."

I didn't quite share his conviction that we would manage to pull that off, but decided that there was no use in telling Nate that now. Instead, I asked what I should have asked over a week ago, when it became obvious that Hamilton would be coming along for the ride.

"Why does he hate you so much? Hamilton, I mean. Yes, I get the resentment because of your former rivalry. And I get how what happened tore your friendship apart. But there's a difference between that, and him outright blaming you for what happened. I don't know how or why, but the more I'm forced to deal with him, the more I think the reason why he hates my guts is also connected to that. You know why, right? Tell me." The polite thing would have been to ask, but really, almost biting it had a way of killing my patience for that.

Nate exhaled slowly, looking from the other cars over to me. "He hates you because I love you."

I shook my head, irritated. "That makes no sense—"

"It makes perfect sense, to him," he corrected me, his voice soft, almost wistful, as it sometimes got when we were dancing around this subject. "He lost the person he loved the most in this world, while you, you're still here, and not just that. I found you, and I made you fall for me, and whatever fucked-up thing keeps happening to us, you're still here. You don't turn on me, and you won't just leave, and as it turns out, again and again, you're damn hard to kill. I got what Decker took from him, and he feels like, of all people, I'm the last who deserves it."

It made sense in a very twisted way, but Hamilton was nothing if not complicated. Completely screwed up, but complicated, even though he loved to pretend he was a very simple, straight shooter. Except for one little detail. "But why?"

I thought Nate wouldn't answer when nothing came for a full minute, but then he forced himself to respond. Nothing good ever came from moments like that, but I felt like I needed to know. "He hates my fucking guts because Decker added one more level to the whole rape shit. One simple condition. If I'd agreed to do it, he would have been satisfied with that. I wouldn't even have had to rough her up too badly. Simply fucking his sister in front of him against her will would have been enough. Obviously, I didn't do it. I wouldn't have done it to anyone, and I knew Hamilton would never have forgiven me. I think he knows that, if that's even possible in a scenario like that, I made the right choice. But he needs someone to hate, and that's my burden to bear. I am deeply sorry for all the pain and grief that has caused you, but unless I kill Hamilton, it won't stop. You can hate me for that, and for making that choice, but if Decker is still alive and we are going to take him down, I need Hamilton with me."

I chewed on the inside of my cheek for a moment, processing this. "Because you need to give him the chance for revenge. Because if you don't, you'll take this guilt to your grave, and if you can avoid that, you will."

Nate didn't answer, but there was no need for it. I didn't want to, but on some level, I got it. It explained so much—also about Hamilton. Like the fact that he was as ruthless as they came, but even he had lines he wouldn't cross, and often deviated where he felt that maybe nobody would notice. I probably owed my life to that not just once, but several times over—at the factory; at our truce at the Colorado base; getting to Canada, and not dying in France or on the way back. Not letting me bleed to death was the first time he actively helped me, but I would have been lying if that made that much of a difference. I hated to admit it, but in a sense, Hamilton had been acting as my disgusting, baleful guardian angel—if only so I could survive and deliver the killing blow to Nate that he, for whatever reason, wasn't ready to deal yet.

And there Sonia was giving me shit for being a dysfunctional asshole after dealing with this for the past several years.

One thing was for sure: whatever Decker was cooking up, wherever he was hiding—he was about to meet his match, and we would deliver the resolution we all so desperately needed. Even if Nate was right and something about this wasn't as it seemed, that didn't scare me. Between the three of us—and the people who would come along with us—we would find a way to deal with anything and everything that he could throw in our way. And we would succeed. Who cared if it was the last thing any of us did? I was more than ready to face the music, and none of us would go down without a hell of a fight.

To be concluded in

ANNIHILATION
Green Fields #12

Acknowledgements

Wow, book #11—almost done with the series!

Yes, book #12 will be the last—and I've already started working on it when you're reading this (on release day). A few weeks ago, that is, since it picks off right where Retribution ends—and may I say so, I'm so psyched about the ending!

But we're not quite there yet, so let's talk about GF#11.

This was an interesting book to write. I thought I would have to make up so much about it—the city with its ravines of concrete and glass, and the tunnels... and a day into researching such things, I happened on an article about the train tunnels underneath Dallas, and that completely blew me away! I've also fallen in love with the actual city, and can't wait to visit it one day. Of course there's plenty of artistic license in the book, but I was extremely happy to find reality had, unexpectedly, handed me the perfect blueprints for once.

I wrote the second half of the book in under a week, so some of the breakneck speed and exhaustion is definitely my own. If there's something like method writing (akin to method acting) this book definitely checked that box. It's one of my favorites, and I can't wait to hear what you think!

My eternal gratitude goes to my editor—she's the best!—and my trusty beta readers, who never fail to amaze me with their willingness to help . You guys are amazing! And what would any writer be without her readers? Let it be said here that you continue to blow me away with your eagerness to get your hands on my next book. Thank you so much!

About the Author

Adrienne Lecter has a background in Biochemistry and Molecular Biology, loves ranting at inaccuracies in movies, and spends increasingly more time on the shooting range. She lives with the man and two cats of her life in Vienna, and is working on the next post-apocalyptic books.

You can sign up for Adrienne's newsletter to never miss a release and be the first to know what other shenanigans she gets up to:

http://www.adriennelecter.com

Thank you

Hey, you! Yes, you, who just spent a helluva lot of time reading this book! You just made my day! Thanks!

Want to be notified of new releases, giveaways and updates? Sign up for my newsletter:
www.adriennelecter.com

If you enjoyed reading the book and have a moment to spare, I would really appreciate a short, honest review on the site you purchased it from and on goodreads. Reviews make a huge difference in helping new readers find the series.

Or if you'd like to drop me a note, or chat a but, feel free to email me or hit me up on social media. I'll try to respond as quickly as possible! If you'd like to report an error or wrong detail, I've set up a separate space on my website for that, too.

Email: adrienne@adriennelecter.com
Website: adriennelecter.com
Twitter: @adriennelecter
Facebook: facebook.com/adriennelecter

Books published

Green Fields

#1: Incubation

#2: Outbreak

#3: Escalation

#4: Extinction

#5: Resurgence

#6: Unity

#7: Affliction

#8: Catharsis

#9: Exodus

#10: Uprising

#11: Retribution

#12: Annihilation

Beyond Green Fields

short story collections

Omnibus #1

Ombinus #2

World of Anthrax

new series coming 2022

Printed in Great Britain
by Amazon

29585002R10189